Queen Bee

Queen Bee

A Novel

Dorothea Benton Frank

An Imprint of HarperCollinsPublishers

QUEEN BEE. Copyright © 2019 by Dorothea Benton Frank. All rights reserved. Printed in the United States of America. No part of this book may be used or reproduced in any manner whatsoever without written permission except in the case of brief quotations embodied in critical articles and reviews. For information, address HarperCollins Publishers, 195 Broadway, New York, NY 10007.

HarperCollins books may be purchased for educational, business, or sales promotional use. For information, please e-mail the Special Markets Department at SPsales@harpercollins.com.

FIRST HARPERLUXE EDITION

ISBN: 978-0-06-291260-2

HarperLuxe™ is a trademark of HarperCollins Publishers.

Library of Congress Cataloging-in-Publication Data is available upon request.

19 20 21 22 23 ID/LSC 10 9 8 7 6 5 4 3 2 1

For Peter

I eat my peas with honey
I've done it all my life
It makes the peas taste funny
But it keeps them on the knife!

—ANONYMOUS

Contents

Queen Bee

Prologue

O f all the stories I've ever told you, this is the one that you're going to remember. This is the one. Hopefully large parts of this will entertain you, because sometimes life goes right off the rails somewhere between hilarity and the absurd and somehow it always happens in my orbit. But there is another story within these pages that might bother you. I know this because this story haunts me. It's the one I can't forget.

I told myself that I should've done something to intervene earlier. But it wasn't my place. I tried polite conversation, I tried impolite conversation. No one would hear me. It bothers me that there was a part of me that didn't want to *see*, didn't *want* to get involved. Was there that part of me? Does that make me complicit? Heaven knows that people in general can rationalize the most egregious behavior in the name of religion, love, the alleged greater good of mankind, or just because whatever it is they're lobbying for is good for them.

For all you know about me, even those I've met in passing, you know I'm not a troublemaker or someone who exaggerates the truth. Okay, maybe I'll embellish a little. But generally, you don't have to make things bigger or more fantastic than they are. Reality has so many surprises and unbelievable situations, it's okay to just lay down the bones.

Maybe I want to tell you this story as a kind of cautionary tale. At the end of the day, you must live with who you've allowed yourself to become. But before you close your eyes for the last time, there will be a day of reckoning, even if it's not the kind we've been taught to expect.

It has taken me a long time to piece together the real truth of what happened, to rationalize that perhaps I didn't have a hand in all of it. But then, I did. Actually, I think you could easily lay half of what happened at my feet. But I digress.

This is a magical tale of love and redemption, of how to heal broken spirits, and most of all, why it's all right to hope for and believe in miracles. It's not just a Lowcountry thing. If this could happen to me, it could surely happen to you.

I said, "People been thinking about and fascinated by bees since forever."

"Yeah?" the boys said. "Like who?"

"How about this? The bee is more honored than other animals not because she labors, but because she labors for others. *That was said by Saint John Chrysostom, Archbishop of Constantinople. He lived from 349 to 407 A.D."*

"That's old," Tyler said.

Chapter One
Meet Me,
Holly McNee Jensen

Sullivan's Island, South Carolina
February 2017

I was standing on our back porch hanging wet dish towels on a swing-arm gizmo, having just finished cleaning up after breakfast. Momma was headed back to bed, where she lived 90 percent of the time, ever since Leslie got married and moved to Ohio with weird Charlie.

I stepped outside and scanned the yard. Mother Nature was clearly losing it, one marble at a time. It was a Friday morning in the middle of February and eighty-something degrees. Eighty-something degrees! When I was a child on this sleepy island, I would've been wearing an overcoat, a hat, and maybe a neck scarf and gloves. I'd be shivering and waiting for the ramshackle school bus to stop at the corner and take me and a hundred other kids to Catholic school, where I would be made to tremble over the painful retribution to come for sins I had yet to commit. Now, people were all over the island, a parade of surfboards and coolers disappearing over the dunes, and on the beach, people half-naked, slathered with suntan lotion, running around like idiots.

Didn't anyone know it was supposed to be winter? And no, I wasn't cranky. There it was! Proof! Climate change.

Flowers that weren't expected to bloom for another six weeks decorated our yard in huge clumps and stands of color. Daylilies, Shasta daisies, and purple smoke reared their pretty heads toward the morning sun and opened wide. My honey bees, who were supposed to be huddled in winter mode, getting their well-deserved beauty rest, had been sending out scouts from the hive all week long to see what was going on. They had to be very confused. I know I was. Something was seriously wrong.

But confused or not, my bees needed attention. I was going to check the hives for the early arrival of—what else—Varroa mites. I was super picky about hive health. These nasty mites were awful! All over the country, varroa mites, along with hive beetles, not to mention pesticides, were trying to put honey bees on the extinct list. If that happened, God forbid, the whole planet would be doomed to starvation. Maurice Maeterlinck said without honey bees, mankind only had four years and then, forget it. Doomsday.

I headed for the backyard shed where I kept my beekeeper suit. Normally, I wouldn't see mites until late summer. But everything seemed so off kilter, I was just being extra vigilant.

"I'll be back in a bit," I called out to my mother.

"*WHAT?*" she screeched back.

Put in your hearing aids, I thought. She probably didn't even know where they were.

"I said, I'm *going* to check the *hives!*"

"Whatever! Suit yourself! Don't be gone long. I'm getting hungry!"

Oh, eat a can of beans, I thought. Didn't I just

feed her? She drove me crazy. My mother, Katherine McNee Jensen, was one colossal pain in the derriere. She kept tabs on me like I was a child (which I was not) and treated me like her personal maid (which I was). If I didn't have a garden and hives to tend and a volunteer job at the library, I'd go right off the deep end. I had been trying to get a teaching job at Sullivan's Island Elementary School for years, and the best I could ever seem to get was the occasional substitute job. Because the island was so popular, there was probably a longer waiting list for teaching positions there than there was anywhere else in the state. And I sold my honey at the island's farmers market and sometimes at the farmers market in Mount Pleasant because I harvested over a hundred pounds, sometimes much more, every year. But eight dollars a jar wasn't going to make me rich. Eventually, I'd get a break.

I let the wooden screen door slam behind me with a loud *thwack* and took a long, slow, deep breath. Rise above! And how was I ever going to get out of her house and make a life for myself? I was going nowhere until she did. So, for now, I was a bachelorette, keeping my considerable favors under wraps until the right man came along. The thought of me having *considerable favors* worth *keeping under wraps* made me smile. Well, to be completely honest, many right men *had* come along, but they kept going, straight to the welcoming arms of my sister, Leslie. And anyway, now I had my neighbor Archie's little boys to keep me busy. I preferred children to adults any day of the week. I'll get to them in a moment. There's so much to tell you.

I want to introduce you to my bees first. Everyone knows honey bees are good for the environment, but few people know why or how their hives are organized. There's a division of labor for every stage of a honey bee's life. Every bee has his or her job to do to ensure they continue to coexist as one. Everything they do is to preserve the colony. Humanity could take a few lessons from them. You'll see what I mean as time goes on, the same way I came to gradually understand them. In any case, I loved the time I spent with my bees because, despite their intense activity, it was so serene. Serenity was in short supply around here. The good news was that there was zero chance of Momma following me out to the apiary. She wouldn't come near the hives out of fear. I keep telling her she's not sweet enough to sting. She doesn't think that's funny.

The apiary was in the back corner of our yard, surrounded by a pale blue picket fence, painted thusly to keep out the haints. *Haints* is a Gullah word for haunts or ghosts. In this part of the world, the Lowcountry of South Carolina, it was generally accepted that a thoughtful application of blue paint would keep a whole array of spirits at bay, ranging from the mischievous ilk to the downright evil. I just happened to like the color. The fence was covered on the inside perimeter with clear mesh to thwart other enemies of the hive—mainly raccoons. My hives were aqua, pale pink, and pale peach. The pastel colors made me feel like I was taking a short trip to Bermuda, and when I looked at them it always lifted my spirits.

I looked up to see the UPS truck pull up to our curb. Andy, our regular UPS deliveryman, hopped off his truck and called out to me.

"Hey, Miss Holly! Sure is a fine day!"

"Yes, it is!" I called back because I didn't want to get into a whole conversation about planet Earth actually having a meltdown. "Your rear passenger tire is about to blow, you know."

"I'll get that checked out! Thanks for the warning!" he called back to me. "I'll just throw this on the porch?"

"That's fine!"

It was probably something from QVC that Momma ordered. That's what she did all day. Sat up in her big bed and watched QVC and ordered large housedresses and sweats decorated with kittens and mermaids, which she thought were stylish and appropriate for church, on the rare occasion that she actually attended Mass. I'm not judging. Okay, maybe I am.

I lowered the veil on my hat and went inside the gate with my lit smoker, not that I ever needed it. It was wise to approach hives from the side so that the guard bees wouldn't be alarmed. I took the cinder block off the top of the first hive and then removed the roof. I kept my smoker handy so that if, on that rare occasion, my girls seemed agitated, a gentle cloud of pine and sage could calm them. One by one, I lifted the full frames. The brood was already growing like mad. Where was the queen? And why was she hiding from me? Another omen.

"Your queen's sure getting busy early this year!" I said, talking to my bees. "Yes, indeedy!"

I replaced the frames and covered the hive, checking the ground for fire ant mounds. There were none that I could find. I filled a pan with water so the bees would have plenty to drink.

There were many reasons and even more suspicions about why you should talk to your bees, too many to ignore. I told them about my mother's illnesses, which I felt positive were psychosomatic, and about my sister's continuing windfall, which bordered on the obnoxious. Sometimes I made up songs to sing to them, like *Leslie's going to Bangkok and Holly's staying home. Les-*

lie's got a brand-new *Benz* and Holly's staying home. I was so grateful no one could hear me, but didn't everyone need a place to vent and be silly? I'd heard stories about people's bees swarming when they were left out of the family loop. I hoped my bees had a sense of me as a part of their colony. I didn't know for sure, but I felt like they knew me. I had enough pluff mud in my veins to consider the possibility of almost anything. Although experience told me that while bees are unbelievably smart about so many things, they don't have emotions in the same way we do. At least not individually. But there is such a thing as hive mentality. I'd seen hard evidence of it many times over the years.

A metal screen door slammed with a clang and inside of a minute, Archie's two little boys, whom I adored, were hanging over my apiary fence. Our house was across the street from theirs on a dead-end road where we had very little traffic. My house backed up to the marsh, which made for spectacular sunrises.

"Here come both sides of my heart!" I whispered to my honey bees.

"Hey! Mith Holly!"

"Hey yourself, Mr. Tyler!"

Archie and Carin MacLean had bought their house and moved in right after they were married. Two years later, Tyler came along. Tyler was now seven, soon to be eight; Hunter, his younger brother, was five. Carin, their mother, had died not long ago in a tragic automobile accident, leaving them in Archie's flustered care, in my care on occasion, and sometimes in extended day care at the island school. Archie kept saying he was going to hire someone to help him full-time with the house and the boys, but that kind of help was so difficult to find and then of course, to trust. For my part? I loved those little fellas like they were my own, and I couldn't understand why he didn't hire me. But he didn't have to, because I sort of did the job for free.

Tyler had curly hair the color of a newly minted penny, and matching freckles of all sizes danced all across his nose and cheeks. He was just adorable and curious about everything. He was also missing four teeth, making him even more precious as he struggled to speak clearly.

"Hey, Miss Holly! Can we see the bees?"

And that was from Hunter, born with an inner daredevil and who was more curious and reckless than his older brother. Hunter's thick, coarse black hair could not be tamed and his blue eyes were a window. From the day he was born, we always said he'd be president of something big or lead a life of crime. He always had at least one Band-Aid on him somewhere. A badge of courage.

"I don't see why not," I said. "What are y'all doing home today?"

"Parent tea-ther meetings," Tyler said.

"Ah! I wondered why your daddy's car was in the driveway. Okay, you both stand right there and I'll show you what's going on."

I drew an imaginary line across the grass. They saluted me and my heart clenched. Tyler and Hunter were just too cute.

I stepped to the edge of the apiary, lifted my veil, and closed the gate. I took my water glass and turned it upside down, capturing a honey bee that was sitting on the roof. Then I slid her into the palm of my hand. My gloves were made of heavy suede and I knew there wasn't a bee among them whose stinger could penetrate the tough cowhide.

"Do either one of you have a magnifying glass?" I asked.

"I do!" Tyler said. "Should I go get it?"

"Yep!" I said. "Quickly!"

Tyler disappeared inside the house and Hunter stared at me like I had just dropped down from the moon.

"Why are you wearing that funny outfit?" he said.

"You know why, young man. So that I don't get stung."

"Momma always said you shouldn't play with bees.

If you're 'lergic you could get Anna flappic shock and die!"

"She was right, sweetheart. Anaphylactic. And yes, you could. But honey bees are pretty tame and they only sting when they feel threatened."

"What about bumblebees?"

"The same. They are both pollinators, and all they want is nectar and pollen. But don't get in their way! Then we'd have a problem."

"What about wasps and yellowjackets?"

"Ah! They're bugs of another color! Mean as the dickens! They can be very aggressive. Never, ever, ever touch their nests. But honey bees? Do you know they're the only bugs who make food for humans?"

"They are? What about crickets? Daddy told me people eat crickets because they're good for you."

"Really? My goodness! I'd have to be awfully hungry to eat a cricket," I said and wondered if they sat around all night watching National Geographic specials on television. "Well, if your daddy said it then I'm sure it's true." His daddy Archie was so good looking he made me stutter and blush. He was also a Harvard Ph.D. Not exactly a dummy. "But we don't eat honey bees. They make food for us. Do you see the difference?"

"Uh-huh." Hunter smiled at me and my heart

melted. "If you ate a bee you might get stung in the tongue!"

"There's no might about it!" I said and smiled at him. "Or in your tummy!"

Slam!

Tyler was headed back our way. I took the magnifying glass from him.

"Tyler? Hold my glass in place so this little bee doesn't fly away. Okay, gentlemen, see there? Look at that! Honey bees are very hairy around the perimeter of their eyeballs. And their eyes have over five thousand prisms! Isn't that cool?"

"Yeah! Wow!" they both said together.

"Here's a hairy eyeball," Hunter said. He stepped back into a warriorlike stance, set his jaw firmly, and frowned at me, staring without blinking.

"That's also known as stink-eye," I said with a giggle.

Tyler said, "How come they have hairy eyeballs?"

"Because they just do. No one seems to have discovered a good reason yet. It could be to discourage dust and other kinds of debris from settling on them."

Tyler added, "How do you know they have five thousand prisms? Did you count them?"

I laughed and said, "No, honey, I read it somewhere. But they're interesting little critters, aren't they?"

Hunter began running in small circles, looking skyward. I mean, how long did I really expect him to pay attention?

"What else do you know?" Hunter said.

"I know you're going to throw up if you don't stop that," I said.

"No! Tell us something else!" Tyler said.

"Well, I just told your brother that honey bees are the only insects that make food for us!"

"Cool!" they said.

"There are still a lot of mysteries to solve about honey bees."

Then the screaming started.

"*Holly! Help me!*" Dramatic pause to gain momentum. "*Helllllppppp!*"

"Coming! Hang on!" I called back. "Oh, Lord," I muttered.

"*Help!*"

"Is that Mith Katherine?" Tyler said.

"Who else would it be? QB! The big queen bee! You boys run along now. She's okay. I promise!" I said and kind of sauntered back into the house at my own pace, discarding parts of my beekeeper outfit as I went through the back door. The boys turned on their heels and ran home. There was little doubt that they would report the bee facts I'd given them to their father. But

I knew that they might or might not relate the story of my mother screaming bloody murder, because she did it all the time. How terrible that it happened so often that everyone took it for granted.

By the time I got to her room, I only had the overalls left to ditch, and there she was in all her glory, crumpled to the floor with her nightgown hiked up around her waist.

"Help me up," she said.

I pulled her nightgown down to cover her lady parts, but there was no chance on this earth that I could lift her bulky weight. I reached for the phone to call 911.

"Pick me up, Holly!"

"Momma, you know I can't do that. You're too heavy."

"That's a damn lie. If your sister was here, *she'd* take care of me one helluva lot better than you do!"

"Well, she's not here, is she?"

I tapped the numbers into the phone.

"What's your emergency?"

"Hey, Darlene. It's Holly Jensen over on the back beach? Momma fell out of bed, and well, you know, *I* can't pick her up."

"Don't you even *try* to move her, Miss Holly. I'll get Anthony over there in two shakes. I'm sure she's okay, don't you worry. How're your bees doing? We sure have been enjoying the honey you gave us."

"Oh, I'm so glad to know that. My bees are fine, thanks. Remember, there's plenty more honey where that came from!"

Momma was instantly irked. "I'm lying here on the floor, maybe near death! And, you're on the phone discussing bees and honey? You've got to be kidding me! What if my hip's broken?"

I thanked Darlene and hung up. She had recently married Mark Tanenbaum, and everyone said she was the most beautiful bride they'd ever seen. He was a handsome devil, too.

"Momma? Your hip's not broken. You'd be screaming in agony. And even if it is, there's nothing wrong with being nice once in a while. You ought to try it."

"Don't be fresh with me. You're only talking like that to me because I'm in a compromised position."

"No, ma'am. I'm talking to you like that because I'm telling you the truth."

In minutes, there was a knock at the door and the voice of Anthony Stith, the head of the fire department, rang out in a melodious but thunderous boom. Boy, that was quick, I thought.

"Anybody home?" he called.

"Back here!" I answered but rushed out to meet him all the same. I pulled my cardigan around me. "Oh, Anthony! Thank you for coming!"

"Happy to help," he said pleasantly.

Momma, for once, said nothing. Anthony stepped into the room. Two EMS workers waited in the hallway with a collapsible gurney. They must've been close by to arrive here so quickly. But then, nobody was that far away from anybody on our tiny island, which was perhaps four miles long, depending on erosion and ac-cretion.

"How y'all doing, Miss Katherine?" he asked.

"Obviously, not so well," she answered, as if it were Anthony's fault she was lying on the floor.

I looked through the window at Archie's little boys chasing each other around their yard.

"They're cute little rascals, aren't they?" Anthony said. "Terrible thing about their momma's passing, isn't it?"

"I'd give anything in the world to have kids like them," I said.

"Oh, please," Momma said. "Children are so over-rated."

"Thanks a lot, Momma," I said and rolled my eyes at Anthony.

He just smiled and, undeterred by her notorious bad manners, knelt by her side.

"Do you mind if I poke around a little bit?"

"Just what do you mean by that?"

Anthony smiled again. "I mean, do you have any pain anywhere? Can you move your arms?"

Momma moved her arms. "I imagine I'm still alive."

"That's good," he said. "Now, can you point your toes?"

She did as she was told, but when he asked her to bring her knee up to her chest, she grimaced in pain.

"I don't like the looks of that," Anthony said. "Now, Miss Katherine, I know you don't like going to the hospital and all . . ."

"Oh, no!" she said, with the smallest objection on record. "Not the hospital!"

He was joking. My mother *loved* the hospital! She thought it was like going to a spa. In fact, she kept an overnight bag packed, just in case.

The fellows from EMS moved in, lowered the gurney to the floor, and between them managed to lift my mother's considerable bulk onto it.

"Get my bag from the closet, Holly! And my medicine. And call Leslie! She'll want to know."

"Yes, Momma. I will."

My sister, Leslie, would not care. The only thing Leslie had ever cared about was getting out of here. And she was reasonably nice to me because I took care of the beast of a mother we shared. I always wondered if Leslie thought I was going to be Momma's nursemaid forever. It wasn't that I wanted such a fancy life. But I did want more than this.

"How is Leslie?" Anthony asked. "She was always such a pretty girl."

Everybody on this island knew Anthony had a sweet spot for Leslie. She was his first sort of serious girlfriend, but she dumped him for Charlie Stevens when his family moved to Charleston in her junior year of high school. Charlie Stevens's family had big money from a string of car dealerships they owned all through the South and the Midwest.

"Leslie's the same," I said. "I'll tell her you asked about her."

God, Leslie was such a dog. If I caught her going wild with Charlie in the back seat of his daddy's car once, I caught her a thousand times. Yeah, Leslie sure did like all that sweaty stuff. Not me. Until recently I was pretty sure it was only for the purpose of procreation. At least that's what the clergy drilled into my head. At school I was so naïve that I believed it. Anyway, as we all know, it wasn't as if I had anyone interested in sharing that sort of experience with me, so there was no point in getting excited about it. At least, not so far. Although I had been entertaining more than a few thoughts about the widower next door. Life could be so easy if he fell in love with me. I could have children without having to give birth. And I would be next door to Momma, who was sure to leave me the house when she went. Wouldn't she? And then I wouldn't have to move my hives.

I grabbed Momma's bag from her closet and her medicine from the bathroom and followed them all outside. They were headed to the emergency room at East Cooper Hospital because that was where you went when EMS picked you up for a ride on this island.

"Now, don't you worry," Anthony said, "we're gonna take good care of your momma."

"I wasn't worried for a moment," I said. "Thanks!"

I got into my car and, as I followed the ambulance over the causeway, thought about the way the water sparkled and how at this time of year it was almost sapphire blue. The sky was strewn with wisps of clouds and the sun was so bright it hurt your eyes to look up. The spartina was still brown. I knew the edges of it were razor sharp, but from a distance it was so beautiful you would love to run your hand across its top as you would a fur coat. The landscape alone would make a poor person feel as rich as cream.

As I passed through Mount Pleasant, whose fast-growing population was being watched by urban developers across the country, I began to wonder about myself and my life in general. Seemed like I was doing that sort of wondering more and more often. It wasn't that I was so miserable or so ungrateful or even jealous of Leslie. It was just that I wondered how a girl like me could ever make her life mean anything.

"Hunter? Did you know honey bees have pockets on their legs to store pollen? It makes them weigh fifty percent more by the end of their day."

"What? They need to go to Weight Watchers!"

"Oh, Hunter."

Chapter Two
Bee Calm

Somewhere between leaving the hospital and arriving at Publix to buy groceries, I made a decision. I was going to invite Archie MacLean and the boys over for dinner. Why not? Carin had been in heaven for long enough for him to enjoy some female company without feeling guilty. And with Momma in the hospital—they were keeping her overnight for observation and to run some tests—the timing was perfect. I was excited about the possibilities of company, daydreaming that the boys were mine and wondering what it would be like to be married to a man ten years older than I was. I didn't even unload my car or take the groceries inside. I was so excited, I'd even coughed up the money for store-bought flowers, a rare indulgence. And, the weather felt a lot cooler than it had been in the morning, which I took as a good omen. In fact, everything seemed like a good omen.

I marched right up their front steps, crossed the porch, knocked on the door, and waited.

Archie answered and, of course, Tyler and Hunter were right behind him, nearly colliding with each other as they sock-skated toward the door across their gleaming heart pine floors. Archie, whose longish hair was sexy as hell, was wearing corduroy pants, a plaid shirt, and a thin cardigan, looking every inch the kindly and distinguished professor that he was. He reminded me of Alexander Skarsgård. I mean, break a sweat.

"Well, hi, Holly," he said. "Would you like to come in? How's your mother?"

"Oh, no, thanks; she's fine. Nothing broken. Her doctors wanted her to stay the night just to be sure she's okay."

"Well, that's good news," Archie said. "I'm sure you're relieved, too."

"Of course," I said.

"Mith Holly!" Tyler shouted. "Come see my map of Italy I'm drawing for extra credit!"

"Cool it, Tyler," Archie said.

I smiled and said, "I was just thinking, wouldn't it be nice if y'all came over for dinner?"

"Well, thank you! I was just going to order a pizza for the kids."

"Well, I'm making chicken and mashed potatoes with little green peas. Nothing fancy."

"That sure sounds better than pizza," Archie said, with a smile so honest and beautiful, it almost made me gasp.

"I hope so," I said.

Tyler and Hunter began rubbing their stomachs and licking their lips while making yum-yum grunts.

"Mmmm! Mashed potatoes!" Hunter said.

"Are you sure it's not an inconvenience?" Archie said. "You do so much for us. I don't want to impose."

"You couldn't impose if you wanted to! Not even one tiny little bit!" I said. "See y'all in about an hour?"

"That sounds fine. Thank you!" Archie said and then turned to his boys. "Gentlemen? Synchronize your watches! We depart at eighteen hundred hours!"

"We don't have watches, Daddy," Tyler said with his toothless lisp. "We're still too little. Remember?"

Maybe I'd buy both boys watches for Christmas. Batman or Mickey Mouse watches?

"Great! See you soon!" I said and left.

I took the bags of groceries from the trunk of my car and hurried inside to get supper started. This wasn't going to be a romantic dinner with candles, but I put on my favorite Tony Bennett album of George Gershwin's music anyway. I just wanted to see how motherhood and marriage might feel. You know, just try it on, like a sweater. Oh, sure, I had made dozens of peanut butter and jelly sandwiches for the boys after school or on the weekends when Archie had an errand to do, even before they lost Carin. I was sure the boys looked at me like an adopted aunt of sorts, because I got plenty of hugs from them. And I had also wiped away buckets of tears when they felt blue or angry or frustrated. In the first days after we buried Carin, I'd taken them casseroles and cake, just like all the other women on the island. It was our tradition, and a nice one, I thought. But this would be the first time I cooked for Archie and the boys in my own house with them all there.

When Momma wasn't ranting and raving, she occasionally delivered some wisdom. One of her favorite sayings had to do with the way to a man's heart being through his stomach. I'd dazzle him with my special chicken dish. I wasn't a gourmet or anything close to it, but I had a way with chicken, thanks to a recipe I'd cut out of *Southern Living* magazine ages ago.

I washed and cut the potatoes into chunks and dropped them into a pot of salted water with their skins left on and set them on the stove on a high flame. I always used a potato ricer on the cooked potatoes that would catch all the skins when they were pushed through. Then I opened the package of boneless, skinless chicken breasts, laid them on paper towels, and blotted them dry. I mixed two eggs in a soup plate with some milk and salt and pepper, and I put a cup of flour on another plate. I sliced a lemon and browned it in some olive oil and butter. Then I dredged the chicken breasts in flour, dipped them in the egg mix, and browned them all, putting them aside to rest as they were done. When we were ready to sit down I'd squeeze the juice of a whole lemon in my frying pan along with a big chunk of butter to make a sauce. Then the chicken would go back in the sauce with the lemon slices to warm it up and coat it all in lemony, buttery heaven. At the last moment, I'd drizzle it with honey and sprinkle minced chives from my garden over the top. Even my *mother* liked it. It was *that* good.

I flipped the album over and set the table in the kitchen, because we never used the dining room, except on Thanksgiving and Christmas. Besides, it was half covered with mail, mostly catalogs my mother refused to let me throw away. She had a black belt in shopping.

The grocery store flowers went into a glass vase in the center of the table. I used our newest place mats and paper napkins folded in triangles. The next challenge was finding four unchipped plates, and to my surprise, I did. When it was all put together, the table looked inviting. Not magazine worthy, but it had a wholesome charm.

By six, everything was ready. A fresh pitcher of iced tea stood on the counter, because of course we drank iced tea all year round. The peas were buttered, the chicken was sauced, and the potatoes were whipped into velvet ribbons. A Mrs. Smith's frozen apple pie was bubbling away in the oven, and it was as domestic a scene as any woman ever set. All I needed was a golden retriever to star in a Martha Stewart tableau. The doorbell rang. On the way to answer it, I glanced at myself in the hall mirror to see that I had forgotten to put on lipstick or to brush my hair and thought, Oh, well, too late for vanity. I bit my lips to give them some color. Didn't Scarlett O'Hara do that when Rhett showed up unexpectedly?

"Come in! Everything is ready! Did you boys wash your hands?"

"Yup," Tyler said. "What's that thmell?"

"Apple pie baking in the oven," I said.

"Yum!" Tyler said and raced ahead.

"I washed my hands two times!" Hunter said. "Can we have pie first?"

"It never stops. My little rule breaker," Archie said and ruffled Hunter's hair. "No."

"Pie is for dessert!" I said. "If you eat your dinner, that is." I surprised myself by saying something that sounded so parental, but when I looked at Archie's face, he was unfazed by my words. The stress of the days since he'd lost Carin was still all over his face.

Tyler was already in the kitchen, having raced ahead, peering into the oven to confirm that there was indeed pie in his future.

"Close that oven door, young man," Archie said and looked at me. "I'm sorry. He knows better."

"It's totally okay," I said. "Now, what would y'all like to drink?"

I poured milk for the boys and iced tea for Archie and me and we sat down to eat. I caught a side glance of Archie and saw that he had double dimples in his cheeks. I loved dimples because I thought they were a sign of being good natured.

"So, boys? Are y'all having a good year in school?" I asked, thinking, That's what a mom would ask.

They both bobbed their heads.

"Well, would you like to tell your dad and me something that's going on? Tyler? You go first."

Tyler, the second-grader, said, "Well, we're learning how to carry one, you know, in math."

"And is that easy for you?" I asked.

"It's not hard," he said. "I'm better at it than most of the kids."

"Great!" I said.

"That's good, son! Keep up the good work!"

"How about you, Hunter? What's new in kindergarten?"

"Hmmm?" he said and looked up to the ceiling to see if the answer was there. In typical baby-of-the-family style, he decided to make it funny. "Well, last Monday our class pet, which is a snake, got loose and Miss Langbein, our teacher, almost fainted. But we found it and put it back, the boys did, that is. All the girls were standing on their chairs pretending to be scared. It was just a little old garter snake."

He snickered.

"How about you, Archie? What's new at the College of Charleston?" I said, feeling like I was doing pretty well as a pseudo parent.

"Oh, interesting and earthshaking things, of course!" he said.

"Like what?" Tyler asked.

Archie looked at them as though they couldn't possibly want to know what was making the earth shake.

"Yeah, Dad, come on!" Hunter said. "Can I please have more mashed potatoes?"

With a nod, I got up and spooned out more potatoes for Hunter and then offered some to Tyler, who bobbed his head in assent. Yes, dinner was going really well.

"Thanks," they whispered.

"Okay. So, this week I've introduced my World Religion 301 honors students to cargo cults."

"What's a cargo cult?" Tyler asked.

For whatever reason, I jumped in and said, "Well, break it down, Tyler. A cult refers to a group of people who believe something that's a nontraditional spiritual set of beliefs."

"Very good!" Archie said. "You get an A!"

"Thank you," I said. "But what's the cargo part of it?"

"In the late nineteenth and early twentieth centuries there were still many indigenous tribes who lived in remote areas, such as islands in the South Pacific. This phenomenon began around 1885, at the height of the British colonization period, and continued on through World War II. With World War II, the Japanese and then the United States needed airstrips to land cargo planes. So they chose a few islands and sent men there to build runways and towers. When our planes began to land there, well, this was a wondrous thing to the native people who had never left the bush. They had never even dreamed about airplanes, much less the manufactured goods the soldiers gave them. After the war, the planes left and abandoned the air bases and there were no more riches coming from the sky."

"Wait a minute, Dad," Tyler said. "Did these people think the guys from the planes were gods?"

"Yes! And after the war, the people felt abandoned and they began to perform rituals to bring the men from the sky back to them."

"So, while the rest of the world was wearing clothes and driving cars made in factories," I said, "these people lived so remotely that the planes, the soldiers, with their uniforms and weapons, seemed like aliens from another planet or gods?"

"Yes!" Archie said.

"Where exactly did this happen?" Hunter said. "I want to pin it on my map."

Hunter and Tyler shared a large wall map of the world in the hallway between their bedrooms.

"Start with the Fiji islands," Archie said.

"We can read more at the library, if you'd like to," I said. "I know I'd like to learn more about them."

By seven fifteen, there wasn't a teaspoon of dinner left in a pot or pan. Tyler and Hunter ate like starving animals, as young boys do, and even Archie had seconds of everything. They insisted on doing the dishes over my objections and order was quickly restored.

Archie and I were standing on the front porch saying good night. It was as dark as pitch outside, with only our porch lights and one streetlight to see where you were going. Tyler had challenged Hunter to a race home and they were already on their porch, calling back to us.

"Is the door open?" Tyler called.

"Yes," Archie called out with a thumbs-up. Then he turned to me. "Thanks for a wonderful supper."

"You're welcome."

"You're so great with kids. Don't you have a degree in early education?"

"Yes."

"Why aren't you using it?"

"If I went to work full-time, who would tend the queen bee? Even in my hives, the queen can't feed herself. My momma's like that."

He gave me an inquisitive look, as though I might be too soft to function in the real world or as though Momma was a bona fide crackpot.

"Besides, I have a dream of teaching at the Sullivan's Island Elementary School, and so does everyone else. I'm waiting for a slot."

"Well, you're a darned good cook," he said.

"Thanks," I said. "Cargo cults, huh?"

"Yeah, cargo cults. I love all that stuff."

"Me, too, I think."

"Where'd you learn to cook like that?"

"I'm self-taught in self-defense."

I could see his eyes twinkle even in the low light. He was probably envisioning Momma frying up some Spam and grits for dinner. Or something worse.

"Once I had a birthday party and the queen baked these casseroles. I remember two things. My sister broke the piñata before anyone else had a chance to give it a whack, and everyone went home with salmonella. She must've left them in the sun."

He was grinning widely. "That must've been some party!"

"The worst," I said.

We just looked at each other for a moment, and then I could see that he was having a carnal moment because he gave me that look. Yes, Archie MacLean, this would be the moment the boy kisses the girl. He cleared his throat instead.

"Well, good night then," he said.

"Good night." I closed the door, leaned against it, and giggled.

Did I really want a guy with graying temples and double dimples? Did I really want those forty-year-old hands on my thirty-year-old skin? Yes, as a matter of fact, I did.

I decided to call Leslie and tell her about Momma. Here's the thing: If I didn't call her, she'd be annoyed with me, saying how could I do such a thing? If I called her, she'd be annoyed.

I poured a large glass of wine to fortify myself, from the box I kept on the pantry floor, and dialed her number. She answered on the third ring. I don't know why, but she always said I should never pick up the telephone before the third ring. Maybe it was because she was always waiting for a boy to call her and she didn't want to seem pathetically anxious.

"Hey, it's me. There's news from the island," I said.

"Hey, yourself. I didn't hear jungle drums," she said, as though she was a comedian.

"Yeah, well, I had to put Momma in the hospital today."

"Again?"

"Yeah. Very dramatic, as usual."

"I'm sure. I already know the answer to this, but is she okay?"

"Of course, she is."

"Well, what happened?"

"She fell out of bed again," I said. "Second time this month."

"She's still there?"

"Yep, they wanted to rule out brain tumor, broken bones . . . you know, a whole litany of stuff."

"Jeez. A zillion dollars in tests for nothing."

"That's what they do these days."

"It's practically criminal. Should I send flowers? I mean, I can do that. No problem. Would it cheer her up?"

"That's your call. Would anything cheer her up besides you coming home? I expect I'll bring her home tomorrow. Maybe send them to the house?"

"Okay. I'll send her something fun. What about getting some kind of guardrails? You know, the kind you use for toddlers?"

I looked at the ceiling. Didn't my sister know how impossibly juvenile our mother was? "Right! Then she'd crawl over them and fall on her head, and I'd really be in trouble. You know, she breaks a hip, pneumonia sets in, and pffft! She's a goner!"

"Well? That's one answer, isn't it?"

"Leslie! You're terrible."

"Gallows humor, sister. Gallows humor."

"Funny but not really. So how are you and Charlie doing?"

"We're fine. Well, I'm fine. Charlie's been acting sort of odd."

"What do you mean?"

"I don't know. Just odd. He wants to go to Atlantic City. He hates gambling! But suddenly, he wants to go to Atlantic City and see a bunch of shows."

"Sounds like fun to me."

"Sounds like fun because you're stuck on that miserable island with the Queen of Mean. You know I don't like all that noise. And all that craziness."

Wait. Was my sister no longer Miss Party Hearty?

"Well, darlin'? Maybe that's why he's got a hankering to go to Atlantic City! To inspire you!"

"To do what? Wear high heels to bed? Get myself a trashy see-through chiffon robe to wear while I fry the chicken?"

"And here I always thought you were the wild one!"

"Well, now you know. Anyway, we're going to Atlantic City next week for four days. I'll let you know how it goes."

"And I'll keep you posted on Momma."

"Do that. I'll call 1-800-Flowers in the morning."

"So, aren't you going to ask me how I'm doing?"

I could hear a deep sigh.

"How are you doing?" she said. "What's new? Nothing, right?" Everyone thought I was a pitiful old maid at thirty.

"Um, actually? I had Archie and his boys over for dinner tonight." Maybe I said it a little too brightly. The minute she heard a drop of happiness in my voice, I knew I was going to get an earful.

Dead silence. Followed by a slowly drawn out, "Really? Is there anything to report?"

"Beyond one marginally awkward moment when he was leaving? Nope."

"Hmm. What did you cook?"

"Chicken. Lemon chicken with mashed potatoes, peas, and hot apple pie."

More silence.

I finally said, "Are you still there?"

"Yeah. Listen, Holly. You're my little sister and I don't want to see you get hurt. Archie has a Ph.D. in world religion from Harvard Divinity School, for God's sake. You're a nice girl and all that, but he's *light-years* out of your league. Can't you see that?"

Two could play this game.

"Jesus, Leslie! I made chicken and mashed potatoes, not lobster and caviar. And I did it mainly for his boys. They hardly ever get a home-cooked meal. Do you know how many pizza boxes are in their garbage?"

"So now you're looking through their garbage cans? Oh, Holly. This is so sad I don't know what to say!"

"No. It is not sad. And no, I do not go through their garbage. They're sticking out of the top of the can, and when I roll ours out to the curb on pickup day, there are the boxes poking out of the cans like a cry for help."

"Oh, okay then. Sorry. Charlie says I always jump to judgment. Maybe he's right. That was nice of you to make them dinner. Did they have a good time?"

"I think so. There's not a crumb left. And they did the dishes."

"You know, Archie's hot. You know that, right?"

"Yes, for an old dude. I'm not blind."

"Don't let him take advantage of you, Holly."

I wanted to say, Why not? Everybody else does. But instead I said, "Oh, please. What's a little chicken between friends?"

Archie was staring at my apiary.
"Ever read David Foster Wallace?"

"No," I said. "Should I?"

"Why not? He said, 'Everything takes time.
Bees have to move very fast to stay still.'"

"He's right. They flap their little wings two
hundred and thirty times a second to hover."

Chapter Three
Buzzing Along

Our old house was a classic clapboard island cottage, painted white some years ago, with a silver tin roof and porches around the front and the back, their floors slanted for runoff during the horrific rains that regularly saturated all the islands. We had working shutters on every window and slim French doors with their original glass from 1860. There was a Pawleys Island hammock, four rockers, and a glider from the 1950s on the front porch. They had more mileage than my sister. A table and four chairs stood on the back porch that no one ever used, along with garbage cans and an old Weber grill. You would say it was comfortable, and it was.

I had slept peacefully, not having to listen for Momma calling me in the night. I was feeling pretty good at first when I turned over in bed and woke up. But as I became fully conscious, I remembered I was irked with Leslie. Why did she always want to make me feel so awkward? What was the matter with her? What was the matter with me for listening to her? Probably a lot. But to be honest, I carried around a nagging feeling inside, like I was still waiting for my real life to begin. Meanwhile, here I was, thirty, with no real career or prospects of one, even though I had that sweet degree in elementary education and was on a wait list for the island elementary school. I was living in limbo, not a thoroughly unpleasant state, but not a very satisfying one, either. In the meanwhile, I told myself as I brushed the tangles of night from my hair, I would continue to do the few things that time allowed me to do and that I liked to do. And maybe I should get another kind of job. Something part-time. Anything that would get me out of the house. I could hire someone to sit with Momma or to check on her a few times a day. It would be good for me. I knew she would scream her head off if I went to work anywhere out of earshot. Maybe if I did, she would regroup and stop pretending to be sick all the time. And hellfire, she didn't own me. The thought of breaking out was so delicious, I could already taste my freedom.

It was a beautiful morning, not as warm as yesterday had been, and I thought that was good. After my favorite breakfast parfait of yogurt, fruit, granola, and my own honey, I dressed and went outside with a big mug of steaming hot coffee. The yard was saturated with heavy dew that would surely evaporate as the sun began its daily climb. By midday, people would be shedding their light jackets and sweaters, but by five they'd be reaching for them again: classic Lowcountry weather.

Archie's car was gone, which meant he had taken the boys to school and then probably gone downtown to the college. I thought about him, wondering what it must have been like to study religion at a place like Harvard, and then to spend your life considering the objects and rituals and beliefs that people held sacred. I had loved our discussion about cargo cults.

Even though I had lived my whole life on this island,

I knew there was life beyond the Vatican. I'd read a little about Tibetan Buddhism and what it meant to be Hindu. And I knew quite a bit about Judaism because Charleston had one of the oldest Reformed temples in the country. Needless to say, because the Holy City's founding fathers' principles were grounded in the belief that all people should worship in whatever manner they pleased, we had an unusually wide variety of places to praise the Almighty. I wondered about how Archie prayed. To be honest, that was between him and his Maker. None of my beeswax, so to speak. On a very odd note, I'd never seen him take the boys to church on Sunday. Maybe at some point I'd gently suggest that the boys were welcome to come with me. That would require a high level of diplomacy, because people got all weird when it came to talking about religion in general, even people with Ph.D.s from Harvard Divinity School. I just really thought children needed to believe in something greater than themselves. Everyone did. If they could manage it, that is.

I took a leisurely stroll through my garden, making a mental list of chores to be done, and, of course, I talked to my bees. They were better company than most humans I knew.

"Good morning, ladies! Guess what I did last night? I made dinner for our neighbors and they loved it! What do you think about that? I made chicken and mashed potatoes and . . ." I went on describing the meal to them and the conversation with my sister. "And she says Charlie wants to take her to Atlantic City. Wouldn't it be fun to play slot machines and see some celebrities and entertainers? Anyway, she thinks Archie is way out of my league. Do you think she's right? I think she's an a-hole. She and Momma are two rotten peas in a rotten pod."

The girls were buzzing all around in the flowers collecting pollen and nectar and I was gently moving among them, pulling some of the weeds that would strangle my flowers if I ignored them. Somewhere over the course of the winter I had decided to get more serious about keeping my garden in flowers all year. If it had color? It counted, especially if it was purple. Honey bees loved purple flowers. I'd plant some things like ornamental grasses that had pink plumes or variegated leaves that changed color with the seasons. And I'd beef up the herb garden because honey bees loved basil, lavender, cilantro, rosemary, and thyme.

"So, yeah, I'm going over to the hospital in a little bit. See how Momma is doing. I'm sure she's okay, but she's no rocking babe anymore and that's when bad stuff starts to happen. She's just in her sixties, but she's old for her age. Personally? I think she's just mad because she's fat. Fat's bad. It leads to all kinds of diseases. Maybe I'll take the nurses a few jars of honey. And by the way, I'm getting a job."

I looked up to see Andy our UPS deliveryman's truck pull over to the curb.

"Morning, Miss Holly! Got a couple of things for you today."

"Well, thanks, Andy. Just toss them on the porch. I'll see about them in a few minutes."

"That's fine," he said and took the boxes up the steps to the front porch. "By the way, you were right about my tire. But it didn't go bad until I ran over a piece of sheet metal on I-526."

"Well, then I'm extra glad to see you in one piece."

His face got all kind of funny looking. "How'd you know that was gonna happen?"

"Andy, it's the most peculiar thing. I looked at your truck and it just popped into my head. *Andy's gonna get a flat in that back tire.* Just like someone was whispering to me."

"That's kind of peculiar," he said and looked at me so strangely.

"Come on, Andy. You've been knowing me for a dozen years. And this *is* the Lowcountry."

"Yeah, I always forget that. You know my people come from Spartanburg."

"Different world up there," I said.

"I reckon so," he said and just stood there.

"Would you like a jar of honey?" I said, thinking it might put him more at ease. "I was just going to get a few from the shed for the nurses at the hospital. I took Momma over there yesterday, and you know . . ."

"Oh, I'm so sorry! Is she all right?"

"Andy, the queen is always all right. You wait here, and I'll be right back."

I hurried to the gardening shed where I kept the jars of honey lined up on shelves. It was also where I kept the equipment that I used to spin the honey from the combs and jar it, too. It could be a very messy and sticky situation if I tried to do it in the house, so a few years ago I just took our old potting shed, painted it in pastels to match the hives, and sort of converted it to suit my needs. It wasn't like anyone else would set foot in there anyway. I grabbed a few, dropped them in a canvas tote bag, and returned to Andy, who stood waiting patiently on the concrete walkway to our front steps. I thought, Someday I might dig out all that awful cracked cement and put in a pretty path of bricks in a herringbone pattern. I'd seen that done in *Southern Living* magazine and just loved it. Maybe Andy would like to help? That made me giggle to myself.

I handed him some honey over pecans, which was just that. Pecans I shelled and covered in honey.

"Here you go! It's good on everything," I said. "Yogurt, ice cream, or a spoon."

"Well, thank you so much! That's so nice of you!" Smiling, he turned to go.

He had a very nice smile.

"Happy to share!" I said and went to the porch to put the packages inside and to get my purse.

I picked up two small boxes from the porch rocker. What had Momma bought now? More tunics? She had so many, she'd never live long enough to get her money's worth out of them. That was for sure. Well, never mind economy. How she spent her money was none of my beeswax, either.

I locked the house, drove over to the hospital, parked in visitor parking, and made my way to Momma's room. I was feeling pretty relaxed and happy until I got there. There stood several doctors with seriously chiseled expressions, like totem poles. I had obviously walked in on something critical.

"Oh, don't pay her no never mind," Momma said. "That's just Holly, my daughter."

"Hello," each one said, and of course I said hello back.

"How are you, Momma?"

"Not so hot. It seems I have a tiny little thing on my liver and something else in my pancreas the size of an M&M. Neither one of these things is good news."

She said it as though she was merely reporting the weather and without a trifling thought about how it might impact me, but then, sensitivity wasn't her thing. But I was so startled that I wasn't sure I'd heard her correctly.

"What?" I said. "Tell me this again?" Suddenly, I was dizzy, and I had to sit down.

"Relax yourself. I'm not dying tomorrow," she said. "These nice doctors want to watch my tumors for a while to see if they change size or if anything pops up somewhere else."

One of the doctors turned to me and explained that the location of the tumors made them inoperable, but they also appeared to be benign. For now.

"What if they're not?" I asked.

"Then we will see changes in their composition pretty quickly. If that's the case, we can radiate them. There's a new protocol for targeted chemo, too. Much less invasive, less downtime."

"My God," I said.

The world changed in that moment. I looked at my mother, lying in her hospital bed, and realized she might be facing something nasty that was going to eventually take her life even if she treated it. It was like a conditional death sentence. She glanced over to me and bit her bottom lip, something she did when she tried to hold back tears. I felt terribly sorry for her then. She seemed as vulnerable as the day Daddy ran off with his physical therapist eleven years ago. Leslie and I didn't blame him. After all, life with the QB was difficult. He had all but vanished from our lives.

I didn't remember the doctors leaving, but I found myself alone with her. I should've asked them for their names and telephone numbers and for a copy of the reports, but I had been so shocked by the news, I had not. She was very quiet, which was completely unnerving. Finally, after a long while, she spoke. She had meditated herself into a ninety-miles-an-hour tither.

"I feel fine," she said in a manic voice. "In fact, I don't feel sick at all. Let's get out of here."

She started to get out of bed.

"Hold on there, Momma," I said quickly trying to maneuver her back under the covers. "I don't think that's how this works."

"What do you mean? They can't force me to stay here! I'm not a prisoner!"

"Well, for one thing, you've got an IV in your arm." I touched her shoulder, encouraging her to lean back against her pillows.

She started to pull it out.

"You watch. In five minutes, they'll march back in here and say they want to do even more tests on me like

I'm their personal guinea pig. I'm not going to have it. Plain and simple. Now, Holly, either you take me home or I'll call a taxi."

"Momma, I . . ."

"Don't 'Momma' me. Pull this tape off and be quick about it."

There was no use in fighting her, but I sure hated it when her manic side got the better of her. On the other hand, she wasn't wrong, really. She didn't have a temperature. There was no visible sign of any real illness. And she was mighty determined. Besides, it did no good to argue with Katherine Jensen when she, pardon the expression, got a bee in her bonnet. I pulled the tape off; she pulled the needle out and put pressure on the puncture point.

"Get me a tissue," she said.

I handed her one and she held it over the wound.

"Now see if you can salvage a piece of that tape to hold this in place."

"Oh, Momma," I said.

Lord, she was difficult. There was no please or thank you to be had. I gave her a piece of tape; she secured it.

"Now, I'm getting dressed," she said. "Do you think I might have some privacy?"

"Of course," I said. "I'll be right outside if you need me."

I stood in the hall outside her door and thought, Good Lord, her doctors are not going to like this. A moment later I heard a thud. I knew that thud. Momma was on the floor. Just to make the situation a little more interesting, when I tried to push her door open, her body was blocking it. I managed to push my head through.

"You okay?"

"Obviously not. My plan isn't working out as I'd hoped."

"I'll get help," I said.

"Damn it," she said.

I hurried along to the nurse's station thinking to myself that it would be so nice if my mother knew how to behave herself. She was always right. She always had to have the last word. But this time, there was clearly something wrong. All this falling business had to have a cause behind it. And normally, whatever our definition of *normal* was, she enjoyed the hospital. She got lots of attention and she didn't have to lift a finger. Maybe she was afraid. Maybe the doctors had given her really bad news before I got there, and her first impulse had been to run.

"Excuse me," I said. "My mother is Katherine Jensen, in room 311. Well, I'm afraid she's had a fall . . ."

The nurse all but sprinted from her desk toward my mother's room, grabbing two others along the way to help her. I got there just as the thinnest health care worker in the world was inching herself inside through the available space.

"Now, just what's going on here?" one of them said.

They pressed the call button and asked for two orderlies to come help. Inside of a few minutes they had Momma back in bed.

"Does anything hurt, Mrs. Jensen?" the head nurse said.

"I'm fine and I'd like to go home, if that's all right with everyone," she said.

"Well, Mrs. Jensen, we have to get the doctor's okay for that. He's got to sign papers to release you."

"We'll see about that," she said.

The nurse looked at her square in the face and said, "Now, Mrs. Jensen. You gonna be trouble for me? My shift ends at five o'clock. Why don't you be trouble for the next shift and I'll bring you all the chocolate pudding you can eat? How 'bout it? Deal?"

My mother, who needed an all-you-can-eat deal like she needed another hole in her head, considered endless chocolate pudding and said sheepishly, "Oh, all right, but only because you asked me so nicely."

The nurse nodded to another nurse, who hurried along to bring my mother the reward for her bad behavior.

"Now, let's get your IV back in place," the nurse said.

Momma held out her hand as though she was offering the nurse an opportunity to kiss the ring of Saint Peter.

The nurse looked at me and said, "She's something else, your momma is."

"You're telling me?" I said.

"You can run along now, Holly," Momma said. "I'm in good hands here."

Peace was restored. I went home to call Leslie.

"I've got another great bee quote for you,"
Archie said. " 'Hope is the only bee that
makes honey without flowers.' "

"Hmmm," I said. "Who said it?"

"Robert Green Ingersoll, known as the
Great Agnostic. Born 1833, died in 1899."

"He was an idiot. Any beekeeper
will tell you there's a God."

Chapter Four
Now What?

I left Momma in the hospital and was driving back
toward the island. She was a funny bird, cutting a
deal with the promise of good behavior for the reward
of chocolate pudding. But the doctors still had to get

to the bottom of her issues. Then I remembered one of the nurses asking her how much exercise she got.

Momma looked at her and proudly said, "None."

The nurse said, "Well, you know, a little exercise is good for you. If you just sit around all day, your muscles atrophy and your mobility becomes really compromised."

Someone else suggested she give herself a couple of daily tasks, like going to get the mail, taking out garbage, or picking up the newspaper. "You know, start slowly."

Momma rolled her eyes heavenward and harrumphed loudly. She was having no part of exercise, if I knew her. And also, it would be a bitter cold day in hell before Katherine Jensen took advice from anyone. But the nurse had offered a point to consider. Maybe balance was the devil behind her falling. That would be considerably better than a brain tumor, which was what I had been thinking she had. Then, in a moment of optimism, I had a thought that maybe her other tumors didn't mean anything. Maybe she'd been born with them. I had heard of that happening. And I wondered how she was feeling about her diagnosis. If it had been me, I'd be terrified to know there was something growing inside of me that would most assuredly kill me eventually unless something else got there first. If

I was possibly facing radiation or chemo or surgery I'd be terrified. Cancer was very scary stuff. But perhaps this terrible news would make her realize she wasn't really living her life. If she would begin moving herself even in the smallest ways, it could lead to getting out of the house to go places besides the hospital. Like, maybe she'd like to go to Gwynn's or to Croghan's Jewel Box just to have her diamond washed. Maybe she'd like to go to church, which would be my first stop if a doctor told me I had the smallest tumor of any kind.

Traffic on the way home was miserable. All through Mount Pleasant, it was bumper to bumper, and I caught every single red light. I decided to stop at the Publix to buy something to make for supper, and on a lark, I took the plunge and filled out a job application. Something told me there was a job waiting for me and that I should seize the moment. I was like the scout bees, seeing what was out there within range of the hive. Sure enough, Publix was hiring and I was given a part-time position in the bakery. Should I take this job? Why not? I thought that it was the fastest interview in history. The pay was only minimum wage, but there were other advantages, like flexible hours. But first and foremost, it was going to save my sanity. Second, I could add the money to my Maserati fund. I had a pipe dream about someday owning a gorgeous sports car.

"You'll be reporting to Andrea Blatt. She's been here forever," Barbara Hagerty from Human Resources said. "I hope you like decorating cakes. We sell a lot of birthday cakes."

"Who doesn't like decorating cakes?" I said, knowing I'd never decorated a cake with anything other than canned frosting and press-on candies that you had to peel off a piece of cardboard that was so stiff that it cracked the decorations. I was so excited, you'd have thought they just made me a network anchor on the six o'clock national news. And I was excited to take a shot at something creative.

"Great! Can you come in tomorrow?" she said.

"Sure! Why not?" I said. "And Barbara?"

"Yes?"

"Thanks," I said.

"Let's see if you're still grateful in six weeks!" She laughed and stood, indicating the interview was over.

"I'm going to go and buy supper now," I said and left her office to forage.

In the produce aisle I was filling a bag with apples and I put them in the wrong cart. Then I walked that cart the whole way up the aisle. Just as I was about to add lemons, I realized it wasn't my cart. I looked up into the face of an old classmate from high school.

"Ted?"

"Holly?"

"Yeah! Wow." Ted's appearance was vastly improved over the years. No acne, for one. "What are you doing here?"

"Manhandling the cantaloupes and rescuing my cart. You?"

No wedding ring.

"Buying groceries?"

"Okay, well, nice to see you," he said and handed me my bag of apples.

"Yeah, you too."

Wow, he got cute, I thought.

Thinly cut pork chops were on special, so I grabbed a family-sized pack of a dozen, a double box of Stove Top stuffing, a huge jar of applesauce, and a bag of frozen spinach and drove back to the island singing along with the radio. I had a job! And I was about to enjoy a perfect meal. I'd fry up some bacon and use that grease to sauté my pork chops. And I'd bought myself wine in a bottle. I was celebrating. A job! I'd been liberated!

When I pulled into the driveway, Archie and his boys were getting out of his car with enormous backpacks that looked like they would topple the boys over from the weight of them.

"Hey, Mith Holly!" Tyler called out.

"Hey, Tyler!" I called back. "How was your day?"

He gave me a thumbs-up. I started unloading my trunk to bring the groceries inside.

"Do you need help?" Hunter yelled at the top of his little lungs.

"Oh, no, I'm fine! But thank you, sweetheart." He was so darling.

"How's your momma?" Archie said, coming over to the low hedge of pittosporum that edged his property. "I thought you might be bringing her home today."

"No, not yet," I said, and somehow my voice sounded strange to me.

"I'm sorry. Have you had bad news?"

"No—well, yes. For the moment, she's all right. But long term? It's unclear."

I relayed the story to him as I knew it. There was no point in sugarcoating the news. In one way, I felt absolutely terrible about my mother's possible illness, and in another way, the news of it and the retelling of it was strangely freeing. Naturally, there was a part of me, that young Catholic girl, that knew I should be ashamed of my black soul that delighted in any part of it. But I wasn't ashamed one bit. I felt like this might be cosmic retribution for her thinking it was all right to steal my independence while she indulged herself in every way imaginable.

"Well, I'm terribly sorry to hear the news. Please

tell your mother I asked about her and that we'll be thinking about her. And you know, Holly, if there's anything I can do, or my boys, please tell us. You've been so great to us since, well, Carin, well, you know."

He still couldn't even bring himself to say what had happened and it had been months and months. He really loved her.

"I know. It was so terrible. But I think we're meant to help each other when life gets too difficult, don't you?"

"If we're able to, yes. It's one of the beautiful things about humanity. We actually can lift each other up. Ease someone's burden. And it's just, well, it's just nice to help others. There's a special joy to be found in service. You know, being useful. Like your hives."

"Yes. Yes, there is something very special about helping each other. Ask my bees. Your boys know that, too, which is sort of amazing, given their ages and all that."

"Thank you. I think they've learned a lot about empathy from you, too, and I'm very grateful. They're good boys."

"They are *wonderful* boys," I said. "Well, now I have to go and call my sister and drop this lovely bomb on her."

"That won't be easy," he said.

I could see him then questioning whether I had the diplomatic finesse to deliver this kind of news in the right way. I looked at him as if to say, If you knew all the bullshit I've had to endure every day of my life, you'd never have a moment's doubt about my capacity to deal with bad news.

"I'll be all right," I said. "And Momma's not even symptomatic of anything yet. But tumors are not a good thing."

I gave him a little wave and turned to go. In the background I could hear Tyler yelling at Hunter for eating the last Oreo. And then I heard Archie telling them to cut it out. All normalcy had not been lost for them. They were coping with their grief because they had each other to pull themselves through each day. But they still bickered, which in an odd way was a good sign.

As I climbed the front steps my legs felt like they weighed a thousand pounds apiece. I realized then that I was exhausted. Of course, there was another package from UPS sitting on the rocking chair on the porch. I went inside, dropped my bag and the package on the dining room table, and took the groceries to the kitchen. I stood at the sink while I absentmindedly filled the kettle with water. Hot tea seemed like a good idea. Hot tea with honey. I wondered then if I should try to find our father and tell him about Momma. But in my guts, I knew he wouldn't care. He wouldn't.

Dad wasn't consciously cruel, but he was cruel nonetheless. He'd remarried and brought three more children into the world. He'd resurfaced long enough to get Leslie up the aisle six years ago. He sure did object wildly and loudly to contributing to Leslie's wedding bills. Eventually he gave in but complained the whole time that Momma should've been saving for Leslie's wedding expenses from the alimony and child support he'd given her all these years, as though he'd given her millions. I wondered then, if I ever married, would he assume he was doing the same for me? Probably not, if it entailed any financial responsibility. I wondered if his new children ever had to eat cereal for supper, as we had, or if they wore hand-me-downs, or if their mother cut their hair. Probably not.

I had long considered myself to be fatherless due to lack of paternal interest. The more I thought about him, the more upset I became. If I ever did find someone to marry, I sure wouldn't let that jerk overshadow my day as he had Leslie's. I'd never forget the gossiping at her wedding. All those old biddies down at Stella Maris saying things like, *Oh, isn't he so good to come back to do this? I always said he was a good man. Well, you know, it was never easy for him living with her. Who could blame him for walking away from her?*

Not that they were wrong, but it sure shifted the tone of my sister's wedding day, putting him in the spotlight. Leslie didn't care. She was marrying the Wallet and she was immune to all else. About six months before the wedding Momma went on a crash diet, determined to look good for the big day. She'd be so drop-dead gorgeous, Daddy would be sorry he left, she said about a thousand times while she choked down dozens of hard-boiled eggs and chomped on celery sticks. When the day arrived, she looked the best that she had in ages, but a magician she wasn't. And don't you know Dad just had to bring his new wife with him? Would you believe Lola was her name? She looked like a young Jackie Kennedy. Momma took one look at her and wanted to just lay down and die. That was the other time I felt truly sorry for her. Getting kicked to the curb in front of Sullivan's Island society is the worst. But being undone at your daughter's wedding by the presence of the stunning woman who stole your husband is horrific. Momma wasn't stupid; she knew he was catting around when she found condoms hidden in the air conditioner when she was changing the filter.

As in many small towns across the country, everyone on this island has something to say about everybody's business. I mean, most of the time I didn't like Momma very much, but I didn't like Dad at all. These were not easy people to like or love. But I didn't want to see my mother publicly humiliated.

It didn't seem to bother Dad or Leslie. Not one bit. I remember I took Momma aside and said, "Screw Dad. Lola's nothing but trash." She burst into tears and I took her to the ladies' room. She washed her face and said, "I think I'd like to eat some cake." That was the end of Skinny Katherine. Pretty soon, Big Mean Momma was back. And maybe that's another reason I didn't leave her. By the time her divorce from Dad was final, she'd had enough rejection to last ten lifetimes. And while we're on the subject of weight? Momma could weigh a thousand pounds if she wanted to, but I had always worried for her health. Nowhere in any medical journal did the experts say that being overweight was a good idea. It was just as dangerous as being too skinny. And now here we were. Momma's health was officially in jeopardy. Of course, while I couldn't swear her weight had a thing to do with it, it couldn't have helped.

The whistle of the kettle snapped me back into reality. I swirled a dollop of honey into the bottom of a mug, dropped a Constant Comment tea bag in, and covered it all with boiling hot water. I decided to call Leslie first and cook supper later. It was still early.

She answered on the third ring. Of course.

"Hey," I said. "You busy?"

"Hey, Holly. No," she said. "What's going on?"

"Well, here's the bad news. Momma's got some itty-bitty tumors in her liver and her pancreas."

"What? Oh, no!"

"Wait, hang on. Don't get upset. The doctors think that whatever she's got is benign, but they want to monitor her. So she's still in the hospital because they want to do some more tests."

"Good grief! How'd she handle the news? Is she hysterical?"

"There was a moment of rebellion."

"Meaning?"

"She decided she was leaving and ripped the IV out of her hand."

"Sweet Mary, Mother of God. What happened?"

"They bribed her to stay with chocolate pudding. Trust me, you don't want the details. It was too stupid."

"I'm sure. So, what do you think? Do you think she's dying?"

"Not a chance. I think the situation is serious but

not dire. I mean, the doctors talked about some new treatment but said it was for down the road and only if necessary."

"Well, that makes me feel slightly better. I don't have to panic and run home?"

"Definitely not. There will be plenty of time to panic. But it's not now."

"I didn't order flowers yet. Should I wait?"

"Up to you. She'll probably come home tomorrow."

"Maybe I'll just send her a card."

"Totally your call."

We chatted about Momma for a few more minutes and hung up. I promised to call her if anything changed. As always, she didn't ask about my life. I didn't tell her I got a job because she would've said icing cakes at Publix was déclassé (which it was not) as though we grew up in the White House. But she came to be self-absorbed honestly, taking after our mother in so many ways. By tomorrow that card would become a phone call. I knew her. She didn't go out of her way for anyone, not even her own mother.

I drained my cup of tea and began digging around in the drawer for a corkscrew, thinking I'd have a glass of wine while I cooked like they did on fancy television programs like Julia Child's. Of course, there was no corkscrew to be found. Then it dawned on me that

Archie probably had one. I'd just go next door and borrow it. He wouldn't mind.

I went straight to the front door and had my hand on the doorknob when I realized this was an opportunity to impress him. I wasn't unattractive, but my appearance was improved with grooming. So I brushed my hair and put on a little lip gloss.

"Better," I said to the mirror.

A few minutes later, I rang his doorbell. He answered and seemed pleasantly surprised to see me there with a bottle of wine in my hands.

"Well! What's this? Are we having a party?" he said. "A bottle of mead?"

Oh! He knew about mead!

"No, sadly, it's just wine. I can't find our corkscrew. Do you have one I might borrow?"

"Of course! Come in." He held the door open and I stepped inside.

"Thanks," I said. "I don't know if I've ever told you this, but I really love your floors."

Maybe saying *love* was overstating it.

"You do?"

"Yes. They're so pretty and they really shine. But not like they've got some fake finish. Do you know what I mean? They have a lustrous quality, like pearls have a luster."

Was I really using a word with *lust* in it? Twice? Did he read into that? His eyebrows were sort of scrunched together. Not good.

"I have kind of a thing for flooring," Archie said. "All these boards are reclaimed from an old house in Walterboro that was being torn down. They're hand-hewed and pegged. You don't see that anymore. They get waxed by hand twice a year. You know, for some guys it's sports cars, although I wouldn't mind a Lamborghini. For me? It's flooring, which is also attainable." He stopped and looked at me. "You might be the only person who ever noticed the patina."

"Really?" I didn't tell him about the car fund.

"Yeah. Come on. Let's pull that cork."

I followed him to the kitchen thinking I was really glad my remark didn't win me a Dork of the Year trophy, because the minute the words left my mouth, I realized they sounded awkward. But that was another reason I liked Archie so well. He never made me feel like I was weird or something.

At first glance, his kitchen was way too sterile. I don't mean too clean, I mean it didn't have a soul. Hunter and Tyler were seated at the kitchen table doing homework. The only small appliances on the counter were a coffeemaker and a toaster. Other than those two things, the counters were bare. And there was no meal preparation in evidence. Were they having pizza again?

"Hey, Mith Holly!" Tyler said.

"Hey!" Hunter said, looking up. "You coming for supper?"

"No, no. Just stopping by for a moment," I said.

"Here it is," Archie said. "Shall I open it for you?"

"Gosh, thanks. Sure."

I was glad he was opening the bottle instead of me. I'd never had a lot of luck with corks. But then, I'd never had many bottles. Wine was sort of new for me. I didn't know much about it except that a glass took the edge off my annoyance when I was annoyed. Therefore, wine was a good thing. There was a popping sound and my visit was about to end.

"Would you like to share a glass with me?" I said.

I don't even know where I found the nerve to ask him. The words just popped out of my mouth.

"Oh! That's so nice of you to ask. But I've got to feed these rascals. It's getting late for their supper."

"Oh! Of course! What are y'all having? For dinner, I mean."

"Well, I was going to, you know, go get a pizza."

"Pizza," I said and just looked at him as if to say, come on, bubba, can't you do better than that?

"Why? What are you doing for dinner?" he asked.

This got the boys' attention.

"Pork chops, stuffing, applesauce, braised carrots, and creamed spinach. There's plenty. Pork chops were on sale, so I bought a slug of them." I was trying to remember if I had another pie in the freezer and I thought I did. Maybe peach? "Give me like forty-five minutes?"

"Oh, we shouldn't . . ." he said.

"Stuffing? Ah, come on, Dad! Please?" Tyler said, his hands folded in desperate prayer. "I can't believe I'm saying thith, but I'm thick of pizza."

"You are?" Archie said.

"I love pork chops," Hunter said with a very sad face. "We haven't had pork chops in years." He slid to the floor and pretended to be unconscious from starvation, or maybe it was malnutrition.

"It's fine," I said. "Really!"

Archie looked at the faces of his little boys and saw that they were missing home-cooked meals.

"Okay," he said. "We'll see you soon."

"Great!"

I hurried home and threw dinner together in record time. The flowers were still fresh and I knew the unchipped plates were on top of the stack. The bacon sizzled in my cast-iron skillet, and I did indeed have a peach pie in the depths of the freezer. Soon our house smelled like bacon and fruit. What could be more mouthwatering?

Over dinner Archie said, "I haven't had pork chops this good since my momma cooked them. I'm not kidding."

"Thanks," I said. "Would you like another one?"

"*I* sure would," Hunter said.

"*Me, too,*" said Tyler.

Archie shot them a stern look and refilled my wineglass halfway. Wine with dinner made me feel very sophisticated.

"Please?" they said.

"Of course!" I said and passed the platter to them, followed by the applesauce and the spinach. "So, I got a job today."

"You did?" Archie said, knowing without me saying a word that my taking a job was tantamount to a full-scale revolution. The QB was going to have a cow.

"Yeah, decorating cakes at Publix. Isn't that crazy?"

"Not at all," he said politely and smiled in a way that said he approved of the revolution.

"Decorating cakes?" Hunter said. "That's the coolest job in the world!"

"My birf-day is in June," Tyler said, implying I should decorate a cake for him.

I smiled at him.

"Well, if I still have this job in June, I'll bring you the biggest cake you've ever seen!"

Tyler looked at me with the sweetest expression and said, "Isn't Mith Holly great, Dad? Isn't she?"

"Yeah, she's pretty great," he said and smiled at me with his twinkling eyes.

"But I still intend to teach at your school when something opens up!"

"Tell us a bee fact," Hunter said. "Please?"

"Well, honey bees were used as the symbol of government by Emperor Napoleon I. Have you ever heard of him?"

"Cool!" Tyler said.

"And the ancient Greeks associated lips anointed with honey with the gift of eloquence—you know, honeyed lips?" Archie said. "And the Delphic bee was the priestess of Delphi!"

"And Utah is the Beehive State," I said.

"It is?" Hunter said.

"Archie? Tell us some more about cargo cults," I said.

"No, really?" he said, obviously flattered to be asked.

"Yeah, Dad!" Tyler said. "Tell us!"

"Well, all right . . ."

Archie went on to embellish the stories about the cargo cults and a mythical character named John Frum while I watched his boys' faces. They were entranced by their father. You could see it in their eyes. This was what they all needed. To be whole. To be a normal family again. I'd brought them together again around a table to talk about their day, to share a good meal, and to give them a chance to feel okay about their lives. They even ate the spinach.

I said, "So, kids, it's not like the bees love the flowers. It's a business relationship."

Tyler said, "What do you mean?"

I said, "Well, the bees use the flowers to get nectar and pollen. And the flowers know the bees will pollinate other flowers as they move around the garden. It's all in the name of self-preservation."

Chapter Five
All the Buzz

I brought Momma home from the hospital the next day and she seemed to be fine. It quickly became clear, to me at least, that she was ignoring her precarious state, because she refused to discuss it. She didn't want to talk about follow-up appointments or doctors or anything at all that had to do with her health in general. Certainly not exercise.

"I can take care of myself," she said.

"Fine," I said. "Let's hope you're right."

Denial set in. She resumed her prone position, changed the batteries in her television remote, and went back to shopping on QVC and HSN.

She also didn't want to discuss my job at Publix. When I told her what I was doing she set her jaw into a lock and barely spoke to me for a few days. That was actually not such a bad thing. In fact, it was peaceful.

I'd gotten in the habit of saving coupons, buying whatever was on sale, and cooking more than we needed so that I could take a meal to the boys. If they couldn't have a momma in their kitchen, they could have me bringing supper. One day, out of nowhere, Momma called me an idiot. After all, she could only be nice for so long. We argued.

"You're making a fool out of yourself," she said, "throwing yourself at that man."

"I'm not throwing myself at anybody," I said. "I'm doing something nice. This is what doing something nice looks like, Momma."

"I'm telling you, Holly, I know men. At some point he's going to feel insulted by all your casseroles and spaghettis. It will be like you think he needs charity or something."

"That's ridiculous," I said. I honestly could not see Archie feeling like that.

"Just don't be surprised."

I told the bees what Momma said. I swear to you the pink hive buzzed in a way that sounded like they didn't agree with Momma. It was like my pink hive had an opinion. I'm not exaggerating. Everyone who knows anything about bees knows that they know how to reach a consensus. For example, when it's time for the older queen bee to be replaced, the worker bees know it. They build new queen cells, load them up with healthy pupae, and flood them with royal jelly. Or, they ball her, which is a term that does not have the naughty connotation that used to travel around with the expression. It's more like a visit from the goon squad. To ball the queen, worker bees cluster all around her, causing her body temperature to rise to the point where she dies, which is bad enough. Anyway, crazy as it may sound, I felt as if my bees were on my side.

I was feeling pretty good about myself and my new-found culinary skills, maybe even a little superior, until the evening I brought them a chicken Divan casserole and Archie met me at the door.

"This has to stop," he said.

"What?" I said and turned every color of red on the spectrum. I felt stung.

"It's not like I can't feed my children," he said.

"Who said you couldn't feed your children?" I said. Now my head broke a sweat.

"It's just bad," he said. "I'm sorry, Holly. It just doesn't feel right to me for you to cook for us all the time. You've got to at least let me pay you, okay?"

"Wow," I said. For once in my chatty life I was at a loss for words. "I don't know what to say."

All at once my fantasy of being Tyler and Hunter's stepmother seemed to lose its footing and fall off a cliff. And I was deeply mortified.

"But you do know how much we appreciate everything you do for us, don't you?" he said, his tone softening somewhat.

"Sure," I said.

"Why don't I give you an allowance of sorts and you spend it. When you run out, I'll give you some more. How does that sound? But only if you're cooking anyway. I don't want to inconvenience you."

"Okay, I guess," I said and still didn't feel any better. There would be no putting the bubble back together again. "Anyway, here's a chicken and broccoli casserole and some biscuits. Just warm it up in your microwave. I can take my Pyrex dish back another time."

"Thanks so much!" he said. His normal chipper mood was back. "Can't you join us?"

"I ate. But thanks." I turned to go.

"You haven't told me," he said. "How's your new job?"

"Chicken was on sale," I said, apropos of nothing except a weak attempt to salvage my pride. "My job is ridiculous, endless entertainment. We've got like six people who rotate between the deli and the bakery. Today one of the younger guys in the bakery went to decorate a birthday cake and the instructions said, 'Just say something nice for Joan.' So he put that on the cake."

"Literally?" He arched an eyebrow.

"Yes. Literally. The cake read 'Just say something nice for Joan.' I'm pretty sure he was stoned. I mean, who wouldn't love this job? It's so creative, it's like the next best thing to restoring the ceiling of the Sistine Chapel."

I said this over my shoulder as I was leaving and inside of a minute I was back on my porch, taking another UPS package inside, leaving Archie to scratch his head, surely wondering what the world was coming to.

I dropped off the package in Momma's room.

"Thanks," she said.

I nearly fainted.

"You're welcome," I said.

"I'm trying to be nice," she said.

Nice? What's next? Would she take up knitting and make me a sweater? Who are we kidding here?

I made myself a cup of hot tea with a big dollop of my honey. Since I'd added a teaspoon to my daily diet in one way or another, my allergies seemed improved. It was just another advantage of beekeeping. I started keeping bees because I loved the idea of other universes. Much like gardening, when you tend beehives, hours can pass without you realizing it. My gardens nourished my bees and my bees propagated my gardens and they both fed me in some spiritual way. I hadn't yet figured out the process of fermenting honey to make mead, but at that moment I wished I had. A big mug of mead might have been just the thing I needed. Mead, by the way, is the oldest known alcoholic drink we know of.

I stared out the window over the sink and thought about Archie. It was upsetting. The offer of money made my intentions feel cheap. I really did need to get my head out of the clouds and accept the fact that Archie did not have romantic feelings for me. I knew he meant well. And it wasn't like I was rolling in money, either. Surely, he realized that and that was why he offered to pay me. If I was going to continue to cook for them, I'd need a calculator to figure out their portion of the food cost. Or I'd just charge him something that seemed fair. By the time I'd finished my tea, I made myself understand why he'd said what he said, but Lord, he had been so abrupt. Men could be like that. Maybe I'd be better off with the UPS man. A gentler and kinder soul, to be sure, but he had thought I was weird because I warned him about getting a flat tire. What was I supposed to do? Not tell him? But the butcher at Publix was pretty cute. I'd have to check his hand for a wedding ring.

The next day was my day to volunteer at the library. I always looked forward to that. For some reason, I'd been asked to do crafts with the children, which of course suited me just fine. Since we were approaching spring, even though half the time it felt like summer, I was thinking about having the children make flowers out of felt by wrapping precut petals and leaves around the ends of pencils and gluing them in place. It was a simple craft that even young children could do, and the pencils would make a nice Easter gift for their mothers or just for them to keep.

I pulled the plastic bin of felt strips out of my sister's bedroom closet and brought it to the kitchen table. When she got married, I decided her closets were going to waste, so I gave the clothes she left to Goodwill and used the space for storage for my craft materials. To be honest, my books filled her shelves, too. As I started sorting what felt I had by color, I thought about all the things that had happened at our kitchen table and silently thanked God the table couldn't talk. I wondered if it remembered the arguments our dysfunctional little brood had pitched back and forth across its old mahogany top. Every disappointment of my childhood was certainly ingrained in it somewhere, along with hundreds of Daddy's fist prints.

For years there had been a sugar bowl in the center that Leslie bought for Momma for some occasion. It was beige crockery, octagonal in shape, and decorated with stamped gold filigree. Not exactly a fine heirloom. But oh, my word! To hear Momma carry on about it, you would have thought it was made by Fabergé, encrusted in real gold and decorated with jewels.

Remembering the moment I dropped it still made my stomach hurt, even all these years later. We were drying dishes after supper. I was wiping off the table, so I picked the sugar bowl up to catch any crumbs with my damp paper towel. My hands were wet. It slipped out of my hand and hit the table. One of the handles popped off in a clean break, and naturally the screaming started. Talk about drama! Daddy walked out. And he didn't come home until very late. And when he walked out for good? That was my fault, too, because

Momma had to spend half her life yelling at me. She spent the other half yelling at him, but somehow that was beneath her notice.

I glued the handle back on with Super Glue, but that wasn't enough to restore harmony. Even now, every time she asked me to pass it to her, she'd suck her teeth and warn me to pass it carefully. Then she'd shake her head as though I was hopeless. Leslie was her favorite. I knew it. Leslie knew it. The whole island knew it.

I was just a kid. It was an accident, but Momma didn't believe in accidents. Neither Leslie nor Momma were very nice to me for the longest time. I'm not exaggerating one little bit. That's how it was.

For me it was a defining moment. As of the sugar bowl break, I began to withdraw from the family bosom. I began to read like a maniac, history and biographies especially. I learned that many of my heroes had challenging beginnings, which gave me hope for my future. I babysat for the island's children and taught myself to do counted cross stitch when I could afford the floss and how to draw with charcoal on a pad of newsprint. I learned to cook and bake by reading *Southern Living* magazine. Slowly, I redeemed myself because there was always a cake available for slicing or a new ornament for our Christmas tree or a new cross-stitched hand towel for the powder room. But by then

I didn't care as much. I'd grown into a citizen of the world, or so I thought, and saw that both Momma and Leslie were always setting me up for a game of Gotcha! To this very day, Momma still gave me suspicious looks, cutting her cold eyes at me, freezing my heart. All of this started over a cheap, stupid sugar bowl.

But the real truth? Leslie looked like a clone of Momma when Momma was a striking young woman. That was the underlying reason for all of their vitriol. I looked like the man who left her high and dry and gave her back the beach house on Sullivan's Island that had belonged to her family for generations anyway. In retrospect, it didn't seem like she got such a sweet deal.

I finally separated enough felt and packed it in a canvas tote bag with my glue gun.

The phone rang. It was probably Leslie, because no one else ever called. It was.

"Hello?"

"Hi. Is Mom awake?"

She sounded terrible, as though she'd been crying.

"Are you all right?"

"Just put Momma on the phone, okay?"

"Hang on," I said. Sure, sweetheart, anything you want, princess . . .

I put the phone on the counter and went down the hall to peek in our mother's room. Before I got there,

I heard the snoring. Great God in heaven, that woman could snore like every hog in hell was singing the "Hallelujah" chorus from Handel's *Messiah.* I went back to the kitchen and picked up the receiver.

"She's sawing logs," I said.

"It's not even ten o'clock," she said in a very whiny voice.

"What do you want from me? What's going on, Leslie? You sound awful."

"You know that trip to Atlantic City I took with Charlie last week?"

"Let me guess. You won a million dollars?"

"No. You wouldn't believe me if I told you, and anyway, I can't talk about it. Every time I . . ."

Then she broke down into tears, sobbing like a baby. Now, we all know my sister was difficult, but I didn't like to hear her cry like this. In fact, I couldn't remember ever hearing her cry like this.

"Leslie, come on now. Talk to me."

"I can't. I'm coming home."

"What do you mean?"

"I mean, clean my room. I'll be there tomorrow night."

Oh, yes, princess, I'm already running for the vacuum.

"How long are you staying?"

"I don't know."

"Is Charlie coming?"

"No. Charlie is not coming. He's going . . ."

"Where?"

"To Las Vegas."

"For what?"

"Oh, hell, you're going to find out anyway. To audition to be in a show. Dressed as a woman."

"I'm sorry. I don't think I heard you correctly."

"You heard me correctly. Charlie is a female impersonator."

"Just get yourself home. We'll get this all sorted out."

Holy hell, I thought. Holy hell.

"There can only be one queen bee per hive," I said.

"But what if another one wants to move in?"
Hunter said.

"Then there's gonna be trouble."

Chapter Six
Bee Truthful

In the morning, I didn't tell our mother anything except that Leslie had called and was coming for a visit, but not that she was coming alone. I didn't tell her about Charlie and what she said he was up to. I'd always thought there was something different about him, like he was hiding something. Dang, I was sure sorry to be right about that one. Frankly, I was surprised. I didn't understand why anyone would want to be a female impersonator in Las Vegas or anywhere. I knew

I'd been leading a sheltered life. My mind just didn't go to things like seeing my name in neon lights. Besides, this was Leslie's story to tell Momma, not mine.

I told my bees all about Leslie and Charlie, but that was entirely different than telling a person. They began doing their waggle dance, which they generally did when they wanted their sisters to follow them to a new location to slurp up nectar and pollen from a different patch of flowers. I like to think they waggled because the news was upsetting to them. Maybe they were warning me to be careful. Did I really want to live with Leslie again? How long was she staying? Did I have any options? Not really.

I worked at the library that day, and Tyler and Hunter were among the dozen or so children who attended the workshop. I sat with them on the low chairs and helped them choose the colors of their petals as I moved from child to child. I'd put together an example to show them what we were going to make. Hunter asked me for a small oval-shaped piece of brown felt. I watched as he attached it to the tip of a petal with a drop of glue. Then a huge smile crossed his face.

"My flower has a honey bee!" he said proudly.

The next thing I knew I was cutting brown felt for all the others until every last child had a honey bee on their flower. I showed them how to mark the body with a yellow felt-tip pen and we added tiny gold wings. No regulation honey bee would confuse these fabric imitations for sisters, but mine might be flattered to know they were so admired. I would tell them tomorrow.

When the class was over, I walked Hunter and Tyler home. There was a Mercedes-Benz with Ohio license plates in our driveway, so I knew Leslie had arrived. She was safe, so that was good. But there was a U-Haul trailer attached to the back bumper. Not good.

"All right, you two! I'll see you later."

"Yes, ma'am!" Tyler said.

"Are you coming for supper?" Hunter asked.

"I don't think so, sweetheart," I said. "My sister just arrived from Ohio for a visit, so I'm afraid I'll be expected to eat with her. I'll see y'all tomorrow!"

"She drove by herself from Ohio?" Tyler said. "That's an awfully long drive!"

"Dad has a girlfriend," Hunter announced. "She has two cats."

"Excuse me?" I said too loudly as every hair on my body felt like it was standing on end. I was caught completely by surprise. "A *girlfriend*?"

"Shut up, Hunter!" Tyler said and looked at me, realizing, even at his age, that I was not delighted to hear it. "She's not a girlfriend, if you know what I mean."

What did he mean? Did *girlfriend* have a new definition?

"She's a dentist," Hunter said. "They got fixed up."

"Well, that's nice. I guess," I said in a voice so low I
could hardly hear myself. "Who stayed with y'all?"

"My teacher, Mrs. Hamilton," Hunter said.

Hunter was oblivious to my feelings, but Tyler knew
I was upset. When my eyes met his, I could see that
he wasn't too happy, either. It was odd for Archie to
ask someone other than me to watch the boys while he
went somewhere. Maybe he hadn't wanted me to know
he had a date. I regrouped immediately.

"Tyler? You know it's good for your father to have
some female company, don't you?"

"Why? He doesn't need anybody else," he said.
"He's got us. And we've got you."

I could almost feel my heart split in two. This little
fellow in front of me had no idea about the needs of
men. He was so innocent, but savvy enough to understand that a girlfriend threatened what status quo
he had with his Dad and brother and yes, in his sweet
mind, even with me. He liked things well enough as
they were. A potential stepmother was very likely an
enemy.

I knelt down to face him at his level and said, "And

you will always have me, Tyler. No matter what happens, you and Hunter will always have me."

Tyler threw his skinny arms around my neck and hugged me so hard. There was nothing to compare to a child's pure affection, but more, this was a little boy who needed love he could rely on, too. He knew what he had with me. So did Hunter. I stood and ruffled Hunter's hair and he looked at me with big eyes that told me he was pretty worried, too.

I smiled at them and said, "Listen to me, boys. This is not the time to panic. And there may never be a time to panic. If there is, I'll let you know, okay? Now, y'all run on home."

I watched them run up their front steps and when I knew they were safely inside, I took a deep breath and climbed my own. So, Archie was dating a dentist. Well, so what. At the moment, I had my own life to deal with. Drama was waiting for me in the kitchen.

My mother, in a bathrobe, of course, sat facing me as I came into the room. She had a very stern look on her face. Leslie's back was to me, but I could see that she had her face in her hands and a box of tissues in front of her, and many balled-up ones were strewn across the table. Ew, I thought, nasty. If I'd ever desecrated my mother's table with a used tissue, she would have chased me the whole way to Siberia with a belt.

"Hey, Leslie! Welcome home!" I said in my most chipper voice. "How was your trip?"

"Hey," she whispered and sniffed. I handed her another tissue. "It sucked."

"Well, it is a long drive," I said.

"Why don't you get your poor sister a glass of water," Momma said. "She's been through a terrible ordeal."

I bit my tongue. Then I took a glass from the cabinet and filled it with water from the tap. In the thirty seconds I'd been in the room, our old family paradigm was resurrected and reinstated. Our mother was the evil queen bee, Leslie was her princess, and I was Cinderella. How stupid, I thought. How stupid.

"Don't we have anything bottled?" Leslie said.

"No. I'm afraid we're living on love around here. No frills," I said. "Just happy faces."

"Now, Holly, don't you come in here and start trouble," Momma said.

"I never should have come home!" Leslie wailed. "Oh, God! What have I done?"

With that, Leslie took her dramatis personae exit like Joan Crawford in some angry-wronged-woman role of hers and slammed the door to her bedroom so hard, it almost jumped off the hinges.

"Well, I hope you're happy," Momma said.

"What are you talking about?" I said.

"This is no time for sarcasm, Holly."

"Did she tell you the whole story?"

My mother sighed so hard then that the National Weather Service issued small craft warnings.

"I imagine certain things were left out. What she did tell me is mortifying enough. Don't you think so?"

"I guess so. I mean, if that's what Charlie wants to do, he should go on and do it. It's still a free country the last time I checked."

"And I'd like to know why you didn't tell me why she called last night. You knew it was important."

"I probably should've left you a detailed note, but you know what you always say about bad news traveling fast. Besides, I thought a story of that magnitude should come from Leslie."

"Well, I suppose you're right, but I would've liked to have had time to prepare myself for the knife she twisted into my heart." Momma had the strangest expression on her face. "In all my days, I've never heard of such a thing."

"Yeah." I couldn't disagree with her. "It's a whopper, all right."

She was staring at the table as though it was taking notes.

"Holly?"

"Yes?"

"Can I ask you a peculiar question?"

"Ask me anything."

"If Charlie wants to be a woman now, but he says he still loves Leslie, does that make him a lesbian? In his head, I mean."

I spun around on my heel and literally gasped.

"Close your jaw," she said. "You'll swallow a bug."

I closed my mouth for a brief moment.

"Good grief! Momma? I don't think he thinks he's a woman. How should I know? I just don't think so. I think he just likes to dress up. But I don't know much about that stuff. I mean, I keep bees, I work at Publix icing cakes, and I volunteer at the library. We hardly ever discuss cross-dressing and gender identity. But I'm not judging here. Maybe he's just having a midlife crisis."

"No, I think this is a real thing he's been hiding for a long time. You do know he wants to stay married to Leslie, don't you?"

What? Stay married? No way! I tried to remain calm.

"No, she didn't tell me that, but I can see why it might be problematic."

"But he wants her to call him Charlene when he's dressed up. Dear God! What next?"

Holy crap, I thought.

"I'd call a lawyer. But that's up to Leslie," I said.

"Thank God they don't have children."

"Well, it would be more complicated; that's for sure. Although, I'd love a niece or a nephew."

Momma harrumphed loudly and stared at me with squinted eyes.

"Who put the bee in your bonnet?" she said.

"No one. I'm fine."

She harrumphed again. She knew I wasn't telling her something.

"What's for dinner?" she said.

"I took more pork chops out of the freezer this morning."

"With apples?"

"Of course." Was she accidentally telling me she liked something I cooked?

"You know, even though it was trouble that brought Leslie home, it's nice to have my girls under one roof."

"If you say so," I said.

"I'm going to go lie down," she said in the weariest voice I'd ever heard. "This is too much for me. Too much."

She wasn't wrong. It was too much. Good Lord, how would we ever sort this one out? Somehow, all the nosy Nellies on this island were going to find out about Charlie and talk about Leslie behind her back.

Eventually, Leslie would hear about it and be morti-fied. I could see the writing on the wall. She was going to have to come up with a story. Maybe she should just tell the truth.

I began peeling the apples into large chunks. I threw some ground sage, cinnamon, and brown sugar on them and browned them a bit in butter in our Dutch oven that was so old I don't even remember life without it. A few minutes later I heard loud thuds, like things were crashing on the floor. I turned off the stove and went to investigate. It was my lovely sister Leslie, the Princess of Pride, tossing my books and bins from her room to mine.

"What are you doing?" I said.

"I don't need your shit all over my room. I've got a whole trailer to unpack. Did anyone offer to help me? Hell, no! I hate this family!"

I decided to use the voice I used at Publix when it was clear I was dealing with a deranged customer.

"Leslie? You're angry. You've got every right to be."

"I'm way more than angry!"

"And you're probably exhausted from your long drive."

"My shoulders are killing me!"

She leaned against the wall and began to weep all over again. Even though she aggravated me to death, I felt sorry for her. Who else did she have in the world? I threw my arm around her shoulder and gave her a squeeze.

"Why don't you go take a good long soak in the bathtub? It would do you a world of good. And if you'll stop throwing my stuff around, I'll help you unload your trailer in the morning. How's that?"

"You're right. I'm sorry. Oh, Holly! My life is one big mess! How could Charlie do this to me?"

"Because you can only hide your true self for so long? I don't know. You want a glass of wine?"

"A bottle and a straw would be more like it."

She attempted a smile, and it was so lopsided and her eyes were so puffy, it made me feel awful for her.

"Archie's got a new flame," I said. "A dentist."

She gave me the funniest look and realized that I had feelings for him. And that I was disappointed.

"Men stink," she said.

"Yeah, but we love the smell," I said.

"We must!"

"Go start your bath and I'll bring you a glass of my best cheap wine."

Tyler said, *"Tell us what happens*
when the queen dies."

I said, "Well, in one scenario, worker bees
will enlarge normal cells to a size that will accommodate
a queen, then flood them with royal jelly.
If more than one virgin queen emerges, they fight
to the death to see who will rule the hive."

"Cool."

Chapter Seven
Bermuda Triangle

Over the next few weeks Archie explored the wonders of his dentist and Leslie wormed her way back into my heart. Deeply destabilized by Charlie's announcement, she began to change, to get nicer, more considerate. For one thing, she stood up for me with our mother.

"Holly's not your personal chew toy, Momma."

"Whatever is that supposed to mean?"

"It means you should quit nitpicking everything she does."

Momma would harrumph, which was still her signature sound of disapproval, and then proceed to ignore us for a while.

She was my sister, after all, so it was nice to see her act like one. And although Charlie made many attempts to patch things up, Leslie insisted she was through with him.

We were sitting on the front porch having a glass of iced tea and talking like sisters do.

"I just can't go back, you know?" she said.

"I get it," I said.

"He's called me twenty times since I left."

"Literally?"

She nodded her head.

"That's a lot," I said.

"Of all the damn reasons my marriage should fall apart, this was not the one I would've picked."

"Me, either. Were there any signs? I mean, there had to be a hint."

"The only sign—well, I don't know if I'd call it a

sign, but well, you know how he was always waiting for his father to die so he could inherit?"

"His dad died a few years ago, didn't he?"

"Yeah, and he inherited a bundle. I say *he*, because he kept all the money in his name. He said I wasn't entitled to his parents' wealth. We needed a new furnace and he said he wasn't spending his money on it until it was actually dead. I pointed out to him that every year we keep pouring more and more money into it, to the point that it's just throwing good money after bad. He said put on a sweater and don't tax it so hard."

"Nice. So, in some way, he was already distancing himself from the marriage?"

"Exactly. Then he lost a ton of weight. And he began coming home later and later. And taking more frequent business trips that now I suspect were monkey business."

"You know, Leslie, I don't care what consenting adults do in the dark."

"Oh, I know that. Neither do I. It seems like half the world is gay or bi or trans something and it's all fine with me. But I don't think it's unreasonable to expect my husband to be monogamous."

"Do you think Charlie is attracted to men? Or does he just want to do this impersonation thing?"

"I think Charlie is a little bit of a smorgasbord at the moment. Eventually he'll settle down and figure it out. He's not stupid. But he's definitely not the guy I married. That's for sure."

"Well, I'm glad you came home. So is the queen."

"Thanks."

"You know people are going to ask. The gossip machine on this island is relentless. What do you want me to say?"

"Tell them I'm available!"

We cracked up laughing.

"No, I mean, what do you want me to say when they ask what happened?"

"Tell them we disagreed about our future together. That's vague enough."

"Come on. We've got to do better than that," I said.

"Tell them I couldn't get along with Charlene. How's that?"

"Good grief!"

We watched as Archie's car pulled into his driveway and the boys tumbled out. They waved at us and we waved back. I'd tamped my enthusiasm for Archie, but I blew a kiss to the boys.

"A dentist," I mumbled.

"You know, you're taking this lying down like a cheap rug. Where's your fighting spirit?"

"What do you mean?" I said and thought, Oh, no, I'm not going to go make myself over and act like I think I'm a seductress.

"I mean, not that I'm such an expert in the ways of romance, as we know, but it seems to me that the woman picks the man. Not the other way around."

"What are you trying to say? I don't know if that's true at all," I said.

"Look, here's the deal. You get married and there you are! The blushing bride! But pretty soon you realize that you're supposed to keep a spotless house, cook fabulous meals, make all the birthdays and holidays gorgeous and unforgettable, have Einstein babies with perfect manners, for heaven's sake never age or gain an ounce, be super nice to his family, and oh, you've got to be a porn star in the bedroom. And you may or may not be required to have a career."

"That sure seems like a lot," I said. "But didn't Charlie help you around the house? Didn't he, like, I don't know, cut the grass and take out the garbage?"

"Are you kidding me? Prince Charles get his hands dirty? Charlie never lifted a finger! He'd say, call somebody!"

"How do you like that?"

"Look, Holly, here's what I'm telling you. If you think you'd like to do all that for Archie, you need to get in there and steal his heart before it's too late. I mean, who knows? Maybe this dentist doesn't have her hooks in that deep."

"I'll think about it," I said. "It sounds like a lot of work for not a lot of compensation."

"It is. That's why I'm never, and I mean *never* getting married again. But I know you. We're as different from each other as we could possibly be. You're a born homebody slash nurturer, and I'm going back to being a party girl. Big time. You won't be horrified if I sleep around a bit, will you?"

What was she saying?

"If you're going to misbehave, please do it in Mount Pleasant. Better yet? Take yourself up the road to Columbia. Okay?" I said and thought, Great. "I'm going to go start supper."

"One must avail oneself as opportunities arise," she said with a smirk. "Geography has no conscience."

"Sweet Jesus, save us," I said and went inside to make pot roast. So much for playing hard to get.

A few days later I was in the yard, pulling weeds, when Archie came home. His boys were at my kitchen table doing their homework. I'd made them a snack called Ants on a Log, which was celery stuffed with creamy peanut butter and raisins dotted across the top. They thought I was the best cook in the world. Of course, I was pretty grimy and a bit sweaty, because when you're serious about weeds, mulch, and vermiculite plus water, you're making mud pies all over yourself. Usually, when I saw Archie, I looked like I had just crawled out of the marsh.

"Hey!" I got up and brushed off my knees when I heard his car door shut. "Tyler and Hunter are in my kitchen. How was your day?"

"Good. Very good. Your flowers look amazing."

"Thanks, I'm working on it. You know, I plant all sorts of things my bees like."

"Well, someday you'll have to tell me all about that," he said and smiled at me.

"I'd love to," I said, and I realized I was staring at him and then repeating myself. "So, it was a good day? That's good."

"Yeah, it was, except for the super pious kid who refused to discuss the John Frum cargo culture. The whole concept of 'myth dream' was beyond his grasp."

"Hmm," I said, unsure if I'd ever heard the term, either. "Someday you'll have to explain more of the finer details of cargo cults to me. I'd love to hear more."

"Sure. How're things at Publix?"

"My days there utterly vibrate with excitement. The work is scintillating," I said and smiled at him. "So, Archie? I heard you have a girlfriend. Is that true?"

"Oh, I don't know about all that. She's the sister of a faculty member at the college. We've had dinner a few times. She's nice enough."

"Nice enough for what?" I said. That sounded awkward.

"For a dinner partner?"

"Uh-huh. My sister, who you might know has returned to the family home indefinitely, wants you to know that if you're about to fall in love, don't do it so fast. There might be other contenders."

I just kind of blurted it out and then my face turned bloodred. His eyes got very large and I could see immediately that he thought I meant Leslie was interested in him.

"Leslie?" he said and sort of gulped and stammered nervously. "No, well, you know, I mean I'm . . . I'm really not on the market at the moment. You know, it's too soon for me."

"I'll tell her that. She'll understand."

How stupid was I? If it wasn't Leslie, then who would it be? Me, obviously. So, shoot me, I let him think it was Leslie.

"What happened? Did she and Charlie call it quits?"

"I think she's thinking something like that. Yeah. She's sort of done. Listen, who knows?" I was leaving the door open for Leslie to better explain it to him. I'd already bungled up everything and I was so embarrassed I wanted to dive headlong into the azaleas.

"That's too bad. Divorce is so hard. Give her my best, okay?"

"Sure! I'll call the boys."

"Thanks!"

"Oh, and I made a beef stew in my InstaPot for y'all! I'll give it to them to bring home."

Leslie gave us an InstaPot last year for Christmas. I finally took it out of the box and now I think I might be in love with a small appliance.

He immediately took his wallet out of his back packet. "What do I owe you?"

"Oh, how about a thousand dollars?"

His expression went dark. He said, "Come on, now. We had a deal about this."

"Okay, how's twenty dollars?" I felt like a mercenary.

"Here's forty. You babysat for them all afternoon."

"Archie, listen. That's too much. But I'll take it, only because I'm saving up for a Maserati."

"You are?" A big grin spread across his face. He knew I was kidding. "I'm a Lamborghini fan myself. I always wanted an Italian sports car."

"Someday! Maybe someday we'll both get what we want. So tell me something."

"Sure," he said.

"What's she like? This woman you're seeing? How do we know she's worthy?"

"Worthy? Of what? An old widowed professor with two kids and a ten-year-old Jeep?"

"Please! That's crazy talk! God, it's so weird how we see ourselves."

"Sharon, that's her name, is actually coming over tonight to watch the Lakers game with us. Why don't you come over for a glass of wine? Starts at eight."

"Good! I'll bring popcorn! See ya in a bit!"

It was already getting dark and I hoped he couldn't see how nervous I became. I must be losing my mind, I thought. Where did all that brave talk come from? I hurried inside as fast as my legs could carry me, leaned against the door, and took a deep breath. I must be crazy. What if Sharon was fabulous? What if I hated her? Why would my opinion matter anyway? Okay, I told myself, get it together. Then I sort of sauntered into the kitchen to get the boys and the stew as calmly as I could. Leslie was there with them.

"Hi, guys! Your dad's home. Gather up your stuff, okay? I've got your dinner in the fridge. Are y'all all done with your homework?"

They nodded like bobblehead dolls.

"They've been at it like demons on a mission!" Leslie said.

"Want to check it?" Tyler said.

"If you want me to check it, it must be flawless!" I said. "But let me see anyway."

Tyler handed me his math worksheet and his list of spelling words. The math was perfect. The spelling words were too easy. Or at least I thought so.

"Ask me anything," he said.

"Spell night."

"N. I. G. H. T. Same as all the other 'ight' words. Light, sight, tight, bright."

"Bonus question. What's the capital of Russia?" I said with a straight face.

Leslie giggled.

"Hey! No fair! That's not in my homework!" he said.

"Okay. For twenty-five cents? Spell 'aardvark'!" I said.

Tyler cut his eyes at Hunter and started to giggle.

"Did you say fart? Miss Holly! That's a bad word!" Hunter said.

"Aardvark? Huh? Is that even a word?" Tyler said.

"It's a aminal," said Hunter, so adorably I didn't correct him. "It eats ants and termites and lives in Africa."

"Oh, yeah?"

"Yeah, and it's got a nose like a pig and ears like a rabbit and its tongue is ten inches long!" Hunter said and stuck out his tongue at Tyler to demonstrate.

Tyler, of course, reciprocated the gesture.

"All right, you two banditos!" I reached in the refrigerator and took out the container. "Let's get you home. Make sure you get your bath. The Lakers are playing tonight and Sharon's coming over."

"Sharon?" Leslie said.

"The dentist," I said.

"I don't like her," Tyler said.

"Me, either," Hunter said.

"Have y'all met her?" I said.

"No, but I already don't like her," Tyler said.

"Oh, come on. You can't dislike someone you haven't even met, can you?" I said.

"I don't like the way Dad sounds when he's talking to her on the phone. He gets all mushy," Tyler said.

"Yeah, and she calls him every five minutes," Hunter added.

Really? I thought. That did not bode well for me usurping the position as front-runner.

"Hmmm," Leslie said.

"Well, I'm coming over tonight, too," I said, "so I'll give y'all a full assessment tomorrow."

"You are?" Leslie said.

"Yay!" said the boys with more enthusiasm than I would have expected.

I shrugged my shoulders at her and shooed them out the door.

"Fix a plate, then nuke it for one minute on high!" I said, calling after them. Then I turned back to Leslie. "They move fast at that age."

"Sweetheart, let me understand something," she said. "You gonna be a third wheel tonight?"

"That appears to be the case," I said.

"Well, for God's sake, go wash your hair. And scrub your nails. You look rode hard and put up wet."

"Thanks," I said.

Sisters.

"Here's a fun bee fact," I said.

"What?" Hunter said.

"Bees are cold blooded. When the temperature reaches below fifty degrees, they can't fly!"

Chapter Eight
Bee Team

It just so happened I had a purple sweater and it was relatively new, the perfect color for a Lakers game. It looked just right with my khaki-colored capris. Leslie loaned me her leopard-print ballet slippers.

"Capris? Really?" she said.

"No?"

"No. What are you? Fifty? Wear my leggings."

"If you say so!" I pulled them on, thinking they were a little immodest.

"Meow," she said. "On the prowl."

"Meow, indeed," I said and shook my head.

I blew my hair out and Leslie flat-ironed it. I actually looked better than pretty good. No one would have ever said I was gorgeous, that's for sure. But I had nice skin that didn't need evening out with makeup. If I used a little mascara, my eyes seemed bigger. And I was a lip gloss fan. I'd have to say my thick hair that was just past my shoulders was probably my best asset.

Leslie was focused on my evening's agenda like a heat-seeking missile.

"We have to have a plan," she said.

"What are you thinking?"

"Unnerve her. Your comfort level with the boys is in the stratosphere. This is her first time meeting them. If she has serious designs on Archie, she'll be on her best behavior. You're bringing popcorn. That's good. Kids love popcorn. I'll bet you twenty dollars she brings him wine and nothing for the kids."

"We'll see. I'm not going to stay for the whole game," I said.

"Why not? Get in there and fight, Holly!"

"I'm just going to stay long enough to ruin her night," I said, adding, "I hope. I've got to pop the corn."

"Well, you'll have to see how it goes," Leslie said.

"In any case, the boys should be the key to Archie's heart. In my opinion, anyway."

"Well, if food was the ticket, I would have known it by now," I said.

"Wow, you aren't kidding. How many times have you fed them?"

"If I had a nickel for every PB and J sandwich I made for the boys, we'd be having this conversation in an oceanfront mansion!"

I threw a pack of popcorn into the microwave, set the timer, and pressed start. Leslie and I stood there looking at each other, waiting for the popping to start.

"What am I going to do with myself?" Leslie said.

"I think you need to get a lawyer. Charlie might be able to keep his parents' money, but you're entitled to something."

"Yes. I agree with that. I don't know if I'm ready for battle," Leslie said.

"That's what the lawyers are for," I said.

"Do I smell popcorn?" Momma appeared in her new housedress, the kind you step into and then you zip it up, of which she must've had a dozen. "Where are you going, missy, all dolled up?"

"I'm going to the ball with my prince," I said.

"Is that a fact?"

Leslie said, "She's going next door to meet Archie's girlfriend and watch the Lakers clobber Atlanta."

"Are we now?" Momma said.

"Good luck," Leslie said.

"Thanks!"

"Wait!" Momma said. "I want some popcorn."

"It's for the boys," I said and took a jar of my honey with pecans from the pantry.

Honestly, I thought.

"Holly, get out of here! I'll pop another package for the queen."

"Thanks," I said, and dropped the honey and the hot popcorn in a plastic grocery bag. "See y'all later."

"Now that's a sweet daughter!" Momma said to Leslie.

Leslie rolled her eyes up in her head.

I crossed the front porch and went down my steps the same way I had at least a million times, but for some reason this time felt different. The hair on the back of my neck bristled. I ignored it, knowing that when my neck hairs bristled, something was about to happen. And instinctively I knew I wasn't going to like it.

There was a dark-colored sedan in Archie's driveway that must've belonged to Sharon. I looked at her car for bumper stickers, because they say a lot about a person's politics and so on. There were none to be found. I climbed the stairs to Archie's house and rang the doorbell. Hunter came flying to the door in his Superman pajamas with Tyler right behind him in plaid flannels.

"Hey, Mith Holly. Game's starting," Tyler said.

"You don't sound too happy, pal. What's wrong?"

"I hate her," he said. "You'll see why."

"Oh, dear. Well, I brought popcorn. It's still hot, so we need to get it in a bowl."

I began walking toward the kitchen and before I got there, I could see Archie with a woman I assumed was Sharon. She had her arms around his neck and she was laying one powerful and prolonged kiss on him. I cleared my throat loudly and walked right on in with the boys on my heels. It was like watching a train derail. I didn't want to look, but there it was. Archie untangled himself from her choke hold and wiped his mouth. His face was blotched with her red lipstick, remnants of something that shouldn't be going on with the kids right in the next room. I hadn't even seen her face and I already despised her.

And then she turned around. To say she was my antithesis is an understatement. She was tall to my short, big boned to my smaller frame, big chested to my average-sized bust, and made up for Mardi Gras.

Her shirt was too tight, her heels were too high, and she had on too much jewelry.

"Hi," she said.

"Holly, this is Sharon. Holly lives next door. My boys adore her."

"As long as you don't, then I don't mind," she said.

Archie was completely fine with the fact that the boys and I caught them kissing. Or if he wasn't, I couldn't tell. Either way, I was irritated.

"Hi," I said. "We just need a bowl for popcorn. Sorry to interrupt."

"Oh, no problem!" she said, smiling like Delilah.

I moved past her as Tyler reached in a cabinet and gave me a large bowl.

"Thanks, sweetie." I ripped open the warm bag, dumped the contents into the bowl, and handed it to Tyler.

"Save me a place on the sofa," I said.

Tyler and Hunter scooted out of the room with the bowl, their mouths already full of popcorn.

"Holly, would you like a glass of wine? Sharon brought a nice red. I just opened the bottle."

I owed Leslie twenty dollars.

"No, thanks. I'll just have some ice water," I said, adding, "And Sharon, I brought you a jar of my honey-covered pecans. It's good on everything."

She took the jar, which also irked me, and studied the label.

"How sweet!" she said, so disingenuously it made me almost sick. "Did you make this yourself? It's so quaint!"

"Holly is a beekeeper, and this honey is from her bees," Archie said.

"Oh, my God in heaven!" Sharon said. "You actually have *bees* next door?"

"Yeah, quite a few, actually," I said.

"Why?" she said. "I mean, I know they're supposed to help things grow and all that, but aren't they a lot of work? And don't you worry about them attacking you?"

"These are honey bees. They don't sting unless they are provoked. They're vegetarian. And they're pretty self-sustaining."

"Aren't there any laws on this island to protect citizens from bees?"

Archie looked at me semi-apologetically. "Well, I've lived here for years and so have the bees, and none of us have been stung."

I narrowed my eyes at her and said, "I think anybody who knows anything about honey bees would say the benefits eclipse the risks by a margin about as wide as the Grand Canyon."

"Still," she said. "Who keeps bees?"

I took a deep breath and thought, This is worse than I thought.

"Well, Charles Darwin, Augustus, Charlemagne, George Washington, Virgil, Tolstoy, Sylvia Plath, and Martha Stewart," I said and took a sip of water. "To name a few."

"By the way, Holly, your beef stew was a hit! We inhaled it," Archie said. "Thanks again."

"Well, thanks! I'm so glad!"

"Wait! You cook their supper? What are you? A caterer?" Sharon said, and I could see she was growing suspicious of me.

"Only to a very small and select few," I said.

There was screaming from the other room. The Lakers had scored and the boys were jumping on the sofa.

"Settle down in there!" Archie shouted.

"I like to cook," Sharon said to Archie. "I'll make dinner for you this week if you'd like."

"Would you?" he said. "What night?"

"Which night works best for you?" she said.

Archie looked at her in that way, the way that told me there was hot mischief afoot. Her hooks were in deep. They were already sleeping together. I knew it in my bones. And there I stood like the proverbial third wheel. Neither one of them seemed to be aware they had an audience.

"Well, when you get that worked out, let me know and I'll watch the boys for you," I said.

"Oh!" Archie said, regaining consciousness. "Thanks!"

"How sweet! You've got a little nanny, a tutor, and a chef all rolled into one," Sharon said. "And you've got me! Aren't you lucky!"

"I am," he said.

I thought I was going to die.

"I'm just going to go watch the game now," I said.

I was thoroughly disgusted. But now that I had a clear picture, I had another problem. Sharon's behavior made me realize how much I cared about Archie. I could see he was heading toward something serious with her. I really, and I mean really, did not want this condescending, arrogant, awful woman to be front and center in Archie's life and most certainly did not want her in the boys' life, either. At all.

I got to the living room reasonably composed, or so I thought, and sat on the sofa in between the boys. They were completely engrossed with the game. But in moments, Tyler sensed that I was seething.

"Was I right?" he said.

I wasn't about to engage in gossip with a seven-year-old boy about the woman who might become his step-mother, but I was sorely tempted.

I just said, "Tyler, these things are hard to figure out sometimes."

And he nodded his head in solemn agreement. A simple answer satisfied him. He knew me well enough, even from where he stood in his young years, to know that I agreed with him. His instincts were excellent. There was nothing to be done about Archie and Sharon. It was going to have to play itself out. I was, after all, the nanny, the cook, the tutor, and nothing more.

Archie and Sharon made an appearance in the living room and soon retreated back to the kitchen where they could talk and be alone. Apparently, Sharon wasn't much of a Lakers fan or a sports enthusiast. I didn't live and die for ball games either, but I loved the occasional basketball game because it was fast and exciting and you could see the faces of the players.

I stayed until the third quarter, when it became clear the Lakers were wiping the floor with Atlanta. I gave the boys a hug and stuck my nose in the kitchen to sign off with Archie and to semi-acknowledge Sharon's prowess.

As I walked home, I knew in my heart that I was no threat to Sharon. And that hurt. Archie was as good as married, and I was going to have that hateful woman as my next-door neighbor forever. And the boys? Oh, this was going to be bad.

Leslie was waiting up for me.

"Glass of vino?" she asked.

"Sure," I said. "This is getting to be a habit."

She poured me a glass and put it in front of me.

"These are stressful times," she said.

"Cheers," I said. "I owe you twenty dollars."

"Cheers. Figures. How did it go?" she asked quietly because my face probably said it all.

I told her every single detail I could remember.

"This woman is insufferable. Even Tyler thinks so."

"He's too young to have an opinion."

"Yes, but there's nothing wrong with his judgment of character. I'm so worried, Leslie."

"This could head south very quickly," she said with concern, agreeing about the urgency of the situation.

"I'm telling you, Archie is down the rabbit hole," I said. "From the looks of things, I'd guess she's screwing him every time she sees him. They're all over each other. I watched the game in the living room with the boys while they drooled all over each other in the kitchen."

"What can we do about it?" Leslie said.

"I don't know. Here's the thing. It's the boys. This woman doesn't give a damn about children. Those boys are going to suffer. And it won't be long until Archie's miserable."

Leslie was quiet then. She was thinking about Hunter and Tyler's welfare. If Leslie knew anything about me, it was that I adored those kids. And even though Leslie wasn't crazy about having her own children, at least so far, she certainly understood crisply how they could be compromised if Archie married the wrong person.

She looked up with a huge grin on her face.

"I've got it!" she said. "I've got the solution!"

"What?"

"I'm going to seduce the shit out of him and wreck their relationship!"

She was so pleased with herself and her marvelous scheme. I was less so. And, excuse me, why was *she* so confident that she could waltz right into Archie's life?

"What? What are you saying?"

"I'm saying I'll take one for the team."

"Really? Can you do that?" Just how far was she willing to go? Knowing her, she'd go as far as it took. I wasn't so sure I liked her plan, but I couldn't think of a better one. "What if he doesn't want to fool around with somebody else?"

"Please! He's a man, isn't he? I've yet to see one say no. Watch him resist. Watch and learn, little sister."

"I don't know, Leslie. This could really backfire. I

mean, if he's in love with her and tells her what you're up to, they could put the house on the market and move to Timbuktu."

"Let's sleep on it and talk some more tomorrow."

"Okay."

We said good night and I slept like a stone, but morning came early. I tossed and turned a bit, watching the rising sun creeping up through the slats of my blinds. I was remembering the previous night and Leslie's plan. Maybe she was right. I was never going to have Archie. But maybe we could stop Sharon from having him, for the sake of the boys. I wasn't pleased one bit with the idea of Leslie putting the moves on Archie. But I'd do anything to get Sharon out of the picture, so I swallowed my damaged pride.

I finally got up and dressed and poured myself a giant mug of coffee. Momma and Leslie still slept. I took my disappointment out to the bees in the haze of early morning's light and told them everything I was worried about. I know it may sound peculiar to say this, but I felt better when I unburdened my heart to them. In my whole life, there had only been two men I'd ever loved: my father and Archie. Both had broken my heart.

I don't want to seem melodramatic, but there were things I just didn't understand about men and never would. How could our father put himself so far ahead of the needs of his daughters? How could Archie do the same thing to his sons? Look at Leslie, Dad. Take a good look at what you did to her. Who did she choose as a partner? And me? I chose an older man who rejected me before he had a chance to consider me. I wasn't even worthy of consideration. Thanks, Archie. Nice job, Dad. Nice job.

"Things happen when they are supposed to, you know," Archie said.

"I don't know about that," I said.

"There's an Indian dude, Srikumar Rao, who said, 'When the flower blossoms, the bee will come.'"

"Oh, please," I said.

Chapter Nine
Leslie Takes the Mike

I had given our seduction idea a lot of solid thought and come to a few conclusions. I'd had enough of my own pathetic marriage to justify trying to stop someone else from making the same mistake. And I knew it was probably immoral to execute the plan as it stood, the actual seduction, I mean. I decided to see how it might take shape, you know, get a sense of where Archie's mind was, and then I'd worry about the morality of it all.

Holly was deeply upset for more reasons than one and I felt it as though it was happening to me. It was awful to see my little sister be rejected by the only man I'd ever seen her have an interest in. Even though I wasn't itching for children and there was a chance I never would, I had a healthy respect for Holly's desire to see these kids be happy.

Holly was right. If Archie married this horror show, they would have to do whatever Sharon told them to do. And if she had children—well, we've all read "Cinderella." It could be a sad situation for the boys. If they gave her too much trouble, they'd wind up at Camden Military Academy, or worse. But in any and all cases, if Archie sealed the deal with her, she'd be able to wield a ridiculous amount of power. According to Holly, Sharon made no effort to endear herself to Archie's boys. I believed her and wondered why Archie wasn't thinking about that.

So, how exactly was I to begin? A lot of naughty ideas floated across my mind and I finally settled on one. I'd start with timing, going outside to get the morning newspaper in a flimsy nightgown when Archie was leaving his house. So I stood at the window and watched and waited. At seven fifteen, his door opened, and he stepped onto his porch. I hurried down the steps and saw Holly was way out, deep in the backyard with her hives, cooing with the bees. Then I leaned over to pick up our paper, giving Archie a clear view of an option to Sharon. I know, I hadn't even met her, but this was war. And remember? All's fair? Then I stood up and pretended to be embarrassed, as Archie was staring at me like I was naked, which I practically was.

"Hi, there!" I said. "Oh, my goodness! You caught me!"

"Good morning!" he replied with a very wide smile. "No worries! How are you, Leslie?"

"Practically naked! I've got to run inside, but I'd love to catch up with you! Been too long!"

"Yes," he said, and then without hesitating, he called out, "Come for supper!"

"Better yet, I'll bring it! Wait until you see what I can do to a chicken!"

I couldn't do diddly-squat with a chicken. I'd enlist Holly's help.

I ran up the steps and inside, closing the door behind me quietly so Momma wouldn't hear. God, I was such a bad girl. And I was out of breath. Maybe I'd join a gym or just take up running. I was still in good shape, but I didn't have the wind I used to have for some reason. Probably pollen. Heaven knows with all the herbs and flowers Holly planted to encourage her bees' honey production, we had an unbelievable amount of pollen in the air all year long.

Wouldn't you know it? I got to the kitchen and there sat the queen. She had a horrified look on her face.

"Would you like to tell me why you're mooning the neighbors? Have you lost your simple mind?"

I swear that woman has eagle eyes in the back of her head and the front.

I dropped the paper on the kitchen table and said, "G'morning! I'll be right back."

I all but ran to my room and threw on a pair of jeans and a T-shirt and brushed my hair into a ponytail on top of my head. One of the few things Holly and I had in common was great hair. At least we were lucky about that. I hurried back to the kitchen, poured myself a cup of coffee, and sat at the table across from her.

"There's an explanation," I said and told her the whole story.

"You girls really are out of your minds. It will never work."

"Why not?"

"Because according to Holly, he's already in love with this horrible Sharon, whoever she is. What you need is a spy."

"Why?"

"My dentist retired and moved to Florida. I need to find a new dentist. Get this woman's last name and I'll go see her, you know, nose around a bit. Save your virtue for the moment. Or at least *try* to. I'll get the story on her. Go get your sister. We've got work to do."

"Okay. But I'm bringing him dinner tonight," I said.

"Then bring the boys over here to decorate cookies or something. That will give you some space to get a read on him. Your sister's so naïve sometimes. She probably just saw them looking at each other with googly eyes. It's a long way from googly eyes to the altar. Let me think this through a little bit. Leslie?"

"Yes?"

"This is the most exciting thing that's happened around here in years!"

"Well, it certainly is a nice diversion for me. I have to get back in the game anyway. This is as good a place to start as any other."

"Leslie?"

"Yes, Momma?"

"I know you. You're hot-blooded. Try not to disgrace the family. Please?"

"Yes, ma'am."

There was nothing like the safety and happiness of children to unite women in a cause, even if they had disparate personalities and goals. Holly, who stopped in to see about the kids after school, found Sharon's business card on Archie's desk and copied down the number and address for Momma. Momma made an appointment for the following day. Holly was shocked beyond belief that Momma was actually leaving the house and even more dumbfounded that she was getting involved in our scheme. I knew Momma's life had become super dull since I married Charlie, but I kept that to myself. Holly was hurt enough as it was.

But Holly was a trouper. She worked her shift at Publix and brought home all the groceries we needed for a great meal.

We spent the rest of the afternoon making chicken parmigiana, which most children love. Then I made a salad of mozzarella balls and the tiniest cherry tomatoes I'd ever seen. And Holly had brought home Pepperidge Farm frozen garlic bread, which is my total favorite. Holly threw together a chocolate cake with a layer of marshmallows inside, which we knew the boys would love. In the end it was decided that the boys would definitely have dinner with Momma and Holly, and I, the family's pinch hitter, would take a picnic over to Archie. And Holly had bought a decent bottle of red wine, hoping it would loosen his tongue and make him want to talk to me.

"You've got to get him to tell you all about Sharon and bring him to his senses," Holly said.

"Yes," Momma said, "you've got to make him see that Sharon is a terrible choice, most especially because of the impact she'll have on his children. If you can't get past first base with him, ask him what he thinks Carin would want for her children. Guilt is a good weapon."

"I'll do my best," I said. "Hopefully, I'll get to home plate."

Surely, Sharon didn't have any real assets that I didn't? I mean, I knew Archie taught world religions and that she was a dentist. Those two professions were galaxies apart. I couldn't see what they could have in common beyond carnal desire. So, around four that afternoon, I took the hot shower of my life, shampooed, shaved, tweezed, moisturized, perfumed, and boofed myself into my former, younger single self, and packed up dinner. Cleopatra could not have put any more intention and effort into the seduction of Mark Antony. The only things I didn't have were a CD of Barry White's and a scented candle.

Momma had been giggling all day at the prospect of how Archie would react to being alone with me. Holly was less enthused, but that was understandable. When they saw me, they stopped and exhaled a whoosh of surprise and anxiety.

"You've got this, sister," Holly said.

"Poor bastard doesn't stand a chance," Momma said.

"Thanks, ladies."

It was almost *go* time. If Holly was right, this might be our only bite of the apple. If she was wrong, I'd have a good time messing with Archie's head anyway. I was just finishing a strategic application of cologne when I heard the boys come in the house. I picked up my purse and went to the kitchen to pick up dinner.

The boys were at the table with Momma and Holly.

Tyler said, "This is so cool to get to go out on a school night!"

Hunter, who was staring at me, said, "You smell really pretty. Do you have a date with our dad?"

This got Tyler's attention right away.

"Do you?" he said.

"Oh, no, sweetie," I said. "I knew your dad a long time ago when y'all were just little bitty babies and had just moved in next door. I haven't seen him in ages. We just want to catch up with each other. That's all."

"That's too bad," Tyler said.

"Why's that?" I said.

"It would be really nice if he'd have a date with someone besides Sharon," Tyler said.

"Yeah, we don't like her," Hunter said.

"Why don't you like her?" Momma asked.

The two boys looked at each other, unsure of how to answer. And then Tyler, being the oldest, spoke.

"You know how some grown-ups don't like kids? You can just feel it? That's her," he said.

"Oh, come on, now." Holly reached over and touched his arm affectionately. "You know, some grown-ups are awkward, but that doesn't mean they don't like you. Sometimes it just takes certain people a while longer to warm up."

"Yeah, maybe," Hunter said, "but some grown-ups think kids are in the way."

Out of the proverbial mouths of babes, I thought.

"I'll see y'all later!" I said.

"I promised to have the boys home by eight thirty," Holly said.

"Thanks for the warning!" I said and winked at Tyler, who smiled at me.

"Behave yourself!" Momma said, and then, realizing little pitchers have big ears, she said to the boys, "Leslie always behaves. I just tell her that."

I picked up my cooler, my bottle of wine, and my purse and left.

Well, I told myself as I walked across the porch and down the steps, if he has on cologne, it is a date. If he's all rumpled and the house is messy, it isn't. I went up his front steps and rang his doorbell. It took him no time to answer it.

"Leslie! Come in! Don't you look lovely!"

"Well, thanks, Archie! It's so great to see you again! Sorry about this morning."

"I'm not," he said.

I leaned in and he gave me a tiny, very chaste kiss on my cheek. He was wearing some lemony-smelling aftershave and a clean shirt. Two points for the home team. The house—well, what I could see of it—was neat and tidy. Two more points.

"What did you bring for us for dinner?" he asked.

Honey, he was smiling from ear to ear. Oh, yeah, Archie, you're going down like a redwood.

"I brought you something you're gonna love," I said.

A little double entendre, why not?

"You did, did you?"

"I just have to warm it up."

Yeah, warm *this* up, I thought.

"Well, let's do it!"

I followed him to the kitchen thinking about how big old mean pussycats torture their mice before they eat them, teasing them. I was hoping I was that cat.

We passed a dining room table covered in mail. It was a bit like our house. Did anyone really use their dining rooms?

"One of these days, I'll clear off that table and start having dinner like an adult. I hope you don't mind eating in the kitchen."

"The kitchen is absolutely fine," I said.

I put the cooler on the counter, where a cheese board sat with a wedge of Brie and some grapes and crackers. And I noticed that he had set the table for us. There were wineglasses and cloth napkins, which I also considered a good sign. I set the oven to 350 degrees and slid my casserole and garlic bread in, thinking it would all warm up in the oven together.

"This is going to take about twenty minutes, I'm guessing," I said.

"That's fine. I opened a bottle of red wine for us," he said. "May I pour a glass for you?"

"Please. That would be lovely. Thank you," I said. "I brought a bottle, too."

"Great! We'll have a reserve bottle. But it's not good to overimbibe on a weeknight. Unless, of course, you feel compelled to overimbibe." He said this smiling, and his eyes just twinkled. "And then, overimbibing is fine."

"Are you nervous, Archie?"

"Um, why, no. Should I be?"

He poured a healthy measure into two wineglasses and offered one to me.

I took the glass from him and said, "Heavens, no! Thanks. Cheers! Here's to renewing old friendships!"

"I'll drink to that! Cheers!"

The edges of our glasses clinked, and we took a sip.

"Cheese?" he said.

"Sure!" I said. "Let me fix some for you."

"Thanks."

We stood there eating rock-hard cold Brie and making polite conversation for a bit until I checked on the garlic bread and decided it was ready. I took it out of the oven, put the salad in a bowl, and fixed two plates of food.

"This looks amazing," he said. "It smells really good."

"Darlin', the Jensen girls know how to put the hurt on a bird."

"They sure do!"

He refilled our glasses and we sat down to eat.

"Bon appétit!" I said.

"You are so right. Bon appétit!" he said, and our glasses touched again.

We took a bite and he said, "This is really delicious."

To which I answered, "I know, right? Here's a piece of unsolicited advice for you, Archie. Never fall in love with a woman who can't cook."

"Really? Why is that?"

"Because if they don't cook, they can't nurture. A nonnurturing woman ain't got no soul."

I realized the wine was quickly going right to my head. I decided to let him talk for a while and I'd just eat.

"Is that a fact?" he said, and he was smirking at me. "How did you and Holly learn to cook as well as you do?"

"It was a matter of self-defense. You probably know our mother is the worst cook on earth."

"I think Holly mentioned that."

"No, for real. She is. But I want to hear about you, Archie. Tell me what's happening."

He sat back and exhaled long and slow.

"Well, it's been almost a year since we lost Carin."

"She was awesome."

"Thanks. We all thought so. And learning to live without her hasn't been easy for me or for the boys."

"Of course."

"Is there more chicken parm? I shouldn't, but I'd really like to have some more."

"Please! I'm flattered! Let me get it for you."

"Thanks. Anyway, we've been moping along, trying to get through the holidays and so on. Your sister has been as good as gold to us. I mean, I don't know what we would've done without her. She picks up the kids from school if the weather is bad, she's helped with homework, made snacks, dinners, and anything she could think of."

"Holly's a rock. And she adores Tyler and Hunter like they're her own blood."

"Yes. I know. And they feel the same way about her. Really, having her with them and us, well, she's been a godsend."

I refilled his plate and put it in front of him. Then I took a bold chance and let my hand rest on his shoulder for a moment before I sat down in my chair again. I could feel him flinch and I thought, Uh-oh, game over.

"Leslie? I feel like I should tell you something."

I smelled bad news, but I pretended to be as serene as Audrey Hepburn in *Sabrina*.

"Lay it on me, brother."

"I've met someone."

"I know. Holly told me. That's so wonderful. The boys mentioned it, too. Sharon, isn't it?"

He breathed a tiny sigh of relief.

"Yes. She's a dentist with a specialty in cosmetic work. She takes athletes and all kinds of wreck victims and rebuilds their mouths. She's very talented."

"That kind of work has to be painstaking and meticulous. I wouldn't be a dentist for all the money in this world."

"Really? Why's that?"

"Well, I think you'd have to have a very exacting personality, which I don't. You know, like a perfectionist, which is a curse, if you ask me. And the thought of getting into other people's germy mouths all day long is unappealing to me. I'm not a fan of blood, either." I shuddered for emphasis.

"Well, she makes me happy. And I guess that's all that matters, right?"

"Um, I'm less sure than you are about that," I said.

"What do you mean?"

His voice had a slight defensive tone, so I softened my response.

"Archie, there's an old saying: marry in haste, repent at leisure."

"I've heard it all my life. There's probably some truth to it. For young people, it makes a ton of sense. But by the time you're my age, you know when something is right."

"Well, in my case, I could've dated Charlie for ten years and not known what he was up to."

"What was he up to? If I may ask."

I looked at him, wondering if I should just tell the truth, and then I started to laugh, and I couldn't stop. He started laughing, too. Finally, he gave me a glass of water and I drank it, calming down at last.

"It was that funny of a breakup?" he said.

"Okay, try this one on for size and tell me what you think. Charlie, who now prefers to be called Charlene, likes to dress up in women's clothes. He's moved to Las Vegas hoping to be hired in a revue of female impersonators."

"You're shitting me."

"Nope. And here's the killer: he doesn't see why that should have any impact on our marriage."

"Great God. And you obviously had no idea?"

"No. None. You could've knocked me over with your finger."

"Is he a dancer?"

"Well, he was one of sorts. Drum major with his college marching band. He likes to do high kicks. This is what I'm telling you, Archie. What's the rush?"

"I hear you," he said. An almost imperceptible amount of doubt crossed his face. "But, you know, Leslie, I'm no prize."

"What do you mean? Are you nuts? You're a total hunk!"

"Please. I'm an old fuddy-duddy with gray temples. I have two children . . ."

"I'm glad you brought them up. Is Sharon the kind of stepmother Carin would want for her boys? If memory serves, your two little guys were the loves of her life, besides you, of course."

"Oh, I think she'd be thrilled," he said, and I got the sense he believed it. "Sharon is accomplished and smart and she's sexy as hell. That's for sure."

Great, I thought. So happy to hear she's sexy. What was I? The Great Sphinx of Giza?

"Does Sharon like them? Do they like her?"

"Oh, I'm sure we'll get that all worked out. But as Sharon says, they're going to go to college and leave me. It would be nice to have a companion for myself."

"Yes, they are going to go to college and leave you. But not for another *decade*."

He got quiet then and reached for the wine bottle to refill our glasses. He leaned back and took a long drink and put it down.

"Ten years is a long time, Archie. I mean, I'd be happier if I knew she was crazy about Tyler and Hunter."

"I'll see about my boys. Don't worry about that."

"Of course, you will." I paused. "Look, Archie. You might think I'm saying this because I'm sour on marriage, and at the moment I have to say, I'm not the biggest fan. If you didn't have kids, I'd say go on and get married and have yourself a ball. But you do have kids."

"And? What are you saying?"

"Well, in our family, we have the opposite problem. Our father just walked out one day and never came back. And there's not a day that goes by that Momma, Holly, and I don't relive the sting of it."

"No, I'm sure it has had a huge impact on all of you."

"I think what I'm saying is that whether the family member is leaving the tent or joining the tribe, all the members of the tribe deserve deep consideration."

"Leslie, you're the first person I'm telling. The boys don't even know. I'm going to ask Sharon to be my wife. We'll get married right here in my backyard the week after Easter. If she'll have me, that is."

The news was going to break Holly's heart, and the boys were going to be devastated. What could we do to stop this wedding from happening?

"Wow. I don't know what to say. It's such a surprise. Congratulations."

"Thank you."

"You're quite certain?"

"I am very certain. She loves me and she wants to make me happy. What else could I want?"

"Listen, Archie, I've never laid eyes on the woman. I'm sure she's perfectly wonderful. Too bad she got to you first, is all I'm saying."

"What do you mean?"

"I think you know exactly what I mean. Holly and I and even the queen want nothing more for you than to be happy. But we want the same thing for Tyler and Hunter. None of us would think less of you if you changed your mind or went a tiny bit slower."

"I hear you. I'll think about what you're saying. But Sharon and I knew each other before we knew each other, you know, in another lifetime. I think we've been together through many lifetimes." He wiped his mouth with his napkin deliberately and placed it on the table, signaling the end of conversation on the topic. "Now, did I see a cake?"

"Sure thing," I said and got up to cut a slice for him. "So you believe in reincarnation?"

"One hundred percent."

"No kidding. Wow. Well, I'll have another glass of wine, if we have any left."

I put a plate with cake in front of him and put his dinner plate in the sink with mine. Things were not going as planned.

I was out in my apiary singing to my bees, "Honey bee!
You stung the heart of me . . ."

Hunter and Tyler popped up, giggling.

"What's so funny?"

"You're singing and dancing!" they said.

"Go ask your daddy to play the Supremes for you."

Chapter Ten
Holly Grabs the Mike Back

I couldn't believe what Leslie told me about last night. She grilled the hell out of him and laid the guilt on as thick as Momma likes her pimento cheese on a Ritz. Worse, Leslie couldn't believe Archie was immune to her charms, however genuine they may or may not have been. The situation was a lot worse than I thought. No man, as far back as I could remember, had ever passed on ooh-la-la with Leslie. And, in my mind, I could see Archie heading to the chapel. I just knew it.

I was in the yard, working my flowerbeds, and had already pulled enough weeds to fill a large paper grocery bag. That amount of volume was usually a whole morning's work, but I'd done it in under an hour. I was in overdrive, and if I didn't get a grip on myself, I'd be so sore tomorrow I wouldn't be able to do a thing. I decided to stop. I made a note to buy Epsom salts at Publix when I went in to work, just in case I needed them later. God, I was turning into such an old woman.

The water pans in my apiary were empty. I turned on the spigot and filled a watering can. Then I put it on the ground and went to my shed to put on my beekeeper suit. As much as I loved my bees, I wasn't taking any chances. If they got a whiff of my pheromones that morning, they might panic and swarm.

Archie was a lost cause as the object of my affection, but the boys weren't. Still, if and when he did marry Sharon, it might be awkward to try and maintain the frequency of my encounters with them. Besides, the decent thing to do was to give her the chance to endear herself to them. She wouldn't be able to do that if I was around all the time. I owed them all some space and time.

I told my bees the whole story of Leslie and Archie and Sharon, and waggle dancing ensued once again. They were telling each other something, but it seemed different than usual.

There were so many interesting things about bee communication within the colony. In the morning, they send out scouts for food sources. On finding it, they drink a bunch of nectar and return to the hive. On reentering the hive, the scout walks straight in, shakes her tummy like mad, and makes a buzzing sound with her wings. The duration of the dancing and shaking and flapping of her wings tells the others how far away the food source is. Next the scout regurgitates the nectar and it's gobbled up by other bees, sort of like a wine tasting. I'd read somewhere that the scouts are also covered in the scent of the flower, which helps the bees know which flowers are the grand crus in the garden. It all makes perfect sense. In fact, life seemed to make more sense in the world of honey bees than in ours.

"What am I to do?" I asked them. "She's a truly dreadful woman of biblical proportions. I'm not kidding. She's so definitely the wrong queen for their hive. I know I only met her once, but she's so wrong for Archie and she's going to absolutely ruin what's left of the boys' childhood. Wasn't it bad enough to lose their mother? A stepmother should be a buoy, a source of strength, but also a chance for those little fellows to have more joy in their lives. Sharon is anything but joyous. The only consolation is that at least they're just next door, so I can still keep an eye on things. But don't worry. I'm going to be very careful around her. I've got to be. She would shut me out if she thought I was doing the least thing to undermine her position. I know that. What do y'all think?"

They just buzzed all around me and then left me to forage. There seemed to be no solution.

Momma had her appointment with Sharon that afternoon. Leslie drove her there, and because Sharon did not know Leslie or Momma from Adam's housecat, she wouldn't have recognized either one of them. I was coming home from work just about the same time they were returning from the city.

"I'm going to make us a pitcher of iced tea," Momma said.

"Perfect!" Leslie said. "I'll cut us a slice of cake."

"I'm starving," the queen said.

"Espionage is completely exhausting," I said, thinking I was pretty clever for once. "How did it go?"

The changes in Momma were remarkable. Since Leslie's return, Momma had not fallen out of bed once. Even more remarkable, she was out of bed *and* dressed appropriately. Now she was making tea. Her life force had begun to flow in her veins again. She was in exceptional humor. Well, I knew why, of course. Since Leslie married and left home, Momma had been in mourning for Leslie, her clone. She had been depressed. Here's the weird part. I didn't mind Momma's turnaround one iota. I'd much rather have her this way than how she had been in Leslie's absence. God, we were such a peculiar family. Now we were engaged in sabotage like the Snoop Sisters. But hey, every family needs a project.

I cut a lemon into wedges and took glasses from the cabinet. Within a few minutes we were recapping the afternoon.

"So what did you think of her?" I asked them.

"She's an imperious so-and-so and I didn't like her one bit," Momma said. "She wanted to put veneers on all my teeth and give me a Hollywood smile. When I told her I didn't need a Hollywood smile, she said, then, I should at least bleach my teeth, and I said what for?"

"She's not telling you the best nugget," Leslie said. "She asked her if she had children and Sharon said, 'That's one pain in my neck I'll never have.' Nice, right?"

"Oh, God, she doesn't want children?" I said. "Don't you think Archie needs to know that?"

"Absolutely," Leslie said. "But how are you going to tell him something like that?"

"Leslie's right," Momma said. "But surely, he's going to ask her how she feels about the boys at some point, don't you think?"

"You would think so," I said. "You would think so. But I don't know what to think anymore."

"It's true," Leslie said. "The whole world seems like it's gone mad."

"Are you talking about Charlie or Archie?" Momma said.

"Momma," Leslie said, "Charlie isn't mad, he's just too odd for me. People should be free to do what they want."

"I know that, but he promised to love, honor, and cherish you in front of every last person I know on this island," Momma said. "He should've told you."

"He's still perfectly willing to do those things," Leslie said. "As long as I'm cool with calling him Charlene and watching him pretend to be Cher or Liza or God only knows who."

There was a pregnant pause in the conversation.

"You did the right thing, Leslie," Momma said.

I said, "Why Archie wants her is inexplicable to me. Carin must be turning over in her grave."

Everyone agreed. What to do? What to do?

"So, Plan A was a bust. And what we learned in Plan B is too hot to handle," Leslie said. "What's Plan C?"

"Plan C is to think about it and tomorrow we'll come up with something," Momma said.

There was a lazy supper of whatever we could put together from last night's dinner with a salad of tomatoes, greens, and red onions. Momma went to bed, Leslie and I cleaned up the kitchen, then we took a glass of wine to the porch.

We sat in our usual rockers, toasted each other, and took a sip.

"At some point in our unremarkable lives, one of us needs to take a course about how to avoid buying bad wine," Leslie said.

"Good idea. I just put a lot of ice in it and then it doesn't taste so terrible."

"That was one thing Charlie knew. Wine, I mean," Leslie said, and paused for a moment. "You know, I don't think Charlie is really so, so odd. I mean, way down deep in his soul. I think he's afraid of life passing him by or something. He wants a thrill. A big thrill. Do you know what I mean? There's something about getting married, buying a house, and moving to the burbs of Cleveland, or anywhere like that, that can feel suffocating."

"I was all set to be suffocated, and nada. Ain't happening."

"Domestic life just doesn't ring his bells. Like, he

thinks his life's over. There are no more big choices at our age. You've made them. Now you have to wait for a promotion to do just what you're doing, except more of it, for some stupid incremental raise. It's a big fat snore."

"You think he really doesn't mean to be a full-time female impersonator?"

"I think he's trying to be outrageous."

"Job well done," I said.

Leslie raised her glass to Charlie, in the darkness.

"That's what I'm thinking."

"Maybe. Are you going to hire a lawyer?"

It was getting dark.

"Not tonight. I'm going to take a walk over to Middle Street and do a pub crawl. Care to join me?"

"Me? Oh, Leslie. No. No, thanks. Maybe some other time."

"I know. But no guts, no glory. Listen, I'm losing my mind staying home every night."

"I'm used to it. Anyway, you go have fun. I'll see you later."

"Don't wait up for me, babe."

Leslie went inside and came out a few minutes later. I could smell perfume, and even in the low light, I could see that she had applied a lot of makeup. And she had changed clothes. It didn't seem right for her to go to the bars alone. I hoped she'd run into an old friend and have a good time remembering the things they did when they were kids or when they went on dates or whatever. She was lonely. I knew what loneliness tasted like. It was bitter, and you wanted to hide it because complaining about it made you look weak and pathetic. But I was used to it. I just called it leading a solitary life. I guessed that the shock of Charlie and the rejection of Archie were the springboards to a good case of forgetting about propriety and all the barriers of the world women endured, although Sullivan's Island was more relaxed about those kinds of societal rules. Good for her! Good for her to get out of this house and out of her box and see what fun there was to be had on this old island, even if she had to go it alone.

But I strongly disagreed with one thing she said. All the big choices about my life had yet to be made. There was a future out there that had yet to be lived, and it was waiting for me to find it.

I checked on the queen and she was lost in the arms of Morpheus, snoring softly like a bear.

After I washed my face and brushed my teeth, I climbed into bed. Maybe I should paint my bedroom walls a new color. I liked that really pale shade of celery green. Maybe even trim it with something besides cream. Like pale yellow? Or maybe I should think about wallpaper. I needed a change. My old mahogany bed needed new life. I didn't even know where it came from. Some long-dead relative, I guessed. Maybe I should paint it, too? And I still had my desk from high school and the same old chair. Maybe I should try to get some money together for a new rug. Suddenly, my bedroom, which had always been my favorite spot in the house, seemed worn. I was feeling so restless that night, my mind still running a mile a minute. When was Archie going to pop the question to Sharon? When was he going to ask her how she felt about his sons? When was he going to tell the boys? How would they react? That was what I worried about the most. I knew they already had serious doubts about Sharon's affection for them.

I must have drifted off to sleep, but around five o'clock, just as the sun was beginning to light the eastern horizon on fire, I woke suddenly and decided to use the bathroom. The house was quiet, as the air-conditioning hadn't kicked into its day cycle yet. The floors were drafty. I thought to myself, Someday, if I ever have any money, I'm going to insulate this place the right way, whatever that meant. Most of the original island cottages had no insulation at all.

I threw a robe around my shoulders and made my way down the hall to the bathroom I shared with Leslie. The door was locked. Something made me look in her bedroom. There she was in her bed, fast asleep. So who was in my bathroom?

Oh, Leslie, I thought, what have you done?

I went back to my room and stood behind my door, peeking through a small opening. In a moment I had my answer as a man emerged, carrying his shoes and tiptoeing as quiet as a little mouse toward the kitchen door. I recognized him, but I didn't say a word. He was a guy Leslie used to date before she met Charlie. I couldn't remember his name. When the moment was right, I cleared my throat to mask the sound of him opening and closing the door. He turned around in surprise and I gave him a little wave. If he had awoken the queen, she would've kicked his butt the whole way to Charleston. And for as much as I thought it was trashy for Leslie to drag some guy home she hadn't seen in a thousand years, I did admire her nerve.

Over breakfast Momma said, "Did y'all hear any noise during the night?"

I said, "I slept very soundly. I didn't hear anything."

"Me, either," Leslie said, lying through her teeth.

"Well, I heard thumping—you know, da dump, da dump, da dump. You know, like, you know?"

"Hmmm," Leslie said and looked at me across the table, crossing her eyes.

I nearly spit my coffee out through my nose.

"Really?" I said. "Could be a mouse in the wall. Or a marsh rat. They always try to get inside when the weather's about to change."

"Yes. And the next time I hear sounds like that I'm going to investigate them with my shotgun!" Momma said and looked at Leslie. "You might want to pass that along."

Hunter asked, "Why do bees buzz?"

I said, "Because they flap their wings two hundred times per second! The flapping makes the buzz sound."

"They must be very tired at night," Hunter said.

Chapter Eleven
The Boys

I saw Archie in the driveway on Sunday afternoon. He told me that he'd asked Sharon to marry him. She said yes.

"Well, congratulations," I said politely.

"Thanks," he said. "You don't seem very excited about it."

"I think it's complicated. Have you told the boys?"

"No. But I'm going to do that tonight over dinner."

On Monday afternoon, I was sitting on the front

porch in the cool air reading the *Post & Courier* when I saw Tyler and Hunter coming down the block. Their backpacks were slung across their backs like Marley's crippling chains. Their young shoulders didn't seem broad enough to carry their troubles, and before they even reached my porch, I read the expressions on their faces and knew they were very unhappy.

Before they reached me, I knew what they would say. They didn't want another mother. Or anyone to try to take Carin's place in any way whatsoever. I understood that clearly. Their point of view was valid. And that was the problem as it stood between them and their father. They didn't want Sharon. Their father did. Sharon, in the best case, was indifferent to the boys.

Leslie was inside sleeping off a hangover. I'd heard her slip in the house at sunrise. Oh, Leslie.

And my mother, believe it or not, had baked cookies for the boys. Okay, they were just the slice-and-bake variety, but for her? This? Are you kidding? We might have been in the End Times. Even Momma, hard-hearted as she may have seemed, felt very badly for the boys.

When the weather was nice, Tyler and Hunter walked the few blocks home from school together. And when Archie wasn't home, they came to my house. It had been this way since Carin died. There was always someone home in our house, so they didn't have to go into an empty house with no one to ask them how their day had gone. Besides, they were too young to be home alone. And since Sharon worked during the week, they would continue to come to my house after school at least until they were old enough to have a key. I hoped.

At that point, because I knew the ball was in play with no chance of a time-out, I had some thoughts for them to help them get through the crisis.

"Well! Hello, gentlemen! How was your day?" I said, standing to greet them.

I folded my paper as though it didn't matter anymore. It didn't. The most important news had arrived in person.

"Terrible," Tyler said.

"Yeah," Hunter said. "Terrible. I threw up my lunch."

"Come here, sweetheart," I said.

"Luckily, he didn't barf on himself," Tyler said.

I put my arms around Hunter and he just leaned into me like dead weight. Poor little fellow.

"All right, now," I said, "Miss Katherine actually baked some cookies for y'all." I held Hunter back and looked into his eyes. "Do you think your tender constitutions can handle warm chocolate chip cookies and a glass of milk?"

"I can," Tyler said.

"I'll try," Hunter said.

"Then let's go inside. Go wash your hands and meet me in the kitchen."

They nodded and went toward the bathroom. Momma was in the kitchen, scooping the cookies onto a platter with a spatula.

"I made a dozen or so. Do you think that's enough?" she said.

"Well, young boys are eating machines," I said. "And these two need some serious TLC this afternoon."

"He told them?" she said.

"Yes," I said. "They're not happy at all."

"How could they be?"

Momma gave me one of her signature harrumphs. We were still incredulous over Archie's judgment. It was still less than a year since Carin died. Nothing, not one thing, about this upcoming marriage felt right.

The boys came in with long faces and slumped into their chairs at the table.

"Hey, Miss Katherine," Tyler said. "How're you?"

"Yeah, hi, Miss Katherine," Hunter said.

They felt hopeless.

"White milk or chocolate milk?" my mother said.

She was going all out.

"Chocolate," they said and then added, "Thanks."

The sighing coming from Tyler and Hunter was profound. They perked up a little when the glasses of chocolate milk were delivered with the warm cookies. They smelled so good, I reached for one. Momma swatted the back of my hand.

"Those are not for you, Holly. If you want cookies, I imagine you know how to bake them?"

I cut her some side eye and she gave it right back to me. Tyler and Hunter giggled and it lightened the mood a little bit.

"She's a mean old thing," I said to them.

"Watch your mouth," Momma said and winked at the boys.

"Okay, let's hear the story," I said.

"My life just blew up," Tyler said.

"Yeah," Hunter said. "Mine, too."

"Oh, come on now," I said. "Look, maybe it won't be a bad thing. Maybe she'll turn out to be a lot of fun. And the next thing you know, you'll both be going to college and then out into the world to do great things!"

"For once, I agree with my daughter," Momma said. "And you know what? Sharon might be really nervous about getting married and suddenly, boom! She's a step-mom, too! It's a lot for her to take on. Think about it."

"That's right," I said. "If you two wanted to make

your daddy happy, and I know you do, you'll be happy for him."

"Yeah, we know all that, right?" Tyler looked at Hunter who was nodding in agreement. "But here's the thing. We don't need another mother. We're fine just like we are."

"I understand, and I see why life's working for you," I said. "But grown-ups are different. Well, not every single one, but most adults like to have a partner. It's normal to want to have someone who likes what you like and wants to do the things you like to do. You know what I'm talking about?"

"And I wouldn't be surprised," Momma said, "if she's more of a partner to your dad than a stepmom to y'all. I mean, I think she's pretty busy and I'd be surprised if she interfered with things as long as they're going along smoothly."

"We'll see about that," Tyler said.

"I don't know," Hunter said.

"Listen, here's my free advice," I said. "Just take things one day at a time. And trust your dad. You know he wants only the best for both of you."

"I know," Tyler said.

"Your dad is super smart, Tyler. I've never seen him do anything crazy," I said. I picked up their glasses and rinsed them in the sink.

"Until now," Hunter said.

"Now, now," Momma said.

In the distance, we heard Archie's car door slam.

"Dad's home," Tyler said.

"Party's over," Hunter said.

They gathered up their things, started to leave, and then turned back to face us. I could see that Tyler's eyes were moist.

"Mith Holly? If things get really terrible, can we come live with you?"

"Oh, Tyler," I said.

"This is still *my* house," Momma said. "But the door is always open for you both."

Then, to my further surprise, Tyler and Hunter rushed to my mother and threw their arms around her. She was breathless from the impact and surprise of it. Before either one of us could think of what to say, they turned and ran out of the house, slamming the screen door.

Momma and I looked at each other.

"What do you think is going to happen?" she said.

"I think that Archie will be happy for a while, but I don't think he could have chosen a worse stepmother for those boys if he'd picked up a stranger off the street. That's what I think."

"I guess we'll find out soon enough," she said.

"You were really sweet to them," I said.

"Well, those poor little guys have been through enough. I just feel for them, that's all. I mean, come on! They've grown up right under my nose. They're just defenseless little boys with no say in the matter. I know that's how these things go, but somehow it doesn't seem fair that they don't even get a vote."

It wasn't like her to be so sympathetic, but there she was, sympathy itself.

"No, it doesn't seem fair at all. You'd think he'd sit them down and talk about it at length. Not just announce it, like here's your new future."

"You don't think he talked to them?"

"No. And I really would've thought there would have been more time spent with Sharon to let the boys have a chance to get used to her. You know? Like movies or picnics? Just something more than this."

"Holly, you don't know men. This is classic. If this marriage is good for him, then it's good for everyone. I'm sure he's thinking the kids will adjust. And to be honest? Most kids do. But then most candidates for stepmother try harder than this one. They try to win over the kids."

"She hasn't done *any* campaigning to win over the kids, as far as I know."

"She didn't have to, because Archie wants this to happen so much."

"Momma? I think you're right. I don't know men. But I know skunk when I smell it."

We heard a shuffling in the hall.

"The family floozy is awake," Momma said.

"Oh, Momma, don't call her that."

Another harrumph.

"Do you think I don't know what goes on under my own roof?" She shrugged her shoulders. "I'm going to go take a nap. All this excitement is elevating my pressure. Too much."

I didn't respond except to say, "Okay."

I took a package of chopped meat out of the refrigerator and reached for an onion. Meat loaf was destined to be the star of tonight's menu.

"We got any coffee?" Leslie said, coming into the kitchen.

Her hair was all tangled, her T-shirt was all baggy over her plaid flannel drawstring pants, and her robe was untied. She was scratching her stomach.

"You look like who did it and ran," I said.

"That's exactly what happened," she said, examining the empty and clean interior of our coffeemaker. "And boy, was it fun!"

"You're terrible," I said. "Coffee's in the cabinet."

"So, what did I miss?" she said.

"Archie's engaged. And he told the boys."

"How did that go over?" she asked.

"Not well at all."

"No surprise there. Nope, none at all," she said and filled the pot with water. "Where are the filters?"

"Pantry. Second shelf."

"So when's the wedding?"

"Soon. As he said. Right after Easter."

"What a sin. Awful."

"I know it's happening, and I know we can't stop it from happening, but I wish something would happen to end the nightmare."

"You know, Holly, I was thinking about this whole deal while I was regaining consciousness from a night of utter debauchery, and . . ."

"I'm worried about you," I said. "It ain't fittin', what you're doing. You're not divorced, you know."

"Let me finish. We can save my eternal soul in a few minutes."

"Continue. You were thinking . . ."

"That in our minds, we may be overblowing this. I think that as long as they don't move off the island, the risk to the kids is probably nominal."

"Leslie, let me ask you something. Would you like to

live with someone who didn't like you? Because that's really the core problem here."

"Well, maybe you can guide the boys to endear themselves to her."

"I think they'd rather take a bullet," I said. "Their suspicions of her and their distaste for her run deep."

"No, really. I'm serious."

"I'm thinking, and I cannot conceive of a single thing they could do. A craft? She'd probably laugh at it. I mean, I could give them flowers from my garden for her or something like that."

The coffee was dripping, and it smelled so good, I decided I'd have a cup as well.

"That's a good start," Leslie said. "Everyone loves flowers."

"It's going to take a whole lot more than flowers to cement that relationship," I said.

I left Leslie in the kitchen and I took my mug to the porch. The fading light of the afternoon was wrapping everything in rosy hues. The truth was that I didn't *want* Archie's marriage to Sharon to work. If I couldn't stop it from happening, then I wanted it to end as quickly as possible.

Unique among all God's creatures, only the
honey bee improves the environment and
preys not on any other species.
—Royden Brown, Author of *The World's Only Perfect*
Food: The Bee Pollen Bible

Chapter Twelve
Roofie

The next day, my cell phone rang, I answered it, and to my utter astonishment it was Sharon. She was not calling for her patient, my mother. She was calling for me. And I knew exactly why.

"Holly?" she said. "It's Sharon."

"Oh, hi, Sharon. What's going on?"

"Well, Arch and I finally decided where we'd go for a honeymoon, and . . ."

Arch? When did he become Arch?

"Oh? Where are you going?"

"Bermuda. And we were wondering if we might . . ."

"How lovely. I've always wanted to go to Bermuda."

She must be calling to ask me to keep the kids while she and Arch went away. Why else would she call? Because she was running a special on veneers? Or Invisalign? Gimme a break.

"Yes, well, you should go. It's completely charming. Anyway, we were wondering if . . ."

"I'd be delighted to take care of the boys." Forever, I thought.

"You would? Oh, that's just great! Another detail to check off the list as done! Thank you so much."

"You're welcome. How long will you be gone?"

"Oh, just a week. You know our calendars are insane and well, I really can't be away for too long. Anyway, this time we want to compensate you. Arch insists."

"I wish he wouldn't," I said.

"Look, we have to spend fifty dollars a day to board my cats. So it only seems fair to give you at least the same for the boys."

I couldn't believe my ears. I knew I was hypersensitive when it came to the boys and this wedding and Sharon and all of it, but to put the boys in a similar category as her cats? Should I have asked if that was fifty dollars per cat?

"I'd be happy to take care of them. Let's just leave it at that. Do y'all have a date yet?"

"Yep."

She gave me the date and I wrote it down. We made a bit of insincere chitchat and a little blah blah blah and finally I managed to get her to hang up. Once she got started talking about herself, it was like a freight train gathering speed. There was just no stopping the thing.

"*Who was that?*" Momma yelled from the other room.

"*The soon-to-be Mrs. Arch!*" I yelled back.

There was silence for a moment. Then she said, "She calls him 'Arch' now? What kind of a stupid nickname is that?"

I could hardly believe the unprecedented words that were on the tip of my tongue, but here they came.

"I agree with you," I said.

I decided to look in her room to be sure she hadn't fainted. She had not.

"So, what's the latest in Peyton Place?" she asked.

"I told her we'd keep the boys while they go on their honeymoon to Bermuda," I said, and I was sure I sounded glum.

Then I told her about the kennel fees and she said, "You know, normally, I'd tell you that you were too sensitive for your own good."

QUEEN BEE · 169

"And that I'm an idiot about men," I said, just throwing it out there to add insult to my own injury.

This brought a small harrumph from the QB.

"I think you and Leslie are right. *Arch* is making a mistake. But you know what? It's his mistake to make. We can't do anything except keep our arms around the little boys and let them know they're loved by us. Archie will regain his senses after he's lived with her for a while."

"I wish I had your faith," I said.

Later on, when I was in the kitchen making dinner, Leslie sauntered in.

"Whatcha making?" she said.

"Something to match my mood," I said.

"Ragout?"

"Very funny. No, I'm making a Portuguese seafood stew."

"So you're stewing over what? Archie?"

"Yeah, it's like my favorite thing these days. Would you believe Sharon called me this morning? I nearly fainted when I heard her nasty voice on the other end of the phone. God, she is so self-absorbed."

"Lemme guess. She wants you to be her maid of honor?"

"You're hilarious," I said, and whispered, "No. You're not."

"Yes, I am," she whispered back.

"She wants us to keep the kids while they go off on their romantic honeymoon to Bermuda."

"Of course, we'll take care of them. We can only pray she dies from sunstroke. Or runs off with a pool boy."

Leslie always took things to extremes.

"Isn't it a sin to pray for something bad to happen to other people?" I said.

"Here, give me the carrots. I'll peel them. Why don't you ever ask for help?" she said, and I handed her a peeler.

"Sometimes it's just easier to do it myself."

"Well, it is not a sin to pray for the bad guys to get it. Go read the Book of Psalms in the Bible. There's one where David asks God to pray his enemies home or something like that. People been praying for their enemies to die since forever!"

"If you say so."

"Charlie called me this morning. Again," she said.

"To talk about what?" I said.

"Nothing in particular," Leslie said. "And that's what's so weird. He thinks everything between us is going to be fine. I told him he's as crazy as hell."

"Hmmm," I said. "How could he think everything is fine?"

"Well, because we still love each other."

My jaw dropped.

"How is that even possible?" I said. Boy, I really didn't understand love at all. Not a bit.

"I don't know, but it is." She was peeling those carrots with a vengeance, long strands falling into the trash. Then she stopped and looked at me funny. "When's the last time you had a professional haircut?"

"I trimmed it last year."

"You cut your own hair?"

"What's the matter with that?"

"I don't know a single soul who cuts her own hair. Are you suffering with some kind of depression or something?"

"No."

"You do realize you could make yourself more attractive than you do. And I mean that in the nicest possible way."

"Why in the world would I change my looks? I mean, who's looking at me?"

"Because, one, you never know who's looking. And two, a good haircut and a little bit of makeup sends a message."

"What does it say? For a good time, call Holly? Can we talk about something else?"

"No, you big dope. I'm just thinking, you don't

know who's coming to the wedding. There might be someone there for you. And if you show up looking like hell, that fabulous guy will be lost forever!"

"I do not look like hell! And I'd be shocked if I liked *any* of Sharon's friends."

Momma waddled into the room and sat at the kitchen table.

"I don't think I'd like any of her friends, either," Momma said. "And Archie's friends are probably too smart for you."

"Momma!" Leslie said. "You couldn't possibly have meant for that to sound as mean as it did."

"What?" Momma said. "What did I say that was so terrible?"

"It's okay," I said. "I'm used to it. I think what she means is that they all have Ph.D.s and I'd feel inadequate around them. They'd be talking about some obscure stuff I couldn't possibly know and I'd be embarrassed with my lowly B.A."

"Just because someone has a huge amount of knowledge on a particular subject doesn't mean they're a genius," Leslie said. "And for what it's worth, I think you have as much raw horsepower as anyone I've ever met with a Ph.D."

"Thank you, sister," I said. "I think."

"I'm just thinking that why not go get a great haircut, get your makeup done, buy a great dress, and let Archie know what he's missing."

"I don't like to relive the past, but I did precisely that for your wedding, Leslie, and then your lovely father showed up with Lola," Momma said. "What's for dinner?"

"Seafood vegetable stew," I said.

"Put in extra potatoes for me," Momma said. "Never met a carb that I didn't like."

"Okay," I said.

"But, Momma, you looked so great in all the pictures," Leslie said. "Holly, it might be fun to get all glammed up. What do you think?"

What did I think? The thought of it made me nervous, that's what. I felt like makeup and fancy clothes draw attention to you, and I wasn't comfortable with attention. But how long had it been since I'd dressed up?

"Well, I might do it just for the fun of it, but I wouldn't be doing it to try and get Archie's attention on his wedding day. That's for sure," I said. "That would be gross."

"Let me handle it," Leslie said. "I still have some friends in the beauty business around here and I still have a few friends on King Street."

"Okay, I'm going out to check on my bees," I said.

"I want you to look fabulous in Archie's wedding pictures," Leslie said, calling after me.

"You're such a good sister," I heard Momma say.

Outside, I told my bees what was happening as I gave them some more water. They were buzzing all around me as though they were paying attention. I was excited to have the boys for a week, but I wasn't excited that this wedding actually appeared to be happening. Then I sheepishly told them about Leslie's proposed makeover. I decided I might as well go along with her scheme because otherwise she'd nag me to death until I did.

I looked over to Archie's house and saw a window screen come sliding down from the second floor and hit the azaleas below. I looked up to see Hunter sitting on the roof. He had climbed out of the upstairs window. He waved at me with a big grin. I ran over to his yard in a total state of panic.

"Just what do you think you're doing?" I called up to him.

"I'm sitting on the roof!" he called back.

"Crawl back inside this instant!" I said. My heart was beating against my rib cage.

"Don't want to," he said. "I'm protesting!"

"Why?" I said.

"Dad's not taking me on his trip to Bermuda! That's why!"

"But it's his honeymoon!" I said. "You're staying with me!"

"I want to go to Bermuda!" he said.

"That's not how this works," I said.

"Tyler said Sharon was marrying into our family and the honeymoon is to celebrate it. If that's so then we, Tyler and me, ought to get to go, too."

I almost couldn't argue with that logic.

"You'll understand when you're a little bit older," I said. "But your dad's right. You boys should not be going on his honeymoon."

"Why not?"

My heart was pounding. Where was Archie?

"Because it's just for the bride and groom! Now go back inside and don't ever let me see you on the roof again!"

He crossed his arms and gave me an angry stare.

"Hunter? Don't make me call the fire department!"

He thought about that for a moment and decided that a visit from the fire department probably wasn't his ticket to Bermuda, so he crawled back inside.

The kitchen door slammed and suddenly Archie was in the yard.

"I heard something fall," he said.

"Yeah, it was a screen. It's over there." I pointed to the bushes.

"Now how in the world did that happen?" he said.

"I wouldn't have the first clue," I said and thought, Wow, Hunter could have broken his neck.

The next day when I saw Hunter coming home from school, I took him aside and explained the concept of Lent to him, that this was a period of time when Catholics all over the world spent some time thinking about their souls and asked themselves if they were living a life that would please the Lord.

"What does that have to do with me?" he asked.

"It means stay off the roof, Hunter," I said. "The good Lord would not be pleased."

"Oh," he said. "You might be right about that."

"I'm actually certain," I added. "So, what are y'all doing for Easter?"

"I don't know."

"Okay. I'll ask your dad," I said.

Hunter ran inside to have an after-school treat with Tyler. Momma was making slice-and-bake cookies again. This time they were blond sugar cookies with the silhouette of a pink rabbit inside and sugar sprinkled all over them. Pink was all they had at Publix. They were out of green and blue.

Soon, Archie's car pulled into the driveway, so I stood to greet him.

"Hi!" I said, popping up from behind the boxwoods like a jack-in-the-box. "The boys are inside with the queen. How was your day?"

"It was a good one. Yours?"

"Another day in paradise," I said and crossed the road to greet him. "Archie, can I ask you something?"

"Sure!" he said. "Anything."

"Do y'all observe Easter?"

"Most years, yes. But since Carin's been gone, I don't think we've been to church at all."

"Well, this Sunday's Palm Sunday, and down at Stella Maris they have an egg hunt for the kids on Saturday. I'd be glad to take the boys, if you'd like me to."

"Oh, that would be so nice of you. Gosh, I'm glad you reminded me about Easter. I've been so focused on the wedding, I forgot all about it. I'd better get Easter baskets for the boys, too."

"We have great ones at Publix. If you want, I can bring home two nice ones and hide them at my house until Easter morning."

"Would you do that? Oh, that would be great! Thanks!"

"Sure! Somehow the holidays seem to have a way of sneaking up on us, don't they?"

"Yes, they do. And this wedding's sneaking up on me, too."

"It's okay to get cold feet, Archie."

"I couldn't do that! Sharon would kill me."

We stared at each other for a minute. I could see I had confused him then. Was I telling him once again that he shouldn't do this? He had told Leslie and me in no uncertain terms that he intended to marry Sharon. Well, then, if Sharon was the right girl for him and his boys, why hadn't she offered to fix Easter baskets for the boys and for all of them to go to church together?

I knew I was an old-fashioned girl who still did things like go to church and plan for holidays. And I wasn't reminding him about it because I thought I was a better Christian. All I cared about was the boys being overlooked and their not being included in a holiday that most of their friends and their families celebrated.

"Well, we're making a traditional Easter dinner for after church. You know, ham, string beans, deviled eggs, potato salad, red rice—all that stuff. Biscuits. Anyway, we'd love for y'all to join us."

Y'all did not include Sharon unless it had to.

"Well, that's awfully nice. I'll have to check with Sharon. You understand, don't you?"

"Of course! Just let me know."

Well, when the jury came in, the verdict read as follows: It would be a great help if I would be in charge of baskets and it would be great if I could sneak them over before the boys woke up. If I wanted to take them to the Easter egg hunt, that was fine. Church on Palm Sunday might work, he'd let us know, but for Easter Sunday, they were going to a gospel brunch at Halls Chophouse.

I outdid myself. I took them to the egg hunt and they had a ball. I let Mass on Palm Sunday slide, because they weren't Catholics anyway. But when the sun rose on Easter Sunday, I had on a rabbit suit, complete with ears and a puffy ball tail. As soon as I saw a light go on at their house, I left their baskets by the front door and sneaked all around the house, tapping on the windows and dropping chocolate-covered eggs on the grass. The boys saw me, of course, and were hysterical laughing. They quickly came outside and chased me, and I threw little foil-wrapped chocolate marshmallow eggs at them, saying things like, *No! You're not supposed to catch the Easter Bunny! It's very bad luck! Run away! Run away!*

I had not counted on Sharon being at their house. Somehow, I had missed seeing her car. She opened the back door, standing there in some Victoria's Secret peignoir set and stirring a mug of coffee.

"Well, Little Miss Bunny Rabbit, aren't you just adorable?"

I stopped in my tracks and stared at her. Suddenly, I didn't care about her anymore.

"Nice job making Easter for these boys, Sharon. Very thoughtful job. You really knocked yourself out!"

Her smile disappeared, and she arched an eyebrow at me. There was hate in those eyes.

Silence hung like something dark and terrible was building. No one spoke.

Before it became horribly awkward, I gathered up my shopping bag of chocolate rabbits and jelly beans and said, "Happy Easter, y'all! Tell your daddy the Easter Bunny was here!"

And like a true bunny would, I hopped my way home thinking Sharon might have Archie for the moment, but the boys were mine.

"Here's another fun bee fact. How about honey bees don't sleep? They stay motionless to conserve energy for the next day!" I said.

"What?" Tyler said. "That's crazy!"

Chapter Thirteen
Any Objections?

Leslie stayed home the night before Archie and Sharon were to be married, probably to give her liver a rest. I was pretty sure the Gentlemen of the Tap were holding a candlelight vigil at Dunleavy's Pub, praying for her swift return. She said she'd been challenging old pals to see who could drink the most shots of tequila and stay on the barstool. I was like, what? You turning into a frat boy? How stupid. And she kept saying she still loved Charlie, but I couldn't tell you why if you gave me a million dollars. In any case, they talked on the phone all the time.

Like I knew she would, Leslie had her way with my appearance, dropping a bunch of money at Stella Nova to transform my looks from the neck up and another small fortune at different retail establishments on King Street to take care of the neck down. This was more money than I had ever spent in one day. Ever. Not even for Christmas.

"Don't worry about it," she said. "I'm sending the bill to Charlie."

We giggled like schoolgirls.

I had to admit I looked pretty amazing; for me, that is. The dress she chose for me was a bold shade of pink, sort of like the color of geraniums. It was linen, sleeveless, and fitted. I could wear fitted clothes because I was on the lean side—probably a result of all that yard work. She found beige strappy sandals with block heels, which were a good idea for an outdoor wedding, so I wouldn't sink into the ground. Lastly, we bought a gauzy linen wrap, in case it got chilly. The haircut was layered a bit, definitely an improvement as it made me look like I had style, something that had totally eluded me for my whole life up to now.

"Who knew you had a figure like this?" Momma said when I tried on the dress for her to see.

"I'll take that as a compliment," I said.

"You need a pedicure," Leslie said.

"Why?" I said.

"Because your feet are gnarly and disgusting. Get in the car."

"Calm down. I have to change first," I said to Leslie. And then I turned to Momma and said, "I guess I'm getting a pedicure."

Momma just shook her head and smiled. She was so much happier with Leslie around.

So I had a pedicure and a manicure, and I had to admit, it was really nice to have somebody rub my feet. I didn't even know they needed it until it was all over, and I felt as light as a dandelion. And the pink polish Leslie chose matched the dress. Of course.

We'd been watching Archie's house as the tent went up, and in the early afternoon, the caterer arrived and more chairs and racks of glasses from a rental company and then, of course, flowers. For as badly as I felt about Archie marrying Sharon, and I was really struggling to get over it, some tiny part of me was excited to be a part of it because, well, I didn't get invited to a lot of big parties and weddings. It would have been much worse to be across the street longing to be a part of it. I wondered if they'd have a band and dancing.

Waiting for the appointed hour seemed like an eternity, but at last it was time to dress and walk over. Leslie and Momma had been invited as well, but earlier in the week they both begged off and sent me to represent the family.

"You don't need me to hold your hand," Leslie said. "In fact, you'll do better without me there. But if there are any hot guys, come get me."

"Don't wait around for that to happen. I fully expect this to be a very dull affair."

"Maybe I'll drop in for a glass of champagne," she said.

The QB harrumphed.

"If I never go to another wedding, it's okay with me," Momma said. "With the possible exception of yours."

I knew the real reason she was staying home was because Archie's wedding would remind her of Leslie's, and I didn't think there was a thing in her closet that would work. The dress she had worn to Leslie's wedding was about five sizes too small and getting smaller every day.

"I'm not getting married any time soon," I said. "But it's nice to know you'd come."

"Listen to you," Momma said. "You're starting to sound like me."

Leslie said, "You look gorgeous."

"Thanks. And Leslie, thanks for all of this. I mean it."

"You're welcome. You know, I know it's going to be awful for you to watch him marry her."

"Yeah, it will be. But I'm going for the children. It's going to be worse for them."

"You're a good woman, Holly. I hope your prince is over there waiting for you."

"If he is, I'll ask him if he's got a brother."

We hugged then, like sisters. Physical affection between us was rare, but Leslie knew I was on edge and I think she just wanted to encourage me to be brave.

As I drew close, I could hear chamber music. Well, I thought, that's pretty classy. There was a crowd of seventy-five or so people, milling around under the tent, talking and claiming seats. I spotted Hunter and Tyler. They were each wearing a navy jacket and khaki pants with a shirt and tie. Their hair was wet-combed. Their loafers were shined. Someone had seen to every detail. Probably Archie. They looked adorable.

"You both look so handsome!" I said to them.

"We're the best men!" they said together.

"That's wonderful!" I said and thought, At least they'll feel like they're a part of the whole event. "That's a very big deal, you know."

"We know. Dad told us that about a million times," Tyler said.

"I'm still mad I don't get to go to Bermuda," Hunter said.

"Oh, come on, now," I said. "Let's put that behind us. And besides, we have a whole week to do things together! It will be better than Bermuda."

They eyed me with keen suspicion, the kind of suspicion only little boys can harbor.

"Like there's anything we can do about anything anyway," Tyler said.

I knelt down to his level and looked him in the eyes.

"Tyler, it's not easy to just trust anyone completely. Believe me, your father has thought all of this through. He only wants what's best for both of you. Someday, when you're a dad, you'll understand just how carefully these choices are made. So promise me you'll both give Sharon a chance, all right?"

They looked at each other. Tyler had his hands stuffed in his pants pockets. Hunter was kicking the dirt and sucking his teeth.

"Okay," Tyler said.

Hunter said, "We'll see. If she's nice to us, then we'll be nice to her."

"No, no, young man. That's drawing a line in the

sand, and that's not how this has to be. You have to begin with an open heart, Hunter. Promise me?"

"Okay," he said after a moment of consideration.

I looked up to see Archie coming toward us. He was drop-dead gorgeous in his tuxedo.

"Is everything all right?" he said.

"Sure, Dad! Let's go get you married off!" Tyler said.

Hunter was less sure but managed a crooked smile all the same.

"Let's go. The sooner you get married, the sooner I get cake!" he said, and he scooted away with Tyler.

I stood there looking at Archie. He was so handsome I wanted to cry. Men in tuxedos were like men in uniform. There was just something so appealing about the formality of it. And he was wearing a Brackish bow tie, made of peacock feathers. I could feel his excitement, and then it all changed. He looked at me then as if he'd never seen me before. We both knew what the look meant. It was recognition.

"You look really, I mean, you're beautiful, Holly," he said.

I smiled at him and said, "I'll still be the girl next door if you ever need me, Archie."

He was quiet then as it all sank in. Perhaps he realized in that moment that he was marrying the wrong woman, but it was too late to do anything about it. And don't you know, here came the bride, a vision of cleavage and bad taste in ecru lace with too many sparkling baubles all over her dress refracting the light like a light saber from *Star Wars.*

"Holly, is that really you? You're so . . . um, pink!"

It's unbecoming for the bride to be a bitch on her wedding day, I wanted to say, but I held my tongue.

Instead I said, "You look lovely, Sharon. What a beautiful bouquet. Congratulations."

I was going to be a lady about it all. People were taking their seats. The chamber music began playing slightly louder.

"Good luck!" I said to them and walked away.

What else was I supposed to do except hide my feelings? I took a seat in the very back, next to an older couple, and waited for the ceremony to begin. The ceremony was being performed by a friend of Sharon's who happened to be a judge. He was standing at the end of the little makeshift aisle with Archie and his two sons. Hunter, of course, was fidgeting, unable to stay still.

First, some older ladies were brought up the aisle. Then two women who were bridesmaids, even though they seemed a little too old to be in a wedding party. And a little tiny golden-haired girl followed them, dropping flower petals. She was walking so slowly and dropping her petals with such deliberation that the guests smiled and chuckled. She couldn't have been over three years old and she easily stole every single heart.

The music became louder again, the guests stood, and along came Sharon, on the arm of a man I assumed was her father. I was puzzled and a little slighted to know that Archie and Sharon's relationship had come this far and I'd never been introduced to anyone in her family. But in my heart, I knew it was because Archie considered any introductions to be unnecessary to a neighbor.

Just get this over with, I thought. Please. Let this be over in a hurry. I watched Archie's face, looking for a crack in his wall. But Archie was too much of a gentleman to be anything else. He smiled warmly at Sharon as she approached him. I could see that he felt genuine affection for her.

The judge invited anyone who had objections or knew of a reason why Archie and Sharon should not marry to speak.

They exchanged vows, and I felt like I was in some altered state of consciousness, watching myself in a nightmare. Suddenly, I noticed a couple of honey bee scouts, buzzing around. Then a few more and a few more. They could only be mine. What were they doing out after dark? I sent them a mental message to go home and not come back here tonight or there'd be hell to pay for them. But I still wished for a disaster to happen; a little one would be fine.

The next thing I knew, the ceremony was over, and Archie gave Sharon a polite kiss. She grabbed the back of his neck and laid one on him that was so French I couldn't believe my eyes. I mean, gross. There was nervous laughter all over the place and I thought, Good, there's something he should notice.

They came up the aisle, smiling at everyone, and went inside, I assumed to sign their marriage license. In moments, waiters appeared with trays of champagne-filled flutes, people were talking, and a party had begun. Everyone stepped out of the tent so that the wait staff could rearrange the chairs and add tables for dinner. Archie and Sharon reappeared and were mingling, followed by a photographer.

Leslie suddenly appeared, and we spotted each other.

"I decided to take advantage of the free cocktails," she said. "How was it?"

"Pretty dismal, from my point of view. I kept wishing someone would call it off."

Just then, a lone seagull flew over and dropped his

visiting card on the back of Sharon's gown. She didn't flinch. He was followed by two others who did the same. Leslie and I looked at each other and burst into subdued laughter, the kind where you chewed on the insides of your cheeks until you tasted blood. Then there was a fourth, which made a direct hit on her head, and bird shit was now running down her face. Understandably, Sharon started shrieking. Had the birds joined forces with my bees?

Waiters rushed to her side with napkins and bar towels. When Tyler and Hunter saw what had happened, they fell to the ground, holding their stomachs and laughing like hyenas. I ran to them.

"Hey! Y'all! Come on!" I hissed. "Yes, it's funny, but only in a terrible, terrible way. But you're not allowed to laugh like this. It's very mean!"

Reluctantly, they got up, and I brushed them off.

"You're no fun, Mith Holly," Tyler said.

"Yeah," Hunter said.

"Wait a minute. You boys promised me to have an open heart, remember? We had a deal, and a deal is a deal."

We looked over to where Sharon was practically getting a bath and saw her crying hysterically.

"I feel bad for her! Don't y'all?" I said. "This night is supposed to be her dream come true! Now, go to her, like good boys, and see if there's anything y'all can do! Offer to get her a glass of water. Hurry up!"

They scurried away and I turned back to Leslie, who was standing with a very tall woman with large hands. She had on a long blond wig, a blue silk dress, pumps, tons of jewelry, thick eyelashes, and enough makeup to put Estée Lauder right into a coma. I looked again and recognized her. Him. Oh, God. I nearly fainted.

"Hello, Holly," said a familiar voice.

"Well, hi there yourself, Charlie," I said. "What a, um, surprise!"

It was my brother-in-law. In full female regalia.

"I guess this makes us wedding crashers," Leslie said, eaten up alive with giggles. "Can I get anyone a drink?"

"Yes, anything with alcohol would be perfect," I said, unable to take my eyes off Charlie.

"I'd like a cosmo, if they can manage it," Charlie said.

"Well, this isn't Vegas, but the Lowcountry can hold her own in the booze department. I'm pretty sure about that."

Just then the photographer appeared with Archie by her side.

"I wanted to be sure I had a picture of us," he said. "And the boys. Where are they? They were supposed to follow me over here." His eyes found Charlie, and his surprise was obvious. "Do I know you?"

"Yes, you do! I'm Leslie's husband." He extended his hand for Archie to shake and Archie shook it soundly. "And tonight, I'm Charlene."

Not to me, you're not, I thought. I was a little confused.

"Well, I'll be damned. Charlene," Archie said. "Of course, you are." He turned to the photographer. "Can we get a picture of the three of us?"

"I hope you don't mind that I stopped in," Charlie said. "I came to the island to surprise Leslie. I want her to come with me, back to Vegas."

"And I'll bet you surprised her, all right," I said.

"No, I'm delighted to see you," Archie said, smiling.

We stood together and smiled, and the photographer snapped several pictures.

"Thank you. I should probably go help Leslie with the drinks," Charlie said and walked in the direction of the bar.

"Terrible thing about the seagulls and all," I said. "Is Sharon okay?"

"Oh, sure. She's fine. Luckily, she has another dress. She went inside to change."

"So, when do y'all leave? I mean, what time? I know it's in the morning."

"At ten. Holly, I need to say something."

I could feel the electricity between us. It was as real and as powerful as anything I'd ever felt.

"No, you don't. You just go and have a great time in Bermuda and don't worry about a thing."

I looked at him, staring straight into his eyes as if to say, You're a damn fool, Archibald MacLean. A damn fool. Did his eyes say he was in agreement?

"So, aren't drones remote-controlled bees?"
Hunter said.

I said, "No. Drones don't do anything except
mate with the queen. And then they die."

"Well, that's stupid," Tyler said.

Chapter Fourteen
The Vapors

Well, Charlie's physical appearance was too much for Momma. When we all got home from the wedding, Momma was in the kitchen. She looked up and gave him the most serious hairy eyeball I'd ever seen her deliver.

"You're not planning on sleeping under this roof, I hope," she said.

"Momma, Charlie is my husband, for goodness' sake," Leslie said.

"Go get yourself a hotel room," Momma said. "I think you've done enough for our family's reputation for one night."

"Momma! That's not nice! You can't treat my husband this way!" Leslie said.

"Charlie, I'm talking to you. Do you have a hearing problem, too?" Momma said.

"No, ma'am. I do not have a hearing problem. But I must say you are hurting my feelings," Charlie said. "However, I will not stay where I am not welcome. Come, Leslie, gather your things. We can go to the Courtyard Marriott."

Leslie looked like she was about to burst into tears. Her fist covered her mouth.

"Oh, Charlie, I can't go with you, you know, like this. I love you. You know I do. But I just can't."

"I see," he said. "And why not? We were just at a wedding."

"That was a bad call," Leslie said.

"Do you not have a mirror?" Momma said. "I think it's time for you to call it a night." She went about ten feet from the kitchen and turned around. "And another thing. You were never that handsome as a man, but, great God almighty, you make one ugly woman."

Momma left the room, presumably to go to her bathroom to try and find ten milligrams of something that would readjust her central nervous system.

Charlie looked at me, pursed his lips, and put his hands on his hips.

"Have you ever?" he said.

I said, "Charlie, sometimes things go your way and sometimes they don't."

"What's that supposed to mean?"

"It means bless your heart," I said.

"Which means?"

"You're an idiot, Charlie," I said. "You can't come around here dressed how you are dressed and expect a good reaction. I'm sorry. That's just the way the world turns."

"I never thought you were so narrow-minded, Holly."

"Don't insult me, Charlie. I'm not narrow-minded one bit and you know it. You're the odd man out here."

"Well, that's an interesting expression. Your mother? Okay. She's from another generation. But I'd have thought you were, well, a lot cooler about the ways of the world."

"Charlie, I have nothing against your lifestyle. How you live is entirely your business."

"Thank you," he said, still giving me some self-righteous attitude. "Although I don't need anyone's permission."

"But you should've told my sister the truth before you married her."

"Maybe we should talk in the morning," Leslie said. "Come on, I'll walk you to the door."

"So, I'm being thrown out into the night? Dismissed like an unwanted visitor?"

"Come on, Charlie," Leslie said and took his arm. "We'll talk tomorrow, okay?"

I said, "Charlie?"

He turned back to me.

"It wasn't a black-tie wedding. You're, like, way overdressed."

He shrugged his shoulders and left.

Well, it wasn't black tie, I thought.

I poured myself a glass of wine and one for Leslie. She would need it. I took a long sip and sat down at the table, waiting for my sister. It was a few minutes before I heard the engine of Charlie's rental car turn over. Leslie came into the room with her arms raised, looking at the ceiling in an expression of *Why me, Lord?*

"Do you believe this night?" she said, taking the glass.

"When Charlie showed up, I thought you were going

to have to send someone to scrape my body up from the ground."

"Yeah, he sure made an entrance."

"The best part though, was the seagulls," I said. We toasted. "Not one but four."

"Agreed, but Charlie ran a close second."

"For sure. Here's what I don't get. Why doesn't he understand that you have your own feelings about his decision to be doing this?"

"You know what? I'd have to say because at the bottom of it all, he's a man like all the rest of them. Part mule."

"There's just so much I don't understand," I said. "So much."

"Yeah, look what you're missing out on." She paused for a moment. "Are you all right? I mean, about Archie getting married?"

"Of course not, but what am I supposed to do?"

"Well, at least you have the affection of his children. They're such precious little boys. They were so cute in their blazers and neckties. Little men."

"I know. It's crazy, but I can't wait to have them for a week."

"Are they staying here?"

"No, I'm going over there. What are you going to do about Charlie?"

"I don't know. I really do love him, you know? I keep telling myself he's just going through a phase or something. But this seems beyond phase behavior."

"Yeah, boy, in my expert opinion? It's beyond phase."

"I mean, if he'd gone out and bought a Harley, it would've been a lot easier to contend with. Or if he'd taken up rock climbing, you know?"

"Of course! The strangest part of this, and it's all pretty strange, is that he doesn't seem to understand why it's a problem for you. Like, why can't you just take him as he is?"

"Exactly. Although he has got to know that this is asking a lot. It's not like he wants to dress up in private, which might be easier for me to adjust to."

"You're kidding, right?"

"Not at all. I mean, I've known him since his family moved here. He was a little femme, but that never bothered me. Now, suddenly, he's a female impersonator out there in the world? I don't understand."

"Maybe because it got dumped on you all at once it's harder to take."

"No kidding! Do you think we might have discussed this bit by bit to give me a chance to get my brain around it?"

"Seems to me that might have been a better choice."

"He wants to flaunt it all over the place. I'm asking you, who comes to Sullivan's Island in full drag and crashes a wedding?"

"Is it *drag*? I thought *drag* was half of the term *drag queen*. And *drag queens* are gay, I think."

"Charlie's not gay. I'm certain of that. But back to my question. Who shows up like that on Sullivan's Island and crashes a wedding?"

"No one that I ever knew. At least, to the best of my limited knowledge."

"What a night," she said again. "Maybe that was just a huge lapse in judgment."

Morning came quickly. I had a little headache from all the wine and champagne I'd consumed at the wedding and afterward, when Leslie and I, incredulous to the tenth power, sat together trying to dissect the brains of Charlie and Archie. I went into the kitchen thinking coffee would clear the cobwebs and a piece of toast might soak up the poison and bring me back to life. Momma was seated at the table reading the paper. The coffee was already made.

"Oh, g'morning! Is Leslie up?" I said.

"No, she's still sleeping. At least she's alone."

I just shook my head and reached inside the refrigerator for the milk.

"I'm going over to the boys in a little bit. Do you need me to do anything for you before I go?"

"No, I'm fine. You sister can help me if and when she decides to rise."

"Did you bring in the paper?"

"I'm not dead yet, you know. I can still go outside and get the paper if I want to."

Maybe she was taking some of the nurse's advice and taking up a little exercise. I didn't say another word about it.

"Well, great. Thanks for making the coffee."

She put the paper down and whispered to me.

"What did you really think of Charlie?"

"I think he's a little cracked. I really do," I whispered back. "His arrival was just so blatant. I mean, where's his consideration for Leslie's feelings?"

"Thank you," she said and resumed reading, satisfied with my answer.

Then she put her paper down again.

"Do you think she's going to patch things up with him?"

"No. I don't. Look, Leslie is super cool with Charlie's choices. She's not super cool having a female impersonator for a husband, especially one who wants to live in drag twenty-four seven."

"I imagine that would be pretty complicated."

I dropped a slice of bread in the toaster and pulled down the lever.

"And I think you might be relieved to know that there was not one single person at the wedding I recognized."

"I was waiting for the telephone to start ringing."

"Well, I'm just saying I don't think Charlie found the audience he was hoping for. What are you reading so intently?"

"The obits. What else? Do you know there are people in here younger than me?"

"I imagine so. Life's a gift, that's why they call today the present."

"You're a regular Hallmark card over there, missy."

"I was just kidding."

My toast popped up. I put it on a paper towel and buttered it. Momma continued reading the paper and I stood eating my breakfast over the sink.

"So I'm working four shifts at Publix this week. They're only six hours each. Do you think you or Leslie could keep an eye on the boys for me?"

"Of course! I think they're going to need a lot of attention for the foreseeable future," Momma said. "I'm sure Sharon is going to try and establish authority over them. From everything I've seen and heard, she's a tough cookie."

"She is," I said and wondered what was going on with me that I was agreeing with Momma right and left. "And thanks. I'm gonna go over there now because I know Archie and his bride are taking off soon. I want to be sure the boys get a good breakfast."

"I know where to find you," she said.

I was just putting some things together to take next door—a book I was reading, my toothbrush, and a pair of pajamas—when the phone rang. Leslie must've picked it up, and a few minutes later she came into the kitchen.

"Is there any coffee left?"

"Good morning!" Momma said. "Decent people have been up for hours, you know."

"It's the weekend, Momma. Decent people also sleep later on the weekends."

"Don't sass me," Momma said. "I can still turn you over my knee."

Leslie rolled her eyes and I poured her a mug of coffee and handed it to her, shaking my head. I thought, Well, that was an ironic thing to say for someone who had spent most of her life in bed until Leslie returned. But when I looked back at Momma there was a tiny smile creeping across her face. She was having fun.

"I'm having breakfast with Charlie this morning," Leslie said.

"Why?" Momma said.

"Because I have to get some things straight between us," Leslie said.

"Good luck with that," I said. "But let me know how it works out. I'll be next door."

I rinsed out my mug and blew them a little kiss.

It was a beautiful day and there was no humidity to speak of. Spring had officially returned to Sullivan's Island. More and more flowers were blooming, and all the bushes had new growth. The azaleas had reached their peak and the magnolias were about to pop open. Confederate jasmine and fig ivy were on the crawl again, climbing and winding around anything in their path. And all those dahlias I planted earlier in the month were coming soon. I was more excited about them than anything else I'd ever planted.

Last spring, just by chance, I'd gone to the Citadel Mall and saw an exhibition put on by the Charleston Garden Club. That was the first time in my life I'd ever seen a dahlia, and I fell in love with them right away. They were so intricate, they almost looked like origami flowers made of tissue paper. And they bloomed in a riot of colors, too many to remember. I decided right then and there that I was going to grow dahlias, even though they weren't fond of our zone or of the coast. So, I worked hard to create the perfect environment for them by mulching leaves and some other organic matter into the soil. I knew they hated hot weather, so I bought a bunch of cheap beach umbrellas to give them shade when it grew too hot, which happened every single year of my life. And I planted the dahlias in a location where they would get afternoon shade. If they didn't bloom, it wouldn't be because I had not tried my best. But if they all bloomed as planned, this summer's garden would stop traffic.

Anyway, my focus for the next seven days was not dahlias but little boys, little boys who needed a truckload of love, and I was ready to deliver. I rang the doorbell and inside of a minute, Tyler opened the door.

"Good morning, best man! How are . . . what's wrong, baby?"

Tyler burst into tears and fell into my arms.

"Tyler! Tell me what's happened?"

"She made us . . . she took all . . . the pictures of our mom and put them away. Now I can't even see a picture of my mom without asking her first."

Then he began to wail. My heart sank. I thought, Oh my God, that's the meanest thing I've ever heard of! But in the next minute, I could sort of see Sharon's point. Only sort of. She was Archie's new wife, and no matter who he married, that woman wouldn't be happy to see pictures of the deceased wife who had been canonized by the entire population who knew her. Still, it was no way to start things off. I thought for another minute and hoped I had a solution.

"Hold on there, sweet pea, I think I have a way to work this out. Where's your daddy?" I pulled a tissue from my bag and gave it to him. "Blow."

He blew his nose and wiped his eyes with the sleeve of his pajamas.

"Upstairs in the bedroom with her. They locked the door."

Well, I knew what that meant, but I quickly changed the subject. But all Tyler knew was that today, and maybe for a long time, he wasn't welcome in their bedroom. There would be no more morning snuggles or tickle fests or pillow fights.

"Did you and your brother have breakfast?"

"We just had some leftover cake."

"Okay, where's Hunter?"

"Watching cartoons," he said.

"Well, why don't we see if we can't rustle up some grub for you two cowboys? Silver dollar pancakes?"

"Yeah!" he said with a big smile.

"Okay! Now! That's the face I like to see! Go get your brother and meet me in the kitchen."

When I got to the kitchen my heart sank again. The cake they had demolished was the top layer of Archie and Sharon's wedding cake, traditionally saved for the happy couple's first anniversary. It had been carefully packed by the caterer. The boys had literally destroyed the box and eaten most of it. I decided to close the box and hide it in the back of the freezer. Sharon was not going to like that at all. If she found out. Which she wouldn't until a year from now. Better yet, I was going to throw it out as soon as they left.

I started making batter for pancakes and took out Archie's largest skillet. The boys came wandering into the room.

"So, listen up, buckaroos, is there any cake in any other part of the house? Even a crumb?"

"Maybe," Hunter said sheepishly. "There might be some on the floor in front of the television."

I glanced at the kitchen clock that hung on the wall over the back door. It was after nine. Archie and Sharon would be downstairs soon. I wet a paper towel, squeezed out the water, and wiped the icing from Hunter's mouth.

"I want both of you to take the broom and dustpan and clean up every single crumb as quickly as you can. Because if there is one crumb left, you both could be in big trouble."

"How come?" they said in disbelief.

"That cake y'all woofed up was a special reserve for your daddy and Sharon's first anniversary."

They looked at each other as terror set in.

"Yikes!" they both screamed and tore out of the room to remove the evidence.

After I tossed the crumbs, I served the boys plates of steaming towers of tiny pancakes drizzled with warmed maple syrup and melted butter with big glasses of milk. They were in heaven.

Archie came down the stairs with luggage and returned upstairs to get more. There was still no Sharon sighting. When Archie came down the steps alone with another suitcase, I met him in the hall by the front door.

"Good morning," I said. I was as cool as I could be.

"Hi! Oh, I'm glad you're already here!"

"Well, I figured the boys needed breakfast."

"Right, of course."

Heaven forbid that Sharon leave the marital chamber to tend to her brand-new stepchildren to let them know she cared about them even a smidgen.

"Archie, can I have a word with you?"

"Of course. Want to follow me? I've got to get these in the trunk. Is there coffee?"

I picked up a tote bag that looked like Sharon's and

wondered if she was taking a bag of bricks on her honeymoon for a special reason.

"We can have coffee ready in five minutes."

He opened the back of his Jeep and the first suitcase went in with a jerk and a grunt appropriate to the size and weight of it.

"Great. What's on your mind?"

"Listen, I know it's not my business, but apparently Sharon took all the pictures of Carin and put them away."

"Understandable, don't you think?"

"Um, I think it's actually a little bit insensitive." Archie stepped back and frowned. "I mean, I found Tyler in tears. Why don't you give each of the boys a picture of Carin to keep in their rooms?"

"I hadn't thought about it that way," he said. "Of course, I'll take care of that right away."

"Great! How about some pancakes?" I said. "And I'll get a pot of coffee going."

"I'll be right there," he said. "Holly?"

"Yeah?"

"Thanks."

"Sure," I said.

I hurried back inside to throw grinds in their coffeemaker, batter in the pan, and two more place settings on the table. Was I really going to cook breakfast for

Sharon? I decided to be the bigger person and just do it. I'd look petty if I didn't. If she didn't want them, she didn't have to eat them.

About ten minutes later, the car was packed and breakfast was on the table for Mr. and Mrs. MacLean. Archie and Sharon came to the table.

"This looks great," Archie said.

"Holly makes the best pancakes I ever had!" Tyler said.

"Better than IHOP!" Hunter said.

"Pancakes? You must be kidding," Sharon said. "None for me, thanks."

Tyler and Hunter looked from Sharon's face to mine and back again.

"Why not?" Tyler said.

"Because pancakes make you fat," she said.

"No, they don't," Hunter said. "I'm not fat. I eat pancakes all the time."

"You shouldn't disagree with me, young man. It's very rude," Sharon said.

The room got quiet.

Archie said, "Hunter, adults have to limit the amount of carbohydrates they eat because the unburned ones metabolize as fat. I don't think Sharon meant to say *kids* shouldn't eat them. You'll burn them off before noon. Isn't that right, Sharon?"

"Perhaps I should have been more specific, but your boys are going to have to learn some manners," Sharon said. "If we're going to get along, that is."

I thought I would really love to fly across the room and strangle her.

"What did I do?" Tyler said. "Why am I included in this?"

"It's a generalization," Sharon said.

"Oh. By the way, what do you want us to call you?" Tyler said.

"Why, call me 'Mother'! What else would you call me?"

How about any of the fifty terrible names that were running through my head?

"You're not our mother," Hunter said quietly and nicely. "Our mother is in heaven with the angels."

"Sharon . . ." Archie said in a kind of a warning to her not to ramp this up to a full-blown war.

"Well, then," Sharon said, "call me whatever you'd like."

I couldn't wait for them to leave.

"Miss Holly? How many drones are there in each hive?"
Tyler asked.

"About fifteen percent of all of them," I said.

"I'm going to pray for them," Hunter said.

Chapter Fifteen
Bliss Week

We stood on the porch, the boys and I, waving at Archie and Sharon as they backed out of the driveway.

"Have a great time and don't worry about anything," I said.

"Thanks for everything!" Archie said to me. "Y'all be good, boys!"

"We always are!" Tyler said defensively, and who

could blame him? Especially after the pile of bull Sharon dropped on him.

"Bye!" Hunter said, disappointed that he was getting cheated out of a trip to Bermuda.

Sharon just waved and gave us that fake smile of hers. I could tell she couldn't wait to get away from us. That was just fine. We couldn't wait for her to leave.

They were finally gone. I knew Archie could not have been happy with the way Sharon spoke to Hunter and Tyler. They'd been married for less than twenty-four hours and there was already an issue.

"Our momma never talked to us like she does," Hunter said, as though he was reading my mind.

"I know she didn't," I said. "But your momma was a very, very sweet lady and she loved you with all her heart. And she was truly your momma. She carried you both in her tummy for nine months and then brought you into the world, which I am pretty sure wasn't an easy thing to do."

"How *did* we get out?" Hunter asked with all the wide-eyed innocence of a little boy.

"Magic," I said, sincerely. "Babies are magic and miracles!"

"Huh," Hunter said, thinking about what I'd said.

"Sharon's not sweet one bit," Tyler said. "Now do

you see what we meant about some people just don't like kids?"

"Listen, do you want to know what I think? I mean, what I really, really, really think?"

"Yeah!" they both said.

"Let's go clean up the kitchen together and I'll tell you."

Hunter made himself busy returning the milk, butter, syrup, and eggs to the refrigerator while Tyler cleared the table, handing me plates and mugs to rinse and put in the dishwasher.

"So what do you think, Miss Holly?" Tyler said.

His top and bottom front teeth were growing in fast and his lisp was all but gone.

"I think I miss the way you used to talk before your teeth started coming in."

"They had a growth spurt. Now, come on. You promised!"

"I think you two are the greatest little boys I have ever known, and I'll bet you that when Sharon gets to know you, she'll think so, too."

"No way," Tyler said.

"But! I think she's super nervous, and that's why she says things that sound a little bit mean. They just pop out of her mouth before she realizes how they're going to sound to you."

"What's nervous got to do with it? We're just kids," Hunter said.

"Yeah, it's not like we're going to bite her or something."

"Well, as I said, she doesn't really know you yet, does she?"

Tyler said, "Why does Dad act so silly around her?"

"That's a harder question to answer," I said. "I don't really know a reason why he does, but you're right, men can get pretty silly around women."

"What are we going to do today?" Tyler said.

I assumed then that my answers had satisfied them.

"Well, we've got to wait for the rental company to take away all the tables and chairs. Then I thought we'd maybe go down to the playground and see what's happening. Maybe get some ice cream. Then we've got to be sure all your homework is done for tomorrow, get some supper, get a bath, and get some z's."

"Where are you sleeping?" Hunter said.

"I don't know," I said. "We never talked about it."

"You could sleep in Daddy's bed," Hunter said.

"Oh, no," I said. "No, no, no. I can't do that."

"Why not?" Hunter said.

"You'll understand someday, but no, I can't do that," I said.

Tyler gave me a sly look that said he had an inkling

of why it might be weird for me to sleep there and said, "Well, I've got bunk beds. Hunter, why don't you sleep in my room and let's give Miss Holly your room? How's that?"

"Perfect! That's a very good compromise!" I said. "Now, let's go check your backpacks to make sure you're ready for school tomorrow."

"I might have been supposed to do a math worksheet," Tyler said.

"Piece of cake," I said. "Let's get on it so it's done."

It didn't take long for the few chores we had to be completed, and the rental company actually came earlier than expected.

"Y'all ready to go for a walk?" I asked.

"Definitely!" Hunter said. "But I want to ride my bike."

"But there's no bike for me!" I said.

"Miss Holly's right. Let's walk!" Tyler said.

There we were, the three of us, strolling down Middle Street toward the playground. Sometimes the boys seemed like they were so very young, and on other occasions, they possessed a depth of wisdom that belied their years. I imagined losing their mother had a lot to do with that.

As soon as the playground was in sight, the boys took off running, hell bent for leather, as Momma said from time to time. I didn't stop them. I intended to let them run and jump and play and get any and all of their anxiety completely out of their system. The great feature that set the Sullivan's Island playground apart from most of the others across the country was the mound that sat smack in the middle of it. It was actually Fort Capron at one time, a fallout shelter at another, and now kids loved to slide down it on sheets of cardboard. It was the closest thing Sullivan's Island had to sledding. The playground had been built over time. First there were tennis courts and basketball courts. Later on a gazebo was built, swings and sliding boards were added, and a playhouse, and all sorts of other opportunities for climbing or digging in the sand. There was something there for children of all ages.

Tyler and Hunter were taking advantage of all of it. I had decided it was best not to bring Sharon up in conversation with them unless they were the ones to do so. In fact, I decided to restrict my thoughts about Sharon to conversations with my bees. I sure didn't want my disappointment in Archie's marriage to be the talk of the town. Not for one second.

The boys seemed to know quite a few of the kids on the playground, probably from school. It reminded me that no parent knows every single thing about their child's life and that eventually, they really will have a whole life for themselves, independent of your orbit. I shouldn't worry about them so much. And then I wondered for a moment if Carin was watching us from somewhere, heaven maybe. How would she feel about Archie and Sharon? For some inexplicable reason I could almost hear her laughing and laughing. And when I had the thought of how she would like me taking care of her kids, I could almost feel her hand on my shoulder in gratitude. It was funny, how connected you felt to the unseen world on this island. But that was the Lowcountry and what it seemed to do to most anyone who would take the time to listen to the muses hidden in the salt air. It occurred to me then that this was another advantage of living here, that edge it gave you, that it made you a deeper thinker. If you wanted to be one, that is.

I loved watching Hunter and Tyler having fun. Someone had a basketball and there was an impromptu game between them all, just shooting hoops, which of course eluded Hunter, who wasn't tall enough to even hit the rim. This was why I wanted to teach. I wanted to be in a world filled with children as they woke up to something new each day and I could help them see their growing sense of reality more clearly. When Tyler and Hunter were good and sweaty and red faced and out of breath, they stumbled over to me on the bench.

"We could probably stand some ice cream now," Tyler said.

"Oh, you could, huh?" I said and smiled.

"Yeah," Hunter said, giggling, "if we had to."

"Then let's go see what wondrous treats are in the freezer at the gas station!"

The walk from the playground to the tiny convenience store attached to the Circle K gas station was only minutes, and soon all three of us were standing on the corner of Station Twenty-two and a Half, devouring some terrible unhealthy combination of sugar and chemicals. They sold great coffee, milk, bread, sodas, and emergency supplies, such as batteries, potato chips, doughnuts, and toilet paper. But the freezer filled with the least healthy of iced snacks was our favorite.

"This is delicious," said Tyler, who was taking down a creamy orange ice cream concoction in a tube.

"Mine's better," said Hunter, who was making fast work of a fudge bar on a stick.

"Let's make a deal," I said, while luxuriating in the awesomeness of an ice cream sandwich.

"What's the deal?" Tyler said.

"If y'all take your baths and get ready for bed early, I'll make spaghetti and meatballs and let y'all stay up and watch *60 Minutes* with me. We can eat in front of the television."

"Do we get garlic bread?" Hunter asked.

"Yes," I said.

"Cool! What's *60 Minutes*?" Tyler said.

"Well, it's only the most interesting program on television, that's all."

"What's it about?" Hunter said.

"That's the thing! It's about new things every single week. Sometimes it's about mountain climbers or the jungle in the Amazon or a symphony orchestra or kids who are prodigies. It can be about anything and everything, but different every week," I said. "And it gives you something to talk about that other people might not know about."

"What's prodigies?" Hunter asked.

"Really super talented individuals," I said.

"You mean like National Geographic programs are different every week?"

"Exactly, but National Geographic deals more with the natural world and *60 Minutes* looks for newsworthy people who are doing incredible things, like inventing things to make the world a better place."

"Sounds too educational," Hunter said.

"I'll give it a shot," Tyler said.

"Wise decision, young man! Let's move on."

The rest of the evening went as planned. Bubble baths were enjoyed. Pajamas were put on. Beds were turned down. Spaghetti and garlic bread filled our tummies. Backpacks were by the door for a fast getaway in the morning. And a whole new world was opened up to them through the ingenious work of Steve Kroft, Lesley Stahl, and others.

I followed them upstairs to supervise teeth brushing and tuck-ins.

"This was a great day," Tyler said, as I helped him comb his damp hair.

"Yes, it was. I had lots of fun, too," I said and meant it.

"Are we gonna get a bedtime story?" Hunter said.

"Sure! Do y'all say prayers before sleep?" I asked.

"We used to say prayers with our momma," Tyler said.

"Would you like to say some with me?" I asked.

"Sure!" Hunter said and launched into "Now I lay me down to sleep" followed by a litany of people to bless.

I made the list. Sharon did not. I didn't mention it. I should've, I know I should've, but I didn't. I just wanted that moment for myself. Was that so wrong?

I told them a story about the American Revolution and the Battle of Sullivan's Island.

"Try to imagine how brave the soldiers were!"

Then we said good night, and I left the door slightly ajar so I could hear them.

My cell phone rang around ten o'clock that night, and I remembered I'd left it in the kitchen. I jumped up from the sofa to answer it, hoping not to wake the boys. Who would be calling at this hour? It was Archie.

"Hi," he said. "Sorry to call so late. I just wanted to be sure everything was okay."

"Oh! Everything here is just perfect. The boys are fast asleep. How's it going there?"

"Not so great," he said.

"Why? What's happened?"

"Well, it turns out that Sharon didn't know that she had a terrible allergy to a certain strain of strawberries. She ate a ton of them and blew up like a blowfish. She's okay, but she's in the hospital. But she could've died. They had to give her a trach."

"Oh, my God! That's terrible!"

"Yeah, it wasn't pretty."

"Are you okay?"

"Who, me? Oh, yeah, I'm perfectly fine."

There was a very pregnant pause. He was not perfectly fine. But I wasn't going to ask why. I knew why, and I didn't want to hear it.

"Okay, then, I'm going to go to bed now. Early call in the morning, you know."

"Where are you sleeping?"

I thought, Why are you asking that? To see if your

pillow smells like me when you get home? What kind of a question was that? I wanted to say, Yeah, I'm sleeping with your pillows and your sheets and I'm rolling all over your bed. Why should I even answer? But I did.

I said, "In Hunter's bed. He's sleeping in Tyler's bunk."

He cleared his throat.

"And everything is fine?"

"Yes, Archie. Everything is fine. The rentals are gone. I took the boys to the park to play. They ran around like nuts for over an hour. Then we had ice cream. I made spaghetti and meatballs for dinner, which they inhaled, and then we watched *60 Minutes*. They took a long bubble bath and then they practically passed out, they were so tired."

"Wow. You're incredible, do you know that?" He didn't say it in just any old friendly tone. He said it like, well, you know.

"Don't play with my heart, Mr. MacLean."

He was on his honeymoon with Sharon, but I was on his brain. Well, wasn't that nice? No. It wasn't.

"I'm not playing with you at all. I am just acknowledging that you amaze me, that you're able to step in and accomplish so much, especially with my boys. It's simply remarkable. Carin was like that. She arranged everything for them."

"Well, I love those little rascals. You know that."

"Yes, and I'm grateful for that, too." There was a long sigh from Bermuda. "I'll check in with you tomorrow."

We hung up and I thought, Holy hell, I need some advice on this one. I'd consult the hives in the morning.

"What happens if the queen bee dies?" Hunter said.

"The colony can't survive without a queen,
so they make a new one."

"How do they do that?" Tyler asked.

"Two parts royal jelly and one part bee magic!" I said.
"Or you can actually buy them."

"Wow," they said. "Cool."

Chapter Sixteen
Bee Advised

Getting the boys off to school was the best start of my day, controlled chaos, but a time filled with laughter. I knew I would miss them until they came home, and I told them so. They blushed, and my heart sent out beams of love like the Care Bears used to do. I was just smitten.

I went back to my house to change clothes, and Momma and Leslie weren't there. I wondered where they had gone. There was no note. They'd probably gone shopping. I was dying to hear what had happened over her breakfast with Charlie. I wondered how he'd shown up and where they'd gone and boy, I would've loved to have been in the booth or table next to theirs! If I'd been the waitress, I'd be refilling their coffee cups every two seconds and then running away to write in a journal. I would have given them the tip back and said something like *y'all gave me more than I gave y'all.* Don't you know that's the truth? But all joking aside, I wondered how Leslie was taking this. She seemed too stoic or something. Numb? Well, I'd be numb for a long time, I think. I just hoped she wasn't too heartbroken.

I showered and changed and went out to my apiary to check on the girls. Time to add another box! Gosh, we were going to have tons of honey this year. Of course, I wound up giving them an earful of Sharon, Archie, and Charlie stories. What a week it had been, and it was only Monday!

I worked my shift at Publix, decorating a hundred cupcakes for a bridal shower with white icing and white crystal-looking sprinkles that sparkled but were edible.

When they were all lined up they looked like a field of beautiful clouds made of glitter. It sounds simple, I guess, but through this almost mindless work I found some creative satisfaction that left me wanting more. Maybe I'd try some designs that were more intricate.

We were having leftover spaghetti for supper, so there was not much need to grocery-shop. But I did bring home milk and a freshly baked apple pie. If this job hadn't done anything else for me, it had turned me on to fresh baked versus frozen, although frozen pies were still a wonderful thing to have on hand in case you had to have pie right that minute. Sometimes I felt like that.

I was home about half an hour before the boys would be there. Leslie's car was back in the driveway, so I left a note on the door for the boys and hurried over to get the latest on Charlie.

"Leslie?" I called her name as soon as I was inside the door.

"In the kitchen!"

Weren't we always in the kitchen?

"So, spill it, sister," I said. "What happened with Charlie?"

"Oh, Lord," she said. "It's complicated like all hell. Sit down."

I took a place at the table.

"No kidding. I'm sure."

"You want tea?"

As you know, in our house that meant iced tea. It could be freezing outside, and we still drank our tea with ice.

"Sure." She poured both of us a glass and sat, pushing the evil sugar bowl across the table to me. "Thanks. Remember the day I broke this?"

"Are you serious? I thought Momma was going to put you up for adoption."

"Me, too. So what happened?"

"I thought about what you and Momma said about full disclosure. Y'all were right. Charlie should've told me before he married me. I asked him that and he said he was afraid to tell me, afraid I wouldn't love him anymore, that he loved me. But this other passion of his never stopped him from being all man in the bedroom, that's for sure."

"Well, I suppose that's good to know."

"We had six years of bliss, him spoiling me to death with cars and jewelry and trips and fabulous dinners, but he never said a word."

"Do you think he was dressing up all the time?"

"Absolutely."

"You've never told me how this all came about in the first place. How you found out, I mean."

"Okay, brace yourself. Charlie was out with the guys one night, or so I thought. Anyway, he was really at a club where female impersonators perform. He was dressed up as Cher and lip-synced "I Got You Babe" hoping to win free drinks. He won free drinks, but he also got a DUI on the way home. He was too loaded to change his clothes at the club. He thought I'd be sleeping at that hour anyway, that he could just sneak in and change in the guest room, but the nice policeman took him to jail and then he called me to bail him out."

"Holy crap! So you go to the jail and there he is dressed up like Cher?"

"All except the wig. He had to take it off for his mug shot."

"So you were pretty shocked."

"You could say that. Yeah."

"Then what?"

"We had words. He felt I was being cruel to him, that if I loved him, I should just love him no matter what he was wearing."

"You know, that actually kind of sounds fair to me," I said, "but I'm not the one struggling with it."

"Well, that's just it, isn't it? He's right. If I love him, I love him. My problem is the deceit. Charlie was always a little bit effeminate. The world knew that. That's fine with me. He played some sports, tennis and golf, and he got along with the jocks. In fact, I always liked him because he was more compassionate or nicer than the other guys. He was a sweetheart. It's why I fell in love with him in the first place. But this deceit was so huge, I just freaked out."

"Well, I understand that. I hate lying. Especially given the nature of the lie. So now what?"

"I don't know. It turns out that he's a super talented lip-sync impersonator. Some big producer in Vegas wants to have him audition for some huge lip-sync group. The money is crazy."

"Are you for real?"

"Oh, yeah. Apparently, there's big money in this business. And here's the thing, Charlie doesn't really need the money. He got oodles from his dad's estate. But pretending to be Cher makes Charlie happier than I've ever seen him. I mean, he's downright dizzy with happiness!"

"Was Cher at breakfast?"

"Good grief, no! We had breakfast at the Sand Dollar on the Isle of Palms."

"Yeah, I can see him getting some heat here." I thought then that perhaps they had made some kind of peace with each other. "So where did you leave it with him?"

"Well, I'm beginning to understand this aspect of

Charlie's personality a little better. And he's agreed to compromise with me on certain things."

"Such as?"

"Such as not showing up unannounced at my mother's dressed as Charlene. I just told him, I said, 'Charlie? My momma's an older lady, from another generation, and she just can't take it. And Momma feels like you duped me by not telling me in the first place. She needs to know you're the same wonderful man that married her daughter.' I'll tell you, Holly, him showing up as Charlene with no warning wasn't nice. I mean, how about a heads-up?"

"But I seem to remember you laughing!" I said.

"Nervously. Because I didn't know what else to do!" she said.

"Yeah, I don't think I would've known what to do, either."

"He wants me to come to Vegas with him to watch this competition."

"Are you going to go?"

"I don't know. I don't know *what* to do."

"Well, let's think about it."

"How did last night go?"

"Terrific," I said and then told her about Sharon's strawberry allergy.

I thought she was going to burst a blood vessel, she

laughed so hard. I mean, she really laughed more than I thought she should have. I wrote it off to her anxiety over dealing with Charlie's new ambitions.

"I know. How terrible, right?" I said. "I'll see you later."

The boys were just coming up the steps and I was almost right behind them.

"Hey! How was school?"

They babbled on while I got the door open and then they followed me inside, still talking a mile a minute.

"Anybody want a snack?"

"Yes!" they said.

"Okay, backpacks down and go wash your hands!"

They scattered like mercury and were back in a flash.

I put sliced apples and peanut butter in front of them on a platter to share, and I sat down at the table with them.

"Okay, Tyler, you first. Tell me every single thing that happened to you today, and make sure you include at least one good thing. Hunter? You should be thinking about what you're going to say."

They told me their stories about math and lunch and recess and what was coming up and who they played with and what games they played. By the time they were finished talking, the platter was empty.

"Okay! Now, who's got homework?"

Worksheets were pulled from their backpacks and they got down to business. I quizzed Tyler with spelling words and helped him complete a two-digit math sheet with and without carrying numbers. Next, I watched Hunter form letters.

"Hunter? Do you know I had the exact same practice paper when I went to school?"

"You did?" He said this in such amazement that I realized he thought I was ancient.

"Yup," I said and crossed my eyes at him.

"You shouldn't do that. They might get stuck," he said.

"Baloney," I said. "Who told you that?"

"Momma," he said.

"Well, then, it's true. Now what else do you have?"

"An Under the Sea math sheet," Hunter said.

"And I have a counting money sheet," Tyler said. "And a sheet on homophones."

"Well, let's get on it so we might have an hour for the playground before supper!"

"Yay!" they both said and focused on the job at hand.

I marveled at the fact that although Tyler sometimes seemed to have all the earmarks of an adult already in place, he didn't yet know how to tell time or the difference in coin values and how they related to basic math skills and social literacy. And it was the same with Hunter. He was still learning his ABC's and how to write his name when otherwise he seemed like he knew everything in the world. I thought then about who was going to help them with this work. Who was going to praise their small incremental leaps and big accomplishments? Would it be Archie? Well, to be honest, he might help with special projects like building a papier-mâché volcano, but it was doubtful he'd be available on a day-to-day basis to help his boys with these small tasks. Would Sharon? The answer to that would be a strong *hell, no* in neon lights.

"I love doing homework with y'all," I said.

"We love doing homework with you, too," Tyler said.

"Yeah, you make it fun," Hunter said.

"Well, listen, when your daddy and Sharon get back, I'll still help you with homework any old time. How's that?"

"Boy, that would be great. I was worried about that," Tyler said.

"You shouldn't worry about anything. It's not a big deal at all," I said. "Okay, let's pack everything up so it's ready for the morning when we make the mad dash! In fact, why don't we go to school on the golf cart tomorrow?"

Big smiles broke out on their faces, as they repacked their backpacks and zipped them closed.

"Can we?" Hunter said.

"Our mom used to take us on the golf cart all the time," Tyler said. "I don't know if it even still works."

"We should find out. I suspect it's probably pretty dirty from just sitting under the house for so long. Let's go find out."

I took a roll of paper towels, a garbage bag, and a bottle of spray cleaner, and the boys and I went outside and under the house to investigate. We lifted the cover off and stood back. The cart was surely in need of some attention, because the seats were covered in mildew stains and the floor was all sandy.

"Ew! Gross," Tyler said.

"It is?" Hunter said. "It looks fine to me."

"Trust me," I said. "It needs some love."

I rolled a half dozen paper towels out for each boy and then for myself. Then I sprayed the seats and seat backs with the cleaner.

"Gentlemen? Let's show this thing who's boss!"

They descended on the golf cart like vultures on roadkill, and it was as clean as a whistle in no time at all.

"Now we need the broom and to get this baby on the charger!" I said.

"I'll get the broom!" Hunter said and took off like a shot.

Tyler plugged the charger into a wall socket and the other end into the cart. We checked the charger, which we should've done first, and, happily, it was working.

"We're going to have new wheels!" I said.

"Can I drive it?" Tyler said.

"Are you sixteen years of age and in possession of a driver's permit or a valid license?"

"Guess not, huh?"

"Guess not," I said.

Hunter returned with the broom and I swept all the sand from the floor of the golf cart in the front and in the back, while Tyler and Hunter wiped down everything else and disposed of the used paper towels. We stood back to admire the fine work we had done.

"Good job, boys! There's a playground in your immediate future!"

Just as we had the day before and as we would for every day it wasn't raining, we walked to the playground, the boys sprinting the last half block or so, and I watched them while they used the swings and sliding board and chased each other all over the place. Someone came with a basketball and of course they began to shoot baskets.

This, I thought, just establishing this simple routine was a big step toward recovering a wounded childhood. We were making it the best it could be.

Archie called later that night. Sharon was out of the hospital and recovering nicely. Her experience had frightened her very badly, he said.

"I'm sure it did!" I said.

"She's driving everyone in the restaurants crazy, though."

"What do you mean?"

"She wants to know where everything on her plate is grown before she'll take a bite of anything."

"Well, in a way it's understandable."

"I don't think she's having such a great time," he said.

Too bad, I thought.

"Well, don't they have carriage tours like we do in Charleston? Take her into Hamilton. There's supposed to be great shopping."

"Yeah, maybe we'll do that. So how are the boys? I should've called earlier so I could talk to them, but we were at dinner. Have they driven you insane yet?"

"Not a chance. The boys are great. The house is fine. Everything is just as you'd hope. So y'all just have fun and enjoy your time together."

"Well, it's only a few more days," he said. "Are you sure you're holding up okay?"

"Are you kidding? I haven't had this much fun since I don't even know when!"

We hung up, and I thought he sounded very glum for a man whose new wife told half the world that all she wanted to do was make him happy. It was awfully soon for the bloom to be off the rose, like they say, but now that she had the ring, maybe this was who Sharon really was.

"You know, honey bees can't survive without strong lines of communication, and the queen substance is super important," I said.

"What's in it?" Tyler asked.

"Pheromones," I said. "Like a smell. It tells all the bees in the hive that everything is all right. Or it sends an alarm."

Chapter Seventeen
Bee Ware

When Archie and Sharon returned from Bermuda it was like a rigid and formal changing of the guard. The boys, of course, flew past me screaming *"Dad!"* He dropped his suitcases, picked the boys up, and swung them over and over. Sharon politely said hello and went into the house, which, for the record, was exactly as they had left it. She would not be able to find any fault with my housekeeping.

"Did y'all have fun in spite of the hospital? You've both got a nice tan!"

"We did," Archie said. "Bermuda is so beautiful, all that aqua water and the cottages all painted in pastels."

"I'll get there eventually," I said. "How about you, Sharon?"

"I wouldn't go back there if you gave me a billion dollars!" she said.

"Why not?" Tyler asked.

"Because I nearly died there! What's the matter with you? Didn't anyone tell you?"

"Sorry," Tyler said, crestfallen. "I'll just be in my room."

He quietly left the kitchen.

Hunter whispered to Archie, unfortunately too loudly, "See? You should've taken us instead."

"Little boy!" Sharon said in a huff. "Archie! Do something!"

Hunter shrugged his shoulders and ran to his room. I was just standing there, so awfully out of place.

"What would you like me to do, Sharon? Cane them? They're just kids."

"I should go," I said, and I couldn't wait to get out of there.

"Wait," she said. "Tell me something, Holly. Were the boys this horribly behaved for you?"

I didn't know what to say, and I sure didn't want to get drawn into a family dispute.

"This really isn't my business, but I think it might help if you tried to understand that children don't always pick up the nuances of adult conversation. They just don't. Tyler probably already forgot that you were so sick. Last week seems like a really long time ago to him, but it's like five minutes to you," I said. "And Hunter still can't understand why he and his brother didn't get to go on the trip to Bermuda. He was actually very disappointed. He thought the whole family should celebrate together."

"I agree with Holly," Archie said. "Try not to have such a short fuse, babe. Kids just aren't wired like adults. They have a different worldview. It's not personal. It's just juvenile."

"Oh, I don't know. Look, I never had kids! What do you expect from me?"

"Kindness," Archie said. "Kindness and understanding."

"Um, I left y'all a pot roast with roasted potatoes and carrots on the stove. I'll see y'all later."

I started walking out, and Archie followed me to the door.

"Holly, thank you for everything. Sharon is just overwhelmed. And wait, I have to give you money. Do you have receipts?"

"Forget it, Archie. Call it a wedding gift. Let me know if I can do anything, okay?"

I left and closed the door quietly behind me. I didn't even make eye contact with him. My intention was to leave them alone until they came to me. There was no more reason for me to cook for them or to do much else for the boys unless asked. And I felt like they probably needed some time alone to adjust to living together. It sure didn't look like they were off to a great start.

Well, it didn't take twenty-four hours for the boys to come banging on our door. They must've just come home from school.

"Hi guys! What's up?"

"You're not going to believe this," Tyler said.

"Yeah, you're not going to believe this," Hunter said.

"Well, come on in and tell me what I'm not going to believe," I said. "There's a lot in this world that's hard to believe."

They followed me to, where else, the kitchen.

"Anybody want cookies?"

"Sure!" they said. "Thanks!"

I poured two glasses of milk without asking and put a half dozen Oreos on the table.

"You have permission to dunk, sirs," I said and gave them a little salute.

"So," Tyler said, "last night I was taking a shower."

"We're taking showers now?" I said. "No more baths?"

"Sharon says baths are for babies," Hunter said.

"Oh? She does?"

"Yeah, she says that they're not sanitary because you sit in your own filth," Tyler said.

"Well, you could rinse off at the end, but what do I know?" I said.

"Exactly!" Tyler said and Hunter bobbed his head in agreement. "So, I'm in the dumb shower and she sticks her hand in the bathroom and turns off the light! She says something like, 'You've been in there long enough! You're wasting all the hot water!' I was like, are you kidding me?"

"Seems excessive to me," I said. "Did you tell your daddy?"

"Of course! You know what he said? He said, 'If Sharon says you've been in there too long, you probably were.' "

"Well, parents are supposed to support each other when it comes to the kids," I said.

Momma came into the room.

"What's new, boys?"

They repeated the story for her. I must say, she was filled with disgust.

She said, "What did I tell you? She's taking over." She poured herself a glass of tea and sat down at the table with us. "But turning off the lights when some-one's in the shower doesn't seem like a nice thing to do. What if you fell? You could really get hurt!"

My ears perked up. Nice thing to do? Suddenly, Momma was concerned with niceness?

"Look," I said, "you see how Hunter has dissolved his whole cookie in his milk?"

The boys giggled.

"Well," I continued, "that's kind of an odd way to eat a cookie. Wouldn't you agree?"

"Yeah," Tyler said. "It's disgusting."

"Okay," I said, bringing this argument to a close, "you've got your deal with cookies and she's got a thing about showers. I'll admit, it's an odd battle to pick. But who knows? Maybe she never had enough hot water when she was a kid or something like that."

"Yeah, maybe it's something like that," Tyler said.

"She did it to me, too," Hunter said.

"Well, so now you know one more thing about her," Momma said. "Just don't stay in the shower so long."

"If it happens again, ask her to set the kitchen timer for you to what she thinks is a fair amount of time," I said.

"You don't understand," Tyler said. "This isn't about water. This is because she doesn't like us."

"Come on, now," Momma said. "Didn't y'all promise to try really hard to give her a chance?"

"I guess so. Anyway, we've got homework. She's coming home early to help us, so I guess we'd better go."

"*She* is the cat's mother," Momma said.

"Huh?" Hunter said.

"You shouldn't call her 'she.' By the way, what are you calling her?"

"Oh! Listen to this! Did we tell you she said we should call her 'Mother'?"

"Yes, I was standing there. Remember?" I said.

"Oh, that's right," Hunter said, looking to Momma to explain. "I said we couldn't call her that because she wasn't our mother, that our mother was in heaven with the angels. She went nuts on us!"

"Yeah," Tyler said. "She did."

"It was awkward," I said.

"Oh, dear," Momma said. "I think it's going to take her a little more time to feel comfortable."

"I agree with Momma," I said, thinking I'd agreed

with her once again and was this becoming a trend? "She needs time."

"So what are you going to call her?" Momma said.

"I don't know. Probably Sharon. She's not ever going to be a momma to us," Tyler said.

"Give it time, sweetheart. Come on, I'll walk y'all home and stay until she gets there," I said.

I walked the boys home and as soon as I opened the door, Sharon's cats appeared and started meowing and meowing and meowing.

"What the heck is the matter with these two?"

"They're hungry," Tyler said.

"Well, then, let's feed the little devils," I said.

The boys and the cats went right to the kitchen and the boys started unpacking their backpacks. I dug around the cabinets, found a container of cat food, and looked around for their bowls. No bowls. No water bowls either.

"Hey, boys, do you know where the cat bowls are?"

The cats were walking in between and around my legs, and I found it unnerving. And annoying.

"Dishwasher," Hunter said.

Dishwasher? I thought and pulled down the door. Well, there were the animal dishes with the family's dishes, and I wondered if that could be sanitary. It didn't seem like a good idea, but anyway, I just took them out and filled one with cool water and the other with cat food and put them on the floor. The cats jumped on the bowls like they hadn't been fed in a month. I was relieved they weren't all over my legs.

The boys stacked up their worksheets and I looked at what they each had to do. Their assignments were light that day.

"Piece of cake," I said. "Let's get started."

The work was quickly completed and just as the last math problem was solved, we heard a car door. The Cat's Mother was home.

"I'm home!" she called out as she came through the door. "Let's get on that homework!"

"We're finished!" Hunter said.

"Yep! All done!" Tyler said.

She came into the room and saw me there.

"What are you doing here?" she said.

"I didn't think it was a good idea to send them into an empty house," I said. What had I done wrong?

"Oh, I see. So I canceled appointments for this afternoon to help the boys with homework and it's already done. That's just great."

I had unintentionally overstepped the boundary, just the thing I wanted to avoid.

"I'm sorry, Sharon. You're right. We should've waited for you. I apologize."

I got up to leave.

"You know how to find the door, don't you?" she said.

Jesus, I thought.

"Sure. See you boys later! By the way, I fed your cats."

I had tried to sound cheery, but I was mortified. I don't know why their homework being done should have made her that angry. She could take the boys to the playground. She could play a game with them. There were a million things she could have done with them, but she decided to be mad instead. Get mad, make everyone uncomfortable—I mean, what's the point of that?

I stopped by my apiary to check the water pans and while I was there, I told the bees the story. I told them that something had to be done about Sharon and if they could think of something to let me know. The bees seemed to be gathering and returning to the pink hive. It was late afternoon and the better part of the day was long gone, but it seemed to be a bit early for them to call it quitting time. Maybe it was going to rain. Bees knew those things, and the inhabitants of the pink hive seemed to be more tuned in to the world than the others. Every hive had its own personality, just like families in their homes. Sometimes, you'd get a queen who was too aggressive, and then the hive followed suit. The only way to correct the problem was to replace the queen. Ideally, you wanted a queen who just laid her two thousand eggs a day and went peacefully and quietly into the night when it was time for the next queen. But the hive was like life everywhere. Imperfect and subject to change.

We still had plenty of daylight left. The closer we got to summer, the longer the days. Winter on the island could be kind of dreary, so I was happy for the extended days.

I went back into the house and reported what had happened with Sharon to Momma and to Leslie, who had just come back from seeing Charlie again.

"She's impossible," Leslie said.

We had all just settled down in the den to watch the evening news or whatever we could agree on. Leslie made cheeseburgers and oven fries for us, which was a change from our normal protein, starch, and vegetable fare. To change things even more, we were eating dinner on TV tables that Momma got somewhere years ago. They folded up and hung on a rack. I'd seen all different kinds and these were easily the cheapest and most rickety, but they did the job. We were the kind of family that didn't replace things that still worked.

So, there we were, watching *Jeopardy!*, screaming

the answers at the television. It was the one show we all liked. Suddenly, there was banging on our door. Not polite knocking. Banging.

I went to answer it, suspecting it was something to do with Sharon.

I opened the door and, what do you know, there stood Sharon, red-faced and stuttering.

"Your goddamn bees!"

"What about them?"

"They shit all over my car. Not Archie's. Not the golf cart. My car! Mine!"

"I'm sorry, what? How do you know it was my bees?"

"Because I *saw* them!" She was screaming at me. "I saw them fly over your fence. There must've been thousands of them!"

I didn't like her tone.

"Would you like to stop screaming in my face?"

I had had it with her.

She stepped back and said at a more reasonable volume, "If this happens again, I'll call the police!"

"Go ahead. Honey bees don't poop in the hive. They take cleansing flights. I've never heard of bees picking out one target. They drop their tiny poops indiscriminately."

"Then how do you explain this?"

"Maybe you're just getting special treatment, Sharon. How would I know? Why don't you ask the bees?"

"I'm taking my car to the car wash and I'm sending you the bill," she said.

"And I'm going to finish my supper," I said.

I closed the door in her face. What was I supposed to do? Go wash her car? Oh, Lord. Did my bees sense something about her? Wait! *Did they understand the things I told them?* I was unsure if I should really believe that or not. Was it possible? Was it possible for bees to step in like that and give the enemy a warning? I leaned against the back of our front door and gave it a few moments of thought. It didn't matter if it was a coincidence or done in collaboration, it had occurred and that much was fact. Just like the bees had appeared at the wedding, disappeared, and then the seagulls stepped in.

"You won't believe what just happened," I said to Momma and Leslie.

"Wait until a commercial, okay?" Momma said. "I'm watching this and I can't hear with you yakking."

When I told them, Momma shrugged her shoulders and Leslie looked at me like I had lost large parts of my mind.

"You don't seriously believe that you told the bees

some trash about Sharon and then as a direct result of that conversation . . ."

"A few thousand of them did a little poop on her car. Maybe the bombing was deliberate. I don't know how the bees understood what I was so upset about, but I'd bet every dollar to my name that they did."

Well, naturally, the next day I reported Sharon's reaction to the poopers themselves.

"Look, I don't know what's happening here, but if y'all pooped on her car deliberately, I'm gonna plant you so much Culver's root and goldenrod you won't believe it!"

Honey bees loved anything with a purple flower. Culver's root was a spiky plant I'd put in near the edges of our marshy backyard. And goldenrod, native to our area, bloomed in a magnificent shade of yellow. The bees swarmed both species, so I knew they had a high-quality nectar and pollen. Christmas would come early for my girls.

"I just want to make you all happy! Even if you didn't do this on my behalf, thank you! Thank you!"

After the bombing of Sharon's car there was a short period of relative peace. I would see the boys a couple of times a week, and sometimes they'd wait at our house for either Archie or Sharon to come home from work. But they had certainly lost a lot of their spark. They were downright sullen.

"Is everything all right at home?" I finally asked.

"It's okay," Tyler said. "I'll be in college in ten years. I'll survive."

That wouldn't do. Maybe my bees needed another cleansing flight.

"Why do they call her the queen bee?" Hunter said.

*"Well, I think it might be because she's
everybody's mother," I said.*

Chapter Eighteen
Expanding Horizons

School would be out for the summer in mid-May. I knew Tyler had a birthday coming up in June, and I was already thinking about the cake I had promised him. My thought was to replicate the island's playground, because we'd had so much fun there while Archie and Sharon were away on that fabulous romantic honeymoon of theirs. I was thinking of using a whole sheet cake covered with green icing on the top to represent grass. I'd ice the sides in waves of blue, to make it seem like the water around our island. I'd already started looking for Lego sets that looked like playground equipment. I could make shrubs and children and even dogs of marzipan and tiny flowers of tissue. I was pretty excited. It was a lot more exciting than *Happy Birthday from the Gang!* on a ten-inch round that, depending on how you cut it, serves ten to fourteen.

When Carin was alive and one of the boys had a birthday, she'd have their whole class over, including their parents. I could still see Carin's beautiful face, flushed with joy as she replenished pitcher after pitcher of sweet tea and lemonade. Or as she stood in the sun, holding her hair back from her face because of a stiff breeze while she listened intently to another parent telling her whatever it was that concerned her. And I could see Archie, grilling hot dogs and burgers by the score, stopping to shake hands with this parent or that one or leaning down to take a special request from one of the children. Carin and Archie couldn't do enough to fete their birthday boys like princes.

I hoped the tradition would continue, because I felt like the more things went on as they had been, the easier it might be for the boys to continue to adjust to and move past all the traumatic changes.

Leslie and Charlie continued to correspond, and the date of his lip-sync competition grew closer. She came to the conclusion that she wasn't going to go to Las

QUEEN BEE • 257

Vegas for this whatever-it-was. But she was developing a broader view on the whole subject.

We were sitting on the porch in the dark, waiting for the stars to come out, just solving humanity's problems.

"Think about Dame Edna," she said to me. "That Australian guy? And what about that whole Monty Python gang? They were always dressing up as women. It doesn't mean a thing!"

"That's true," I said. I had to agree with her about them.

"And they're hilarious! It turns out that as Cher, Charlie is hilarious. I mean, who knew?"

"Really? How weird is that? Like Clark Kent has superpowers when he's wearing his cape?"

"Sort of. But yeah."

"The human mind is fascinating. If I had it to do over again I might be a neurologist or a psychiatrist. You going out tonight?"

"No, I think I need to spend some time really thinking about where my marriage is going. You know? And what do I want my future to look like?"

"You say that like you're in charge of it," I said.

"What? My future? Of course, I'm in charge. And, darlin' Holly, if you don't think you're in charge of yours, we've got a lot of talking to do."

"I could probably use some direction, because I think I may have painted myself into a corner."

"Well, then, we'll have to find a way for you to paint yourself out. I mean, your life should make sense. Example, if you look at Charlie's new lifestyle objectively, you can break it down to the point where it makes perfect sense," she said.

"Oh, please. Let me hear this new slant on the world," I said.

"Well, let's start with the things Charlie never told me about his childhood," she said.

"Wait a minute, I want to check the sky." I got up, stepped outside, and looked up. Only half the stars were visible, so I went back to my rocker. "Okay, I'm ready."

"Well, he was attracted to pretty things—you know, jewelry, perfume, or just good smells in general."

"Like what?"

"Well, fresh baskets of laundry that were still warm. He didn't like the smell of people's sweat. Apparently, when he got around anyone working in the yard in the heat of summer or around his father after a long tennis match, the smell of body odor made him nauseated."

"Can't say I'm a fan, either," I said.

"Well, anyway, that extended into high school. You can imagine, the locker room was disgusting to him. He had no desire to play sports other than tennis or golf. He was drawn to music and theater and the arts. On and on it goes. Dad's wool suits were scratchy. Mom's silk dresses were super nice to touch. Trying them on was even better."

"Where are we headed here?" I said.

"He was just simply never comfortable in the role of All-American Boy. But All-American Girl didn't appeal to him, either. He says he always felt stuck somewhere in the middle. He always liked girls and was attracted to girls and girl things. And he loved musical theater, especially when he was cast in something that required costumes and makeup—like pirates or some Greek play where they wore togas. It was why he became the drum major in our marching band. And, gosh, he was so good at it. Do you remember?"

"That's true. I remember him being all enthusiastic and twirling that big baton down the center of the football field at halftime. Always smiling. Yeah, he was a natural for that job. And I've gotta say that he *was* the most spirited drum major I've ever seen. He got everyone up and out of their seats, cheering like crazy!"

"That's just it. It makes him so happy to be somebody else for a while, especially if it involves impersonation of a big female star. I don't want to deny him that. Who's getting hurt?"

"No one, as far as I can see."

"I think he's just having fun. You know, you talk to bees. That honey you harvest gives you a thrill. Lucky for you that your thrills are within the boundaries of society's norms. There are so many people who suffer. You know, all the stigma, bias, and even hate crimes when all they're trying to do is be happy and not hurt anyone else."

"So you think Charlie's really a straight guy who just likes feminine things?"

"Yeah. I think this is how he was wired. Charlie is a good guy and we really love each other. But there *are* going to have to be some concessions."

"I understand. Like showing up at the wedding, un-invited and unannounced, all glammed up?"

"Exactly. I'm thinking if I could tell myself that when he dresses up, he's putting on his work clothes, like a costume, then maybe we could work something out. There's a time and place for everything, right?"

I didn't say a word. I could only imagine what she had put herself through to come to that conclusion.

"I don't know if that is how this works, Leslie. It may be that he wants to be Charlene more and more. Or it could be that Charlene gets boring and he'd prefer to be Charles. In a smoking jacket. With velvet slip-pers. I have no idea. But I sure do admire the hell out of you for trying so hard to find a solution. This is not your regular marital problem."

"I know, but I can't just throw us away, you know?"

"I know. You shouldn't. And look, not everybody wants to be a stevedore. People come in every size, color, and way we can imagine."

"Well, that's sort of the way I'm seeing it," she said.

"Look, you're my sister. Whatever you want to do, you know I'm going to support your decision."

This may not have looked like progress to the conventional world, but it was. Leslie had gone from an emphatic *this ain't happening no more* to a *let's talk about it*. Even Momma was going through some kind of evolution in her thoughts.

"I give my girl a lot of credit," she said over coffee the next morning.

"Yeah? How come?" I said and peeled four strips of bacon into my favorite cast-iron skillet.

"Because she's willing to really dive into this and try to resolve something instead of just running away, although she did have a couple of runaway nights there."

"Momma!" I said. "I think it would be best to view those few indiscretions another way, like maybe therapeutic?"

"If you say so. Want to bring in the paper? I forgot."

"Sure," I said. "I'll be right back. Watch the bacon for me, okay?"

I went outside and picked up the paper and here came Archie with the boys. Another day was beginning.

"Good morning! Not much school left!"

"Nope!" Tyler called out. "Five more days!"

"Freedom!" Hunter yelled.

"In the car," Archie said. "How are you, Holly? I haven't seen much of you lately."

"You mean since my bees dropped their you-know-what on Sharon's car?"

"That was unfortunate," he said. "And of course, it wasn't your fault."

"Duh, Archie." I gave him a smirk. "So, listen. That young man in your back seat is having a b-day soon, if I recall. Is there a party? Can I do the cake?"

Tyler had a huge grin on his face.

"Gonna be eight!"

"I know! That's so amazing!" I said.

Archie got the funniest look on his face.

"It's probably best if you discuss that with Sharon," he said.

I wanted to talk to Sharon like I wanted to have dinner with Satan and all his buddies.

"Well, maybe just ask her to let me know," I said. "Y'all have a great day!"

I turned and walked over to our house and climbed the steps without looking back. So that's how it was now? Sharon was the go-to person? I told myself if I didn't hear from her in a few days, I'd go over and see what the story was.

"What kept you so long?" Momma said. "Your bacon is done."

I told her about our exchange. She shook her head.

"Will you pour me some more coffee, please?" she said. "Sharon is the worst."

I refilled her cup and said, "This is news?"

Leslie walked into the kitchen, took a mug, and filled it.

"G'morning! What's going on?" she said.

We told her the story and she rolled her eyes somewhere up in her head.

"Oh, God. It's always going to be something with that beast," she said. "And she's cut off Archie's *cojones*. He's going to go along with whatever she wants."

I thought it was funny that Momma used to be the beast. Now Sharon was. But why was Archie letting Sharon call the shots?

"It's a shame," Momma said. "Such a shame. Do you think you might share your bacon, Holly?"

"Sure," I said and gave her half of what I'd fried. "You want toast?"

"I think I would," Momma said. "Thank you."

Hello? Who are you aliens that took my mother? Can you keep her? This one's halfway nice.

"You're welcome," I said and dropped two slices of white bread in the toaster.

"I've gotta go and pack," Leslie said.

"Really? Where are you going?" Momma said.

"Vegas, to see my husband. I'll be back Sunday," she said. "He has been begging me to come since the first day he got there."

"Well, you tell him I said, if we're going to have a female impersonator in the family," Momma said, "he'd better be the best damn one the world has ever seen!"

"Oh, Momma!" Leslie said. "That is like the sweetest thing you've ever said to me."

I thought I had better go lie down.

Leslie left for Las Vegas, and I didn't hear anything from Sharon over the next three days, so I took a deep breath and called Sharon that night. She answered on the first ring, but I didn't read anything into that.

"Sharon? Hey, it's me, Holly."

"Hi, Holly. What's going on?"

"Not much. How are y'all doing?"

"Great, thanks."

"So I was just thinking about Tyler's birthday. It's right around the corner."

"I'm aware," she said.

Ooooh, boy. I thought. This is not going to go down as I had hoped.

"I'd like to make a cake for him and I wanted to make sure it was all right with you."

"Of course! By all means. Make him a cake. That's very nice of you."

"Well, I'm delighted to do it. So, if you could just tell me how many people you're expecting at his party so there's enough to go around."

"Let's see. Well, my parents, so that's two, my aunt and uncle, so that's four, Archie, me naturally, and of course the boys. That's eight."

I was a little stunned.

"What about Tyler's friends?"

"You mean you're thinking we should have fifty children running around, screaming and making a mess? No, no. In my family, birthdays are strictly for family only. I would send cupcakes to school, but school is out for the summer."

"I see. Okay then. I'll make a cake for eight."

"With a little extra for my family to take home."

"Sure thing." Was she kidding? "What day are y'all

celebrating?" It was all I could do to hide the disappointment in my voice.

"Oh, I think Sunday afternoon would be nice, say early dinnertime?"

"Okay, I'll drop it off after church."

His actual birthday was Thursday. What in the world was going through her head? What planet was she from? She was all set to deny Tyler a birthday party with his friends when every single child in his class had a party. But Tyler should celebrate four days late with her parents? I was furious. There was nothing I could do. Nothing. Except, I told my bees.

"There's no fourth floor in the Nobu Hotel,"
Charlie said.

"Why not?" I said.

"Because in Asia the number four is bad luck,
and in this town they don't tempt luck!"

Chapter Nineteen
Leslie and Cher

I am telling you that when I got off the plane in Las Vegas I thought I would die from the spectacle of it all. There were slot machines all over the airport and a kind of excitement in the air I'd never felt before. You could see the anticipation in the faces of arriving passengers that they were about to have the vacation of their lives. And win a fortune. And others waiting at gates filled with disappointment.

I spent a little time talking to a guy next to me on the plane, and he said he came to Las Vegas all the time. He said every night he'd see a show, have a big dinner, and then go to the casinos. Every night would be different entertainment, a different restaurant, and another casino. He was meeting his brother there, who was coming from just north of San Francisco. They did this every year without their wives, just the two of them. I thought, Well, why not? But Las Vegas didn't really hold a lot of appeal for me. Okay, I'd never been there, but gambling wasn't my thing. I was doing this for Charlie. My sweet Charlie.

And Charlie was excited. He met me in baggage claim and was talking nonstop.

"Kiss kiss!" He kissed my cheeks and continued. "How was your flight? Don't you look wonderful! Do you have luggage?"

"No, just this roller," I said.

"Well, did you eat? Are you starving? The Mexican food in this town is AH-mazing! Or would you like sushi? I could always eat sushi."

"I'm fine, Charlie. I ate."

"Okay, well then, let's get a move on!"

He took my roller and I followed him through the terminal and out to the parking garage. He was walking so fast I could hardly keep up with him.

"Charlie! Slow down!"

"Oh, sorry, Leslie. I guess I'm excited to show you everything."

"Well, so far, even the airport is pretty colorful!"

Charlie stopped at an unfamiliar car, a bright red Toyota RAV4, unlocked it, and raised the hatch door. He put my suitcase in and slammed it shut.

"New car?" I said. Charlie usually drove a luxury car, so I was a little surprised.

"Yeah, a new car for the new me."

I thought, Oh boy, exactly who is this *new me* going to turn out to be?

"So the climate here is one of the best things to recommend it. I mean, it's hot like hell in July, but it's hot in Maine in July, isn't it?"

"Yes. And I think it's pretty dry here, too, isn't it?" I said.

"Yes, you'll have great hair here."

He drove, talking the whole time about all the things he loved about Las Vegas.

"I rented an apartment, too. Wait until you see it. It's very tiny, but until I get to know the town, it's very centrally located to the Strip and all that."

"You rented an apartment? Charlie, we have a house in Ohio."

"I'm aware," he said. "But I have to tell you, you

couldn't pay me any amount of money in the entire world to shovel snow again."

"You never shoveled snow. Not once. I did. And salted the walkways and steps."

"Well. It was a pain in the neck to deal with all your complaining about shoveling it then."

"Oh, Charlie." What was he saying? "Are you saying we should sell our house in Glenwillow?"

"Not today. But if my plan works, yes, we should. You'll like it here so much better. We're close to Sedona, you know. A mere four-hour drive. We can go sit on the vortex and meditate."

"The vortex?"

"Yes, the vortex. Sedona, Arizona, is in the Verde Valley, which is one of the most spectacular places on this entire planet. Think Wile E. Coyote. But there is the spot called the Red Rock that some people think is an alien spaceship or a portal to another dimension. It's very popular with psychics and artists. Sedona used to be full of old people and hippies, but now it's got more private jets coming and going than you can count."

"What makes it a vortex? I mean, isn't a vortex something that's moving? Seems to me that the desert is pretty still."

"I think you're right, and I don't know why they call

it that, either. But it's supposed to be a place where you meditate more deeply and maybe the cosmos speaks to you."

"Yeah, well, right now the cosmos is telling me that you're losing your grip on reality."

We were driving along the famous Strip, where all the big casinos and hotels are located. It was very garish and loud. Not historic Charleston one teeny bit.

"No, I'm not. Isn't this something?"

"You know, maybe it's the Catholic girl in me, but I feel like if I look this place square in the eyeball, I'll be turned into a pillar of salt."

He laughed and then I did, too. All Las Vegas was, really, was an adult Disneyland, where new crazy dreams were born and other, old, worn-out dreams came to die. Treated with the right amount of self-control, it might be fun.

"A pillar of salt, indeed!"

We were then on West Flamingo Road and we turned on Arville Street.

"We're almost home," he said.

I thought, Yes, your home. Not mine. Yours.

Finally, he turned onto West Rochelle Avenue and into his apartment complex, called Rancho del Sol. The landscaping was really beautiful. And the buildings were lovely. No one ever said Charlie had bad taste.

"This looks very nice, babe," I said. "You have a pool, I hope?"

"We have a pool!" he said. "And tennis courts and a gym and a party space and a beautiful terrace where we can sit outside in the shade or the sun and have a glass of some wonderful California agricultural product."

He pulled into a parking space. We got out, and Charlie got my bag and rolled it up to his front door. He unlocked it and went inside. It was fully furnished. In white. And chrome. No plants. No artwork. But a huge television over the fireplace. And a lot of mirrors.

"Where did you get all this?"

"It's all rented until we make up our minds," he said. "Except for the television. I bought that. And the stereo and some linens and kitchen stuff. What do you think?"

"I think it could benefit from a woman's touch. It's a little cold."

"Yes, but considering I've only been here for ten days, it's not bad, right? And it's only temporary. At some point, we'll want to look for a house."

I looked all around and said, "No, it's not bad at all."

As usual, Charlie was operating on a lot of assumptions. I thought about strangling him for making all these decisions that truly did not include me, and I thought about telling him that this felt like I had moved from wife and lover to friend status. But maybe that's what he was telling me. Anyway, I had come here to support him in his performance, and that's what I intended to do. I could choke him before I left on Sunday.

"So what's the plan?"

"I have to be at the club by six. Competition starts at six thirty."

"Okay, are you ready for this?"

"I'm ready and I'm excited. You see, this is all part of my master plan. Instead of working retail or working in my family's business, I'm going to make it on my own as a female impersonator. I'm going to get a full-time gig doing this and support us with money I earn."

"Charlie, you know I love you, right?"

"I depend on it."

"Let's just take this one step at a time. Let's focus on tonight."

And we did. Charlie put on his full Cher costume, complete with false eyelashes, enough makeup for ten women, and fake-diamond bangle bracelets over his elbow-length gloves. The dress was pretty simple, a long gown of black jersey knit shot through all over with tiny black jets that shimmered. It was the wig that did me in. When Charlie put the wig on, he was more Cher than Cher. After we practiced his routine four times at his apartment, we went to the club.

"I'm nervous," he said.

"Listen, make your nervous energy work for you and keep your eyes on me."

"Okay."

I took a seat in the audience and watched: Cher, Cher, Judy Garland, Judy Garland, Diana Ross, Barbra Streisand, Gaga, Gaga, several Bette Midlers, and ten more Barbras. Finally, my Cher came on. "Gypsys, Tramps & Thieves" was a great choice because it had more soul than a lot of Cher's other hits. And Charlie had everyone on their feet clapping and whistling by the time he was done. I gave him a thumbs-up from the audience and he blew me a kiss.

It was another Cher who took the prize that night lip-syncing "Believe," which was perhaps more of a crowd-pleaser, but Charlie came away with a thousand-dollar prize for best new talent.

"What did you think?" he said, hungry for praise.

"I think you've got a whole new life in front of you, Charlie, and I love you and only wish every good thing in the world for you, but . . ."

"You're going back to Charleston."

"Yes. Yes, I am."

"There's only one queen bee in each hive," I said.

"How come?" Hunter said.

"Because somebody has to be in charge."

Chapter Twenty
Wigged Out

I knew it was the boys' last day of school. How did I know? I knew because I paid attention, that's why. Was Sharon there to help the boys clean out their lockers and cubbies? Of course not. Did she ask me to go help? Nope. Was every other parent or nanny there to help them? With little gifts for the teachers, and taking pictures, and bringing treats for the end-of-year class parties? Of course! So when Sharon got a call from the school that she was remiss in her duties, she had to

276 • DOROTHEA BENTON FRANK

leave her office and go. According to Tyler, she wasn't too happy.

I knew this because she dropped the boys off at my house. She was going back to her office. And, as it can be in May, it was an unusually hot day. That kind of weather drives the bees from the hives because it's too hot in there. Generally, what they do is find a cool spot and hang together in a formation that looks like a beard. That day they were hanging on the live oak tree in our backyard. If Sharon had seen them, she might have gone running and screaming to the police station.

"Come in! Come in!" I said when I answered the door. Tyler and Hunter ran by me, headed straight for the kitchen. There on the table was a cake that said *Congratulations Tyler and Hunter! Another Great Year in School! Happy Summer!* Of course, it was a full sheet cake, because I needed the room to write all that I wanted to say.

I had a big flat-bottomed basket, and in there were plates and napkins and plenty of small cold bottles of water, stacked up, ready to go.

"Want to take all this over to the playground and see who shows up?"

They were twitching and moving their weight from one foot to the other.

"Yeah!"

"Okay, but go to the bathroom first, okay?"

"Okay!"

They scampered like puppies, bumping into each other to see who would get there first. I was very pleased with myself in that moment.

This time we took their golf cart since we had so much to carry. Don't you know half of their classmates were there at the playground? Tyler and Hunter were so excited. I pulled over and stopped, and they jumped off the cart and ran ahead, emptyhanded, I might add.

The kids were literally jumping up and down like mad and screaming, "No more school until August!" and "It's officially summer!" We, the adults, looked to each other, remembering our own youth and how exciting it was to consider the promise of summer and all it might bring—vacations, days at the beach, flip-flops, sleepovers with friends, barbecues, fish fries, baseball games—there was an endless list. For me, I could remember trying to get the perfect tan without burning. Leslie, of course, had a tan after one afternoon on the beach. I used to be jealous of all those things, but these days I just remembered them and said, I'd so rather be me.

I took the cake over to the picnic table, went back for the plates, napkins, and water, and got it all organized. Tyler came running over with a couple of boys.

"We're ready!" Tyler said.

"Aren't you going to introduce me to your friends?" I said.

"I'm Tommy and this is Brian," Tommy said, before Tyler could respond. "Are you the nanny?"

"Nope," I said. "I'm the next-door neighbor sort of aunt and sort of really great friend."

Tyler gave me a huge hug and Tommy threw him a little grief.

"Hugging your *best friend*?" Tommy sang it in baby talk.

Tyler spun around on his heel and said, "Oh, yeah? Well, who bought *you* a cake?"

"No one! I see your point, sir!" Tommy said.

"I'm Brian," Brian said. "And I would like a piece of cake, please."

"Brian has the best manners in our class," Tommy said solemnly, as though this was simply a goal beyond his reach.

"Well, I'll tell you what. If you boys will go tell everyone there's cake and water bottles, I'll give you the corner pieces! They have the most icing."

It didn't take two minutes for every kid on the playground to appear, hovering like locusts.

"Okay! Anybody got a peanut allergy?"

No one said a word.

"Anybody gluten free or vegan?"

Sounds crazy, but you had to ask these days.

There being no allergies or health concerns that fessed up, I had one last announcement.

"When you're done, what are you going to do with your plate and napkins?" I pointed to the giant trash barrel to help them out with the answer.

"Put them in the garbage!" came the loud response.

Two of the other women there supervising their charges stepped in to help me.

"Hey, I'm Alice," one of them said. "This is so nice of you. How can I help?"

"I think we need more cake in our lives," I said. "It's nice to meet you. Pass out cake to all these varmints?"

"Happy to! More cake in our lives sounds excellent!"

"I can give out water bottles? Hi! I'm Maureen Thomas," the other woman said.

"That would be great," I said.

I thought to myself then that these were two ladies I'd probably like to know. They had just stepped right up to help. I liked that. It wouldn't kill me to have a few friends. But, as we all know, ever since Leslie married Charlie, I'd been captive. Well, enough of that. Momma was completely ambulatory. She didn't need a nurse. What she needed was the same thing I needed—more fun. Plain and simple. We *both* needed more fun.

"So do you live on the island?" I asked Maureen.

"Yes. My husband and I just moved here from Nashville. He's working for Boeing."

"Wow, that's a heckuva commute for him."

"Well, we wanted Matthew to be able to attend Sullivan's Island Elementary School," she said. "You know, you make all sorts of unbelievable sacrifices for your kids, right?" She sort of laughed.

"Yeah. Living on the island is a terrible sacrifice."

And she added, "And I inherited this big old house on the beach when my grandmomma went to her great reward."

"How cool is that? Well, the school is absolutely idyllic, like something out of a dream."

"It is. So, are Tyler and Hunter yours?" she said.

"Sadly, no. They're my next-door neighbor's children. Their mother was killed in a terrible car accident . . ."

I told her the story because she seemed to want to know the details.

"I heard about this. How awful. And he's already married again? Pretty quick, huh?"

"I thought so, but it's really none of my business," I said.

"Well, what's she like?"

I thought about it for a moment before I spoke because I didn't want the story to travel. But on the other hand, why not stick it to Sharon with a total stranger? Just a little.

"The real reason I brought this cake to the park is because Tyler's birthday is next Thursday and he's not having a party because *she* doesn't believe in them."

"So she's a big ol' bitch?"

"Kind of the biggest one I ever met," I said. "She's having her parents and her aunt and uncle over for cake on the Sunday after his birthday."

"And that's it?"

"Yep."

"Poor little guy! Oh, I just hate that story," Maureen said.

"Me, too."

We stood there and watched as Tyler ran around with Brian, Tommy, and her Matthew. And twenty other kids were playing tag, shooting hoops, and just generally having the time of their lives. On further inspection, I saw Hunter was hanging upside down on the jungle gym.

"Hunter!" I called out. "Get down from there!"

"He'll break his neck," Maureen said.

"No, he won't. He's part monkey. *Hunter! Get down this instant!*"

Hunter climbed down by grabbing the bar from

which he was hanging and doing a flip, squarely hitting the ground like a junior Olympic gymnast.

"Kids," she said.

We both grinned and shook our heads, but I hoped Hunter did not see that. He didn't need an ounce of encouragement.

There was a magical Lowcountry mood that afternoon, as though the invisible sirens of Sullivan's Island were poised to swoop down from the tops of all the bushy palmetto trees on the island to claim the boys of summer as their own. It made my heart swell to see all their energy and happiness. It was a snapshot I'd never forget.

Maureen said, "His birthday is next Thursday, you said?"

"Yes."

"Then why don't we throw him a surprise party at my house?"

What an amazing idea. Amazing.

"Maureen? I think I want to be your best friend. Brilliant idea! When Sharon finds out, she'll kill me. But this would be the first year of his life without his mother, with no real party and no friends to celebrate with. So let her kill me."

"I'll be your best friend. And, just so you know, I'm not afraid of her."

Maureen was right. What could Sharon do?

"All righty then. Let's do it! I'll bring the cake."

"I'll get pizza and sodas," she said. "We should invite a few parents, too. You know, to supervise."

"And a teenager who's a certified lifeguard?"

"Excellent idea!"

Over the next half hour our plan came together. Tyler and Hunter would think they were just going over to Matthew's for a swim and maybe supper. They should arrive at three. The other kids would get there at two. They would hide in the bushes, jump out, and yell *surprise!* Tyler was going to lose his mind! I was getting excited. And I loved having a secret. We exchanged phone numbers and promised to talk over the next week.

We chugged slowly along Middle Street as we tried to take the golf cart home. The battery was dying.

"As soon as we get home, I'll put it on the charger," Tyler said, sounding very much like an adult.

"You are such a good helper, Tyler!" I said.

"I'm a good helper, too," Hunter said.

"Of course you are, sweetheart!"

It was somewhere around five o'clock. Archie and Sharon's cars were in the drive. I was carrying leftover cake and surplus plates and napkins over to our house. Sharon met the boys on the porch.

I heard her say, "Dinner is at five o'clock. You *know* that. It's five thirty. The kitchen is closed. Sorry. There will be no dinner for either one of you."

"But we can't tell time!" Tyler wailed.

"Then I suggest you learn how."

She had to be the worst woman in the whole entire world to step into Carin's shoes. What in the name of everything holy did Archie see in her? I went inside and called Domino's, paid for a pizza with my credit card, and told them to deliver it anonymously to Tyler. It was really my fault that they were late. I didn't know about the dinner rule. But a pizza would send a strong message.

I waited and watched. Fortunately, it was Archie who opened the door when Domino's arrived. He took the pizza and went inside. I wondered then if he knew it was from me. He was so dense these days, he probably thought it was a gift from the heavens, like manna.

Next Thursday couldn't get here fast enough. But Sunday came first, and that meant Leslie's return. She came rolling in around four in the afternoon. Momma and I were in the kitchen, drinking tea and waiting for her.

"So? How was it?" I asked.

"It was insane, just as you'd expect. Charlie won a special award for emerging talent. A thousand dollars and a trophy. He had a ball. I was completely over-whelmed by the spectacle of the whole thing."

"A little more detail would be nice," Momma said, in her more caustic voice, because she had been starved of Leslie's company for a few days.

"Well, let's put it this way. If you went to a bar with impersonators on the outskirts of Charleston, you'd have one level of costume. You know, a nice gown but maybe the wig might be of a type that is natural hair, trying to pass for Ann-Margret when she was young."

"I wouldn't know," Momma said.

"But when you go to Las Vegas, the ladies there have on *extraordinary* wigs, eyelashes so long and thick they're like awnings, glitter in their makeup and on their bodies, gorgeous gowns like they wore in the old days of Hollywood, and so much jewelry it borders on garish. They've got huge attitude that's regal but naughty and sassy at the same time. And most of them have hilariously funny personalities. I think quite a few of them started out doing stand-up and for one reason or another, they graduated to impersonators who also do stand-up."

"Did you take pictures?" Momma said.

"Of course!" Leslie said.

"Let's see," Momma said.

Leslie clicked around on her phone and then slid it

over to Momma. I got up and stood behind her so I could see them, too.

"You were not exaggerating," I said.

"No, she did not stretch the truth," Momma said.

From one to the next, the ladies were stunningly beautiful, and you could not tell they weren't women. Then we came to the pictures of Charlie. He paled by comparison in terms of hair, wardrobe, and accessories. Momma sat back and considered his pictures for a moment or two, and then she scrolled back to the others.

"I used to sew, you know. In fact, you know I always wanted to be a pattern maker."

I had forgotten that, but it was true. When Leslie and I were little, Momma had at least three Singer sewing machines, always trading up. But what was she saying? Was she offering to sew for Charlie?

Then she scrolled back to the other female impersonators.

"Looks like Charlie's wearing a prom dress next to those other ladies," she said. "I can't stand by and let him look like that. He'll never get anywhere if that's what the competition looks like."

"What do you mean?" Leslie said.

"I mean, I could probably make a few gowns for him

every so often when he's got a new show coming up. It might be fun, and he'll certainly be no more worse off than he is in this getup. What do you think?"

"You mean you'd come to Las Vegas and stay with us and do this?" Leslie said.

I was just trying to keep my jaw off the floor.

"Yeah, that's exactly what I mean. I wouldn't be moving in with you permanently, but I couldn't really do this for him from this island, now could I? And we need to find him a wig maker. Farrah Fawcett he isn't, with all those wings and wisps. He looks like a refugee from the 1980s."

Okay, it wasn't lost on me that my mother now fancied herself to be a fashion maven. And she expected us to believe her.

Leslie did.

"Oh, Momma! That would be so wonderful! Charlie will be so thrilled! The thing is, the gowns *have* to be custom! Oh! I can't wait to tell him!"

She ran from the room to call him.

"Let me get this straight. You're going to get on a plane and fly to Las Vegas and live with Leslie while you sew for Charlie."

"Yes," she said.

"Okay," I said and thought, Now I've heard it all.

"Don't ever eat bananas around a beehive," I said.

"Why not?" they said.

"Because the smell of them
might cause the bees to swarm."

Chapter Twenty-One
Splash!

Momma was out shopping for luxury fabrics with Leslie. That whole situation still boggled my mind. If you'd told me a year ago my momma would get out of bed, I'd have said, fat chance. And if you'd told me she'd be designing and making evening gowns for her son-in-law's lip-sync competitions, I'd have thought you'd lost your damn mind. But then, Momma would do *anything* for Leslie. And it turned out that Leslie would do just about anything for Charlie.

So I was on my own to take up a small problem with Archie. His car was in the driveway. He must not have had classes that afternoon. I walked across the street and rang their doorbell.

Archie answered after a few moments.

"Hi, Holly! What's going on?"

"Archie? Is there a place we can talk without being overheard?"

"Sure," he said and stepped out onto the porch, closing the door behind him quietly. "Is something wrong?"

"I'm not sure where to start. Tyler is a popular kid, but I assume you know that. Hunter is as well."

"I assume they have friends at school," he said.

I thought, The thing to say would've been, *I know they have a lot of nice friends. They used to come here all the time.* But the waters had been sullied and all the rules had changed. Now, maybe they had friends at school. And they were no longer welcome.

"Yes. They have a lot of them, good kids from nice families. Anyway, there's a new child, Matthew, who's just moved here from Tennessee. His dad works for Boeing. His momma's name is Maureen Thomas.

Maureen inherited a big house on the beach over at Station Twenty-seven from her grandmother. In an effort to make friends for her son, she planned a birthday party for Tyler."

"When is this party supposed to take place?"

"This afternoon."

"Well, Tyler's in lockdown."

"Again?"

"Yeah."

"So I suppose Maureen went to great effort?"

"Yes." I was quiet and just stared at him for a few minutes. "Balloons, a lifeguard, twenty kids . . ."

"Well, this is a dilemma." He stared at me, seeming lost.

"I know," I said. "Look, Archie. This will be the first time in his life he hasn't had a birthday celebration with his friends. And I know it's none of my business, but does the punishment fit the crime?"

He paused before answering me.

"Between us? I thought being grounded for a week was too harsh. But I have to back up Sharon, even when she's over the top, or else it undermines our relationship. You understand that, don't you?"

I chose my words carefully.

"What I understand is that it's a little boy's birthday today, who barely a year ago lost his mother, who's got to be on his mind, especially today, and that he's got a stepmother that may not be the perfect fit. And no matter what he did or said, this punishment isn't going to make him love Sharon. It's only going to make him miss his own mother even more."

"Did you ever think about becoming a child psychologist?"

"I've toyed with a lot of different ideas about my future. But do you see what I'm talking about?"

"I'll call Sharon and see if I can get him some time off for good behavior. Maybe even get the whole sentence commuted."

"There you go! Great! Thanks, Archie."

"It would be a shame for Tyler to miss his own party." He looked at me in such a funny way, and then he said something so stupid, I almost fell off the porch. He said, "Why do you care so much?"

I wanted to say, Why don't you care more?

"Because I really love Hunter and Tyler, that's why. I have since you and Carin brought them home from the hospital."

Archie stood there on the porch, reminiscing.

"I miss her, you know?" he said.

"I know. Everyone does, but I think your boys might miss her the most."

Archie nodded his head.

"Thanks, Holly. Somehow I always find myself thanking you for something. What can I do to make up for all you do for us?"

Well, I thought, you could toss Sharon off the top of the Ravenel Bridge into the Cooper River and let the sharks eat her. That would take care of it.

"You know, before you got married, I had a conversation with the boys. They both said they didn't want another mother, that they liked things just as they were. Y'all had a boys' club, in their mind anyway. Just you and them against the world, and together, nothing would ever hurt them again. With Sharon on the scene, they lost that, too. Do you see what I mean?"

"Do you think I made a mistake marrying Sharon?"

"Do you?"

"No."

"Well, then . . . good." I looked at the ground as my face got red and hot. "Maybe, if you wanted to do something, just try to temper Sharon's rules and regulations. There might be a few that could be loosened up a bit."

The look on his face said that I might have won Tyler a reprieve, but I had inadvertently embarrassed Archie by implying he wasn't giving enough vigilance to what was going on. He knew that I knew he had simply turned the boys over to Sharon to raise like house plants. He also knew I knew she was doing a terrible disservice to two little boys who deserved one helluva lot more than they were getting.

"I can take them over to Maureen's if you'd like," I said.

"Let me talk to Sharon first," he said. "I'll call you, okay?"

"Sure," I said. I went down the stairs into the yard and turned back. "Archie?"

He just stood there looking at me.

"It's his birthday. Come on. He's just a little boy."

"I'll call you," he said.

What else could he say?

I went home and called Maureen, telling her every detail.

"So that's the latest," I said.

"What do you think?"

"I think that if she doesn't let this child come to his own birthday party, I'll be so furious with Sharon, I'll rip her head off. How's that?"

"I'll help you."

And so, I waited and waited and waited.

I went out to my apiary to check on the girls. Naturally, I told them everything. My cell phone rang in my back pocket. It was Archie. I took off my gloves and answered it.

"Sharon said no," he said.

"Are you serious? You *can't* be serious!"

"She really feels very strongly that Tyler needs to learn a lesson. Holly, he called her a terrible name. He can't do that."

"So let me get this straight. Hunter is going to Tyler's birthday party without him?"

"When she found out there was a party for Tyler and that she had not been told the truth, she was furious. Hunter isn't going, either."

"Why?" I asked.

"Because she thinks they both knew and didn't tell her."

"It's a surprise party, Archie."

"She's got the final word, Holly. She's coming home at two thirty to talk to him."

"Y'all are unbelievable." I hit the end button. I turned back to my hives, told them the story, and said, "What now?"

It didn't take long for me to get an answer to that question. At precisely two thirty, Sharon pulled up in the driveway. My bees from the pink hive bearded her car, so many of them that all the windows were covered. I could see them leave the hive as they flew over in a swarm. She started blowing her horn over and over.

"Help!" Sharon was screaming bloody murder. "Help! Archie! Help!"

The bees were undeterred. Archie and the boys came running out of the house and stopped dead in their tracks when they saw what was happening.

"Call the police!" she was screaming. "Call them!"

She turned her windshield wipers on and began spraying them with the wiper fluid. This infuriated the bees, who quickly flew away and joined their sisters on the sides of the car.

I saw Archie give Tyler a push to come over to our house, presumably to get me. Maybe he thought I could do something.

I met him at the door.

"What's going on, Tyler? Happy birthday, by the way."

"Thanks! There's a billion bees that have Sharon trapped in her car! Dad says for you to come quick!"

"I'll be along in a minute. Let me get my suit on."

He followed me through the house and out the back door to my shed.

"I don't know why he thinks I can do a thing about it," I said. "Now, Tyler, I want you to stand way back from her car, okay? Maybe my smoker will help. Maybe it won't. Let's hope."

I pulled my veil down and lit my smoker. When I got to the scene, Sharon was beyond hysterical.

"You're a menace!" she was screaming at me. "I'm going to sue you for a million dollars!"

"Good luck with that," I said and started smoking the girls. They began to land on me, and when I had them all, and I estimated ten thousand or so, I simply began walking them back to their hive.

"The bees are all over her!" Sharon screamed. "Oh, my God! She's a freak!"

"No. I'm not. I'm a beekeeper," I said calmly.

A few bees, which might have been affected by the windshield washer fluid, hung back.

"Maybe that will teach her a lesson," I said quietly to them. "I love you, girls!"

They buzzed all around me in a waggle and returned home to their hive.

It goes without saying that Tyler was allowed to go to his party with Hunter and all charges against him were dropped by his jailer. Archie told me that he'd had a chat with Sharon and told her she was being too strict. She was so upset about my bees swarming her car that she relented. I drove them to Maureen's with the cake tucked away out of their sight in the back of my SUV. Sure enough, it represented the Sullivan's Island playground, with a tiny marzipan Tyler playing basketball with Matthew and Brian, and Hunter hanging upside down from the monkey bars.

Tyler shrieked with delight when the kids yelled, *"Surprise!"* There were presents and pizza and cannonballs into the pool. They played Marco Polo until the adults couldn't stand it for another minute. They dried off and sang "Happy Birthday" loud enough to wake the dead; Tyler blew out the candles and they all ate cake. The parents took pictures of everything. Tyler's parents weren't there, but he was absolutely beaming with happiness. That was all I wanted to see. If Carin was watching she'd be pleased.

Maureen finally got around to asking me how I got Tyler out of restriction and to the party.

"I had just about given up and I thought, Well, we'll have the party anyway," she said.

"You're right. My honey bees helped me."

"You keep honey bees?" Alice said. "I love them!"

"No, how wonderful!" Maureen said. "They're the most fascinating little creatures, aren't they?"

"Uh, yass. Listen to *this* story."

I told them about the bees and how I talk to them. Then I told them the story about how they used Sharon's car for target practice on their cleansing flight and about how today they swarmed her windows. They didn't know how to respond to the implications of what I had just told them.

"Well, first of all," Maureen said, "I can't even begin to tell you how happy I am we put this little shindig together for Tyler. That is one precious little boy."

"He was tickled to bits," Alice said.

"And don't you know he was probably missing his momma today?" I said. "It's his first birthday without her."

"Poor baby," Alice said. "Well, time for me to go."

Alice gave Tyler and Hunter a ride home with all of Tyler's gifts, and I stayed behind to help Maureen finish cleaning up. Everyone else had said good-bye and gone home.

"Those kids are going to sleep like stones tonight," I said. "They hardly got out of the pool, except to eat."

"Yeah, they will sleep good, but my yard looks like we were hit by a tornado!" Maureen said.

"Don't worry," I said. "We'll make it all go away. I need a big black garbage bag."

She handed me one and I started wadding up wrapping paper and ribbon.

"I'm not worried in the least! But now that I have you alone, I want to ask you something."

"Sure! Anything."

"Do you think the bees acted in response to the stories you told them?"

"Maureen?" I laughed and shook my head. "You're going to learn all about the Lowcountry. You're not in Tennessee anymore."

"That's for sure, but you didn't answer my question."

"Okay, here's what I think. I think there is no scientific proof anywhere, in any written record, that bees can do your bidding. It's impossible. They have hive mentality, and they only work to preserve the queen and the hive. They can't decide, oh, that Sharon is a terrible wretch who needs to know we're onto her psychodrama. That's not what bees do. It's not their nature."

"Okay. But aren't there bees that kill?"

"Yes. African bees are super aggressive. But honey bees are sweethearts. Anyway, Maureen, you did a really good thing today."

"So did your bees," she said.

"I know."

"Guess what happens to the drone bees?" I said.

"What?" Hunter asked.

"When it cools off in the fall,
they get thrown out of the hive."

Chapter Twenty-Two
The Vapors (Part 2)

When I got home, there was a police car in front of Archie's house. I thought, Oh, come on. Really? What was the point of that? I went in our house. Momma was in the dining room. She had pushed all the catalogs and magazines aside and was spreading swatches of fabric by color group.

"Hey!" I said, curious to see what she had brought home.

"Hay is for horses," she said.

"Fine. Did you and Leslie have a successful shopping trip?"

"Well, we got started. It's a big project, you know."

"No, I *do* know!" I said.

She said, "Well, do you know why the authorities are parked in front of Archie's house?"

"Maybe."

"Would you like to share?"

"My bees from the pink hive might have bearded Sharon's car with her in it when she refused to let Tyler go to his own birthday party."

She smiled wider than I had seen her smile in years.

"I see. Isn't this a pretty shade of green? Very dramatic," she said. "And you're leaving out some details, I think."

"Maybe."

"Why don't you get your poor old mother a glass of tea and we can chat for a few minutes."

"I'd be delighted to," I said. "Where's Leslie?"

"In her room, on the phone with Charlie. What else is new?"

I poured two glasses of iced tea for us and just as we sat down, the doorbell rang. I knew it was the police. Hopefully, someone I knew. It was.

"Well, hey, Ted," I said with a big old innocent smile.

"Hey, Holly," he said with a smile to match mine.

I'd seen him at Publix. We had gone to high school together. I used to let him copy my biology homework. He was a hottie then and he was still a hottie. His blue eyes were almost translucent. Like me, he never dated anyone back then.

"Come on in. I was just getting ready to have a glass of iced tea with Momma. Can I pour a glass for you?"

"That would be awfully nice. Today sure was a hot one."

Ted followed me to the kitchen where Momma sat, waiting. She looked at him suspiciously.

"It sure was," I said. "Global warming's here. Almost a hundred degrees in the shade."

"Hey, Miss Katherine. How are you doing?" he said politely.

"Hey, yourself, Ted Meyers. Sit down. It's too hot to stand."

"Yes, ma'am," he said and took a seat at the table.

There was an awkward silence that hung in the air like something sweet and sour.

"So? What brings you to our door, Ted?" I said, placing a glass in front of him on a paper napkin. "Would you like a slice of the remains of Tyler's birthday cake?"

"Sure, thank you. Who says no to cake?" he said and then cleared his throat. "It seems we had an incident with your bees this afternoon."

"They were bearding from the heat," I said. I sliced a piece of cake and put it on a plate, handing it to him with a napkin and, of course, a fork.

"Sorry?" he said.

"When the temperature in the hives goes over ninety-three and a half, some of the bees go hang out somewhere else to let the hives cool down. Then they go home and some others leave."

"And it's called *bearding*?"

"Yeah, kind of a funny term, isn't it? Sugar?"

I pushed the sugar bowl toward him and watched him load four spoons of sugar into his glass. I gave him an iced tea spoon. He'd be stirring that much sugar until next week if he wanted it all to dissolve.

"Mrs. MacLean told me she was swarmed."

I sighed as wearily as I could muster.

"Mrs. MacLean is as crazy as a low-flying loon," Momma said under her breath, just loud enough for us to hear her.

"Momma!" I said in mock horror. "Ted, I'm not surprised. But of course, she's dead wrong. Lots of people don't know the difference between swarming and bearding."

"Can you enlighten me? I'm just a police officer, you know, keeper of the peace. You're the beekeeper."

I laughed a little, trying to keep it light.

"Sure. When bees swarm they make a loud roar. My bees were quiet. That's a sign. Also, swarming occurs in the spring. Not the summer. I just changed the bottom of the hive to a screen to give them more ventilation. They're happier now."

"She claims that the bees swarmed her car, causing her to become hysterical."

"That she got hysterical is her own mental problem. For the most part, honey bees are harmless."

"She had to take something and lie down."

"She lies down a lot," Momma said. "That's how she hooked Archie."

"Momma!"

"Sorry," she said.

Ted smiled and I blushed.

"She says you caused the bees to swarm her in retaliation for her putting Tyler on restriction and refusing to allow him to attend his birthday party because he called her a bad name."

"Good Lord, Ted! Did you hear what you just said?"

"I know." Ted smiled at me. "And I said it with a straight face. Good, right?"

"You always were the best actor in the whole dang school. I think I'll never forget you singing "Maria" in *West Side Story.*"

"Somebody call Hollywood," Momma mumbled.

I kicked her under the table and cut my eye at her.

"Well, thanks, Holly." He ate the last of his cake.

"Anyway, she called me a bad name, and did I get to put her on restriction?"

"She did?" Momma said. "What did that Jezebel call my daughter?"

"She said I was a freak, a menace to society, and that she was going to sue me for a million dollars."

"She said that? I ought to go over there and slap her face!" Momma said.

"Oh, Momma, she was just being crazy," I said. But I did love it that Momma defended me.

"Where in the world did Mr. MacLean find this new wife of his?"

"An online Transylvanian dating app," I said. "Listen, she's not from here, you know? She doesn't understand the first thing about nature or children. It's pitiful."

"No, she's not a Lowcountry girl. That's for sure. Still, I have to ask, is there a way to keep the bees away from her? Apparently, she's terrified of them."

"That's her mental problem, not mine, but I'll mention it to them when I check the hives in the morning," I said.

"Tell all the palmetto bugs to get off the island while you're at it, okay?" Momma said. "And to take the coyotes with them."

"You bet," I said.

Ted laughed at that and stood to leave. I walked him to the door.

"Thanks for the cake and the tea," he said. "Did you know they made me the interim chief?"

Our chief of police on the island had retired at the end of last year.

"No! I had not heard that. Congratulations!"

"Yeah, they got a search going, but my hat's in the ring, too. You never know."

"That's right, you never know. Wow, wouldn't that be wonderful?"

Ted had always been a dignified guy, very smart and not impetuous. I thought then that he would make an excellent chief of police. There was nothing bubba about him.

"It sure would be."

We stood on my top step, looking toward Archie's house.

"That woman's a nightmare, Ted. Between us, that is."

"Yeah," he said. "Doesn't take much to get her all worked up, all right. Your momma's still a character, isn't she?"

"Oh, she's that and a whole lot more."

Why was he so slow to leave?

As though he read my mind, he said, "Well, thanks again. I'll be seeing you around the island, I guess."

"Anytime," I said and slipped by him and back into the house.

"Hey, Holly?"

I turned back to him.

"You think you might like to go see a movie sometime?"

"I might."

"Well, now I know where to find you."

"Hey, Ted?"

"Yeah?"

"How's the competition for the job of chief?"

"I don't know. Probably stiff. I mean, who wouldn't want to live on Sullivan's Island?"

"Sometimes I wonder about that," I said. "Well, listen, if we can do anything to help the process along, just let us know, okay?"

We waved to each other and I went back inside. I had a thought then that maybe he had a very good chance of getting the job. Why not? He'd been doing it for months anyway. Pretty long interview, I thought.

Momma was still in the kitchen and now Leslie was there, too. She was starting supper. That was one of the nice things about her return, having help in the kitchen.

"So what's new with Charlie?" I asked.

"You wouldn't believe it," Leslie said. "He's got it in his mind that since he's got a private seamstress, aka Momma, that she can make Christian Siriano–esque costumes for him."

"Who's he?" I said.

"I guess you don't watch the Oscars, huh? So he wants her to come out to Vegas, see a few shows, and get inspired. He's going for it, Momma. Because of you!"

"I guess I'm going to spend my evenings in Las Vegas with a whole lot of Liza Minnellis," Momma said. "I'm going to lose my mind."

"You'll have a blast!" I said. "Just do it."

"Have you taken leave of your senses?" Momma said.

"Absolutely not," I said. "Here's what I've been thinking. A while back, I came to the conclusion that what we need in this family is more fun. Months and years are slipping away, and none of us are getting any younger, you especially, Momma. And what are we doing? I was thinking maybe we should take up bingo."

"Bingo," Momma said, as flat as a pancake.

"Yeah, that was before *this* opportunity popped up," I said.

"Let me understand where you're going with this," Momma said. "It's either bingo or Vegas?"

"No," I said. "Listen, didn't you tell Charlie if he was going to do this, he'd better be the best?"

"Yeah, Momma," Leslie said. "You did say that."

Momma fidgeted around in her chair, and I could feel a grumble coming on.

"Yes, uh-huh, you sure did," Leslie added.

"So, Momma?" I said. "The same goes for you."

"What do you mean?" she said.

"I mean, you don't even know what the competition looks like!" I said. "How can he be the best anything if he doesn't have the best-informed support team?"

"All right," Momma said. "You're right. You win. Leslie? You coming with me?"

"Of course!" Leslie said. "Charlie's flying us out and putting us up. He's even bought you a portable sewing machine and he's having a form made."

"I'm assuming the form will have breasts?" Momma said. "And that he's doing something about foundation garments that will compensate?"

"I'm sure he is," Leslie said.

"Good grief," I said.

"Pack your hearing aids and your swatches!" Leslie said. "Las Vegas, here we come!"

This new aspect of our family life was still something of a challenge for me. But when I thought about it, we'd all come a long way since the cat jumped out of the bag and into the spotlight. Maybe I was too old-fashioned for my own good. But when I thought about Momma in Las Vegas going to these types of shows, impersonators at the top of their game, I wondered just how eye-opening it would be for her. She was about to become a woman of the world. She sure couldn't wear her sweats with the kittens on them. Momma was going to have to buy a few things for herself, too. And meanwhile, I'd just be here, on the island, keeping bees and mooning over a married man and his crazy-as-hell wife. Or would I?

"One of the things that amazes me about honey bees is how they all take care of each other. They're selfless. They feed the queen, they hunt and forage for each other, they take turns guarding the hive. Amazing."

"They're like you, Miss Holly," Tyler said.

Chapter Twenty-Three
Bee Have

It took about a dozen trips to Chico's and Belk's for Momma to get some kind of a presentable wardrobe together, which Charlie, bless his heart, paid for. Then Robin Harris at Stella Nova gave her a haircut and highlights that were beyond a transformational experience. I barely recognized my own mother with makeup on.

"Momma! You look like a total babe!" I said.

"Oh, go on now with your foolish talk," she said, and

as the good Lord is my witness, she blushed. I would've thought her blushing mechanism dried up decades ago.

"Doesn't she look amazing?" Leslie said.

"*She* is the cat's mother," Momma and I said in harmony and laughed a genuine laugh.

We looked up Christian Siriano online and printed quite a few of his costume sketches for reference. And we looked up and printed pictures of every major female impersonator in the business for inspiration as well.

"We're going to need a resource for exotic feathers," Momma said. "And did anyone find a wig maker?"

"Charlie's got a wig person. Look, he sent me some pictures last night. Look."

I looked at them, too. These weren't normal wigs. They were beyond Marie Antoinette. Way beyond.

"Wow," Momma said.

"I know, right?" Leslie said. "Crazy!"

So Momma and Leslie flew to Las Vegas with light hearts and heavy bags. Reportedly, Charlie couldn't wait for them to arrive, and to demonstrate his enthusiasm, he picked them up in a stretch limo with a bottle of Veuve Clicquot champagne and Lalique flutes. When I spoke to them, even Momma was giggly with excitement.

"We're going to our first show tonight! I can't wait!

Oh, Holly! You have to see this place to believe it! You're in France, Italy, and Egypt all at the same time! You're going to have to come for a visit!"

Momma hadn't produced that many exclamation points in one statement in all her life as far as I knew.

"Maybe one day," I said. "You two have fun, okay?"

I had zero interest in Las Vegas.

Later that night, the pictures started coming, and they were almost unbelievable. I'd never seen so much glitz and glam. Literally, everything was shiny. Every building, every column, every fountain, and boy, there were a lot of those. There were mirrors everywhere. Women in stiletto heels—most of them, in fact. High-end retail stores were everywhere, ones I'd only ever heard of in magazines. And then there were the female impersonators. Holy whopping hell! You couldn't make this stuff up. They were the fanciest, most glamorous, most artfully accessorized impersonators you could even imagine. Boas. Headgear that ranged from demure fascinators to tribal headdresses. Gowns of gold and silver lamé with burnouts, and jewels? Diamonds like door knockers. Ropes of gorgeous pearls. Tiaras fit for true royalty. Their makeup? Airbrushed and flawless. The pageantry of it all was intoxicating. Momma's eyes must've been spinning in her head. Leslie had to be giddy and Charlie so happy to have them there and especially to be on good terms with Momma again, because she was going to put him on the map.

And, just to be clear, neither Charlie nor anyone in Las Vegas had ever heard of matte finish.

I was sort of enjoying my peace and quiet, and I had no idea when Momma and Leslie were coming back. I should have known the peace wouldn't last too long. The next morning I was cleaning up my breakfast dishes and I heard the front door open and slam shut.

"Miss Holly! Miss Holly! Where are you?"

It was Tyler and Hunter, of course.

"In the kitchen!" I called back.

"I just can't take it anymore," Tyler said and burst into tears. "We can't stay long because she just went to CVS."

"I can't take it, either," Hunter said and started to cry.

"Come here, you two." I put my arms around them and let them cry it all out. What had happened? When I thought they were winding down, I said, "All right, now. Tell me what's the matter." I reached for a box of tissues and gave them both a couple. "But first, blow!"

They blew their noses and their breathing gradually returned to normal. They handed me their tissues and I threw them in the garbage. I poured two glasses of apple juice and put them on the table in front of them.

"Okay, sit down at the table and talk to me. What's going on? It's a gorgeous day and you both should be outside! Why aren't you over at Matthew's swimming? Or down at the playground?"

"Because *she* won't let us. Her parents and her aunt and uncle came on Sunday and *she* didn't like how we behaved. We're on restriction *again!* We didn't do anything wrong. I promise! We didn't!"

"All Tyler did was ask her old aunt if she had brought him a birthday present. And she didn't. And so we both got in trouble."

I noticed suddenly that Hunter had some pretty good-sized bandages on his shins. These were not ornamental. And his elbows had huge bandages on them, too.

"What happened to you?"

"I fell off my bike," he said. "And it hurts, too. I hurt everywhere." I thought he was on the verge of tears, but he just sighed with so much sadness, I prepared myself for a terrible explanation, because this was all wrong.

This was a kid who could ride a bike with no hands. And turn corners. As we all said, he was part monkey.

The hair on the back of my neck stood up. I knew intuitively I wasn't getting the whole story.

"Want to tell me what really happened?"

They looked nervously at each other and didn't answer me.

"Okay, Tyler. Let's move on to you. What's going on?"

"Sharon just did something that was so terrible." He stopped and looked at Hunter. "We have to tell Miss Holly, Hunter."

"What did she do?" I said.

Hunter still wasn't talking, but he nodded consent to Tyler.

"I'll tell her. Hunter was riding his bike, see? But when she told him to stop and come inside, he took off as fast as he could."

"Because there was no reason why I shouldn't be riding my bike!" Hunter said. "It's summer!"

"She did room inspections and didn't like Hunter's. It wasn't perfect enough for her. So she took his bike away until his room passed inspection."

"I'm not even six years old! I can't change the sheets! It's too hard! I can't reach the washing machine buttons and I can't read what they say anyhow! And the vacuum cleaner is too heavy for me!"

"Inspections?"

"Yeah, she says she didn't marry our dad to be a personal maid to us."

"Anyways," Tyler said, "she jumped in her car to follow him to make him get off the bike. She pulled around in front of him. Hunter didn't have time to stop and so he flipped over his handlebars and got all cut up on the road. I saw the whole thing happen."

"She didn't even say she was sorry," Hunter said. "She said next time, I'd listen to her, wouldn't I?"

"Does your father know about this?" I asked.

"No. He only knows what she said," Tyler said.

"She told him a lie. She said she followed me and got there just in time after I fell off my bike," Hunter said.

"She didn't say it was her fault that he had the accident in the first place," Tyler said.

This was a clear case of reckless endangerment of a minor, and who knew what else?

"I hate her guts," Hunter said.

"Me, too," Tyler said. "It's like living with the devil. My little brother could've been killed! What if he had landed on his head?"

Tyler wasn't wrong.

"Okay, what would you boys like me to do? Would you like me to tell your father your side of the story?"

"Yeah, but she'll kill us if she finds out we told on her," Hunter said.

"Nobody's killing anybody," I said.

"We won't get out of the house until school starts!" Tyler said. "And Dad doesn't listen to us anymore!"

"We'll see about that."

"He just goes along with whatever she says," Hunter said.

I believed them, and any fool could see they had no advocate. These boys needed family therapy. So did Archie and Sharon.

"Let me talk to your father," I said. "He listens to me. Sometimes."

They drained their juice and put their glasses in the sink.

"Thanks, good luck," Tyler said. "Things are really terrible, Miss Holly."

"I hear you, sweetie. It's going to get better."

They literally ran home in fear that Sharon would come home from the drugstore and discover them missing. And why had she left them home alone, anyway? I was tempted to tell Ted. They were still too young. Surely Sharon knew that.

The more I thought about it, the angrier I became. I went out to the apiary to check on the bees' water supply and, of course, laid the whole story at their fuzzy little feet. Not just the pink hive, but the other two as well. I was talking to myself all over the backyard.

What the hell was the matter with Archie? And what was the matter with her? Eventually I came to the conclusion that I'd talk to Archie. If he didn't want to hear it, I'd take it to Ted. This was too important to let slide.

I waited for a time when Cruella de Ville's car was gone and Archie's car was there, and boldly, I rang his doorbell. He answered and invited me inside.

"No, I think it's better if we speak where we can't be heard. Why don't we sit on your porch?"

"Sure, okay." He came out onto the porch but made no sign that he intended to sit. Instead, he crossed his arms over his chest and leaned against the banisters. "Maybe I'd rather stand. I've been sitting all day, grading essays."

"There's something I have to talk to you about, and I don't think you're going to want to hear it."

"How could that be?"

"You know your children love me, don't you?"

"That goes without saying," he said. "They adore you."

"As I do them. And I hope you know that I would never tell you something taken out of context to excuse or to enhance anyone's innocence or guilt, right?"

"My God, Holly! Get to the point."

"Okay, here it is. Sharon cut Hunter off with her car and that's what caused his accident. Not the other way around, that he had an accident and she arrived to save him."

"Oh, come on now, Holly. She wouldn't lie to me."

"Really? Okay. I'm not going to go into this any further. But you ought to know, Archie, this is endangerment of a minor. I'm not going to stand around while these boys are in harm's way and do nothing about it."

"Why are they in harm's way? Because Sharon's trying to make them responsible for cleaning their rooms?"

"Archie, Hunter and Tyler can't read the washing machine buttons."

"Then all they have to do is ask for some direction," he said.

"And if they get home at five minutes after five, do you really think they should be denied dinner?"

"That's a bit too much, I agree," he said.

"And should she really turn the lights out when they are in the shower?"

"She was just trying to make a point about using too much hot water."

"What if they slip and fall in the darkness? Do you know what percentage of head injuries come from bathroom accidents?"

"I suspect more come from football," he said. "Look, I know Sharon's a rough taskmaster, but this house has never been cleaner. Even the dining room table is cleared."

"Your house might be clean, but your boys are miserable."

"Why in the world would they be miserable?"

"They feel they are being distanced from you, and they sure as hell don't feel loved by her."

"Holly, that's quite a mouthful."

"Yeah, it is. Can you imagine what it would be if I filled in the details?"

"It wouldn't be a story I'd relish hearing about my new wife, I'm sure. But I will be more vigilant and I will try to give the boys more time."

"Why not have a boys' night once a week? Give them a chance to talk to you without her there."

"Not a bad idea."

He looked at me in such a way that I could tell he was absolutely unconvinced that I had told him the truth about Hunter's accident.

"You don't believe me about Hunter and his bicycle accident, do you?"

"Look, I think you are very well intentioned. If I didn't know you had genuine feelings for my boys, I'd be furious right now. And I'm not. Not a bit. And I think my boys are on a mission to get rid of Sharon, for whatever their juvenile reasons might be."

"Okay, I've said my piece. Good luck to you, Archie."

"Hey! Why are you saying good luck like there's something terrible looming?"

"Because there is something terrible looming, Archie. I feel it in every one of my bones."

"Really?"

"Look, she's accusatory, self-absorbed, defensive, judgmental, petty, dishonest, and unkind, so I don't like Sharon, your boys don't like Sharon, Leslie doesn't like Sharon, and even my momma doesn't like Sharon. The bees don't like her and even the seagulls don't like her. None of us, the humans that is, see this situation improving. We all see it as going downhill. So good luck."

"I see. So are you saying you don't want to sit for my kids in the future?"

That was his biggest concern?

"I would never say no to doing *anything* for those boys. And you know it. But sit for them? I wish they lived with me. And so do they. Figure it out, Archie. You've got a ticking bomb on your hands, because this is only going to get worse unless you step in."

"Look, Holly. You're a nice girl. You mean well. But you should never assume to know how things really are under someone else's roof."

Don't condescend to me, bubba, I thought.

"That's right. And you're a nice boy." I thought, Think about *that* one, old man. "Unless a person is absolutely certain things are way off kilter, it's always better to mind your own business. And I am absolutely certain."

"Well, you've given me a lot to consider," he said.

This entire conversation was all in one ear and out the other.

"Archie, I've known you since the day the boys were born. We've never had a serious difference of opinion."

"Are we having one now?" he said and had the audacity to smile at me.

"Yeah, we are. You may think this is a joke, but no, sir, it is not. We're having a huge difference of opinion."

I walked down his steps, across the road to my house, and went inside. I sat down at the kitchen table and had a long-overdue cry. After about thirty minutes, I lifted my head to see my bees, bearded on the window screen over the sink.

Suzanne said, "Do you know there are about
a thousand people living underground in Las Vegas?
They're in tunnels."

"No way," I said.

"Way," Charlie said.

Chapter Twenty-Four
Leslie, the QB, and Vegas

There would be no grass growing under our feet. Momma and I didn't waste a moment in getting down to business. In the first few days we were in Las Vegas, we found a fabric store and bought a bolt of muslin, shears, thread, tailor's chalk, and everything else she would need to get started. There were sketches of costumes taped all over the walls of Charlie's dining room, which was now transformed into a pattern and sewing room. Momma measured and remeasured Charlie from one end to the other, noting everything on a legal pad.

"I love your apartment, Charlie," Momma said, while hooking up the back of a bustier we'd bought to give Charlie a bit of cleavage.

"Why, thank you. It's just for now, but the view of the desert is quite nice. Especially the sunsets."

"You're getting too skinny," Momma said to him. "There's not enough meat on your bones to achieve the desired effect."

"I have to be svelte for this plan to work," he said. "Ow! That's too tight!"

"Pride knoweth no pain, Charlie boy," Momma said. "Suck it up! I still can't believe I'm doing this."

He was caught somewhere in between strangulation and suffocation.

Charlie looked at me and said, "She's trying to kill me. You know that, don't you?"

I knew no such thing.

I laughed and said, "Oh, Charlie. I'm afraid Momma's right."

And did we shop? We found fabulous women's shoes in Charlie's size and so many wigs we couldn't decide, so we bought them all, and we had an appointment with an award-winning cosmetic artist who was going to give Charlie a distinctive look. And at Momma's insistence, he hired a personal coach to work on his dramatic presentations of Cher, Judy Garland, Beyoncé, and anybody else he felt he might like to lip-sync to. He was good, but he'd have to be drop-dead amazing to break into the *really* big time as he wanted to.

Momma and Charlie were out shopping again, so I called Holly to see how she was holding up. She told me about Hunter's accident and the words she'd had with Archie. I was flabbergasted.

"This makes me absolutely sick inside," I said to her.

"Me, too," she said. "It's like something really terrible is going to have to happen before Archie will wake up."

"Don't say that," I said.

"Here's what I don't understand," she said. "Hunter's accident would've been the perfect moment for her to take this banged-up little boy in her arms and say she was so sorry. It could've been a turning point for them instead of a hundred more nails in the coffin. But that's not what she did. This is what happens to people who can't ever be wrong."

"You're right, of course. They always blame the problem on somebody else."

We were quiet for a moment.

Then Holly said, "Something awful is going to happen. I just know it."

"You and your premonitions," I said. "Let's hope you're wrong for once."

"I'd love to be wrong."

"On a lighter note," I said, "Charlie is beside himself with all the attention he's getting from Momma and this army of people they're calling in to help him literally get his act together."

"Is she having fun, too?"

"Are you kidding? She's the stage mother for him that she never was for us," I said. "She made me laugh so hard yesterday when we were shopping. She said to him, 'Now, Charlie, remember, the higher the heel, the more flattering it is to your calf muscle.' I thought I'd lose my mind. Can you believe she even thinks of things like that?"

"We always forget that back in the day, the QB was a stunner."

"That's true. She was. Well, Project Charlie is sure resurrecting her."

"That's good to hear," I said. "So how's it going between you and Charlie?"

"That is a much harder question to answer. It's like, the overwhelming majority of drag queens I'm meeting are one hundred percent gay. But Charlie says he just wants to be a female impersonator. Gay's cool, though. Listen, whatever Charlie decides he is becoming, I'm still going to love him. In fact, there's an old female impersonator here, Suzanne Velour is her stage name, who's taken a shine to Momma and flatters her so much that Momma's sort of smitten with her. Suzanne bought Momma's drinks all night last night. And the night before."

Suzanne Velour was approximately the same age and girth as Momma. They acted like they'd known each other all their lives. In fact, anyone who knew Momma at all might say they'd never seen her so compatible with someone.

"Momma doesn't drink," Holly said.

"Well, honey, she was knocking back mimosas like she grew up on champagne. Anyway, I imagine at her age she'd be happy with a platonic relationship. And, here's the thing, I suspect I'm headed down that road with Charlie, you know, that maybe our job here is to help him step out of the closet with his dignity and his relationship with us intact. If that is what he wants."

"And if you have a full understanding of the lifestyle, and see it for what it really is, that then you won't judge him?"

"That and more. I don't think Charlie wants to see

our relationship sour and get bitter. And he's working really hard for that not to happen."

"You're not going to know what's cooking in his head until he does, so you may as well relax and try to have fun," she said.

"You know what?" I said. "You're right! Last night we went to the Miss Behave Game Show, which was so hilarious I thought we'd die, and then tomorrow we've got a reservation at the Drag Supper Club. And we're wait-listed for tickets to Divas Las Vegas. I'll tell you, Holly, this crazy world of drag queens and female impersonators and the whole lot of them is a universe unto itself. It's fantasy and drama and humor all rolled into one. And it's super fun. At least, as a spectator, so far."

She said, "Send pictures!"

I promised I would, and we hung up.

And as day rolled into night, there was plenty to photograph. Sometime in the afternoon, Suzanne Velour called Charlie to speak to Momma. They had just arrived home with an astounding amount of shopping bags.

"What?" Momma said. "She wants to talk to me?"

She dropped all her bags on the floor.

"You need your own cell phone, Momma," I said.

She took Charlie's phone and I heard Momma say, "What? Italy? But I don't have a passport! Oh! Oh!

I see! You had me going for a minute, Suzanne. Yes, I think we can be ready by eight. That was my new friend, Suzanne. She's taking us all out tonight. She said we should get gussied up. What does getting gussied up mean in Las Vegas?"

"It means, get fancy!" I said. "I'll do your makeup, if you'd like."

"Well, someone had better take over for me. All I've got is a bottle of Oil of Olay and a Chapstick," she said. "But I have those Eileen Fisher black silk pajama pants with the tunic. Maybe we can dress that up."

"Oh, Momma," Charlie said. "Don't you worry! We're going to have you looking like a queen!"

"That's what Holly and I call her, you know," I said.

"That's right," she said. "You girls!"

"Actually, Momma, we call you the QB, for queen bee."

"I've heard you two mumble it," she said, obviously pleased instead of irked. "I think I kind of like that name! Although I have a very small kingdom with very few minions."

"Well, you've got us and Holly, and I'd say that's not a bad start," Charlie said. "Now let's get you dressed!"

"Charlie?" I said, with some trepidation. "Are you going out tonight as Charlie or Charlene?"

"I don't know," he said. "Do you have a preference?"

"Why don't you try Charlene?" Momma said.

Please someone come and get my dead body off the floor.

"Because if Suzanne shows up in drag then we're just having a girls' night out!" the now and forever QB said.

"That's hilarious, QB! I love it!" Charlie said.

As he applied his own makeup, he began to gradually and ever so subtly wade into the waters of Charlene's personality, which I'd noticed he did from time to time. The changes were extremely subtle. There would be more expressive hand gestures, more gentility, and a different posture. I had to say, I liked Charlene just as much as Charlie. Charlene was merely Charlie completely relaxed and at home with himself. Charlie with his guard down. Charlie in perfect humor. But also Charlie exuding confidence. Were these changes so odd? When I put on new shoes or had my hair blown out by a pro, I felt more confident, too. So what was the big difference? The whole world of female impersonation fascinated me. Well, Charlie fascinated me, probably because I loved him so much. This whole new aspect of him was incredible.

By eight o'clock we were all set to go out for a night on the town. Charlie had decided on a cosmetic transformation instead of a complete change.

"You know," he said, "I have a few things for the stage but not a lot for dinner. So, I'm thinking this black shirt and pants with ballerina flats, lots of bangles, and this scarf tied like this." He stopped and looked in the mirror. "Dear Lord! I look like that old dame Anita Bryant in the orange juice commercials from a thousand years ago!" He quickly untied the scarf and tossed it on a chair. "I need a little black dress."

"What is your problem?" Momma said. "You're beautiful!"

He looked in the mirror again.

"Wasn't it Coco Chanel who said to ditch one accessory before you walk out of the door?" He said. "Or was it Wallis Simpson?"

Would a straight man know this? I asked myself this, knowing the answer was, who's to say?

Suzanne rang the doorbell promptly at eight.

"Hello, lovelies! Our gondola awaits! Don't you look chic, Miss Katherine?" she said to Momma.

"You may address me as Queen Bee, or Miss QB!" the QB said with the most mirth I'd ever seen her show in my entire adult life. "Are we ready, ladies?"

"We are," Charlene/Charlie said.

We stepped outside. Suzanne drove a 1960 convertible Cadillac. It was jet black and as long as a city block. The rear end featured shark fins, and its interior was white leather with red piping. It was a treasure.

"Wow!" I said. "What a fabulous car!"

"Thanks, honey. She's my fave. I got her from Jay Leno." Suzanne touched her fender with tenderness. "Okay! Our first stop is the Venetian! I have a reservation for us at Sushi Samba. You'll love it. It's absolutely divine."

"Sushi?" Momma said.

She wouldn't eat raw fish on a bet. Suzanne sensed Momma's concern.

"There's also Bouchon or Morels if you would prefer," she said.

"Oh, that's okay," Momma said. "I'm sure there's something on the menu for me."

And off we went into the night.

We gave the car to the valet service and entered yet another world. The lobby of the Venetian was unlike anything I'd ever seen, even in the movies. Opulent would not begin to cover it. The Uffizi Gallery in Florence was a total snore next to this. The ceilings were indescribably high, vaulted, painted with murals, trimmed in gold; there were mirrors everywhere, fountains, and, of course, the Grand Canal, complete with gondoliers. Whew! Momma and I were simply dumbfounded.

"Holy Michelangelo, Batman! We're not in Gotham anymore!" Momma said.

We stopped dead in our tracks and looked at her.

"Momma? Did you just make a Batman joke?" I said.

"It's a good one," Suzanne said.

"Thank you," the QB said.

Charlene and I exchanged looks of surprise. It seemed that Momma's younger personality, the light and carefree one, might have been resurrected.

We found the restaurant and were taken to our seats immediately. Suzanne ordered sake for all of us.

"Don't let this stuff fool you," she said. "It's potent."

The menu at Sushi Samba had just about everything in the world on it. A lot of it could have been written in Greek, unless you ate Japanese food frequently and knew the terminology.

Suzanne said, "Why don't I just order for the table and everyone can help themselves to some of everything?"

We all said that sounded fine to us, as Suzanne had been coming here for ages. So she quickly began to rattle off our order to our server. She ordered edamame and Berkshire pork belly ramen to begin. Next, she ordered toro, hamachi, unagi, udama, and uni. Those were all various creatures coming to us straight from the sea. Then she ordered some traditional rolls and two kinds of tempura.

"You must be very hungry," said our waiter.

Suzanne twisted up the side of her mouth and looked at him and said, "Yes, as a matter of fact. We are."

The food began to arrive, platter after platter.

"It's too pretty to eat," Momma said.

"Oh, darling," Suzanne said. "Take a picture with your iPhone and just dig in!"

I pulled mine out and recorded the moment for posterity. And I snapped pictures of Charlene, the QB, and Suzanne.

The warm sake was replenished over and over.

With just a little coaxing from Suzanne, Momma ate tuna sashimi and loved it.

"How come I never knew about tuna . . . what do you call this?" she said, and I laughed. Momma's eyes were being opened to the larger world, bit by bit.

"Sashimi," Charlene said.

"No more calls," Suzanne said. "We just lost a virgin."

Momma gave Suzanne the hairy eyeball. And Suzanne burst into laughter.

"I love a woman with some spunk!"

"Delicious," she said and turned to me. "I'd like a picture of me eating this. Do you think you can manage that?"

"That sounded pretty harsh, darling," Suzanne said. "Is everything all right?"

"It did?" Momma said. Then she turned to me and said, "I just want to remember this night and I began to panic that after dinner it would all be over. I'm sorry."

"It's okay, Momma! Smile big! Charlene, you and Suzanne get in the picture, too! One, two, three!" I clicked the button a few times.

"The night's young, Miss QB," Charlene said.

"And miles to go before I sleep!" Suzanne said.

"Robert Frost?" Momma said.

"Whose woods these are I think I know . . . ?" Suzanne recited the whole poem "Stopping by Woods on a Snowy Evening," and Momma fell in love a little more.

"Miss QB? Here's another fun fact. Every single day of the year sixty thousand pounds of shrimp are consumed in Las Vegas. That's more than the rest of the country combined!" Suzanne looked from face to face, seeking a bit of acknowledgment.

"Oh, please," Charlene said. "Suzanne wins every trivia night contest in Nevada!"

"Yes, I do!" Suzanne said. "Ask me anything."

"Tell us the weirdest thing you've ever heard," I said.

"Hmmm," she said. "That's a tough one. Okay, here's something. How about in 1980, they had to suspend a bunch of hospital workers for betting on when a patient would die? And a nurse was actually arrested for murder, having killed a patient so she could win? How weird is that?"

"That's out there," Charlene said.

"If that's not the work of the devil, what is?" the QB said. "Is there more sake?"

"Yes, but the larger question is," Charlene said, refilling Momma's cup, "do y'all want to ride the gondola down the Grand Canal indoors or outdoors?"

We finished all the sake and almost everything else, paid the bill, and made our way to the gondola passenger station.

"Thank you, Suzanne. That was absolutely fantastic!"

"Not exactly Shem Creek, is it?" I said.

"No. It's another world," Momma said in agreement.

Suzanne bought tickets for us, and after a few false starts and more than a few promises to save her if she fell in, we finally got the QB into the gondola, too. It was doing some serious wobbling. But then, to be honest, Suzanne was no skinny Minnie, either.

"I thought we were going to lose you there for a moment," Suzanne said. "Come on now, sit right here next to me."

As we drifted along the Grand Canal, Momma was strangely quiet, but smiling, and she seemed awfully happy. She was probably half in the bag, I thought.

"What are you thinking about?" I heard Suzanne ask Momma.

"I'm thinking this is my wildest dream, except I'm alive and in it, and how in the world would we top this?"

"Well, there's the zip line on top of the Rio Hotel at the Voodoo. I was thinking we could knock back a couple of Witch Doctors and go for it," Suzanne said.

"Witch Doctors?" the QB said.

"House cocktail," Charlene said.

"Zip line?" the QB said.

"Yes, they put you in a harness four hundred feet above the ground and then you jump off the roof and go thirty-three miles an hour for a third of a mile. When it stops, you return to the roof facing backward," Suzanne said. "It's lots of fun and very safe."

"You must be as crazy as every devil in hell to do

something like that," the QB said. "I think I'd rather just drink a Witch Doctor. That sounds more sensible to me."

We all laughed at that.

"They have another cocktail that's really famous," Suzanne said. "It's called the Love Potion."

"Is Suzanne gay?" I whispered to Charlene. "Because he's acting very straight."

"Suzanne? Oh, no! He's *totally* straight. He's just a female impersonator, like me. He always wanted to be the next Dame Edna. But then, who doesn't?"

More than a few people, I thought.

"Yeah, well," I said, certain then that I had seen it all, "the next Dame Edna is kissing on your mother-in-law!"

And the QB was loving it. There was no one I could tell who would believe it.

*"Okay, so here's a really fun bee fact.
Honey is nectar that has been chewed and
regurgitated over and over!" I said.*

"Ewwwww! Bee barf!" Hunter said.

"That's right," I said.

Chapter Twenty-Five
Gone Boys

Little boys are fragile creatures. In our society we rear them to rise above emotional outbursts, to be the stronger sex, to bravely go to war, even though women make up about 20 percent of our armed forces now. But inside their hearts, all small humans are the same—tender and sweet and in need of just as much guidance in forming values and learning manners, and for someone to shape their ambition, hear what's on their heart, and do something about it. They are just trying to navigate their way into the world, and it's impossible to do it alone and do it well. Children need advocates.

The terrible truth of Tyler and Hunter's new reality was that they had no advocate. Sharon, in a short span of time, had moved into their lives and manipulated everyone in such a way that any disagreement about the slightest thing was deemed a betrayal and punished.

There was too much sadness in them, and Archie refused to see it. And with every passing day those boys came to me, I could see their zest for life diminishing. I would try to cheer them, but eventually I realized it was to no avail. They could not be cheered. They had all but stopped complaining about Sharon because they said they knew nothing was going to change.

They were at my house while Sharon and Archie went shopping for a new mattress. Had they already worn out the one they had?

"I'm just trying to get through the summer. Someday, I'll never have to see her again," Tyler said.

"I can't even look at her," Hunter said.

"Have you had a boys' night out with your dad?"

"We were supposed to, but then she found some reason why he couldn't go," Tyler said.

"Oh, who cares?" Hunter said. "He'd rather be with her anyway."

"You know, boys," I said, "it's not unusual for new-lyweds to want to be alone a lot of the time."

"That's not the problem. The problem is there's no room for us," Tyler said.

"No, the problem is," Hunter said, "we're not wel-come."

"That's absurd," I said, having heard enough. "And I have to tell you, I don't think it's true. It may be somewhat true on certain days in certain situations, but it can't be entirely true. If it was, you'd be heading to a boarding school."

"So now you don't believe us?" Tyler said.

"Tyler? You both know I love y'all from the bottom of my heart, don't you?"

They said, "Yeah, we know."

"What I'm seeing from where I stand is different than what you see. I see that you are having a really terrible time trying to adjust to your dad's marriage. And I see that you both are looking for solutions and can't find them. It's not an unusual problem, do you know that?"

"Not really," Tyler said.

"Yeah," Hunter said.

"Well, we need a solution, because I can't take your

unhappiness much longer," I said, and then thought it probably wasn't the most empathetic thing I'd ever said. "What's your plan for this weekend?"

"Nothing," they said.

"Okay, so why don't I call Maureen and see if we can't go over for a swim or all of us maybe go to a movie?"

"Okay. If she'll let us go."

"*I'll* ask her. So, for now, do y'all want to make milk shakes?"

That perked them up, and I said a little prayer of thanksgiving.

"Do you want to scoop the ice cream?" I said to Hunter.

I didn't tell him it was frozen yogurt.

"Yeah!" he said.

Frozen yogurt, milk, chocolate syrup, ice, and a shot of vanilla went into our blender and Tyler flipped the switch. The blender made so much noise, you couldn't hear yourself think. The next thing I knew, Archie was standing in my kitchen. When we turned the blender off we turned to see him there.

"I guess you couldn't hear me knocking," he said.

"Hi, Dad," Tyler said.

"You're right! We didn't," I said. "Would you like a part of a chocolate milk shake?"

"Does this mean we have to go home?" Hunter said.

"I'd love a swallow or two," Archie said. "I haven't had a milk shake in probably twenty years."

Tyler, sensing a good mood in his father, quickly got another glass and said, "Then you have to have one! It's the best!"

Hunter said, "Miss Holly's milk shake is better than McDonald's!"

I poured a glass for Archie and he took a sip.

"This is amazing! Why have I deprived myself all these years?"

"Have a seat!" I said.

Tyler said, "Give Dad the rest and me and my brother . . ."

"My brother and I . . ." I said, correcting his grammar.

"My brother and I can make another one."

"Have at it!" I said. "You know what to do."

Archie and I watched as Hunter and Tyler put all the ingredients into the blender, covered it, and turned it on. The high-pitched noise was deafening as the hard ice was crunched over and over by the blades and turned into snow, thickening the shake. When the racket died down, they turned the blender off. I got up to help them pour.

"That's heavy," I said. "Let me give you a hand."

I poured the creamy shake out into three glasses and refilled Archie's glass with the balance.

"Well, isn't everyone having a party this afternoon?"

We looked up to see Sharon in the doorway.

"We just made milk shakes. Can we offer you one?" I said.

"You must be kidding," she said. "Do you know how many calories are in those things?"

I wanted to say, *A simple no thank you would've been nicer.* But I didn't.

"It's delicious," Tyler said.

Sharon looked at him and did not respond. Instead, she took a bite out of Archie.

"I sent you over here to get them and instead I find you here all cozy."

"That's right," Archie said. "I am enjoying a moment with my boys. Is that all right with you?"

She was so flustered because he didn't jump up and kiss her behind and grab the boys by the neck and drag them out into the street that she turned on her heel and flounced out of the house.

"Bye-bye, Sharon," I said and gave a tiny wave to the thin air. "See ya."

Tyler started laughing. Then Hunter got the giggles.

Archie looked at me and said, "She can be a little demanding."

"Really?" I said. "I hadn't noticed." I'd had it with him. I was furious.

Now Tyler and Hunter became hysterical laughing.

"Calm down, boys. You're going to make yourselves sick!" I said.

Archie stood up. "Well, it's time to go home and face the music."

"Thanks, Miss Holly!" the boys said together.

I said to them, "You boys run ahead. I want to talk to your dad."

They put their glasses in the sink and ran out of the house.

"So, Archie?"

"I know, I know," he said. "Marry in haste, repent at leisure."

"Well, there's that, but I was thinking of something else."

"What?"

"Where is your spine?"

"What?" He looked very annoyed.

"Just what I said. You can't let Sharon continue like this. She's a tyrant! The boys can't have a milk shake? You should go tell Miss Perfect that they were made with skim milk, frozen yogurt, sugar-free chocolate, and Sullivan's Island ice cubes, which might or might not be the most suspicious ingredient."

"I'll tell her."

"You're missing the point, Archie."

"What?"

"Your boys are depressed. They need help. Professional help. I'm not kidding."

"Oh, come on."

"Ask yourself this. Are they enjoying their summer? Who's taking them swimming? Who's having their friends for sleepovers? Or camping out in the backyard? Where's their vacation?"

"I think they're doing fine. This has been a tough adjustment."

"My point is this. They're not adjusting, and I really think that if you can't bring *yourself* to stand up to Sharon, you need to take them to see someone who can teach them coping skills."

"Well, I'll think about what you've said."

With that, he got up and left. I realized a few minutes after he left that he was seething with anger. I had said some outrageous things. I knew that. But if I didn't tell him, who would? Well, guess what? I was seething, too. I went out to my yard and saw that my dahlias were beginning to open. They were already astonishing. I checked my bees' pans for water. It was as hot as the hinges on the back door of hell. Sometimes late afternoons were more unbearable than midday. I refilled the pans and muttered to myself and the bees.

"This woman is a scourge. She has got to be stopped before she totally ruins this family. But what can I do? Nothing!"

Later in the afternoon, I turned on my sprinklers and went back inside. If I ever won the lottery I was going to put in an irrigation system. On a timer.

I went back inside, and a few minutes later I heard a woman's voice screaming. Where was it coming from?

I went out to the porch and realized it was coming from Archie's house, so it had to be Sharon. What was her problem this time?

As I was walking down my steps and toward their house, I noticed a swarm of bees returning to the apiary. To the pink hive. Uh-oh, I thought, what were my naughty bees up to now?

I heard a siren coming in our direction and assumed the siren was related to the screams, because that's what a smart girl I was. Sure enough, the police car arrived and out stepped Ted Meyers. He wore a serious expression.

He waved to me, went up Archie's steps, and knocked on the door. Someone let him in. I waited. About twenty minutes later, he came out.

"Hey, Ted!" I said quietly and motioned for him to come over to my porch. He approached my steps.

"Hey there, Holly. Sure is a hot one, isn't it?"

"Sure is. So what's going on over there?"

"Well, Archie's new wife says that when she went into her bathroom there were thousands of bees in there, just sitting quietly all over everywhere."

"Did you see them?"

"Nope. Not a one. I don't know if she sees things or what, but something's definitely wrong over there." He made a circle with his finger beside his head, the international sign for insanity. "She says the bees are after her, trying to make her lose her mind."

"That's not likely," I said. "African bees might kill somebody, but honey bees? Not a chance."

"I know. I looked up honey bees on the Internet. Boy, you can find out just about anything online these days, can't you? Anyway, your little critters are just about completely benign. And they're good for flower and vegetable garden production. And their honey should help to relieve allergies for other island residents."

"I feel like I ought to give you a gold star, Ted!" I said and laughed.

I was relieved to have an ally in law enforcement. I had no idea how crazy Sharon might get.

"I'm off on Tuesday. Want to get some dinner?"

"Sure. Why not?"

I had a date. Damn. Oh, my God. I had a date. Yeah, but it was Ted. No reason to get nervous there.

That night, while I was having a glass of wine and making a list of things I needed to do, I got a text message from Leslie.

Send Momma's sweats and her sneakers. She's staying for a while and so am I. Charlie's contest is in two weeks and he's not ready by a long shot. News flash! Momma's got a beau.

Next, a picture appeared in my feed. I wasn't sure what I was looking at. And then came the explanation.

That's Momma with Suzanne Velour.

What the hell, Momma? What the hell?

I texted back, *Is Suzanne Velour a woman?*

No, came her reply. *She's a heterosexual man who's a super successful female impersonator like Dame Edna.*

Oh, I feel much better, I texted back.

I laughed. I hoped they both stayed in Las Vegas until they sowed all their wild oats. I had enough excitement in my life. And I had a date.

"Ever hear of a gangster named Bugsy Siegel?"
Suzanne said.

"I think so," the QB said.

"He named his casino the Flamingo after his
girlfriend, because she had long legs . . ."

"Like a flamingo?" the QB said.

"Yeah, like you and me!"

You could hear them laughing in Arizona.

Chapter Twenty-Six
Char

In the morning, Charlie and I were on his tiny terrace enjoying a cup of coffee and some cinnamon
rolls when Momma burst through the French doors
making a very dramatic entrance.

"Good morning, possums!" she said.

"I was about to come and check for a pulse," Charlie said. "Good morning!"

"It's good to be alive," Momma said and gave each of us a peck on the cheek.

"Come sit," I said. "I'll get you a cup."

"Thank you, sweetheart," she said.

I went inside to the kitchen and got a cup and saucer, a plate and napkin, and hurried back to them.

"I've been giving your act a lot of thought," the QB said to Charlie. "In fact, I've hardly slept a wink."

"What are you thinking?" Charlie said.

"Well, I made it my business to watch every bit of Dame Edna on YouTube and her Web site and anything else I could dig up, and suddenly I have a much better understanding of what you're after. Suzanne's idea, of course," she said.

"What do you mean?" I said.

"Forgive this old bee, but I've never given two minutes of thought to the difference between drag queens and female impersonators. I live on Sullivan's Island and the subject seldom comes up in conversation. But coming here and meeting Suzanne and seeing what you're doing and then Dame Edna? Honey? That guy is the glue that put it all together for me!"

"Hallelujah!" Charlie said. "He's making wads of money and having a ball while he's doing it!"

"But here's what he's got that you don't."

"What?" I said.

Charlie held his breath.

"He's got a shtick!" Momma said. "That's Yiddish for having your own act."

"I know that," Charlie said.

"Actually, I knew that, too," I said.

"Well, Suzanne explained it all to me," the QB said. "We stayed up watching Dame Edna until I understood what it was I was watching."

"Dame Edna is the gold standard," Charlie said.

"Agreed," Bee said. "Suzanne agrees, too. Here's the thing. Dame Edna's been entertaining family and friends by dressing up in all sorts of costumes since she was a child. She has extensive history in theater and film, which you don't have."

"He was our drum major with our marching band," I said, hoping to add some credibility to Charlie's résumé. "And we know he's a helluva lip-syncer."

"These are helpful, but they are not the things that will catapult our sweet Charlie to the big league. But we came up with something that might."

"Well, for the love of all that's good and holy, spill it!" Charlie said.

"You lip-sync Cher's songs, and these are your favorites, correct?"

"Yes," Charlie said.

"What if you were her identical twin sister, who actually wrote all those songs and Cher stole them, having heard you singing them in the shower?"

"What?" I said. "That's crazy."

"No, it isn't. Think about it," Momma said, stirring cream into her coffee like one of Macbeth's witches tending the cauldron. "If you have a character that's only yours, then you can build a shtick around it!"

"Dame Edna calls her fans possums and refers to her outrageous eyeglasses as face furniture," Charlie said.

"So what if you compared Cher having sex with Sonny to landing on an aircraft carrier?"

"Oh, God!" Charlie said. "That's priceless!"

"Poor Sonny," I said, envisioning Sonny's landing in Cher's Netherland the way a small plane is snagged by a wire across the landing deck of an actual aircraft carrier.

"You could say you dated him first," Momma said.

"Momma? You're right!" I said. "There are lots of possibilities of things you could drop into a monologue, in between songs, or take little pauses."

"Exactly!"

So, until noon, when Charlie had a block of time reserved with a theater coach, we built a character that Charlie felt comfortable enough to become. His humor surfaced along with his sense of irony and satire. It was like unlocking Pandora's box, except there were no evils to be released, only humor, and it didn't take long for that humor to become outrageous.

"Just imagine actually being Cher's identical twin sister!" said Suzanne, who had come by to help, laden with pastrami sandwiches and the best half-sour pickles I'd ever had, a rare find in the Lowcountry. "You can have costumes for the Sonny stage, the Gregg Allman stage, the Hollywood stage, the Broadway stage . . . I mean, you've got a treasure trove. But so you know, you'd also be seventy-two if you were her twin sister."

"Cher is immortal," Charlie said. "I could be her twin at every stage of her life, couldn't I?"

"Now you're thinking like a superstar!" Suzanne said, and we all applauded.

We gathered at the kitchen barstools, Suzanne helping Momma hoist herself up.

"Wooo!" Momma squealed.

Suzanne must've taken a little grab.

"Suzanne!" Charlie said. "The QB is still my mother-in-law!"

"Sorry," Suzanne said and shook her head to mean no, she wasn't sorry.

Momma giggled, something I had hardly ever heard her do.

"Cher was born Cherilyn. I could be born Charlene!" Charlie said. "Oh, I knew that was the right name for me!"

"I think you should go by Char," I said. "Char! Cher's Long-Lost Twin!"

"Agreed," Charlie said.

"Now we're having real fun," Momma said. Suzanne winked at her.

"You know, Cher actually does have a half sister named Georganne," Charlie said.

"Let's not confuse the situation with facts," Suzanne said. "But it's worth noting that one of the reasons Cher has enjoyed such a long, successful career hinges on her ability to roll with the times, change with the times, you know, reinvent herself whenever it was time to do it."

"That's it," Charlie said, "and her self-deprecating sense of humor. She had perfect timing, and speaking of timing, it's time for my drama lesson."

"I'm coming with you," Suzanne said. "You need supervision. Let's lay this whole concept on the coach and see where it goes."

"Excellent idea," Charlie said. "See y'all later."

They left and I turned to Momma. I had questions, but I wasn't sure if I wanted the answers.

"I think we should use this time to examine the lyrics of Cher's top ten greatest hit songs and change them to be Char's lyrics," Momma said.

"That's a stroke of brilliance, but while we have this time alone, would you like to tell me what the hell is going on between you and Suzanne?"

"Baby girl? I'm taking a walk on the wild side!" Momma was beaming from head to toe. "I'm breaking loose from all those rules and regulations and expectations. I'm a liberated woman!"

I wanted to tell her she'd done all that years ago. I wanted to say, maybe we should think this through a little better. I wasn't convinced that Suzanne's intentions were sincere. I didn't even know what Suzanne's real name was. And I wasn't sure if Momma had a goal in mind, in terms of Suzanne. But I neither said nor asked any of those things.

Instead I said, "Momma? I'm with you, girl!"

For the next few days, while Momma sewed hippie vests and bell-bottoms, we turned Cher's songs into Char's music. "Bang Bang" became "Dang Dang." "I Got You Babe" became "I've Got Your Babe." "The Beat Goes On" became "The Cheat Goes On." "Baby

Don't Go" became "Baby Please Go." We did this until we had enough material for thirty minutes onstage. The music was interjected with monologues about what it was like to live in Cher's shadow and all the things Cher did that were never supposed to be revealed. It was a hilarious act worthy of any small club, straight or otherwise.

Charlie worked with his coach every day, until he could recite his monologue without cue cards. Charlie was becoming so much more than a female impersonator. Charlie was a star. Not a megastar, not an icon. Not yet. But a budding star. You could smell success all around him. All he had needed was guidance and encouragement. Charlie was going places, and all of us were brimming with excitement to see where it would lead. And his confidence was growing.

Charlie had *become* Char. We wanted her to live in character all the time so that it would become second nature to her. And she did.

"The change in Charlie is incredible," Momma said.

"Char is a goddess," Suzanne said.

"Suzanne? Baby doll? That might be slightly overstating things," Momma said.

"Bee, baby? She's gonna be a goddess if it's the last thing I ever do," Suzanne said.

"Listen! I'm on the team, okay?"

While Momma sewed up a blue streak, and Suzanne and I reworked lyrics, Char and her drama coach cruised the bars and clubs and made tons of phone calls, on a mission to find out when there would be good opportunities for her to audition. Finally, they came up with a plan. Char's first appearance would be in a club where many new artists tried out their acts. A date was set. A few solid and reputable booking agents were invited to be in the audience without Char's knowledge.

"I don't want her to have any more anxiety than she's already got," Suzanne said.

"Good call," I said.

Suzanne suggested that when Charlie was dressed as Char, we should use feminine pronouns and that seemed right to me and to Momma. And now that she was Char all the time, she was she all the time.

The day before her showcase I said to Char, "Okay, you have to do your nails. And that includes your feet."

"I've never worn nail polish," Char said.

"I don't know how you missed it, but now you're going to, so let's go."

"I'm nervous," Char said when we were in pedicure chairs in the salon Suzanne sent us to.

"Me, too," I said. "But you know what? You're going to be okay."

"Easy for you to say," she said.

"Look, I've thought about this. If the show goes well and an agent appears to book you a pile of gigs? Great! If an agent never appears, I still love you."

"I love you, too," she said, and the relief that flooded her was obvious.

"This is not a contest with an approval trophy from me, Momma, or Suzanne. It's more like a little dream coming true. Don't let the what-ifs eat you alive and take all the fun out of it for you. This is supposed to be *fun*. Remember that."

"What if Cher's in the audience?" Char said with a nervous laugh.

"What if Dame Edna's in the audience?"

Realizing that the odds of their making an appearance were a billion to one, my Charlie, soon to be the world's Char, relaxed again.

"You're right," she said. "I'm worried about nothing."

"That's right," I said. "You're worried about nothing."

There was one rehearsal in the actual space with the lighting manager and the sound engineer.

"How did it go?" I asked when she came in.

"I'm as ready as I'll ever be."

The evening of the showcase arrived and we went to the club on the early side so that Char would have some time to get comfortable in the space. She wasn't the only one performing that night. There was a ventriloquist, a magician, a vocalist, and our Charlie. Char. There would be no costume change for Char, so that minimized the stress.

"How do you feel?" I asked her.

Char said, "You know what? Strangely enough, I'm pretty calm."

"Good!" Momma said. "You know what, Char?"

"What?"

"You're going to be fabulous. I just know it. The costume alone should cinch it!"

She was only teasing. But can we have a word about her costumes? They were amazing. The gowns Momma made were in various stages of completion. For tonight, Char looked exactly like Cher had looked in her Sonny and Cher days. She wore vertical-striped low-rise bell-bottoms, a white shirt with billowing sleeves, a brown suede vest with long fringes, platform Kork-Ease shoes, and a headband worn Native American style over her long black wig, which was parted in the middle. She had hoop earrings, a long chain with a cross, and bangles on both arms. She wasn't quite Cher; she was Char.

Momma had never been more supportive of Holly or of me at any moment in our lives than she was of

Charlie in that one. But she knew what a chance Charlie was taking. Either Char had the talent or she didn't. Even if there was no agent present in the audience, the club manager had been around long enough to recognize talent. He would make calls. Suzanne explained that in Las Vegas, just like in Hollywood, everybody's in the racket for all they can get. So yes, club owners acted as managers and managers acted as agents.

Momma and I found a table and ordered iced tea. The tired waitress looked at us like we were crazy.

"Y'all never heard of iced tea?" Momma said and gave her some side eye.

"I'll see what I can do," she said.

Finally, Suzanne returned and sat with us. The club began to fill up for the first set and we began to get excited.

"You know, when Charlie arrived in Las Vegas," Suzanne said, "I thought he was a lost little lamb."

"Not anymore," I said.

"Not anymore is right," Momma said.

Boy, had this family changed with the times, and Momma was all smiles, agreeing with everyone all over the place. Well, that was Suzanne's fault.

"Your mother is a beautiful woman," Suzanne whispered to me while the magician was pulling scarves out of audience members' ears.

"Thanks. Suzanne? What's your real name?"

"Buster," she said. "Buster Henry. Retired military."

"No shit," I said.

Suzanne smiled like the Mona Lisa and said, "Yeah, no shit. I got sick of uniforms."

"Okay," I said. "I can understand that."

"Costumes are more fun."

What did it say that in such a short period I'd become accustomed to being with this lifestyle that was so foreign to mine? And what about Momma? Her transformation from an impossible old crank to a woman of a certain age with a reservoir of juice worthy of a squeeze was, well, nothing I ever expected. I wondered what Holly would say if she could have seen all this.

We suffered through the vocalist who tried to kill our love of music in general with her rendition of "Fascinating Rhythm," with a truly lame tap routine interspersed between lyrics. The poor thing was out of breath and someone finally gave her a glass of water and helped her off the stage.

Then the stage went dark as the sound engineer began to play a medley of Cher's music, one song leapfrogging to another, growing into a crescendo until, boom! The lights came on and there was Char, back to the audience, and as she turned she looked more

like Cher than Cher. People began to clap spontane-
ously, and Char hadn't really done a thing. But she had
that something, that special something that stars have.
Presence. Stage presence.

"Good evening, everyone! I know what you're
thinking. No, I'm not Cher. I'm Char, her identical
twin sister! Isn't that insane? I'll bet she doesn't even
know she's got one!"

The whole club was totally mesmerized. Even the
club manager leaned against a wall to watch and the
bartenders stopped taking drink orders. Char had
them right in the palm of her hand.

She explained how her evil twin stole all her music
and said that now, she was going to give us the real lyrics to "I Got You Babe."

She was so damn good, I had tears running down
my face. So did Momma, and Suzanne was about to
pop out of her cocktail dress, her chest was rising and
falling so fast. People were screaming and cheering,
and when the song was over there were calls for more.

"Encore! Encore!"

"Oh, darlin' little precious gems! I didn't come here
with just one story. Do y'all want to know who the real
tramp in the family was?" Everyone laughed. "Uh-
huh. You heard it from me! And how about the original
lyrics to 'Bang Bang'? Are we ready?" The lights went

low and Char lip synced the Cher version but they had cut Char's changes into the song so that it sounded like Cher singing Char's song.

"How did they do that?" I asked Suzanne.

"I wouldn't know, but then, there's a lot of magic out here. Smoke and mirrors."

When it was all over, the crowd stood and roared with applause and whistles. We clapped so hard, our hands stung.

Momma said, "Well, y'all, a star is born."

"Honey never goes bad. Did you know that?" I asked.

Ted said, "I want to hear all about honey bees."

Chapter Twenty-Seven
Ding-Dong

Ted was picking me up at six. I didn't have the good sense to be nervous about having a date. I just told myself I was going out with a friend, because in my mind that's what he was. Nonetheless, I did all the things to prepare that I'd watched Leslie do in our youth. The date ritual. Shower, hair, shave, moisturizer, and a measure of cosmetic enhancement. I wore a simple sundress and flat sandals that were a natural color. I borrowed one of Leslie's purses and a spritz of her cologne.

Promptly at six, the doorbell rang, and I wouldn't say I sprinted to the door, but I got there quickly. I didn't wait the suggested three beats that Leslie did, like her three rings on the phone before answering. What was the point in delaying the fun?

"Hey!" I said. "Don't you look nice?"

"You, too! Are you ready to go?"

"Yep! So, what's the plan?"

"Dinner at the Shem Creek Bar and Grill, watch the sunset, and then I don't know. We'll see how late it is, I guess?"

"That sounds lovely," I said and locked the door to the house behind me.

"Great!" he said and held my car door for me, closing it when I was comfortably seated with the skirt of my dress neatly tucked under me.

Ted's car was precious—a Japanese import, red and loaded with gadgets. The lights were on at Archie's house and yes, I had a moment where I hoped he could see me going out with someone. *That's right, Archie! I have a date!*

Now, that whole southern thing about gentlemen holding chairs and doors for ladies might seem dated to some people, that the fair sex couldn't manage a chair or a door for themselves, bless their sweet little heart-shaped peach kernels. To me it said a mouthful of other things—that your momma raised you right, that you had respect for women and deferred to them by allowing them to enter a home, a store, a restaurant, et cetera, before the man and then to take their arm and fold it over yours to ensure steady footing, and finally, it was just a tiny bit of refinement that wasn't hurting anyone and made you both seem like you didn't grow up in a barnyard, even if you did.

We were passing over the causeway and couldn't help but notice the water on either side was almost even with the road. One more inch and the causeway would be a washout. Then, for a moment, I felt overwhelmed, as though something terrible was all around me, something as dark as death itself. I must have gasped.

"You okay?" Ted said.

"Yeah, I'm fine. Just sometimes I get these weird premonitions and I have to figure out what they mean."

"Such as?"

"Oh, Lord, if I start telling you this stuff you're going to say, well, now I know why *she's* not married!"

"No, I won't! I love all that spiritual business."

"Sometimes it's useful, but most of the time it's just ether garbage, floating around."

"What was on your radar just then?"

"It was pretty dark, I mean dark like death, and this overwhelming feeling of, well, pressure on my chest and not being able to breathe."

"How awful."

"Must be a full moon," I said.

"Yes, tonight is the peak. It's also when all the nuts come out of the woodwork and do crazy stuff."

"Like what? Howl?"

"Exactly. I wouldn't be surprised if your new neighbor was outside spinning around and howling at midnight."

"Let me just tell you, Ted. That woman is bat shit crazy, sorry for the foul language."

Ted threw his head back and laughed.

"I love that you're apologizing for saying a bad word! And, by the way, I think she's probably delusional."

I did not tell him that I had seen my bees leaving her house. That they had been in her house and that she didn't make it up. Sharon was not someone I wanted anyone to hold in any kind of esteem.

"I don't know if she's delusional, but she does other things that border on cruelty."

"Really? Such as?"

"She's made Archie's boys miserable in every way she can."

"Why would she do that?"

"Because she's incredibly selfish and puts herself ahead of everyone. And she never wanted kids."

"Whoo-hoo! I touched a nerve here, didn't I?"

"Ted, did you know Carin? Archie's deceased wife?"

"I didn't know her, but I knew of her. I mean, I remember that she was very pretty and she loved her family. She was always at the oyster roast and she decorated her golf cart with the boys for the Fourth of July parade. Her Halloween house was a favorite stop on the island. You know, that sort of thing."

"Yes, she did all those things, but Carin was also the most loving mother I have ever seen. The loss to these boys is so horrible. And this Sharon is Halloween every day of the year."

"That's too bad for the boys. Poor little guys. Give me an example."

Then I thought it wasn't good to talk about Sharon like this. "Listen, I could tell you a pile of stories about Sharon, but it won't change anything."

"It might," he said.

"It would just be hearsay," I said. "But it wouldn't hurt anybody if the Sullivan's Island Police Force kept an eye on her."

"I will make a note of that."

We pulled into the parking lot of the Shem Creek Bar and Grill and got out of the car.

"I love this place," I said as I crunched along the gravel. "Best hush puppies ever."

"I could eat a truckload of them, that's for sure.

But I'm partial to those little bitty crab cakes they make."

"Love them, too! And the oysters! I don't know where they come from, maybe the May River, but oh, man, I love them on the half shell. Do you love oysters? And clams?"

"I do!" Ted said. He stopped and held me at an arm's length. "Holly Jensen?"

"What? What did I say?"

"Nothing. You're just a breath of fresh air," Ted said. "That's all."

"Oh. Gosh. Thanks!"

We had to wait a few minutes for a table, but then we were seated in the back room over the dock. The restaurant was bustling, as it always was. A waiter with a tray loaded with platters of fried seafood passed and suddenly, I was ravenous.

We were looking at the menu and there were so many great choices, I couldn't decide.

"If I don't get some food right now I'm going to start crying," I said and then looked up at him. Ted was staring at me. "Not really."

"It's okay. My stomach is growling like an idiot and I'm starving, too."

"It's the smell. There is nothing on this planet better than the smell of fried shrimp that were swimming this morning."

"Except for a perfectly grilled steak," he said. "I know red meat's bad for you, but oh, momma, there's nothing better than a big old bone-in ribeye."

He had said, oh, momma. Really? Oh, momma? He was definitely a nerd like me. I started smiling and thought, Wow, I like him a lot.

"You know, I make chicken that's so good it borders on the obscene, but I never really got into grilling."

"Well, I'll tell you what. Next time we get together, I'll show you how to grill a steak to perfection, and the time after that, you can make your badass chicken, pardon the language, and I mean badass in a good way."

"Of course," I said and giggled. "But what makes you so sure there are more dates in our future?"

"Because I can tell you like me," Ted said and grinned at me. "Don't you?"

I couldn't stop smiling.

"Maybe," I said and turned red. "Maybe not."

"Okay," he said. "We'll see what we see."

Our server appeared and Ted ordered two Corona lights with lime and cold mugs, and two fried seafood platters, basically enough food for four people.

"Beer! What a great idea!"

"What do you usually drink?" he said. "I'm sure we can change the order."

"No, beer's great. Really! But that's a lot of food, don't you think?"

"So we'll take it home. Tell me the truth. How come you're not married yet?"

"I don't know. You'd think someone as cool as me would've been snatched up the minute I graduated from college, right? How about you?"

"The same. Did you ever have any serious boy-friends?"

"Nope. Not one."

"How can that be?"

"I think I'm too shy or something. How about you and women?"

"I dated a girl in college for a long time, but she and I just wanted different things out of life."

"Like what?"

"You're pretty nosy, aren't you?" He was smiling, so I knew he didn't mean it.

"Yeah, maybe. So tell me what she wanted that you didn't."

"She liked television, I like to read. I like to cook at home. She liked to go out all the time. I'm a dog per-son. She was a cat person. When we went somewhere in the car, she had to listen to the oldies station and sing along with every single song."

"That's the worst! It's like being held hostage and if you say anything, you're the jerk, not them."

"Ah! It sounds as if you have some experience in this area?"

"Yeah, my brother-in-law."

"What's he like?"

I leaned back against the well-worn leather booth and considered his question. I wasn't required to answer every single question in detail, and I liked Ted. So I gave it a moment's consideration and threw what I thought was a pretty sassy answer out there for him.

"Ted? When I'm sure you're desperately and hopelessly in love with me, I'll tell you all about Charlie. In the meanwhile, let's talk about you."

"There's not much to tell, ma'am. Not much at all."

The waiter delivered our beers and we poured them into our chilled mugs. We toasted each other.

"I know that you sat behind me in English class and that you were a sensitive young man. I remember your poetry."

"Oh, now I'm blushing! My poetry was terrible."

"That's why it's so memorable!" I laughed and reached across the table, giving him a little push on his arm. "Just kidding!"

"Oh, Lord," he said. "Hey, here comes our food."

"Good thing, I was about to faint."

"Don't worry, Holly. I can give mouth to mouth. It's all part of the job."

Mouth to mouth. Oh, God! Was I expected to kiss him? How was that going to go? To say that I began to feel some stress would not do my shaking body any justice at all. I was coming undone. Why hadn't I gone out with any of the ugly boys who'd asked me to go on a date, so I wouldn't be such a newbie? Why had I saved kissing a boy until now? He wasn't even a boy and I wasn't even a girl. We were well into adulthood!

"Hey, are you okay?" he said.

"Um, sure," I said. "I'm fine."

"No, you're not. You're all flushed. Did I say something stupid?"

He reached over and put his hand on the back of mine.

"No, not at all. I'm the stupid one," I said.

"Your hands are like ice, Holly. Tell me what's wrong. Please."

"Oh, hell, I may as well tell you." I took a deep breath and a big sip of beer. "When I told you I've never had a serious boyfriend, I wasn't exaggerating at all. In fact, I've never had a boyfriend, period. I know that seems crazy, but there are reasons why, other than me being picky and shy. But there it is."

It was his turn to lean back in the booth and take a deep breath. And he got awfully quiet for a while. Then he leaned across the table.

"Holly? Are you a *virgin*?" he whispered.

"Yeah, sorry."

"Wait a minute. Don't apologize for that. Are you kidding? You know, sometimes I have night duty and I get the pleasure of riding around the island and tapping on the car windows of couples engaged in, you know, having sex. Can I just tell you how many of those are the same people all the time except they're with somebody else?"

"Good Lord," I said.

"Yeah, it sort of cheapens the whole thing, doesn't it? There's nothing forbidden anymore. People are doing drugs, getting drunk, full of road rage, and generally acting like there are no rules. And those are the people my parents' age! You go on the Internet and there are oceans of people filled with hate, saying things I've never wanted to even think. And to perfect strangers! I think it's totally gross."

"Yeah, it's pretty disgusting," I said. "It all makes you wonder what ever happened to having morals and integrity. Or kindness. Not to bring up my lovely neighbor again, but kindness toward these boys? She doesn't have an ounce of it."

"Holly, when I said you were a breath of fresh air, I wasn't kidding."

"Really?"

"Yes, and don't worry. I don't have any crazy expectations."

"Well, that's good, because I wouldn't have the first clue how to meet them."

"Can we eat now?" he said.

"Please! And let's change the subject."

He had this smile. One that was going to be stuck in my head. And those eyes. He had those translucent blue eyes. And he had my number. Boy, did he ever.

Dinner was so much fun. Once we changed the topic of discussion to other things, we found an easy rhythm. He thought my stories about my mother, the queen bee, were hilarious, and I thought his stories of the old island residents were wonderful. I told him about my stupid job that I loved at Publix and he told me about the summer he learned to surf.

On the way home, we drove down to the tip of the island to look at the sky all streaked with red and then purple and then pink and marveled at the power of nature and we watched the sky become dark and the stars come out, countless stars twinkling all around and above us. And yes, of course, that's when he kissed me. It was not what I expected, but if it had not happened then I knew it never would.

"I knew you couldn't resist me," I said, still trying to catch my breath.

"You were right," he said. "Let's get you home."

When we turned on my block at Station Twenty-three, there was an ambulance and a fire truck at the end of the block. My heart was in my throat. Had something happened to one of the boys? I couldn't bear to think about it.

"I'm on it," Ted said and stomped on his gas pedal, screeching to a halt in front of Archie's house. "Stay in the car."

"Okay," I said.

Please don't let it be the boys! I thought and prayed. I waited while he went inside and I worried, praying like I had not prayed in my life.

Soon, two EMS workers came around from my backyard with a body in a body bag on a gurney. It was an adult.

At the same time, Ted came out of Archie's house and walked up to the side of our car and leaned inside.

"Sharon's dead. They think she was stung to death by your bees. Archie found her in your backyard."

"Oh, my God! That just can't be!"

*"Bees gorged with honey are less likely to sting," I said.
"My hives are full of honey."*

*Ted said, "There's going to be an autopsy.
It's going to be what it is, Holly."*

Chapter Twenty-Eight
Bee Cool

Ted went back inside Archie's house to be sure Archie and the boys were okay for the night. He told me Archie was terribly upset and it would be best if I stayed in the car and didn't make contact with them.

I called Leslie on my cell. Leslie put me on speaker.

"You're not going to believe what's happened here."

I quickly told them the story and they were horrified.

Momma said, "Her family's going to blame you, you know. Get ready for a lawsuit."

"Momma! Don't say that! How can they sue me? On what grounds? And what would they get? Three hundred pounds of honey?"

Then Leslie told me about Charlie's huge success in his showcase, which of course I was happy to know, but given the weight of the moment, I couldn't get too excited. My mind had been racing while she was going on and on about Charlie and Cher and now Char, and I finally had to stop her.

"Leslie, listen to me. I might be in huge hot water. Sharon's death might be ruled a negligent homicide or involuntary manslaughter, and then what?"

"Well, then, do what Momma said and get a lawyer. You're a big girl; call someone!"

"Leslie, I don't even know a lawyer."

"Well, sister? I'd Google it, then. Let us know what happens, okay?"

"Sure," I said and pressed the end button.

I was shaken. Leslie had not expressed any concern or sympathy. But she probably had no more of an idea on how to handle this pickle than I did. Maybe because they were on the other side of the country, it didn't seem real to them.

I was feeling very alone in the world. Very. Archie didn't want to see me? I needed a lawyer? What kind?

The car door opened. It was Ted again.

"So," he said, "there will be an investigation, of course. I don't want you to get upset, but you might be implicated. I don't know how they can accuse you of anything, except keeping bees that may or may not have turned into a malicious private nuisance."

"My bees have never been malicious. And they've never been a nuisance," I said and then reconsidered. "Okay, they used her car as an outhouse and they bearded her car, but that's normal behavior for bees. She did not get stung."

"The coroner most likely will be calling for an autopsy. In a few days, we'll know whether it was bee venom that killed her or not. I expect the odds are that it *was* the venom, because she was an otherwise healthy young woman."

"With a very unhealthy mind," I said.

"Listen, Holly, want to be smart? Don't talk to anyone—from any kind of media. And hire a lawyer first thing in the morning. A criminal lawyer. And here's my number if you need me. You know Darlene, our emergency dispatcher? Her husband, Mark, might be able to help. Come on, I'll walk you to your door. And stay away from your bee yard. It's a crime scene that needs to be combed, and you sure don't want to be accused of tampering with evidence."

I'll admit, I was in total shock. How was I supposed

to sleep that night? I sat by my kitchen window and stared at Archie's house for hours. His lights were on, too. I wrote a text message to him that said, I'm so sorry. If I can do anything, please tell me. And then I deleted it. If he wasn't texting me, why should I be texting him? I was so confused about Sharon's death.

Sharon was dead, but Hunter and Tyler were saved. And did my bees in the pink hive do it? Had they heard everyone's cries for help to the point that they just decided to intervene? Had anyone seen what happened? What was Sharon doing in my yard in the first place? Why wasn't anyone asking that? Was she taunting the bees? Trying to harm them?

I made a cup of chamomile tea, hoping it would help me sleep. I went to bed, but sleep was not mine to be had that night. I caught twenty minutes here and there, but something would wake me up again. A noise. A foghorn. The screech of an owl. The howls of coyotes as the Lowcountry crept toward dawn. Finally, I heard the newspaper brush my driveway and I went outside to pick it up.

There was no sign of life at Archie's house. It was seven thirty. I assumed Archie would be taking the day off to arrange Sharon's funeral, to write an obituary, to order flowers, and to do all the things that are necessary when there's a death. I went back inside and dropped the paper on the kitchen table. I was exhausted.

My phone rang. It was Darlene.

"Bad news travels fast, doesn't it?" I said. "Who did you hear it from?"

"It came over the wire from the call center. Are you all right?"

"I don't even know the answer to that. But I do know that I need a lawyer."

"That's why I'm calling. Mark is free this morning, which is so weird because he hasn't had a free morning in months! But he wanted to know if you'd like him to come over and talk to you."

"Oh! Yes! Please! You have no idea how frightened I am by all of this! I'm supposed to go to Publix this morning, but I think I'm not going in. I'll call them. Thank you, Darlene! And tell Mark I said thank you, too!"

I dressed quickly and tidied up the house. And I put up a large pot of coffee. The day would be fueled by caffeine. Then I called Publix.

"Is Andrea in?" I asked.

"Not until ten," came the answer.

"Well, it's Holly Jensen. I can't come in this morning. We've had a tragedy and I have to be home."

"Oh! I'm so sorry! What happened?"

"I am not supposed to comment. I mean, I'm sorry, I can't comment because it's a police matter. Anyway, if Andrea has any questions, just ask her to call me, please?"

"Sure thing."

I knew that within thirty minutes every single person who worked or shopped at Publix was going to know something big and really terrible had happened on the island. And that it had something to do with me.

The doorbell rang at nine. It was Mark Tanenbaum, Darlene's husband. He was a nice man with age-defying looks, a very successful lawyer and in amazing shape for his age, which I guessed was somewhere around fifty.

"Good morning," he said. "May I come in?"

"Please! And thanks for coming!" He followed me to the kitchen. "Coffee?"

"Yes, please. Just black. By the way, your garden is unbelievable."

"Thanks."

"How's your momma?"

"If I told you, you wouldn't believe it."

"Really? Is that a good thing?"

"She's fine. She's with Leslie and her husband in Las Vegas."

I poured two cups and put one in front of him. Then I sat down.

"Las Vegas. That's a crazy place, eh? We had an ABA meeting out there a few years back. It was like, wow!"

"That's what they tell me," I said.

He took a small notebook from the chest pocket of his sport coat and a pen from another.

He took a sip of the coffee and said, "This is really good coffee. Starbucks?"

"No, Folger's. This is some mess," I said.

"Well, Darlene told me what she heard on the wire, but why don't you tell me what happened in your own words and then we can see what to do."

I gave him the sequence of events, but I didn't tell him about the more mystic aspects of my bees or that they might be responding to my pleas for help in ways that they could. It just sounded too crazy. But I did tell him about the bees dropping tiny bombs on Sharon's car and about them bearding. And I told him about Sharon's personality and how I thought she was way too uptight. And I mentioned her strawberry allergy.

"So it's clear there was no friendship between the two of you."

"No."

I told him about my relationship with Archie's boys and Archie and that I had been good friends with Carin. I might have mentioned something about Sharon being a complete paranoid, germophobe, and perfectionist. Maybe.

"She wouldn't let the boys bring library books home because they had been touched by other people who might have filthy germs," I said.

"Really. Wow," Mark said.

"I know," I said. "Wow."

"Criminal law isn't really my area of expertise, but until we're sure you need one, I'll represent you on the house. I'm not going to stand back and watch an old island family's daughter get pushed around, and that's what happens if you don't have legal representation. I don't think any charges have been filed, but I will stay on it and find out."

"Oh, Mr. Tanenbaum, I can't tell you how much I appreciate this."

"Call me Mark. Mr. Tanenbaum is my dad." He smiled and I thought, What a lovely man. "In the meantime, talk to no one. Do not give a statement to the police or the press or say a single word on social media, understand? As far as I can see it, I don't think any crime has been committed here."

"Good. Mark? Why was she in my yard?" I asked.

"I don't know. No good reason I can think of. Did anyone see her?"

"I don't know. I was out on a date with Ted Meyers."

"No kidding. Well, in your best interest, I'd say no canoodling with him, either, until this is all sorted out."

"That's a shame," I said, thinking, I finally have a fish on the hook and I have to release him?

"Look, Holly, you don't want to get into a he-said, she-said thing with the chief of police, temporary or not. Basically, from here on in, I speak for you. And I think for you. Here's my card. You can text me or call me any time of the day or night, but please, if it's possible, let me get my beauty rest."

I smiled then and said, "Mark? Am I in trouble?"

"I don't think so. I think you should relax until I let you know otherwise. Holly, I'm an old-school lawyer. I like to see all the facts and then we go from there. So far, we don't have all the facts."

"Will you tell me what you find out?"

"Absolutely. As soon as I hear something, you'll be the very next to know. I'll call the coroner's office this morning. Now, I've got to go to the gym. I've got a young wife, you know what I mean?"

"I'm pretty sure I do," I said and laughed. I felt so much better. "Thanks, Mark."

I walked him to the door and as I glanced at my backyard, I noticed crime scene tape everywhere and three men in bee suits walking around, looking in the bushes.

"Mark! Wait! What's all that tape and who are those men?"

"They would be crime scene investigators investigating a would-be crime scene. Don't worry about them. They're actually on our side."

"Okay," I said. I wasn't so sure.

"I'll call you later," he said. "And stop worrying. You'll get wrinkles."

I smiled. He was actually pretty sweet.

"Thanks."

I stretched out on the sofa thinking I might catch a nap. I couldn't tell you how much time went by, but when I woke up, it was dark outside, well past the cocktail hour, and Archie was at my door. He didn't ring the doorbell, he was just calling my name, like Stanley calling Stella in *A Streetcar Named Desire*.

I got up to let him in and he stumbled into my hallway.

"Archie? Are you a little bombed?"

"I'm impaired. I won't deny it." He blinked his eyes as he struggled to focus in the light. "Can I have a moment of your time?"

"Of course," I said and looked outside to be sure he wasn't being followed by television cameras. The coast was clear. "Would you like some coffee?"

"Prolly not a bad idea," he said. "Oh, hell, Holly. I'm a widower *again*!"

I began walking toward the kitchen.

"Yes, and you know you have my condolences, Archie."

"Yeah, yeah. Listen, I know you didn't think much of Sharon."

"It doesn't matter what I thought of her," I said.

I filled a filter with ground beans and the well of the coffeemaker with water and flipped the switch.

"Of course it matters!" he said. "It matters what you think and it matters what my boys think. And I didn't listen to anybody. And now she's dead. I must be some kind of a bad luck charm."

"That's crazy talk."

When the coffee was done, I filled a mug and sat down at the table with Archie.

"Thanks," he said.

"Drink up," I said. "So, is there a plan in place for a funeral?"

"Yeah, her family is planning it. They don't want any input from me."

"Hmm," I said. "I know what that's like."

"Right? Holly, I've treated you awfully bad, and my boys, and I'm sorry."

"Who's watching the boys?"

"That woman Maureen has them both at her house. She's got that kid Matt?"

"Are they spending the night there?"

"Yes."

That was good. His sons didn't need to see him as drunk as a dog.

"I'll call her. I think you should be getting on home now. Tomorrow's probably going to be a tough day, okay?"

"Okay. You'll call Maureen?"

"Yes, I'll call Maureen." I stood up, a message that this visit was ending. "I'll walk you out."

"Thanks. Thanks for the coffee. You're a nice girl, Holly. Did I ever tell you that?"

"Thank you, and yes, I think you've said it before. Now let's get you up."

"Okay, I'm going."

Somehow, by God's grace, he got to the front door and left. I called Maureen.

"Maureen? Hey! It's me, Holly. Y'all okay?"

"Yes, and what a terrible thing. I mean, nobody liked her, that's for sure. But, damn! Death from a thousand bee stings? How awful!"

"Is that the story going around? Well, here's something we don't know. Maybe it was the bees, maybe it wasn't, but I can't imagine that many bees would sacrifice their lives to get rid of her. And if it was bees, and she was allergic, it would only take one. The queen is the only honey bee without a barb on her stinger. She might have done it, but I doubt it, because she doesn't ever leave the hive except to swarm. Swarming season ended months ago. So I guess we'll see when the autopsy comes back. And when they examine the findings in my yard. If it was my bees, there'll be carcasses all over the place."

"Are you pissed about something?"

"I don't know," I said. "Maybe. I'm just waiting for the morning papers. Give me a shout if you need me."

I was sort of pissed that my bees would take the blame when, if her death was the result of bee stings, they were probably only defending their hives. That finding, blaming my bees, could lead to passing laws against beekeeping in residential areas, which would be a terrible thing.

"You do the same," she said.

I went back out to the front of the house to lock up for the night and noticed that my hammock appeared to have an occupant. It was Archie. He'd made it past my front door but not down the steps. It was a warm night. I took a picture of him with my iPhone and sent it to Mark. I just left him there. Hopefully, by the time I got up in the morning, he'd be gone.

I had a moment then to reflect on how many nights I'd gone to sleep wishing I was in his arms, and I thought I wasn't so sure about that dream anymore. I wasn't so sure about anything.

Chapter Twenty-Nine
Strut Yo Stuff, Sugah

I was waiting for Char to come out of the bedroom, where she was trying on Momma's latest creation. It was sensational in muslin, which was phase one to making a custom gown as complicated as the one Momma and Charlie had designed. The entire gown was first constructed in muslin, an inexpensive fabric, to be sure it draped properly. So if it looked good in cheap muslin, I could only imagine what it would look like in celery green metallic lamé.

I was so surprised by what Holly said, and I knew I didn't respond with the right amount of concern. She must think I'm a coldhearted bitch. I wouldn't blame her. Sometimes I was one and I knew it. I don't know why she irked me so. Okay, yes, I know why she irks the ever-loving hell out of me, and when I tell you why, you can add petty and judgmental to the long list of my poor qualities.

My little sister was a martyr. I don't know why she always acts like she's being persecuted, but she does. She doesn't want to stay home with Momma? Well, Momma ain't home, so honey, go on, go over the causeway and go get that life you're always mumbling about not having. And even if Momma does come home, there's no one keeping you locked in, is there? Well, to hear her tell it, she was going to be blamed for Sharon's death, which was absurd.

And she's afraid of her own shadow. She's never even had a parking ticket, much less a speeding ticket. The only people she's really comfortable around are generally under five feet tall. Go figure that one out. Except for Archie.

And this stupid torch she's been carrying for Archie? He's not even that interesting, if you want my opinion, unless you are all hung up on the history of religion, which I am not. Although he was soon to be on the market again.

Sharon was dead? Found in our yard? It didn't make sense. I'd call Holly as soon as I had a little time and see what the whole story was. But hey, ding-dong, the witch was dead. A cause for discreet celebration to be sure.

The bedroom door opened and Char stepped out into the living room.

"Wow!" I said. "Just wow!"

Celery green was definitely her color.

"You look like a movie star!" I said.

"Thanks!" Char said. "I love that it shimmers when I walk. Watch."

Char sashayed through the living room to the front door and back to the bedroom.

"I hate to tell you this," I said. "But this apartment is no longer worthy of your star power."

"As soon as I have my own little club, we'll move," Char said. "Your mother is Christian Siriano!"

"I'm happy with it," Momma said.

"You should be," I said. "Wait until Suzanne sees this!"

I still could not believe that Katherine Jensen and Suzanne Velour, aka Buster Henry, USMC, Ret., were a number. Do you think the ladies of the Stella Maris Altar Society would understand? Approve? It was just such a long jump from lying in her bed, picking at Holly over every little thing, and satisfying her longings with catsuits. And by *catsuits,* I don't mean the kind Lola Falana made famous representing Tigress perfume a thousand years ago. I mean the fleece variety with kittens all over them.

And now she was designing and making spectacular costumes for *Char*. Talk about a 180: she was simply not the same woman. I couldn't see her ever living on Sullivan's Island full-time again. Not after this. Side note? She was also the happiest I'd ever seen her. Maybe Suzanne was just so outrageous, which she was, that Momma couldn't resist. Who knows? Anyway, I wasn't about to suggest a return date to the Lowcountry for either one of us.

Momma seemed more tired than usual. She had purple circles under her eyes. Her spirits were high, but her energy seemed a little tapped out. But then, we were out every night, doing one crazy thing or another. We went to see a show called Le Rêve, which is this underwater tango that's about true love versus dark passion—a hard choice if ever there was one. We'd been to the Burlesque Hall of Fame, we'd played miniature golf at a Kiss-inspired course and shot our golf balls through Gene Simmons's head, and we'd had a tour of the Neon Boneyard. Pretty exciting stuff for a couple of home girls from the Lowcountry.

There had been a scout in the audience the night of Char's showcase. And don't you know, Char had been quickly picked up by the William Morris Endeavor agency. Now she had professional representation. Naturally, they had a huge legal team to go over contracts and a bookkeeping department to keep the clubs and casinos honest. Well, at least the clubs and casinos would be honest with Char. Suzanne predicted that soon Char would have a big-time manager and a choreographer who would help her shape a more professional and polished act, maybe give her a live backup band. As soon as the word hit the streets that there was a new talent in town, all these folks would be coming out of the woodwork. They would offer so much more than Suzanne could provide, more by a ridiculously wide margin. And Suzanne would conclude that she was just happy to have been a part of the launch.

"You know," Char said yesterday, "having my own orchestra would be my dream come true."

"With a horn section?"

"I was thinking xylophone and maybe strings?"

"A retro act, like Duke Ellington and Lionel Hampton?"

"Exactly!"

"Hmmm," I said. "That's something to work toward."

All the shows and clubs we'd been to were so over-enhanced with digital images and digital music and crazy lighting that it all looked and sounded a bit like the same electronic mix. Something retro might be new, if that made any sense.

His first gig was at Divas at the Linq.

"No point in starting small," Suzanne said to Char.

We had seen the show one night and it was mind blowing. Frank Marino was the emcee of the best show of female impersonators in Las Vegas. Divas Las Vegas. He was a spectacularly handsome man but a wickedly funny and beautiful Joan Rivers. And he had the widest variety of the most talented impersonators in Las Vegas. What set Char apart was that she wasn't trying to be Cher. Cher impersonators were a dime a dozen, like Elvis impersonators. Char's fictitious life as Cher's long-lost identical sister gave her a creative edge of authenticity over just a regulation female impersonator, if there was such a thing.

And as the day wore on, I couldn't stop thinking about Holly. What if she was really in trouble? Momma was taking a nap, Char was in rehearsal, so I finally had some free time to call her.

"Holly? I can't get you out of my mind. Are you okay?"

"Well, until they get the results of the autopsy back, it's unclear. But it's not my fault if my bees swarmed her. How could it be? I mean, it's not like bees take orders."

We were quiet then, because we both knew she

talked to her bees the way other people talk to a therapist.

"It's not like anyone could prove it," I said, "even if you did. My sister, the bee whisperer."

"And there's no precedent. I checked. I mean, her parents could file a civil suit. You can sue anybody over anything. Here's the thing: even though this is not my fault, I still need a lawyer."

"This is some world we live in, isn't it?"

"Sometimes, it's a little unbelievable. How's Momma?"

"She's having the time of her life. She's sewing like mad, and laughing all the time with Suzanne, her friend, who's taking her all over town."

"Unreal," Holly said.

"Is there a funeral for Sharon?"

"Not until the coroner releases her body."

"We want to send flowers," I said. "Do you know when that might be?"

"Nope. But it was in the *Post & Courier* this morning. Anytime there's a police investigation, it's in the paper."

"Did the police come to you?"

"I was on a date with the acting chief of police when it happened."

"*You* had a date?"

"Yeah. Stranger things have happened. Ted Meyers, a guy I went to high school with. He's really nice."

"I might remember him. Holly? Do you need me to come home?" I said.

"Absolutely not. My friend Darlene, her husband is a lawyer and he's handling it so far."

"Okay."

"Really, I'm fine. If I wasn't, I'd tell you."

"Have you seen the boys?"

"No, only in passing but not to talk to. I'm keeping myself busy. Don't worry. There's not a weed in our entire yard."

I was certain that was true. Holly took all that energy of hers and spent it rage-gardening and on her bees. It bordered on obsessive behavior. And sometimes it surprised Momma and me to admit it, but the honey from her hives was the best honey we'd ever tasted. It just had a sweeter and smoother flavor. Holly said it was because of her herb garden, that her bees loved the pollen and nectar from rosemary and thyme when it was in flower. Holly was insistent that her bees' favorite herbs and flowers had everything to do with the honey's flavor. Momma and I just let it go and ignored all the bee facts she tossed around, because, you know, Holly was a little odd and neither one of us really wanted to fight over every single thing because she didn't like to fight like we did. Momma and I could disagree about something and then go on about our business, agreeing to disagree on whatever the argument was about. Holly would carry the disagreement on her heart like irreparable scar tissue, a wound that would cut her tender spirit into ribbons. And that's why I was worried about her. I had my issues with my marriage, to be sure, and I'm sad to say they seemed to be growing. I was happy for Charlie to be Char and I was amazed by her talent, but as I had long feared, the more she became Char the less appealing she was to me as an intimate partner. What was I going to do? Leave Momma with Suzanne and go home? To what?

Momma got up from her nap and found me on the patio, drinking iced tea and just daydreaming.

"Oh, hey! How was your nap?"

"Truth? I don't feel so well. I think I'd better go home."

"Momma! Sit! What's happened?"

"I just feel bloated and I don't know what that means. And I'm worried about Holly."

"She's fine, Momma. I talked to her."

"She's my daughter and I know her better than she knows herself. I've completed three gorgeous gowns for Char. Char is fine. Holly is not fine. And neither am I."

"Drones have no stingers.
So they can't defend the hive," I said.

"That's awful," Tyler said.

Chapter Thirty
Bee at Peace

I couldn't believe how annoyed Char was with me when I told her I was taking Momma back to Charleston.

"Momma doesn't feel well, Char," I said. "And I've got a bad feeling that Holly's in trouble."

"You're my wife! You can't just walk out on me again! I thought we'd reached an understanding."

"You understand what *you'd* like me to accept, but you *don't* understand that *I* just can't bite into this thing like a Krispy Kreme donut. I love you, Char, I always will. But, and I can't believe I'm going to say this, this whole lifestyle is too crazy for me. I wish you well, you know I do. I have to take care of my family now. Someone has to take care of them."

"So that's it? Good-bye? After all we've been to each other?"

"It's good-bye for now. You know Momma had a bad report from the doctor. If she's not feeling right, she should go and see them. She has not complained once since she got her diagnosis. If she's complaining now it's for a reason."

"Yes, but I have my opening this week. I need you here for good luck!"

"I want to, but my mother needs me, and I can't believe you'd say something so selfish."

"Okay, you're right. That was beneath me. So, if it turns out that the QB is all right, will you come back?"

"I can't promise that now," I said. "You know that."

"Leslie, we have a problem," she said.

"Oh? Is there news?" I said.

"Look, Leslie, I can feel it. You're not attracted to me, physically, when I'm Char."

"Yes, that's true. But I do love you."

"Well, since this is a time for truth telling, I guess you should know I've always been happier as a woman."

"In my heart, I've known that for a long time," I

said, knowing this was finally the end of us. "But it's important for both of us to be happy. Don't you agree?"

We hugged then and we both choked back tears.

"It's okay, Charlie. It's okay."

"I know I've disappointed you," she said, "and I'm sorry. So damn sorry."

"Char? It's okay, baby. Just go be the biggest Char you can be! And I'll—well, I guess I'll always be your biggest fan."

We hugged again until we were both okay and then Char, not Charlie, was out the door. My heart was a little heavy, not too terribly crushed to bits, because being with her during this time had shown me what I already knew on instinct.

Char left to go work on her act with her drama coach and a special production manager from the Divas. Now they were incorporating old film clips of Sonny and Cher behind her as she performed. Her act was growing into something a lot more sensational than any of us had imagined that it might. And quickly. But her new production manager said that Char was taking to the stage like the proverbial duck to water, and he saw no reason not to go all out for Char's debut. Naturally, Char was thrilled, as we all were.

But I had to get back to Charleston, and forgive me if I sound like Holly, I just had a feeling that the sooner

I got home, the better. I just felt a nagging pull, way down inside of my gut. And as any old salt will tell you, when the Lowcountry calls you home? You had better go.

When Suzanne got word we were leaving, she came by. She was very upset, too, so I tried to explain to him the whole story about Holly and the bees and Sharon and Archie and the boys. And about Momma's health.

"Honey, if you can clean up that mess, you can negotiate lasting peace in the Middle East." She just shook her head and said, "Where's your momma? I want to talk to her."

Momma was in the bedroom, packing. I watched as Suzanne knocked lightly on the door and heard Momma say she should come in. The door was closed for a long time. Meanwhile, I got flights for us for the following day and decided to pack as well.

Suzanne came to my room and said, "I talked to the QB. Get her home and call me, okay? I want to know what's going on. And if you need me, I'll come in a heartbeat. You hear what I am telling you? A heartbeat!"

"I promise. I will."

I looked at her and realized her eyes were filled with tears. When I saw Suzanne upset, I began to choke up.

"I'm scared for her," she said.

"Me, too," I said and put my arms around her, giving her a solid hug. Then we sat down together on the end of my bed. "Char's mad with me for leaving."

"Oh, she's a big old brat if ever there was one. Don't worry about her. I'll straighten her out."

"I think we're all done."

Suzanne just patted the back of my hand and nodded her head. "It's all going to be okay. Now, may I drive my favorite ladies to the airport?"

"Oh! That would be so nice," I said.

"I love you girls, you know? I really do."

"Oh, Suzanne."

"I'll tell you what. You and your momma put on your best dresses and I'll take you to Morels Steakhouse over at the Venetian for a nice dinner tonight. My treat. Tell Char if she can rip herself away from the full-length mirrors to come and join us."

I giggled then. It was true. Lately, Char was finding mirrors to be fairly irresistible.

"We might have made a monster," she said.

"We may have done just that," I said and thought about Suzanne's generosity. "This is so nice of you to take us out. I'll miss you. Momma will miss you more, of course, but I'll miss you a lot."

"I'm not going to know what to do with myself when y'all are gone."

"She's even got you saying 'y'all,' " I said. "And you want to know something crazy?"

"Sure."

"I'm using all feminine pronouns with Char, as I should. At least I think I'm supposed to. And I'm using them for you, too, but it doesn't feel right."

Suzanne laughed so hard then, I thought she'd have to sit down and catch her breath.

"Leslie? You may call me however and whatever pops out of your mouth. I know this crazy world of Las Vegas isn't like home. And I know you both love me to death. And I love both of you to death. People are too screwed up over being politically correct all the time."

"Thanks, Suzanne. Momma and I feel like a couple of country bumpkins next to all this glamour."

"Well, don't. I think you're fabulous!"

At eight that night we were seated at a gorgeous table in Morels. The QB ordered lobster, I ordered a small filet mignon, and Suzanne and Char ordered rib-eyes.

"I never have lobster," Momma said. "I just never think to order it."

The truth was she never went anywhere where lobster was on the menu. In fact, she seldom went anywhere at all.

"The queen should have lobster every single night if

she likes," Suzanne said, smiling at Momma with all of her heart.

"And champagne?" Momma said.

"Darling, you're the queen bee," Suzanne said and touched the back of Momma's hand tenderly. "And the queen will always have champagne if that is what she wants!"

"Agreed!" Char said.

Sometimes, there's a sixth sense that kicks in when someone around you is deathly ill, and it seemed to me that Suzanne was acting on that instinct. It didn't matter. We would know soon enough. The Doctors of Death at MUSC would tell us. But all that was to be on another day. I sat back in my chair and looked at the four of us. What a foursome we were! Char had certainly been a wonderful host. And Suzanne, too. Suzanne and Char could teach the South a thing or two about how to show amazing hospitality.

"Suzanne, I cannot even begin to tell you how happy I am to have met you and to spend this time with you," I said. "I hope you're going to come and visit us on Sullivan's Island."

"When things get dull, just give me a call," she said and winked at me.

"I can see the two of us," Char said, "taking a walk over to the Obstinate Daughter for a martini."

"Finally, a restaurant in your name," the QB said, deadpan.

I bit my lip so I wouldn't laugh.

"The Obstinate Daughter?" Suzanne said. "That's the name of a *restaurant*?"

"Yes," I said. "During the American Revolution the Carolinas refused to surrender and so the press in England began to refer to us as the Obstinate Daughter."

"Brilliant!" Suzanne said. "The Brits have always had a way with words."

"Do you think that's a true story?" Char said to the QB.

"I'm only sixty-four, not two hundred and forty something," Momma said with a sniff.

"Oh! My apologies! I thought you were there! Right on the front lines!" Char said with a look of mock horror.

Even the queen laughed.

It wasn't easy saying good night, and it wasn't easy saying good-bye at the airport. Not at all. Char had stayed behind, still pouting because we were leaving. When she told me she wasn't coming I thought, Oh boy, she still has a lot of growing up left to do. I didn't like who she was becoming, which was a completely self-centered pain-in-the-neck diva. She was all over Momma when she was sewing for her but pretty much uninterested in her well-being. What did that say about her?

I got our boarding passes while Momma stood with our bags, saying good-bye to Suzanne. There was definitely something cooking between them. I thought that after our father left us, Momma would never let another man into her heart. But Suzanne was solidly in Momma's heart and most likely got in there because she was so completely disarming. Having had next to no exposure to female impersonators beyond Monty Python on television, Momma had let her guard down around Suzanne, and was probably as confused about her sexuality at first as I was when Charlie came clean with me. But now she knew better and was having a difficult time leaving her.

Suzanne was standing there, her head wrapped in a black silk kerchief and wearing only minimal makeup, looking more like Johnny Depp's chubby father than anyone else who came to mind. That would be Johnny Depp in *Pirates of the Caribbean,* not *Edward Scissorhands.* The effect of Suzanne's style of dressing was not unnerving at all. In an unusual way, it was damn sexy. She was a Venus flytrap and Momma was her bug.

I looked around and decided that the Las Vegas airport personnel had seen it all. From Elvis impersonators traveling in costume, to queens of every stripe, to big winners wearing diamond-encrusted Rolexes and big losers crying in their beer, the Las Vegas airport was as diverse and exciting as the Strip itself.

But for all the excitement and off-the-wall experiences we'd shared in Las Vegas, there wasn't anything to prepare us for what we found when we got home to Sullivan's Island. It appeared that Holly was reading a statement to members of the media, gathered in our front yard. There was a man standing beside her, who I assumed was the lawyer she had spoken of. Our taxi pulled into the driveway and I all but jumped out of the car and ran toward the front steps where Holly stood.

"That's all," she said.

"No questions," her lawyer said. "Thank you for coming."

They turned to go into the house, and as it became clear nothing else was going to happen, the media began to disperse.

I ran right up the steps.

"Holly! What the hell?"

She turned on her heel.

"You're home! Oh! I am so glad to see you, Leslie! Where's Momma?"

"Paying the taxi driver. Can you help with luggage?" I said.

"I'm Mark Tanenbaum," her lawyer said and extended his hand. "Where's the taxi? I'll get the bags."

I shook his hand. He seemed like a nice man.

"On that side of the house. I'm Leslie. Thanks."

In a few minutes, we were all in the house, bags delivered to bedrooms, and we gathered in the kitchen around the table, where much of our lives seemed to play out.

Holly took a pitcher of tea from the refrigerator and filled four glasses with ice. Mark sat in Momma's usual chair and she harrumphed loudly. Instinctively, Mark got up and sat in another chair.

"Tea, Momma?"

"Thank you," Momma said. "Now, would one of you like to tell me what's going on or should I watch the six o'clock news?"

"This is the craziest thing I've ever heard of, Mrs. Jensen," Mark said. "I've been a lawyer for over thirty years."

"Can you cut to the chase, please?" Momma said. The queen was not amused.

"Yes. The parents of Sharon MacLean told our chief of police that they're filing a civil suit against Holly blaming her for the wrongful death of their daughter. They are seeking damages of one hundred million dollars."

"Good luck with that," Momma said. "This child doesn't have a pot to piss in or a window to throw it out of, pardon my language."

"Doesn't matter," he said. "Next they'll file a suit against you for harboring a criminal and for keeping a public nuisance, namely the beehives. That is, *if* they can find a lawyer to take the case."

"That's ridiculous," I said.

Holly said, "It is the craziest, most over-the-top bunch of bull I've ever heard."

"No lawyer will represent them and no judge in Charleston will hear the case," Mark said. "It's going to get thrown out of court. Watch. You'll see."

"And where does Mr. Archie stand on all of this?" Momma asked.

"Behind his curtains," Holly said.

"Probably sucking his thumb," I said.

"He's radio silent," Mark said. "Not a word. But that doesn't matter. I'm just waiting to see the CSI report and the autopsy. We should have that any day."

"He probably doesn't know what to think," I said. "What about the boys?"

"Well, it's another transition for them," Holly said. "They've been waving at me from next door with smiles as big as Texas."

Tyler said, "Do bees have friends?"

*"No, they work together as a team. But in many ways,
human beekeepers are their friends, because
we keep their hives free of mites and beetles."*

*"It's a good idea to have someone watch
out for you," he said.*

"Yes," I said, "it surely is."

Chapter Thirty-One
Stop and Smell the Roses

Leslie took Momma to see her doctors and I stayed
home to work in the yard, which had become a
veritable horticultural miracle. I knew the bees were
so relieved to be rid of Sharon that they were cross-
pollinating like madwomen, hopping from one flower

to the next, waggling and leaping in joy, bringing about an insane profusion of blooms. Those dahlias that I didn't think would thrive were flourishing as though I had fertilized them with unicorn droppings and irrigated them with the tears of saints. Cars stopped to take pictures, and I gave away armfuls of flowers every day. It seemed that the more flowers I cut, the more flowers bloomed. I finally put a sign in the yard that said, *Help yourself to a few.*

I was just handing a large bouquet to a carful of curious members of the Sullivan's Island Garden Club when Mark pulled into our driveway. He got out of the car sporting a broad smile, which had to mean the investigation had gone our way.

"Hi!" I said. "What brings you to my neck of the woods?"

"I have some very good news for you," he said.

"Should we go inside?" I said. "Would you like a glass of iced tea?"

"Why not?"

It was a hot August afternoon and let me tell you, August on Sullivan's Island was like the seventh circle of hell.

We went inside. He followed me to the kitchen, where I pulled a cold pitcher of tea from the fridge and filled two glasses.

I pushed the sugar bowl and a dish of lemon slices across the table to him.

"I have a friend who works at the county morgue. It always pays to have a friend in places like that. Anyway, she said Sharon died of a heart attack. Natural causes. There was no evidence of a single bee sting, not a drop of venom in her blood. They've released the body to the funeral home."

It wasn't my bees!

"Hallelujah! My bees are innocent."

"Right."

"No kidding! Wow! But why would someone her age have a heart attack? She wasn't even old! She was like forty-one or -two."

"Well, she may have had that thing Tim Russert had. The widow-maker, except hers would've been the widower-maker. Anyway, don't matter. It wasn't the bees that did her in."

"Then why was she in my yard?"

"Because *she* was trying to kill the bees."

"She was? Why? Why in the world would she do that?"

"Who knows? The crime scene guys found a power spray gun she must've thrown into the oleanders. It was filled with a mixture of soapy water and a neonicotinoid like Ortho Bug B Gon, which is what people use to kill bees."

"That awful . . . well, she was awful! Sorry."

"If I had to guess, I'd venture that she came over here with the intention of wiping out the bees, she sprayed the hives, the bees got crazy and started coming after her. Then she started running and had a heart attack and boom, dead body in the backyard. But we will most likely never know the truth."

"You've got some imagination," I said. "You should write a book!"

"What? You don't think that's a plausible scenario?" Mark said.

"I wouldn't know. But I do know that if I was Sharon, I wouldn't be taking on almost two hundred thousand bees with one little spray gun."

"Two hundred thousand? How many hives you got?" Mark's jaw was somewhere in between the table and the floor.

"Three. The real number is probably closer to one seventy," I said. "But there's not a doubt in my mind that she didn't know that. She probably thought that maybe there were a thousand or so in the hives. Most people do."

"Just so you know, we're not entirely out of the woods

yet. While I know there's not a judge that would hear the case of you telling the bees to kill her, to some people you've got something potentially dangerous in your yard, and there's still the civil suit from her parents."

"Let them sue me. What I really cared about was Archie and his little boys, and I've lost them now. It's not even my fault."

"That doesn't seem right," Mark said. "I'll bet they come around. Give them some time."

I looked at Mark, and I hoped I didn't seem ungrateful, because he had gone to an awful lot of trouble on my behalf.

"Mark, I hope you know how much I appreciate what you've done for me. For my whole family, really. I just wish we could make the rest of this nightmare go away."

"Well, we got rid of the criminal piece of Sharon's death, and I'd call that a good start." He winked at me. "My grandmother was a beekeeper. Kept bees for probably fifty years. So I know how it is with honey bees. Around here, anyway. But I never realized she kept that many bees, I gotta say."

So he knew.

"Maybe it was just a coincidence. And I don't think they would've swarmed her—if they did, that is—unless she provoked them, which she did. In any case, she shouldn't have been sneaking around in my back-yard."

"Agreed. So, I've got to push on. I've got depositions all afternoon. Nothing as colorful as this, however." He stood to leave. "Now, should anyone from the press or television call, tell them you're not talking except to say it's a great relief to know that the bees had nothing to do with Sharon's death and that you offer condolences to her family as well as Archie's. And not one more word after that, okay?"

"Okay. Come on. Let me cut some flowers for Darlene. I'll give you a container of water to put them in."

"That would be awfully nice. Thank you."

I sent Mark away with dozens of roses and dahlias and he couldn't get over the fragrance. He said they smelled like heaven. I had to agree.

I looked over at Archie's house. I couldn't understand the silence. At this point he had to know the truth about what really happened. Why didn't he want to talk to me? Maybe he was freaked out that he had to go through another funeral. Maybe he was unhappy that the boys weren't mourning Sharon. Maybe he was embarrassed that he hadn't done enough to protect his boys. Maybe, maybe, maybe. The fact was that their curtains were closed, and I only saw the boys as they ran to and from the house.

Hunter had finally healed well enough to be back on his bicycle and tearing down the street with Tyler in his wake. I called Maureen to give her the update and see what she might know.

"No kidding. A heart attack! Wow," she said.

"Yep, and she was the one trying to kill my bees, not the other way around."

"I'll be darned. Well, the boys have been over here a lot, swimming and playing with Matthew. They seem to be fine. In fact, they seem the happiest I've seen them since Tyler's birthday."

"I'll bet so. Now, there's going to be a funeral, and I'm sure I'm not welcome there, even though she was the one trespassing with bad intentions."

"That's nonsense, Holly. You should absolutely go to the funeral. If you don't, you'll look guilty."

"Maybe," I said. "You know what? This might sound crazy, but in some really weird way, I feel like I'm being punished for Sharon's bad behavior. Is that my imagination or does the world just have to have someone to blame?"

"I know what you mean, but I think that once the truth gets around, people's suspicions will go away."

"I hope you're right."

I was working on convincing myself of my complete innocence and doing a so-so job of it. I wondered what would happen if I tried to enlist the bees' help with Archie. Maybe I'd just go sit with them for a bit and calm myself.

I felt a little shaken that the boys transferred their affection for me so quickly into a friendship with Matthew, but then I knew in my heart that all those little boys ever wanted after they lost their mother was to feel normal again. Sharon in their lives was a thousand steps backward, but a friendship with a classmate who had a nice family was a much-needed leap forward. Still, when I should've been congratulating myself on a job well done—that is, helping the boys survive their hideous stepmother and their useless father—I couldn't help missing having them around. Or being needed.

Leslie and Momma came in around four o'clock.

"I'm exhausted," Momma said. "Let your sister fill you in. I'm going to lie down for a bit."

"Okay," I said and turned to Leslie. "What did the doctors say?"

"There's a slight change in the tumor on her liver and they want to zap it with a targeted chemo."

"What does that mean?"

"Well, it's pretty incredible, really. They snake this probe through your groin to the exact position of the tumor and then they give it a shot of chemo, killing it."

"I thought they said her tumor was benign," I said.

"I guess they saw something to the contrary this time," Leslie said.

"When is this supposed to be happening?"

"They're going to call her in the morning with a time. Actually, it's not supposed to be a big deal. They do the procedure, which takes about an hour. Then they keep you overnight just to be sure you're stable. Then you go home."

"What if the tumor grows back?"

"Then they do it again, I guess," Leslie said.

"Man," I said. "Momma's brave."

"What choice does she have? This is the latest medicine there is for what she's got."

"I just—I don't know. It scares me, you know?" I said. "So listen, I've got news, too."

"Tell it," she said.

"Sharon died of natural causes. Not one bee sting. The coroner's office released her body."

"Dear God! What a relief! You going to the funeral?"

"I don't think so. Maybe I should send flowers," I said.

"Send flowers? You could just donate flowers! What the hell is going on in our yard?"

"The bees are pollinating like mad, probably celebrating the death of the evil one. But, if there is a funeral, I don't feel good about going. I don't want to see her parents."

"You're chicken shit, you know that? They won't even know who you are. I'll come with you."

Sharon's obituary was printed in the *Post & Courier* the next morning and it also gave the details of her funeral. There was to be no wake. And Momma was to go into MUSC the day following the funeral.

"She was a Catholic!" Momma said. "What do you know?"

"You never know," Leslie said. "She sure didn't appear to be a devout anything except a dedicated pain in the butt."

"Amen to that. Momma? If your tumor was a big panic, your doctors would have you there, like, right now," I said.

"That's true! That's got to make you feel some better," Leslie said.

"Oh, yeah, I feel really great about having a cancerous tumor on my liver," she said. "I should call Suzanne. I promised I would."

"We've got to get you your own cell phone," Leslie said.

"I have a very strong feeling that you're going to be fine," I said, even though I had no such feeling.

"Sweet Mother of God, I hope you're right," Momma said.

And then there was the discussion of the funeral.

"The gates of hell opened wide when she croaked," Momma said. "I smell sulfur."

"Momma! You know it's bad luck to speak ill of the dead!" I said.

"I'll take my chances," Momma said.

"Sulfur," Leslie said. "You're terrible."

The QB harrumphed.

"What am I going to wear to this?" I said.

"Wear your beekeeper getup," Momma said. "You know, make a statement."

"Boy, Momma, you're on a roll today!"

Leslie said, "If I were you, I'd wear anything but black."

"Too bad I can't wear that pink dress," I said.

Even Leslie agreed. "It's a bit bright for a funeral. Let's dig in my closet. I might have something."

There was a navy linen sheath dress we decided was just right. And my neutral sandals from the wedding were fine with it.

"Well, it's a good thing we're about the same size," I said.

"Wear sunglasses," Momma said. "Be mysterious."

"Was she like this in Las Vegas?" I asked.

"*She?*" Momma said.

"We know. We know. Meow," Leslie said.

Momma cleared her throat. "I think we should all go to the funeral. After all, we are their neighbors."

What Momma really meant, and she had not taken this position often, was that she wanted to be there if anyone tried to corner me or blame me. I had my mother and sister on my side.

"Dial Suzanne for me," Momma said.

Leslie did and handed Momma the phone. Momma got up and headed to her bedroom to have a private conversation.

"Momma's sweet on Suzanne, whose real name is Buster."

"No kidding?"

"Yeah. Like seriously sweet."

"Wow."

The next morning at nine thirty, we piled into Leslie's Benz and rolled down Middle Street to Stella Maris Church. The bells in the tower were ringing a mournful dirge.

Everyone on the island loved a good funeral, and given the circumstances of Sharon's death, it was no surprise that the church was packed to the rafters. And it was the second time Archie and his boys were burying someone in a short period of time. I recognized many people from part-time teaching at the Island Elementary School, and I assumed there were a lot of Archie's colleagues present as well. There were many massive flower arrangements on the altar and the tone was appropriately somber.

Archie and his boys followed the casket up the aisle and were seated in the front row on the left. We were in the back of the other side of the church. Momma and Leslie were giving tiny smiles of recognition and little waves to people whose eye they caught. I was engrossed in prayer and self-examination. I was deeply troubled by the reality of Sharon's funeral and the fact that whether or not I was directly or indirectly involved, there was still suspicion, even in my own conscience, that some of the responsibility for her death lay at my feet. I knew that in the weirdest way it was true. I begged God's forgiveness. And I even asked God to forgive Sharon. That was the best I could do for her. If the situation were reversed, I doubted she would pray for me. And I prayed for Carin then, too, hoping that she'd ask the good Lord to forgive me. I knew that she had no anger toward me. In fact, I could still feel her gratitude.

Finally, the Mass was ended and the processional took Sharon's casket to the waiting hearse, which would then take her remains to be buried in Mount Pleasant.

I watched as Archie and his boys walked together, followed by her parents and close friends and family. It had to be an awful ordeal for his boys, as I was sure they were reliving their mother's funeral.

We did not go to the cemetery. I delivered a sheet cake to the house for all those who would stop by to help Archie and the boys get through the remainder of the day.

I watched from my living room as dozens of people came and went from Archie's house. There were at least ten or so kids at any given time, running around their yard. It was good to see children there again, to hear their laughter and to see Hunter and Tyler at play, just being kids.

Around seven that night I got a text message from Archie.

Thanks for the cake, it read.

You're welcome, I answered.

I guessed then that the door was open to me again. As much as I had once wanted to be with him, that day I decided to let him come to me. I stopped blaming myself then, because what was done was done and it could not be changed. And I also knew that the hive had a will of its own.

"How do the bees get the nectar out of the flowers?"
Hunter asked.

"Well, they can fold their tongue like a
drinking straw and then they suck it out."

"Like this?" He rolled his tongue
and made a great slurping sound.

"Yes," I said and thought he was priceless.

Chapter Thirty-Two
Good to Bee

Leslie and I were up early and driving Momma to MUSC first thing in the morning. I'd had no further communication from Archie. And I was pretty sure Leslie had not been in touch with Char. Our focus was all on the QB.

"Did you talk to Suzanne?" Leslie said. "Does anyone want me to stop at Dunkin' for coffee?"

"Yes, of course," Momma said. "I talked to Suzanne."

"I wouldn't mind an iced coffee with cream," I said.

Leslie pulled into the drive-through lane at Dunkin' Donuts on Coleman Boulevard.

"Y'all want anything else?"

"I wouldn't shoot you if you got me a glazed doughnut," I said.

"You've got it," Leslie said. "Actually, that sounds pretty good."

"I'm not allowed food or drink," Momma said.

"I know," Leslie said. "I'll get you doughnuts when this is over. So what did Suzanne say?"

"She wanted to come," Momma said. "I told her no."

"Why?" I said. "I'd love to meet her."

"Well, you might meet her sometime but not today. I'm too nervous about this procedure to play hostess."

"I understand that," Leslie said. "But if Suzanne were to come, I doubt she'd be expecting you to show her the town."

"Exactly, and I'd want to. I mean, after all she did for us in Las Vegas."

Leslie gave our order and we drove around to pay.

"Did Char come up in conversation?" Leslie said

and handed the person at the window a twenty-dollar bill.

Leslie handed me my coffee and a small bag and dropped her change in her bag. I put the coffee in the cup holder and took the paper wrapper off the straw, stabbing the opening in the top of the cup. I couldn't get the doughnut in my mouth fast enough.

"Of course," Momma said. "Suzanne said Char wishes me luck and sends her love to you. I told her about the autopsy and the police finding and she was very relieved for us."

"That's nice," I said, "but I still have the threat of that civil suit."

"You've got to stop worrying about that," Momma said. "It may never come to pass, and you'll get a hundred gray hairs for nothing."

"That's a decent piece of advice, Holly," Leslie said.

"I suppose it is," I said. "You know, there's this piece of me that wishes life could go back to before Sharon met Archie. I was so much happier."

"And I was a lot happier before I found your father's condoms in the air conditioner filter."

"And I was a helluva lot happier before Charlie became Cher's long-lost identical twin!"

"I guess we all have our problems," I said.

"I've been telling you girls that for years," Momma said.

We got to MUSC, found parking, took Momma in, filled out all the forms, and then we waited an eternity until they came to get her.

"Good luck, Momma," I said. "I know you'll do fine."

"Thanks, sweetie," she said and gave me a hug.

Leslie said something similar, and Momma hugged her, too. The attendant asked her to sit in the wheelchair and then wheeled her through the swinging doors.

"She called me *sweetie*," I said.

"I know. She must be terrified. I'm calling Suzanne," Leslie said. She got up and walked outside to get better reception.

I waited a few minutes, then I checked my cell phone for messages. There was a text from Archie.

At some point I'd like us to talk.

That was it. So I texted him back.

Sure.

I figured short and sweet was the best. I didn't gush all over him. I didn't even ask what he wanted to talk about. Sharon wasn't even in the ground for forty-eight hours and he needs to talk to me? About what?

Leslie came back.

"That was quick," I said.

"I left a message," she said. "What's the matter?"

I showed her Archie's text and she sucked her teeth, making that *snick* sound.

"You want to know what I think?"

Leslie had bailed on Team Archie when he rejected her.

"Of course I do!"

"I think he's wondering if you're going to pick up where you left off with helping him with the kids."

"I have no intention of doing that."

"Good. Can I ask why?"

"Well, it's a funny thing. I was watching the boys on their bikes the day after Sharon died. They were happy and laughing, on their way over to Matthew's house. I felt like, okay, they're fine, and I don't have to hold them up and feed them and all that. I mean, if Archie needs a sitter or a tutor and I'm around, then fine. But I keep thinking about Archie and I keep trying to understand, how and why did he let Sharon treat his boys the way she did?"

"Because he's a spineless idiot?"

"Or something very close to it. That was my thought. And when I tried to talk to him on the boys' behalf, he didn't listen to me. He thought I was being dramatic or something. I mean, I spoke to him on several occasions and really laid it on the line and still, he was not moved."

"Well, we already know he's got lousy judgment."

"I think it's worse than that. Remember I told you I had a date with this guy I used to go to school with? The acting police chief?"

"Yeah, I remember. What about it?"

"Well, he made me see Archie in a new light. Archie is a taker. He would take and take and take and then go off and marry somebody like Sharon. Ted, the guy I went out with, is a giver."

"My Charlie was a taker of the first order."

"Yeah, well, I think I like givers better than takers." Then I told her about Archie at his wedding and his phone calls from Bermuda. "It made me super uncomfortable."

"What's the matter with him?" she said very quietly. "He knew before he married her that he was making a mistake and did it anyway. Then he goes on their honeymoon, carrying a torch for you. You tell him the awful things Sharon is doing to his little boys and he ignores you. He's just off base all over the place. I think this guy needs a strong dose of reality check and therapy."

"And this from a Harvard Ph.D. in religion. Shouldn't he have a more reliable compass?"

"Yes. Yes, he should."

"Anyway, I sort of feel like I did my thing with the boys. They're fine and on their way. They know where to find me."

"I hope this guy Ted remembers where to find you."

"Oh, I expect now that the Sharon disaster is pretty much behind us, I'll hear from him."

"Wait a minute. Was he ignoring you until he found out her death wasn't your fault?"

"Good Lord, no. Let's be honest, we don't get too many suspected homicides on the island. He was probably pretty busy figuring things out. Anyway, we'll see."

Leslie gave me a funny look.

"What?"

"I think I like you a lot better without Archie monopolizing your brain."

"I think I like me better, too."

We waited, reading magazines, checking e-mail, pacing until after noon. There was still no word on Momma. I went to the desk to ask.

"Let me check," the attendant said and made a phone call. "Last name of the patient?"

"Jensen. Katherine Jensen."

She repeated Momma's name into the phone and was told to wait. A few minutes later she had our answer.

"They just took her in. They had an emergency and had to take the OR for that. So, they're a little behind. Don't worry. She'll be fine."

I wondered how many times a day she said, *Don't worry, she'll be fine.*

"Thanks." I went back to Leslie. "They just took her in. Some emergency caused a slowdown. Anyway, how long is this supposed to take?"

"Less than an hour. Maybe a little longer."

I looked at my watch. It was close to one.

"You want lunch?" I said.

"Sure. Let's walk over to Melfi's. New place. Food looks amazing."

"Let's go."

Melfi's had the feel of a clubby but super hip Italian trattoria that welcomed all comers. It was a neighborhood place but also a destination. The food was wonderful. Their wide variety of pasta was all made in house. But Leslie and I were feeling like pizza. We ordered a Mrs. Melfi's Pie to share and salads with Italian dressing.

"Iced tea is fine for me," I said when our waiter was ready to take our drink orders.

"Me, too," Leslie said.

"Very good," our waiter said and left.

"What do you think the odds are that Momma will wake up and be pissed that we're not there?" I said.

"We can say we went out to get her something to eat," Leslie said. "That will make her happy."

"Great idea. Let's take her something," I said. "So, Leslie, what are you going to do about Char?"

She sighed a huge sigh and looked at me with so much sadness.

"I'm going to let her open her show, send her a big bouquet of flowers, and pray she does great. And in a few weeks, I'll call her and tell her that I think it's best if we dissolve our marriage and go our separate ways. That's my plan."

"I sort of figured that's where you were headed. I mean, divorce is messy, but you've got to settle things so you can move on."

"Exactly. And let me tell you, she doesn't want to be burdened with a wife, or a wife in name only. She needs to spread her wings and fly."

"So do you," I said.

"Um, so do you," she said. "Look, for the foreseeable future, I'm going to be living at home. If there's somewhere you want to go, you know, like, to live in Atlanta or something, now is the time you should give it some thought."

"You want to know what's funny?"

"God knows, I could use a laugh. What's funny?"

"I've spent the last eight or so years, ever since I graduated from college, complaining about being stuck on the island. Why couldn't I have Archie? And now that I can probably have him or move to anywhere that strikes my fancy, I want to stick around and see where this thing with Ted might lead. Besides, who would take care of the bees?"

"Oh, the irony of it all!" Leslie said with a lot of drama. "I think the bees could take care of themselves."

We ate our pizza, moaning about how delicious it was, and there wasn't so much as a piece of crust left. On the way back to the hospital we picked up a sub sandwich for Momma. When we arrived back to the family waiting area in the hospital, there was an old pirate sitting there reading a *People* magazine with a very large bouquet of flowers resting on the seat next to him, probably intended for his wench. I wondered who in the world he could be.

"Suzanne!" Leslie said.

I nearly fainted. This was Suzanne?

Suzanne Velour was in the building! She jumped up from her chair and hugged Leslie so hard, I could hear her vertebrae crunch.

"Leslie! Oh, my dear girl! I'm so glad to see you!"

"I can't believe you're here!" Leslie said.

"I took the first plane I could get," Suzanne said and then turned to me. "Holly?"

"Yes. That's me," I said and giggled.

"Oh, sweetheart, I'm so happy to meet you!" Suzanne said.

I thought, You know what? Okay, she's a little peculiar, but she's very nice.

"Tell me about the queen. What's the story?"

We told her all we knew, and her concern for Momma was real.

"So, this is not the cure. It's just a treatment of this episode," she said.

"Yes," Leslie said. "At least that is how I understood it."

"Well, then," she said. "That settles it."

"That settles what?" I said.

"I'm staying with her until the bitter end. That's what."

Leslie and I just looked at each other and then back to Suzanne in disbelief.

"I know what you're thinking, but I'm going to tell you something you don't know. I am so in love with your mother, I can't see straight. Deeply and truly in love. She has more spunk and wicked sass in her than any woman I've ever met. She makes me laugh from head to toe and she makes me happy like I haven't been since, well, in too many years."

Leslie was the first to speak.

"Well, then, Suzanne Velour? Welcome to the Low-country!"

I thought, Oh boy. How's this going to work?

"Did you know that monarch butterflies migrate?"
I asked Tyler. "It's another reason to plant goldenrod.
They love it, too."

"Where do the butterflies go?" he asked.

"Some go to Palm Beach," Suzanne said.
"The rest go to Boca."

"Don't listen to her," I said and laughed.

Chapter Thirty-Three
Bee Leave

Momma opened her eyes and saw Suzanne before she saw Leslie or me. She closed her eyes again, opened them, and smiled.

"Suzanne," she whispered with so much tenderness, I couldn't believe my ears.

"My dove, I'm right here," Suzanne said. "Just rest."

And that was a preview of how the following days would unfold. Suzanne, true to her word, never left Momma's side except to get something Momma needed. We picked up an air mattress from Bed Bath & Beyond and Suzanne slept on the floor right next to Momma's bed. Momma's procedure was more invasive than they thought, there was more cancer than the PET scan showed, and so her recovery time would be longer. The good news was that her team of oncologists at MUSC were confident that they'd gotten it all.

Word got around that Momma had had some kind of surgery, and of course, people came to call. They brought casseroles, shrimp salad, cold salads, pound cakes, tomatoes or basil or peppers from their gardens—the usual things. Suzanne was the gatekeeper, deciding who Momma could see and how long they could stay.

Maureen was the first to knock on our door the day we brought her home. She came with brownies and curiosity. If Suzanne's appearance surprised her, she didn't show it.

"How's the queen?"

"She's doing just great, but she tires quickly," Suzanne said.

"That's probably the anesthesia," Maureen said.

"My mother was a nurse. Once a patient reaches a certain age, it's harder to get over the anesthesia than it is to get over the surgery."

"That seems to be the case," Suzanne said.

"Don't let it scare you if she seems a little out of it," Maureen said.

"If she hasn't scared me up until now, I doubt that she ever will," Suzanne said.

I walked Maureen to the door, and we stopped to chat for a few minutes on the front steps.

"Suzanne, huh?" she said.

"Aka Buster Henry, retired military. Got sick of uniforms. Likes costumes better."

"Well, she might be a little strange, but she sure is devoted to your momma," she said.

"I know. And you know what else?"

"What?"

"If I haven't learned anything else this whole year, I learned that love comes in every color, shape, and size," I said.

I was thinking about not only Suzanne's affection for Momma but Leslie's for Charlie, and mine for Archie and his boys, and his for Sharon, and my recently piqued interest in Ted.

"How are the boys?" I asked.

"Tyler and Hunter live in my pool now," she said

with a laugh. "I know it's not my place to correct them, but I had to tell them to stop saying how happy they were that Sharon was dead."

"That's appropriately terrible," I said with a smile on my face.

"Have you seen Archie?"

"Not even a sighting in passing. You?"

"Nope. Poor devil," Maureen said.

I looked up at the sky. Even at four o'clock in the afternoon, it was blazing blue.

"I don't know if I'd call him a poor devil," I said.

"Why not?"

"I must be getting old," I said.

Maureen looked at me and said, "At a certain point we all put away our rose-colored glasses, right?"

"You have to stop reading my mind, Maureen!" I laughed and she gave a little chuckle. "And I always thought I needed to get far away from here to understand the world a little better when all the while . . ."

"All the answers were right here under the freckles on your nose?"

"Yep." I shook my head. "Isn't that something? Oh, I expect there are things to see that are worth the trip."

"Definitely." She smiled. "Hey! Have you ever been to Italy?"

"Italy! No, can't say I have. Only through the magic

of Hollywood. But I think it might be super fun to ride on a Vespa and throw coins into fountains. How about you?"

"Me, either. But! I was going through the mail I usually throw out, and my alma mater is hosting a trip through Rome, Venice, and Florence, ten days, two thousand, all inclusive. Even airfare. Want to look at it?"

I thought how much money was in my Maserati fund and I couldn't remember. And then I said I might.

"Can't hurt to look," I said. "Italy. Wow."

"I really want to go, but I don't want to go alone," she said. "I'll bring the brochure over or I'll text you the link."

"Sounds terrific, and hey, thanks for the brownies."

"It's nothing. I'm glad your momma's home and that it went well."

"Yeah, so are we. See you later!"

I went down the stairs with her and then I went around the house to put some water in the bee pans. I heard Archie's Jeep coming from down the street. He needed a new muffler. It wasn't any psychic ability that told me that. It was the awful, earsplitting rumble of his vehicle. I got my shears from the shed and began cutting some flowers for Momma's room. I knew almost to the second how long it would take him to stop, get out, and slam the door. I had become so accustomed to listening for his sounds, I could recognize his footfall on a gravel driveway. I didn't look up to greet him. In the past, I would've fluttered and flittered, finding an excuse to speak to him. Now I ignored him and felt fine about it. He must've thought I was deep in thought, because he called out to me sort of loudly.

"Hi, there!"

I could hear him thinking, Where's my adoration?

So I looked up from my flower beds and said, "Hi!"

He took that as an invitation to come over to my side of the flower beds.

"Boy, look at this! Your flowers are just spectacular!"

"Thanks!"

"Listen, I wanted to talk to you about something."

"Sure," I said.

Then he stepped back.

"Wait, are you upset with me for some reason? Is there something I've done? The boys?"

"No, why?"

"I don't know. You just seem, I don't know, different somehow."

"Archie, I'm fine. Momma had sort of a major surgical procedure yesterday and we brought her home today. She's resting. Her friend from Las Vegas flew in to help take care of her. And then, you know, just ten days ago, I was under suspicion for Sharon's demise because I trained my bees to sting her to death, even though she was prowling around my yard at night with the intention of killing them. But other than that? Things are good."

"Yeah, that was pretty crazy, wasn't it? Well, I wanted to talk to you about Sharon's cats. I thought you might like to have them. I'm allergic, you see, and . . ."

"Have you lost your mind?" I just stared at him. "I mean, I'm waiting to see if her family is going to file a civil suit against me. You do know that, don't you?"

"I heard something about it, but that would just be ridiculous, don't you think?"

"Of *course*, it's ridiculous!" I knew my voice was elevated. "Give the cats to her parents!"

"Well, see, I was hoping you'd take them because the boys sort of like them and then they could visit them every now and then."

I couldn't believe what I was hearing. (A.) Was he really going to try to use me again? And (B.) Why would I want anything that had anything to do with that horrible wife of his? And (C.) Not even if he paid me fifty dollars a day to board them would I touch her cats.

"Really? Archie, do you want to know what I think?

I think you should go home and get out all the pictures of Carin you locked away and put them back where they were. Then maybe you ought to take your boys on a vacation somewhere to rebond with them. Go camping, go to Disney World, but do something for *them*! Sharon's cats? No, thank you. Not in a million years."

"This is about the civil suit, isn't it?"

I just stood there for a minute looking at him. I was seething. After all I had done for him and the boys? And to be treated the way I was treated by her while he stood by and said nothing? Never mind all the horrible things he allowed her to do to his own boys. And now, for me to be threatened by her family? Now, I should take Sharon's cats? I mean, in theory, I like cats just fine. Dogs, too. But it's a huge commitment of years to make when you take in an animal. If I wanted to have cats, the cats I'd have would definitely never have been hers. And did he really think there was no damage done to his boys by Sharon that might need to be repaired? Oh, my God! Was he this stupid? Could he possibly be this incredibly stupid?

"Holly? Are you talking to me or are you just going to stare at me?"

Don't get indignant with me, I thought.

"I'm just wondering about something."

"What's that?"

I said, "How in the name of God did you get into Harvard?"

I said this without malice. I really wanted him to see how unforgivably and insensitively dense he was.

Tiny little lights began to come on in his mind.

"Okay, I'll tell Sharon's parents to back off."

I wasn't going to be so easily appeased.

"Maybe you should have told them that before the threat of it ever reached my door." I gathered up my bucket of flowers and shears and turned to walk away from him. "See you around, Archie."

I went in the house and there stood Leslie and Suzanne giving me a whole lot of quiet applause, huge hugs, and lots of *atta girl!*

"How did you hear everything?"

"Darling, you were right under your momma's room. We opened the window and we could hear every word as though you were in her bedroom with us!" Suzanne said.

"You were marvelous! Oh, my God! Suzanne and I were dying!" Leslie said. "Momma wants to tell you something. Hurry!"

I put the bucket of flowers on the floor and the shears on the hall table and went to her room.

I opened her door. She was propped up in bed.

"Come sit here on the side of my bed," she said.

Of course, I did as she asked.

"What's up?" I said.

"I want to tell you something I should have told you a long time ago." She took my hand in hers and held it. "I'm so proud of you. You told that Archie MacLean just what he's needed to hear from you for a very long time. It takes nerve to tell somebody where the bear goes in the buckwheat and I could not have done a better job myself."

"Thank you. I just got sick of him thinking I'd do anything on earth for him when he did nothing for me."

"But you should take Sharon's cats? I could only imagine what was going on in your head when he said you should take them, so his boys could come visit them once in a while. That was *rich*!"

"He's so thick in the head, he didn't think he was asking for much at all. He hasn't got the first clue how to take care of anything or anyone except himself. Not even cats. Much less his poor boys."

"Yes, sweetheart—and yes, I'm calling you sweetheart—if you'd allowed yourself to become actually involved with him in an intimate relationship, you'd have been deprived of any emotional support just like his boys are. You would not have been cherished by him."

"I see that now."

"I want more for you, Holly. You are such a lovely

young woman in every single way and you deserve so much more than a man like Archie. What I've learned and what your sister has learned, both of our lessons coming at a very high price, is the importance of choosing wisely."

"It's true."

"Now, go fix my flowers and hurry up. I need to feel some love."

I smiled then and so did she.

Of course, the second I opened her door, Leslie and Suzanne nearly tumbled over themselves to get out of the way.

"Let's get a glass of tea," I said, picked up the bucket of flowers and my shears in the hall, and they followed me to the kitchen. "Did y'all think I wasn't going to tell y'all what she said?"

"We just wanted to hear it for ourselves," Leslie said. "She was actually sweet to you."

"Yeah, I only had to wait thirty years," I said and laughed. "And when I think of all the days and nights I wasted thinking about Archie and literally worshipping him from afar, it's just too stupid. Too stupid."

I put the bucket of flowers in the sink and gave it a few inches of water.

"Oh, I disagree with that," Suzanne said. "I don't think you should ever regret loving anyone. Love is such a miracle. You'll never know for sure, but maybe you loved him the best he'll ever know. And maybe when he thinks about it, he'll be a better person for it."

Leslie took the pitcher of tea from the refrigerator and put it on the counter. I got three glasses from the cabinet and filled them with ice.

"I'm not sorry I married Charlie," Leslie said. "I loved him, but I'm not sure I made him a better anything."

"Can I ask you ladies something?" Suzanne said. "It's about that pitcher of tea."

"What about it?" I asked.

"Is it magic? I mean, it's the best iced tea in the world. But, like, does it refill itself? It never appears to be empty."

"It never is," Leslie said. "If it was, I think we'd all shrivel up and die."

I said, *"Did you know you can use honey on a cut*
or a scrape and it will keep germs out?"

Hunter said, *"Is that why they say*
go lick your wounds?"

"How old are you?" Suzanne said. "Who is this kid?"

Chapter Thirty-Four
Bee Happy

Momma was out of bed and Suzanne was completely dedicated to her full recovery.

"We're going to take a stroll down to the Obstinate Daughter, that charming little spot named for Char, and have some lunch."

"I don't know if I can walk that far," the QB said.

"Go!" I said. "If you need me, call me. I can come pick you up."

With that assurance, Momma nodded at Suzanne and they were off.

"I wonder what Jacques and Jonathan are going to say," Leslie said.

Jacques Larson, the executive chef, and Jonathan Bentley, the general manager, were in charge of almost everything about the restaurant, especially the image. If they looked at Suzanne and loved her, she and the queen would receive the royal treatment—a great table, focused interest on their comfort and enjoyment, and countless freebies from the kitchen. If not, well, I'd get a call soon.

"Um, I feel like every kind of superstar that passes through Charleston goes there, so they're used to characters showing up at the door," I said. "I'm not worried."

While they were at lunch, Ted called. Finally.

"Officer Meyers? I thought maybe you were ghosting me," I said.

Leslie, who was standing by, wasn't used to me being even remotely clever. She gave me the strangest look.

He asked me if I would like to have dinner and I said, "Sure. When?"

He said, "I was thinking about tonight."

"Why not?" I said. "What time?"

"How's six? I'm done at five and I just have to shower up. I think six is safe," he said.

"I'll see you then," I said and pressed the end button. I must've been smiling in a way that Leslie was unfamiliar with, because she still had this very weird look on her face.

"This is your guy," she said.

"Don't be ridiculous," I said. I blushed and broke a sweat. "I don't have a guy, and I don't need one, either."

"Uh-huh," she said. "You're not the only one in this family who can predict things, you know."

"I know that."

The fact was that most of the women in our family on my mother's side had some kind of weird gift. My grandmother used to dream about hearses driving by and she'd know someone was about to drop dead. If the dream was accompanied by a death knock the next day—that is, a loud knocking on your door but no one's there—then she knew it was a family member. My aunt, the QB's sister, who'd gone to her reward years ago, could tell you who was calling before the telephone rang. And she could predict rain by the shape of the crescent moon, and the gender of unborn babies. And me? I knew that eventually I'd be teaching at Sullivan's Island Elementary School because I could see myself in the classroom there. And I knew my bees heard me. And a few other oddities. But I couldn't see myself married to anyone. I sort of hoped Leslie was right.

Suzanne and the queen arrived home about ten minutes before I was to go out. They had been gone all afternoon.

"Hey! Did y'all have fun?" I asked.

"It was fabulous," Momma said.

She was literally beaming. So was Suzanne. My antenna went up. Leslie wandered in.

"How was lunch?" she said.

"Shockingly delicious!" Suzanne said.

"We ate so much we decided to walk it off. So we walked out to the beach and down the island."

"Then we crossed the dunes at Fort Moultrie, and I learned all about cannonballs bouncing off the palmetto logs of the original fort during the Revolution."

"And about Osceola and the Seminoles!" Momma said.

"And about Fort Sumter. Don't forget the *Hunley*!" Suzanne said.

"It sounds like y'all had a perfectly marvelous afternoon!" Leslie said.

"We did," Suzanne said. "And I asked the queen to marry me."

"And I said yes!" Momma said. "I'm going to make Suzanne my king!"

Hmmm, I thought. Really? How's that going to work? Then I thought, Why not?

"Jesus!" Leslie said and staggered backward as though she might faint. "I sure didn't see *that* one coming!"

After a moment's pause, I thought it was just about the coolest thing I'd ever heard.

"Well, I think neither one of y'all ought to be wearing white. But I'll make the cake! Congratulations!" I gave Suzanne a hug and said, "Welcome to our crazy little hive!"

"And when is the wedding to take place?" Leslie asked.

"I don't know!" Suzanne said. "I have to get a diamond and wedding bands. Any suggestions where to go?"

"Oh, honey, there's only Croghan's Jewel Box," Leslie said. "I'll take y'all there tomorrow."

"And we need a marriage license," Momma said. "And witnesses. Oh! Y'all will do that for us, won't you?"

"Of course!" Leslie and I said.

"And I need a dress," Momma said.

"So do I!" Suzanne said. "Just kidding."

We all about died laughing, of course. But it was serious business and we all knew it. I hoped that Suzanne was in it to cherish—a new word for me—Momma for whatever time she had remaining with us and not to stake a claim on whatever she had when she left us. Momma needed a prenup. I'd call Mark.

Ted was at the door.

"I'll see you kids later!" I said and sailed out with the least amount of fanfare possible. We had a lot to discuss.

He closed my car door, walked around his side, and got in.

"So, what's new?" he said.

"How much time do we have?" I said. "There's so much going on that my little head is spinning."

I looked over at him and he looked back, and those ice-blue eyes of his gave me a shiver.

"You cold? Should I adjust the AC?"

"No, I just had a thought. Anyway, where are we going?"

"I thought we should go someplace where people can't see their new chief of police drinking alcohol, so we're going to Bowens Island."

"Ted! You got the job! Oh! I'm so happy for you!"

"Yep! I got the job! Town council voted, and they're paying for housing on the island as a bonus. Now, it's not oceanfront and it's not huge, but it's big enough for a small family."

"A small family?"

"Yes. Now that my future seems to be secure, I'm thinking I should probably be looking for a wife."

"Oh, I agree."

"You do?"

"Yeah, I just hope our children have your eyes."

He laughed so hard and then so did I that we both had tears coming down our faces. It was such a bold thing to say that I wondered where Little Miss Demure went.

"That's hilarious!" he said. "I can't believe you said that!"

Well, at least he didn't pull over to the side of the road and tell me to call an Uber.

"Ted? It's gonna be what it's gonna be. I think that's how life is, if you're paying attention."

"I can't believe it, but I agree with you. We should just enjoy each other and see what the plan is when it's time."

Something in me had changed when Archie asked me if I wanted Sharon's cats. I thought then that if I didn't start saying what it was that I wanted, I shouldn't expect to get it. Archie got so off base about me because I let him be so off base about me. I was never clear.

We rode in amused silence across the bridges and causeways until we reached Folly Road and Bowens Island. Then we went inside, got a table, and looked at the walls, which were covered in graffiti.

"This place makes me wish I'd brought a set of Sharpies," I said.

"Well, you go writing on the walls and I might have to take you into custody, ma'am."

"I think this place encourages bad behavior," I said. "And I might like to be in your custody. You never know."

"I knew I liked it here," he said. He was quiet for a moment and then he said, "You know, Miss Jensen, you might just have a little devil in you that's ready to dance."

"Ted, I'm thirty years old. You know I never squandered my flowers, so to speak."

"Squandered your flowers? Oh, God! Holly! Where do you come up with this stuff?"

"Because I'm a big nerd. DuBose Heyward. You're not the only one who wrote lousy poetry."

"DuBose Heyward who wrote *Porgy and Bess* with George Gershwin?"

"Fun fact. It was his wife, Dorothy, who adapted his book *Porgy* for the stage, and *Porgy and Bess* was born. Gershwin's musical came later, and it made less money than Dorothy's production. But he was a genius. They all were, actually."

"I can't wait to hear what qualifies as genius in your mind."

"You're kidding, right? The guy was one of the greatest composers of the twentieth century! *Rhapsody in Blue, An American in Paris,* "Funny Face," "Love Is Here to Stay," "I Got Rhythm" . . . need I say more?"

"And I imagine you know all the lyrics to all the songs?"

"Of course!"

"The same way I do with Cole Porter?"

"What?"

"I've worn out three vinyl albums of *Ella Fitzgerald Sings the Cole Porter Song Book.*"

We were a match made in heaven. I hoped. Everything with Ted was as easy as everything with Archie had been circumspect. Laughter came easily. Kindness was in abundance. And we had a lot in common. Not to mention no small amount of heat for each other.

After devouring platters of fried shrimp and fish with french fries, coleslaw, and hush puppies, all washed down with a few Budweisers, we paid our bill and went out to the deck to watch the sunset.

"Would you like another beer?"

"Oh, no, I'm just fine. Dinner was delicious," I said. "Thanks."

"And it was great fun. So, tell me what else is happening in Holly World."

"Just this afternoon, my momma got engaged to an old female impersonator named Suzanne Velour. Looks like she's going to beat me to the altar."

"Excuse me? Can you back up just a bit? A female impersonator?"

He started laughing so hard, I thought I might have to call EMS. I laughed with him because on the surface it seemed, well, unimaginable that a crabby old ultraconservative divorcée of a certain age from a place like Sullivan's Island should wind up married to a female impersonator named Suzanne Velour.

"Yep, isn't that crazy? But that's my momma. She's the queen bee in our hive and she's going to do as she pleases."

"It's out there. And you approve?"

"At first I was like, whoa! But after some consideration and seeing them together? You do know that right in the middle of that whole insanity with Archie's crazy wife Sharon, we had to take Momma in for surgery? She's got some kind of liver cancer."

"No, I'm sorry. I did not know that. Is she all right now?"

"Yes, I think so, until it comes back. Anyway, Suzanne flew in from Las Vegas and never left her side.

And she makes Momma so happy. You should hear them laughing."

"Okay, so there's a missing piece to this picture. How did your mother come to know a female impersonator from Las Vegas? Some underground version of Match.com?"

"Ah, yes! That little detail. So, remember my sister, Leslie?"

"Sure. She was a pretty girl. She married that guy Charlie and moved to Ohio, right?"

"Correct. But then, after six years of married bliss, Charlie revealed a little secret he'd been keeping from Leslie."

I unpacked the rest of the story and Ted was stunned.

"You've got to be kidding me, right?"

"Yeah, I know it's a lot to process."

"Wow," he said.

"And then there's me. I keep bees, as you know. I decorate cakes at Publix and I volunteer at the library. And sometimes, when all the stars are aligned, I get to substitute-teach at the Sullivan's Island Elementary School. I am officially the most boring person in my family."

"I think I like you just as you are. Don't change a thing."

"I won't, because I don't think my family needs another ounce of drama."

The horizon and then the sky put on a show of such spectacular dimensions that all the color of my family story paled. I wasn't embarrassed. What was I supposed to do about them? The good news was that Ted seemed much more amused than horrified. And when he took me home, there was an extended period of time spent in the car saying good night. I floated into bed that night. This was love, and I was astonished by its power. More than that, I was happier than I'd ever been. Where was Leslie? Her bed was empty. Hmmm.

"Did you know honey never goes bad?" I said.

Ted said, "No, I did not know that. That's amazing."

"You're amazing," I said.

Chapter Thirty-Five
Forever Bee

I got up on the early side of morning, as I usually did. To my surprise, Suzanne was in the kitchen. She had made coffee. Suzanne in the morning, reading the paper wearing a terrycloth bathrobe, was a lot less theatrical than Suzanne in the afternoon or evening. Her gray hair was all spiky, and without all that eyeliner and mascara, she looked more like a kindly grandfather.

"Good morning," I said.

"Good morning. There's coffee."

"Thanks! Did you sleep well?"

"I did, but your momma had a bit of a night."

"What do you mean?"

"Well, we might have overdone it yesterday. I'm guessing she doesn't get a lot of exercise."

"You could say that," I said. "Want a little more?" I filled my mug and was ready to top off Suzanne's.

"Sure. Thanks," she said. "She was full of aches and pains. I found some ointment in the bathroom and rubbed her legs. Then she slept well after that. She's still asleep."

"Well, I'm sure she's still getting over the surgery, too."

"That's what I thought also," Suzanne said and re-folded the front section of the paper. "Did you have fun last night? Who was that nice-looking man you didn't introduce me to?"

"Oh, Lord, Suzanne, I'm sorry! That's Ted Meyers. He's the chief of police on the island. I think I'm going to marry him and have his babies. I'll be sure to intro-duce you to him the next time he's here."

"I see. And how long have you two been seeing each other?"

"Last night was our second date," I said, knowing she'd think I was jumping the gun.

"You Jensen girls don't mess around, do you?" She was smiling. "Get right down to business."

"Nope. No flies on us."

Leslie tootled in.

"G'morning!"

"There's coffee," Suzanne said. "So, when everyone's caffeine intake has been satisfied, there's something we should discuss."

"Fire away," I said.

"Lay it on me, baby," Leslie said.

"Okay, well, here it is. I know I've come along late in the game, and I'm also keenly aware that the dress code of Sullivan's Island isn't the same as Las Vegas. They don't have a lot of men like me around here, so I want you to know, I'm going to tone it down a bit. You know, for the sake of propriety."

"Don't change a thing!" I said. "Screw the neighbors!"

"Yeah! Screw the neighbors!" Leslie said. Then she got a peculiar look on her face and said, "Uh, actually, Holly, you and I should probably have a chat later."

"Fine," I said. "Whatever." I knew *exactly* what she did last night.

"Anyway," Suzanne continued, "I adore your mother, as you know. One of the other reasons I want to marry her is so I can have the legal right to make decisions about her health care with the two of you. As an equal partner."

"I had not even thought of that," I said.

"Me, either," Leslie said. "But you're right."

"But I think we should have a prenup to protect her assets. Not mine. But I don't want anyone to think I want to take anything that is hers and rightfully yours. For me? I have much more to protect than she does, but I have no heirs. If I get hit by a truck, you ladies can divide the spoils among yourselves."

"I love you, Suzanne," Leslie said.

"Me, too," I said.

"Call me Buster from now on."

"I can't," I said. "You'll always be Suzanne to me."

"You'll ruin your mystique!" Leslie said.

Suzanne laughed.

"Okay. Well, then call me what you'd like. The reason for this is in my experience I knew a young lady I dearly loved who became deathly ill, and, not having any family, I volunteered to see her through her illness. That was all fine, as long as she was conscious. But when she became unconscious, and because she had no living will, the end of her life was disastrous. It should've been a peaceful end that followed her wishes. I cannot go through that again and I cannot leave the queen."

"Oh! What a terrible story! I'm so sorry!"

"So I'm wondering if you have a family attorney I might use to draw up a simple document for us."

"I'll call Mark," I said. "He's not a wills and estate lawyer, but he'll know someone."

"I'm going to go about my morning toilette, and then I'd love some company to purchase a rock for my dove that's worthy of a queen!" Suzanne stood and put her cup in the sink.

"Hey, Suzanne?" Leslie said.

"Yes?"

"You're the best."

Suzanne left the room, and when she was out of earshot, I said, "And are you the worst?"

"Maybe." She looked at me apologetically. "How was your date with Ted?"

"Well, we talked about marriage, if that's what you want to know."

"That's good. Very good. I'm telling you, that's your husband."

"I think you're right, weirdly enough. He just seems absolutely right for me." I looked at her. I knew my sister. She couldn't bring herself to tell me what she had done, so I helped her into the confessional. "Archie?"

"Yeah."

"Good luck with that nightmare."

"You don't mind?"

"Hell, no. Not even a little bit. But it's nice of you to ask, even if it's after the fact."

"I think I can help him," she said.

I began to laugh. And laugh and laugh.

"No, you *can't* help Archie MacLean! You might have some fun with him. You might be really good for his boys. But you can't *change* that son of a bitch. Just have fun and don't worry about where it's heading."

"You're sure? God, I need a lawyer now, too."

"Ask Mark. With all the business I'm sending his way, maybe we can get a family discount. You know what else?"

"What?"

"For about a hot minute I thought Suzanne was marrying Momma for this house. I wonder what's in her asset column?"

"Cars, I know for sure. Probably some kind of a ranch. Who knows? She'll tell us, if we ask."

"Ask her when you go to Croghan's."

"You're not coming?"

"No. I'm going to stay and see about the queen."

"You're a good woman, Holly Jensen. I hope Ted knows that."

"I have definitely fallen for him. He's such a stand-up guy."

"Gosh. I wonder what that's like?"

"Well, you won't find out with Archie, that's for sure."

"I'll be careful."

"Just be good to those boys, okay?"

"I'll have no problem with that."

In the next hour, Leslie and Suzanne were gone to the city and I checked my hives for mites. No mites. No beetles. There was a lot to tell the bees that morning, but I had decided I'd better be very careful what I said to them. My hives, as we know, were dead serious.

I went inside and Momma was up and dressed. And wearing her hearing aids, as she had been since Suzanne arrived.

"Hi! How are you feeling?" I said. "Did you get enough rest?"

"Oh, I slept like a little lamb," she said so sweetly, it alarmed me. "Can you believe I'm getting married?"

"Yes, because Suzanne is a living doll. Let me tell you all she told us this morning."

"Why don't we have a nice glass of tea and maybe some toast and discuss the wedding?"

"Let's do!"

I put bread in the toaster and Momma poured tea.

We sat and talked and I told her every single thing Suzanne said to us and that I thought Suzanne was an angel straight from heaven, albeit no halo and wings, and dressed rather oddly.

"We told her to just be who she is. If she wants to

tone it down, tone it down, but not for our sakes. She's such a great character."

"This island has always had its share," Momma said. "Now, tell me about Ted."

"Well, I think he's just my perfect speed."

"I've got a good feeling about him, unlike that nut bag next door."

"Leslie can have him."

"Nuts are her specialty."

"Momma! You are so bad!"

"I know. When are you seeing him again?"

"Tonight and hopefully every night for the rest of my life."

"Oh, Holly, my sweet girl. I've wanted someone like him for you for the longest time. And you know what the nicest part is?"

"Tell me."

"I've got a sweet husband on the horizon, so do you, and with any luck at all, I might live long enough to hold a grandchild in my arms."

"I think Suzanne has every intention of keeping you in this world as long as possible. And I'd love to see that day come to pass as well. Grandchildren, that is."

"You know, when you weren't around, I went and talked to your bees, too. I didn't go inside the fence, of course. But I talked to them plenty."

"You did? About what?"

"About whatever was on my mind. I spoke to them the same way as you did."

"How do you like that? So do you think they hear us? Do they understand us?"

"What do you think?" she asked.

"I know with certainty that they do."

"I thought that's what you would say."

"But they don't act on command, you know."

"No, they act as one. And that's what we're going to do from now on. This family is going to act as a family. That's how the bees survive, and that's how we will, too."

"One team, one dream?"

"Are we having another Hallmark moment?"

I smiled at her smiling face and said, "We are."

Momma had brought back the tender side of her I'd rarely witnessed in all my days. But there it was. Suzanne had appeared and vanquished the crank.

That night, after Suzanne spent at least four hours scrubbing it, our old Weber grill was put into use. Dressed in khaki shorts and a blue polo and looking like most of the men on the island, Suzanne was going to grill steaks. She still had on bracelets and earrings, but she cleaned up good. I told her so.

"You look very nice tonight," I said.

"There's a store called M. Dumas right near Croghan's. They fixed me up."

"Well, they did a good job. I think it's a good sort of compromise you've got going on there."

"Well, now that I know I'm auditioning tonight for the possible role of father-in-law, I figured I'd better give it my best effort."

Ted was coming for dinner. In a moment of near total insanity, Leslie invited Archie. The boys were at Maureen's house. Against Momma's complaints, I cleared off and set the dining room table. This was going to be a classy night if it killed me. I wanted us to show well to Ted. I cut flowers for the table, dahlias and roses mixed with rosemary and thyme, and they were so beautiful and fragrant, I could scarcely believe they were from our yard.

Leslie put potatoes in the oven to bake and I made a salad and a salad dressing with honey, remembering to shoot the bees a telepathic *thanks*. And Momma, deadly as she could be in the kitchen, blew the dust off her old copy of *Charleston Receipts* and very carefully followed the recipe for pickled shrimp.

"I think it's important for Suzanne to think I can cook."

"She'll know better soon enough," Leslie said, and we both giggled.

"*She* is the cat's, um, wait . . . oh, forget it!"

Even the queen had a laugh.

"Don't either of you bad girls tell her anything different, y'all hear me?"

We had wine to pour. Wine in bottles. Actually, good wine. I say this because Suzanne went to a real wine store and brought home six bottles. There were châteaus, not flip-flops, on the labels and I couldn't pronounce the names, so it had to be pretty good stuff. And she brought a bottle of champagne that had to be for a toast, which was my clue that the ring would be on Momma's finger that night and we would all be properly hydrated. This was not to be our normal dinner, to be sure.

"We should be drinking mead!"
I said after two glasses of wine.

Everyone stared at me and told me it
was a ridiculous idea, except Ted.

"I think it would be fun to ferment honey,"
Ted said. "Let's try it!"

That's just one reason why I love him.

Chapter Thirty-Six
Bee Joyful

We were not party-hosting people. In fact, the last party I could remember that took place under my mother's roof was the one when everyone got sick when I was a child. So Leslie and I were not well versed in the hospitable ways of normal southern women. In addition to a copy of *Southern Living,* I had my hands on a copy of *Southern Lady* I picked up at Publix, which seemed focused on dinner parties and brunches and how they should look.

After I ran the vacuum, dusted everything in sight with Lemon Pledge, and made a centerpiece for the dining room table, I went digging through Momma's china cabinet and buffet drawers to see what I could find. In the top drawer, I found a tablecloth and eight napkins, still in their original cellophane wrapper, never used. I couldn't remember where they came from, but they were going to have a debut that night.

"Momma? Didn't we used to have silver flatware?"

She was in the kitchen peeling shrimp while the ceiling fan overhead moved the paltry air around.

"My mother's. It's in the bottom of my closet, inside the American Tourister red suitcase, under a blanket. Why?"

"I thought it might be nice to use it. Why is it buried in your bedroom closet?"

"To hide it from the robbers! Why else?"

Of course. Why else? Our house was the last house on the island that would entice robbers. And besides that, there were very few crimes ever committed on the island anyway. The occasional speeding ticket. The occasional DUI. But robberies? Nope. I heard about somebody stealing tomatoes from their neighbor's bushes, but that was probably kids, doing something stupid on a bet. I mean, Momma didn't need to hide the silver like they did during the Civil War. Honestly.

I went in her closet, which had not been cleaned in a dozen or more years, and located the suitcase. Inside, just as she said, was a felt-lined box of silver flatware and serving pieces. It was blue with tarnish.

"Good Lord," I said.

I didn't have the time to polish it all by hand. And then I had a thought. There had to be a fast way to clean silver. I went online and found a solution that seemed too good to be true. But since I had nothing to lose, I tried it.

I took Momma's biggest pot and filled it with water. Then I put it on to boil. Next, I crumpled aluminum foil—shiny side out—and dropped a few balls of it into the pot. Then I added about half a box of baking soda. When the water came to a boil, I carefully lowered in the silver and let it boil and bubble for about five minutes. I must say, the fragrance was that of rotten eggs, but if it worked, who cared? Momma, Leslie, and Suzanne stood there the whole time like a Greek chorus telling me this would never work. That the only way to polish silver was elbow grease.

"What's that horrible smell?"

"You need that expensive pink stuff and a whole afternoon," Momma said.

I removed each piece with tongs, and voilà, it was all as good as new.

"Really?" I said. "Apparently not."

I laid it all out on dish towels and began drying it and buffing it with a soft cloth.

"I'll be damned," Suzanne said.

"Would you look at that?" Leslie said and picked up a cloth to help me.

Now the dining room tablecloth had something else to make it sparkle. And of course, Momma had wedding china that had not been used since her wedding, just sitting in the china cabinet, all stacked up, collecting dust. There was nothing wrong with it a little soap and water couldn't cure. And besides, I only needed six place settings. That simple task took fifteen minutes with Leslie's help.

"Should I put them on the table?" she asked.

"Why not? Sure!"

"Who's coming to dinner with all this hurrah?" Momma said.

"Well, there is the queen to be considered," Suzanne said.

"I just felt that with all the trouble Suzanne went to scrubbing that awful old grill of ours plus buying wine and steaks, and the fact that Archie and Ted are coming to dinner, that maybe we should put our best foot forward," I said. "I think the table looks really beautiful. Come see!"

Momma followed me to the dining room and was speechless for a moment.

Then she said, "I don't know why we don't do this all the time! It's so pretty! Nice job, girls!"

"Thank Holly," Leslie said. "This was all her idea."

"I don't know. I sort of miss Catalog Mountain," I said and laughed. "We're missing one thing."

"I can't imagine what," Momma said.

"I'll be right back," I said.

I went to my room and unplugged my portable turntable and brought it to the kitchen. We were going to have dinner with George Gershwin. I texted Ted, *Bring your Ella vinyl!* He texted back, *You bet!* I plugged it in and put an album on and dropped the needle in the first groove. "Rhapsody in Blue" began to play.

"May I have the pleasure of a dance, my dove?" Suzanne said.

"Of course!"

For the next five minutes or so, Suzanne waltzed Momma around the kitchen table. She was an amazing dancer—Suzanne, that is. Momma followed her lead the best she could, blushing and stammering while Suzanne nuzzled her neck and she blushed some more.

"Too precious," Leslie said.

"Should we have cocktails in the kitchen or on the front porch?" I said.

"I vote for the kitchen, so I won't miss any of the conversation while I'm grilling on the back porch," Suzanne said.

"Yes, and I think it's too hot on the front porch," Momma said.

"And we have a ceiling fan in here," Leslie said.

"Then the kitchen it is," I said.

It was five o'clock. Ted and Archie were expected at six. I took the Jarlsberg out of the refrigerator, so it wouldn't be as hard as a brick, and put it on a cutting board with a box of crackers. Then I lined up the wine bottles and a half dozen wineglasses and remembered I couldn't find a corkscrew the last time I looked for one.

"Leslie? Please see if you can find a corkscrew, and if you can't, ask the Scarecrow to bring one. Please? I'm going to go and change."

The Scarecrow was the guy in *The Wizard of Oz* without a brain.

"Good one," Momma said.

I stopped in my tracks and looked back. She gave me a thumbs-up.

I got to my room and stopped again. Something had changed in the house. I wondered what it was and finally, I realized what was different. Everyone was happy. That may seem to be an overly simplistic way to state the very complicated facts, but it was the truth. That happiness was so hard won. I had scars to prove it. We all did.

I took off my dirty gardening clothes, rinsed off in a fast shower, and put on a clean sundress and sandals. I couldn't wait to see Ted. I could've waited a long time before I saw Archie, but if I guessed correctly, he was going to be here a lot, sniffing around for Leslie like an old hound dog. What can I say? It had always been this way. She was Brigitte Bardot to my Tammy Tell Me True. She was wired in a way that was the complete opposite of me. And did it really matter to me if Archie wanted Leslie and not me? Well, there was a smidgen of a sting to it, but I had Ted, and I didn't have to change myself for him to like me. In the cool of the afternoon, that matters just a whole lot more to me.

Ted and Archie were prompt. Leslie answered the door and I remembered she had not really been introduced to Ted. Although Ted knew Archie, because of Sharon's hysteria and, ultimately, her death. So I hurried out to meet them to make sure that Ted was introduced to Suzanne as well.

"Hey!" I said to Ted. "Don't you look nice? Hey, Archie."

"Hi, Holly. It's nice of y'all to have me."

Leslie smiled at Archie like a large, slinky, satisfied feline. Archie gave her kind of a lascivious look. Ted caught it, raised his eyebrows, looked at me, and handed me his Ella Fitzgerald album.

"There you go!" I said. "Y'all come on in!"

All at once the physical differences between Archie and Ted were crystal clear. Ted was a younger man, muscular and fit. His hair was close cropped and he was tanned. Ted was a well-made specimen. Archie's posture wasn't as sturdy as Ted's and he looked pale and unkempt instead of like the Sexy Professor. And he had a little belly I'd never noticed before. The truth was that Archie was a lot less appealing, to me, anyway. Leslie seemed to be less picky.

Archie, who had brought his corkscrew, shook hands with Suzanne and said, "I'm sorry, I didn't catch your name?"

Suzanne said, "I'm just the proverbial boy named Sue. Me and Johnny Cash."

"That's funny," Archie said. "Miss Katherine? I heard you were under the weather? I hope you're feeling better now."

"I've never felt better," Momma said. "Thank you."

Suzanne turned to Ted and said, "And you've got to be Ted."

"It's a pleasure to meet you," Ted said and extended his hand for a shake.

"Thanks, son," Suzanne said and shook his hand soundly without batting an eye.

Leslie began filling glasses halfway with wine and handing them around. Ted, who in my experience was a beer drinker, took a glass and thanked her. I put the music on and soon Ella's rendition of "All Through the Night" filled the room.

"That's our song," I said to Ted.

"So, young man," Suzanne said to Ted, "do you know your way around a grill?"

"I think I might," Ted said. "Can I give you a hand?"

"You sure can. Grab that tray of meat and follow me outside." Suzanne passed me and whispered. "Love this guy. He's a dream."

Momma picked up a shrimp on a toothpick and said to Archie, "I pickled these today. May I offer you one?"

Memories of Momma's gastronomic prowess must've crept into his tiny mind because he said, "I'm going to wait for dinner, but thank you. Big lunch."

"So, did you find a home for Sharon's cats?" I asked.

"Yes, I gave them to one of my students," he said. "I'm really more of a dog person."

"That's nice," I said.

"Oh? Do you have a dog?" Ted said, as he came back into the kitchen for the peppermill. "I've got a golden named Stubble."

"Stubble?" I said. "That's a funny name!"

"Well, his snout always looks like it needs a shave. That's why." He went back to the porch.

"I love goldens," I said to the room.

Ted stuck his head back in and gave me a wink. He had a golden, we had a song, and it was all good.

We made it to the table, which everyone complimented, and sat down to eat. I had plated the steaks and potatoes in the kitchen and brought the salad bowl to the table. Everything smelled delicious and it was. There wasn't a lot of chitchat because we were all busy eating, but as Suzanne finished her steak she said, "I'd like to propose a toast to the Queen Bee."

She stood and raised her glass and walked around the table to Momma's side. She placed her glass on the table and reached into her pocket, producing a small velvet sack.

"I bought champagne for a very special reason," she said and sort of dropped to one knee with a small grunt, hanging on to the arm of Momma's chair. "This will make it official." Out came a beautiful diamond ring, and she put it on Momma's finger. "Katherine Jensen, will you make me the happiest person alive and say yes?"

Momma's eyes filled with tears and she blurted her response.

"Yes! Yes! Yes!"

Momma got up, helped Suzanne up, and they hugged. We all clapped and cheered. Archie and Ted got up and shook Suzanne's hand and kissed Momma's cheek.

"I'll get the champagne!" I said and hurried to the kitchen.

Ted followed me. I reached in the refrigerator, took out the bottle, and handed it to him.

"I'll definitely break something with an exploding cork."

"I've got it." He easily removed the cork with the smallest pop. "Isn't that something? Your Momma and—was it Sue?"

"Suzanne," I said.

"Well, whatever. Still. There's nothing like love."

"Yeah, I think I just found that out. I mean, really found it out. Sort of."

"You are the one, you know," he said.

It was a reference to the lyrics of "Night and Day," or so I thought.

"I love Cole Porter, too, and Ella? Wow, what a voice!"

"No, I mean you and me. This is it."

"Oh, *that!* Oh, yeah, I know that. But they're waiting for champagne."

"Don't steal your momma's night. But soon?"

"Yeah, sure, big shot. We'll see," I said and hoped he meant it.

We stole a quick kiss, then went back to the dining room and poured champagne. I put on *George Gershwin's Great Hits* and the first song to play was "Love Is Here to Stay."

There was more toasting and lots of good wishes. The rest of the evening was spent, as it should have been, in a beautiful and prolonged dream about love and happiness.

Finally, Leslie said, "I'm going to walk Archie home."

We all knew what that meant.

"Thank you for a wonderful night," Archie said. "And congratulations."

"You're welcome," Momma said, grinning like an eighteen-year-old blushing bride. "I'm going to help my fiancé clean the kitchen."

"I'll be along in a minute," I said, with the intention of walking Ted to his car.

"Good night, y'all!" he said. "Thanks for a great night!"

One of those star-filled skies was waiting for us outside, the kind you only see in a magazine with the pictures taken by super powerful telescopes.

"Look at that, would you?" he said. "It's hard to believe it's real."

"Yeah," I said. "Sometimes I like to come out and look at the stars and just lose myself in them."

"We should do that," he said. "You know, take a blanket down to the dark end of the island on a clear night, lie there, and just get lost in the stars."

I looked at him and a thousand things raced through my mind. The main one was I knew that if we did that, I wouldn't honestly be wearing white on my wedding day. Now that I had waited so long, I wasn't budging.

"After we're married," I said. "I'm not that kind of girl. Sorry."

"Oh, God! Of course! *Only* after we're married!"

"Make it soon, okay?" I said. "Good night."

"Where do you think you're going so fast?"

All I can tell you is that it took Ted Meyers, chief of police, about two minutes to leave me breathless, weak in the knees, with an unfamiliar clench in an area I did not know could clench involuntarily. I felt like my bones had turned to jelly.

"Well, I just learned something."

"What's that?"

"Why people lie down to you know, you know . . ."

"Yeah, I think it's so they won't fall down."

"You'd better get out of here."

"I'll be back, Little Queen Bee."

"What is that supposed to mean?"

"You need your own hive." He smiled. "And I'm going to give it to you."

"G'night!" I said and thought, Holy shit, there's sex in my future after all.

Epilogue

Sullivan's Island
April 2019

Leslie finally divorced Charlie, who, as predicted by everyone involved, went on to become wildly successful as Cher's long-lost identical twin sister, Char. We were actually all delighted for her. And Leslie's involvement with Archie became more serious. Who cared? They were both happy. The boys were happy. But she would not marry him.

"I'm just dividing my time between our house and his. That's enough for me. You think I want to be his third dead wife? No way, baby. Uh-uh."

In the Lowcountry, we believed bad things happened in threes. Becoming the third wife of a man twice widowed was a terrifying prospect.

"I don't blame you," I said.

But good things also happened in threes. I had so many good things happening around me and to me, I wasn't quite sure where to start counting. I'd started teaching at Sullivan's Island Elementary School eight months earlier, and I loved it. Because of that and a few other details, I couldn't go to Italy with Maureen, but Ted promised to take me there someday.

"When's the baby coming?" Tyler asked.

"Any day now," I said.

Last fall, Ted gave me a diamond ring. It wasn't huge, but it wasn't too small, either. We got married as soon as we could, right after Suzanne and Momma. Everyone knew we would run to the altar because our pants were on fire. We had a small ceremony at Stella Maris Church. Monsignor Ben Michaels performed the ceremony and Lynn Bagnal played the organ. Leslie was a maid of honor and, in a surprise choice, Ted asked Suzanne to be his best man. They had become very close. He had taken to calling her Suz, which Suzanne said suited her better anyway. It was a gender-neutral name. So first Suz walked me up the aisle to give me away and then she stood by Ted.

My friends from Publix and school came and, of course, friends of Ted's, lots of folks from the township office and the police force, our neighbors, Maureen, her husband and son, and Archie and his boys. Archie and his boys bought us a remote-controlled toy Maserati as a wedding gift and I thought it was really sweet. Of course, Mark and Darlene were there, too. Afterward, we had a small reception at home with wedding cake from Publix, finger sandwiches, and champagne. It was simple but beautiful, and exactly what we wanted.

My garden was a botanical wonder that season, with so many gorgeous roses and dahlias, still in bloom, as though they were staying in bloom, waiting for my wedding to happen. They filled every container we owned, and I even made my own bouquet. I decorated my beehives and the fence around them with yards and yards of white tulle and bouquets of herbs. And of course, I got a sense that the bees were pleased for me. I really did.

Don't you know that when we announced we were going on a short honeymoon to Bermuda, Hunter wanted to come.

"Aren't we related yet?" he asked with those gorgeous eyes of his.

"You are such a little charmer," I said and tousled his hair.

The boys had survived the reign and wrath of Sharon and appeared to be unscathed.

"I'll take you to Bermuda this summer if you have a good year in school. And Tyler, too, of course," Archie said.

Leslie shot Archie a hairy eyeball.

"And you, too!" he said. "Of course!"

There must've been some magic in the coral sand where we stretched out on beach towels to watch the stars in the night sky over Bermuda, because I came home with a little biscuit in my oven and a whole lot smarter about what goes on between the sheets. All I can say is that I wish I'd taken Ted more seriously in high school. I would've married him the day we graduated and dragged him to bed every chance I had. All those wasted years of self-deprivation! Ah, well. Deprivation no more!

When we got home we moved my hives to Ted's backyard, which was now our backyard, and he quickly constructed a fence to keep Stubble from getting into trouble. Stubble became my constant companion. The bees buzzed around and bearded some, but overall, after a bit, they settled down and got back to the business of foraging, pollinating, and making delicious honey. I kicked up some dirt in the long-neglected flower beds and said I could get them going again. I did, and by April, our yard looked like somebody loved it. We were only a few blocks from Momma, in case, well, you know, if something happened and she needed us.

What of Momma and Suz? If laughter and happiness were the best medicines, then Suz was going to keep Momma alive on this earth forever. I'd never seen her so happy. And oh, interesting side note, all those pounds on Momma just melted away. Suz had her walking all over the island and the result was astounding. Her doctors told her to ditch her blood pressure meds and her statin. She was delighted. And there had been no recurrence of tumors.

"I feel so much better!" she said every time someone told her how great she looked.

I prayed that the good Lord would give her plenty of time to be together with Suz. She deserved happiness. We all did. I just never believed that we, the crazy bunch of outliers that we were, would find it so happily and completely.

It became obvious that I needed to go to the hospital to deliver our baby at about four in the morning on May 14. My back had been killing me all week. My ankles were swollen, and I was just generally uncomfortable all over. I labored until around noon and then, by the grace of God, I delivered the most exquisite baby ever born.

"It's a boy!" my doctor said. "A little fat guy, and he's perfect!"

Ted cut the cord and fainted. He was out cold on the floor of the delivery room and had a small cut in his forehead.

"I thought he was the chief of police!" a nurse said.

They revived him, got him up and into a chair, and gave him a cold cloth and a Band-Aid.

"What are we going to name him?" Ted said.

"He's Theodore, my love. He looks just like you."

"Okay," he said. "Theodore. I've always wanted a son."

I was just so glad I'd have two Teds to love. What could be better? We brought him home and laid him in his bassinet and I thought my heart would burst from all the love I felt for my little Ted. I stared at him for days on end and walked around in a fog of joy.

I could go on with this story forever. You know it wouldn't be hard. There will always be shenanigans to entertain you from the islanders like Leslie, Momma, Suz, well, all of us, and our friends, too. That's what it is to live in the Lowcountry. The colors are a little brighter. The air is a little sweeter. Jokes are funnier, love runs deeper, and life overall is richer. But I have a baby to feed and a gorgeous husband who'll be wanting dinner, too. Who knows? Maybe we'll be back another time. Remember Tolstoy? He said something pretty clever. He said, "One can no more approach people without love than one can approach bees without care." Wouldn't the world be a better place if we took that tiny bit of advice? The hive has many lessons to teach us. This was only one of them.

Acknowledgments

There was an unusual amount of enthusiasm for this book from the very beginning. Many people gave me their thoughts and wisdom to make *Queen Bee*, we all hope, worthy of your time. The world around me is suddenly filled with beekeepers, honey bee keepers to be exact, all of them filled with hope that *Queen Bee* will gently enlighten and inform my readers on the importance of honey bees to our food supply and the beauty of the natural world while I'm telling you a story about human frailty and cowardice confronted with unstoppable and sometimes very unlikely love and devotion.

I began my research with *BUZZ—The Nature and Necessity of Bees,* a recent work of nonfiction authored by Thor Hanson. I bought a copy and was given two more. If your curiosity leads you to only read one book on the subject of honey bees, it has to be this one. I read it in two days, took copious notes, and quickly came to understand that honey bees have much to teach humanity. In fact, a lot more than I thought.

Then, as my list of questions grew, a dear friend and former beekeeper, Dawn Durst of Sullivan's Island, South Carolina, introduced me by phone to Jerry Freeman of Hamburg, Arkansas. Jerry had a saintly patience in all our conversations until I finally came to understand the risks our honey bees face and what might be done about it. He is the inventor of the Freeman Beetle Trap, a remedy to hive beetles. His website also offers plenty of sound information on Varroa mites and on beekeeping in general. You can visit Jerry at www.freemanbeetletrap.com.

And finally, in the category of Things Bees Do to Amaze Us, I owe a word of thanks to Allan Perry Hazel and his charming wife, Judy Hazel, of Sullivan's Island, South Carolina, and Ted Shrensel and his lovely wife, Bettie Frank-Shrensel, of Montclair, New Jersey. Both of these beekeeping couples had some hilarious stories to tell about hive personalities and the personal habits of bees. So, thanks to y'all, some of the funnier aspects of beekeeping will reach lots of people.

There's another huge acknowledgment owed to

Emma Waters and all the fine folks at the Savannah Bee Company first for having such a wonderful and informative website and for your generous sponsorship of my Fan Fest 2019, but perhaps most important for your generous support of The Bee Cause project that brings bees into classrooms all over the country to teach children about the critical importance of honey bees in our lives and in the environment. And also to Tamara Enright of The Bee Cause. Part of the proceeds from books sold during my book tour this year will support the work of The Bee Cause as well. My team from William Morrow is mighty proud to know you and to congratulate your fine work. In addition, special thanks to J. L. Napolski and all the nice people at Dixie Vodka for their support of book tour and Fan Fest. You have most definitely put the fun back in book tour. Ahem.

For years I have offered various nonprofits around the country the opportunity for one or more of their patrons to appear in my books as a character as a way for them to raise money. The winner never knows if they'll be a good guy or a bad guy. They take their chances. This year the Naples, Florida, Friends of the Library brought two of their supporters to immortality. Holly McNee Jensen and Leslie Stevens. Holly and Leslie, I gave you both starring roles and I hope you enjoy this crazy duo. And Carin MacLean, who generously gave to my old grammar school, Stella Maris/Christ Our King in Mount Pleasant, South Carolina, I hope you enjoy your pedestal and I'm sorry, well, I should've sent flowers. Last, I'd like to thank Stubble the dog's owners for their generous support of the Montclair Art Museum, Montclair, New Jersey. Although I have barely met any of these kind and generous souls, and Stubble not at all, I am sure they are nothing like the characters they portray. What we do know about them is that they support the arts, literacy, and education, a worthy pursuit all around. And so I salute y'all and thank you again on behalf of these fine institutions. On a side note, my sister Lynn tells me she was stopped by a friend at her bridge club who said her daughter was very upset because she was supposed to be a character in this book or last year's (details were unclear) and I asked her to find out who this was and I'd take care of it right away. Well, that never happened. So if you are that person, please contact me on Facebook or Instagram with a little bit of validation and we can remedy the situation.

Sometimes friends and acquaintances just show up in my pages. Usually it's because I'm thinking of them but always because I need another name for a character. This time, Andrea Blatt, Barbara Hagerty, Joanne Langbein, Anthony Stith, and Darlene and Mark

Tanenbaum slipped in and I hope y'all get a kick out of seeing your name in print. And Darlene and Mark, special thanks for keeping me hydrated and fed during the last days of writing this book.

Then there are those to thank for various reasons. Thank you, Harlan Greene for your excellent advice I took to heart and tried very hard to adhere to. Thanks to Martin and Toni McKerrow of Nantucket Island, Massachusetts, for their amazing hospitality and also to my writer pal Elin Hilderbrand for her insanely wonderful blurb for this book. I owe you one! Thanks to Judy Linder, my great cousin, for helping find fun bee facts and connecting them to the chapters and huge thanks to my fabulous daughter, Victoria Frank Peluso, for so many things I can't even remember them all—help with proofing, bee facts, social media, brainstorming, and for our first children's book, a true collaborative effort, *Teddy Spaghetti,* which we hope will be published in the summer of 2020 by the children's imprint of HarperCollins. And it should be obvious to Margaret Anastas, our children's editor, that we love her to bits. Yes, we do. Victoria and I are super excited to work with you.

And heading over to the floors of William Morrow, let's start with Carrie Feron, my fearless editor, the one I adore. Our fifteenth book together? Where does the time go? Your thoughts, ideas, and advice always bring me to a richer and more satisfying story for the enjoyment of so many others and I am deeply grateful for all of it. And I am also seriously grateful to Asanté Simons, assistant extraordinaire to my fearless editor, for the endless questions she answers and the many things she does to keep me above water. And let us not forget to blow a kiss to Michael Kelly! No reason. Just blowing kisses.

To the William Morrow team: Brian Murray, Liate Stehlik, Kelly Rudolph, Julie Paulauski, Kathryn Gordon, Kate Hudkins, Lisa Sharkey and the whole team at Studio 16, Frank Albanese, Virginia Stanley, Andrea Rosen, Josh Marwell, Andy LeCount, Carla Parker, Donna Waikus, Michael Morris, Rachel Levenberg, Gabe Barillas, Andrea Molitor, copyeditor Greg Villepique, Jennifer Hart, Rachel Levinger, Nyamekye Waliyaya, Suzanne Mitchell, and last but Lawsa not least, Brian Grogan: thank you one and all for all the miracles, and for your amazing support. And to our new secret weapon, Gretchen Koss of Tandem Literary. Girl? You killed it last year! Let's do it again!

Speaking of powerhouses? Deep bows and many curtsies to genius, Suzanne Gluck, my agent at WME, and Andrea Blatt, of course! Many thanks to Michelle Feehan of New York and Matilda Forbes Watson, London. And thanks to Sylvie Rabineau and Hilary Zaitz Michael of WME Los Angeles. Y'all are the best!

Let us not forget Patti Morrison, my book tour buddy who keeps me out of trouble. Well, mostly. Anyway, many thanks for your excellent friendship and humor!

And then there are the extraordinary booksellers, and I mean every single one of you across this big wonderful country of ours, I thank you from the bottom of my heart, most especially Margot Sage-El and the Jedis of Watchung Booksellers in Montclair, New Jersey, Vicki Crafton and her wonderful booksellers at Litchfield Books in Pawley's Island, South Carolina, Jonathan Sanchez of Blue Bicycle Books in Charleston, Wendy Hudson from Mitchell's Book Corner on Nantucket and all the wonderful people from the Nantucket Book Festival and Jacquie Lee, who, lucky for me, always finds a way to enhance book tour or my life in general. I love y'all and you know it's true.

To my growing family! Carmine and Victoria and that precious angel from heaven, Teddy Peluso, whom we all adore—as y'all know, I love y'all so much! And Liam and Maddie Frank—I love y'all so much and miss you every day. And to Brian and Roberta Benton and Matthew and Danielle Benton and of course, little Luke, you all inspire me and fill my heart. And to my amazing husband, Peter. Mr. Frank? There are no words to describe my enormous love for you, but love you I do with all my heart, and all of you with all I've got.

Finally, to my readers, to whom I owe the greatest debt of all, I am sending you the most sincere and profound thanks for reading my stories, for sending along so many nice emails and posts and for coming to my book events. Y'all are the why of why I try and write a book each year. I hope *Queen Bee* will bring you lots of happiness and give you a thing or two to think about. There's a lot of magic down here in the Lowcountry. Please come see us and get some for yourself. I love you all and thank you once again.